Kingslayer seemed to fuse itself to Davi's fingers, but he no longer cared. He'd given himself over to the weapon's dark influence and would gladly pay any price for the power that coursed through him—for the quickened reflexes, the incredible physical strength, the heightened senses.

And the hot, sweet blood that soaked his gloved hands.

Someone stepped into the circle of carnage, a familiar tall form. The dim memory of his Red King made the duke hesitate.

"Give me the sword," the red-bearded man said with infinite calm.

Davi shook his head. "No. It needs me."

"*I* need you, my duke."

Jealous, Kingslayer hummed the louder to block the voice and sooth this descendant of the Dark King. Its song filled Davi's head, demanding the blood of this man as well. And when Gaylon Reysson, Red King of Wynnamyr, reached out to take the sword, the boy-duke swung the blade high.

Other TSR Books

STARSONG *Dan Parkinson*	**WARSPRITE** *Jefferson P. Swycaffer*
ST. JOHN THE PURSUER: **VAMPIRE IN MOSCOW** *Richard Henrick*	**NIGHTWATCH** *Robin Wayne Bailey*
BIMBOS OF THE **DEATH SUN** *Sharyn McCrumb*	**OUTBANKER** *Timothy A. Madden*
	THE ROAD WEST *Gary Wright*
RED SANDS *Paul Thompson and* *Tonya Carter*	**THE ALIEN DARK** *Diana G. Gallagher*
ILLEGAL ALIENS *Nick Pollotta and* *Phil Foglio*	**WEB OF FUTURES** *Jefferson P. Swycaffer*
THE JEWELS OF ELVISH *Nancy Varian Berberick*	**SORCERER'S STONE** *L. Dean James*
MONKEY STATION *Ardath Mayhar and* *Ron Fortier*	**THE FALCON RISES** *Michael C. Staudinger*
THE EYES HAVE IT *Rose Estes*	**TOKEN OF** **DRAGONSBLOOD** *Damaris Cole*
TOO, TOO SOLID FLESH *Nick O'Donohoe*	**THE CLOUD PEOPLE** *Robert B. Kelly*
THE EARTH REMEMBERS *Susan Torian Olan*	**LIGHTNING'S** **DAUGHTER** *Mary H. Herbert*
DARK HORSE *Mary H. Herbert*	**THORN AND NEEDLE** *Paul B. Thompson*

KINGSLAYER

L. Dean James

KINGSLAYER

First Printing: June 1992
Printed in the United States of America.
Library of Congress Catalog Card Number: 91-66501

9 8 7 6 5 4 3 2 1

ISBN: 1-56076-398-1

TSR, Inc.
P.O. Box 756
Lake Geneva, WI 53147
U.S.A.

TSR Ltd.
120 Church End, Cherry Hinton
Cambridge CB1 3LB
United Kingdom

For my father, Frank Alden Buckley James

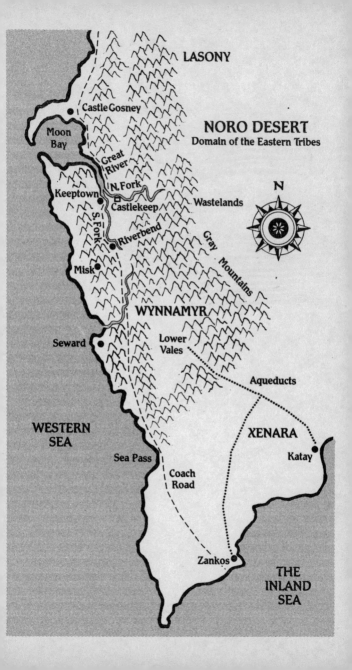

Prologue

In Castle Seward's murky depths, the darkness throbbed and writhed. Faint illumination came from the phosphorescent mosses that clung to the slick, wet stones of the walls, but the old wizard was unhampered by the perpetual night of this place. His inhuman eyes detected far more than visible light, and though centuries had passed since last he'd followed these twisted, narrow corridors in the castle's lowest level, they were well known to him.

At last the passageway ended, and a single ruby eye winked to life before the sorcerer. He clutched the small stone pendant on his breast as a disembodied voice, gentle yet impersonal, rumbled in the dark.

"Who approaches Solstad? Identify yourself."

It spoke in a lilting tongue that carried nuance in tone as well as in word.

"I am Sezran fon Holdred fen Tantal," the old man answered in the same tongue, but the taste of the words was bitter.

The voice altered. "Stand where I may see you, master."

Sezran moved before the red eye. Immediately, the smooth section of wall before him dissolved and revealed a small, crowded chamber with two contoured chairs. Panels of lights blinked slowly on every hand. The wizard stepped inside, then took a seat on the nearest chair. Carefully he settled back and, with a palm, pressed the corner of a flat metallic plate that edged the armrest. A whirring came from above his head, and a thin wire encircled his brow, tightening.

"Command link," he murmured.

A diagram of the ship's systems appeared behind his eyes, each system working at the low end of normal range. Sezran studied the slow monotonous loop of the star drive display. "Run . . . engram, Kesric, Holdred, six-two-three-eight point four-two-one."

A swirl of white light filled his mind, then resolved into an overview of Kesric, the capital city on Holdred, his family's world. The great sculptured towers had been built on a high barren escarpment as close to the heavens as possible. Starlike, the city glittered in a long summer's dusk. The sky to the west lay crimson and gold with the setting sun. Now inner vision blurred, and a deep throb started beneath the wizard's feet—an ancient, vivid memory. Thunder clapped, followed by a sudden breathtaking heaviness, and the ship seemed to launch into the sky. Kesric dwindled quickly, replaced by the curve of an oceanless, ocher planet, and then, a black, black night with myriad stars.

Sezran thumbed the disengage key, and the wire loosened on his head. These were only memories of a distant place in an even more distant time. The ship remained as it had for over a millennium, buried deep below the castle.

"Are you lonely, Solstad?" the sorcerer asked.

"No, master," the ship answered. "I wait."

Of course. Solstad simply waited. It would wait a thousand thousand years if need be. Anger seeped into Sezran's calm, and the Sorcerer's Stone on his chest glimmered blue. This was his fault. Long ago, he had delivered them here—himself and a sister. Sezran, a man of technology, had been enthralled with this primitive world, with its magical forces and short-lived sentient species.

Misk had warned him, had even tried to stop him, but the temptation had been too great. He had taken the gem that powered Solstad's star drive—the black gem that wove both time and space—and offered it to the king of this realm in exchange for a Sorcerer's Stone and knowledge of its magic. With the ship's black gem, Sezran had forged a sword that controlled the fire of the stars, then placed it in the hands of a human, a madman, who had sought to destroy his own world.

The ancient wizard stepped down from the command chair and, without a backward glance, left the ship and its winking lights, his mind on the present. For a millennium, he had waited even as Solstad waited, though far less patiently. A new sorcerer-king had risen to take up Kingslayer, at last. The sword would destroy this king as it had the first, and this time, Sezran would be there to reclaim what was rightfully his.

One

The royal hunting party of five, after so many fruitless quests, had flushed a stag with an impressive rack of antlers on the thickly wooded hillsides across the river from Keeptown. Drunken and loud, the members pushed their tired, sweated horses at breakneck speeds down the snow-covered slopes in pursuit.

Gaylon Reysson, king of Wynnamyr, led the group on a young, half-wild sorrel mare that fought him nearly every step of the way. He struck the animal on the flank with his bow when she tried to dodge right through the trees, to a place where the terrain was less rugged.

"Arlin!" the king shouted, gusts of vapor curling back into his bearded face. "Cut him off at the river! Head him east! East!"

Arlin D'Lelan, a young, dark-haired nobleman from the southern nation of Xenara, let out a whoop and drove his horse through a tangle of whitethorn toward the riverbank. Gaylon laughed, giddy with icy winter air and brandy. Behind him came a familiar squawk of distress, and he pulled the mare up hard, then reined her about. Karyl of Oakhaven, the king's untitled third cousin, lay sprawled on the frozen, snowy ground. The redheaded youth's mount dragged him downhill by one rein.

"Karyl!" cried Marten Pelson, earl of the Lower Vales. "When are you going to learn to ride?"

They were all laughing now—all but Arlin, who, intent on their prey and the king's orders, still crashed headlong toward the slushy black waters of the river. Gaylon spun the sorrel and put the spurs to her.

Karyl scrambled to his feet. "Wait!"

"Meet us in town," the king called back.

"Town?" Marten echoed breathlessly.

"Town!" Gaylon sent the mare at a run westward through the woods, parallel to the north fork of the river. The others followed with noisy glee.

His bow and quiver slung across one shoulder now, the king pulled the wineskin from the saddle's pommel and tipped it to his lips. It was a much practiced feat performed with a skill none of his young bravos had mastered—not at a hard gallop over uneven ground. Still, as much of the distilled wine splattered the front of his heavy bearskin coat as found his mouth.

Rinn, a simple tailor's son, blond and lanky, drew abreast on a raw-boned black gelding. With a grin, the king slung the skin at him. The young man snatched it from the air, then swerved around a massive grandfather oak. The road into Keeptown lay just ahead. Gaylon sent his mount up the steep side of the roadbed just as the stag clambered up from the river. He spurred the mare again and got their quarry turned onto the bridge, its splayed hoofs churning the ice-encrusted snow.

Arlin arrived, face red with cold, teeth chattering. Rinn and Marten thundered with him over the icy wooden planks toward the unsuspecting town.

"Rinn! The grocers' alley," Gaylon called and circled a hand over his head. The tailor's son nodded, then turned his horse into the narrow passage between the tall stone buildings on the left. The king slowed, and his small entourage dropped back as well, still hooting joyfully at each other. The few people on the main street scattered before the stag. Women, outraged, drew small children into door-

ways. Before the milliner's shop, a pony waited, harnessed
to a cart. The little animal spooked at the stag's approach
and galloped away, the cart bumping behind. Bolts of
brightly colored cloth were left scattered in the dirty snow.
The shaggy-maned deer gave the cloth and the irate milliner a wide berth, but was forced on by the riders.

"What are we doing?" Marten asked as he came alongside the king. "Shoot it and be done. We've already run
the creature so hard the meat will be foul."

Gaylon ignored him. Rinn had arrived at the far end of
the street and stood blocking it. His horse's flanks heaved
with exertion, and the young man pushed tangled blond
hair from his face. On the near corner, a faded wooden sign
rocked in the cold wind. The Stagg Tavern, it read.

Arlin, dark eyes aglitter, let loose with another unbridled whoop. "You're a great and glorious madman, milord!"

The king, with a dramatic flourish, pulled the glove
from his right hand, and the gray stone in the gold ring on
his forefinger flashed suddenly blue. The tavern doors
slammed open under his magical command. Exhausted
and left nowhere else to go, the deer turned and lunged
over the threshold.

"Here!" someone cried from within. "By all the gods,
what's this?"

"Hey!" Karyl, his cap gone and his bright red hair loose
around his plump face, arrived, panting harder than his
mount. "Where is it? Where'd it go?"

Arlin chuckled. "Inside the tavern. Be a good lad, go in
and buy it a drink."

"It went in there?" Karyl looked doubtful.

Something fell with a crash in the tavern, and two dis-
gruntled customers shot from the doors. A good deal of
shouting began inside. Gaylon stepped down from his saddle and threw Karyl the reins.

"Hold the horses."

"Why do *I* always have to?" the redhead groused while Arlin, Marten, and Rinn passed him their reins as well.

The king entered first, both gloves caught in one hand, his bow and quiver still across a shoulder. At the far end of the wide room, the deer stood, nostrils flared and head cocked, its great rack threatening the heavyset man behind the bar. The barkeep had only a broom to brandish.

"You!" he cried when he saw the young men. "I might have known."

Gaylon threw a glance at the half-dozen mounted stag heads that lined the walls. "I thought you might like another trophy, Tassic."

"Here, good fellow," Arlin said and foolishly stepped up to the counter beside the deer. "Let's have an ale for my friend and me."

"Arlin!" Marten snapped.

The stag swung its head, caught the young Southerner in the forks of its antlers, and pinned him to the front of the counter.

Instantly the king had bow in hand, an arrow nocked and loosed in one smooth motion. The feathered shaft struck the deer just behind the shoulder and drove deep through the rib cage to puncture heart and lung. The animal bellowed, then twisted to the side and collapsed on the worn floorboards, dead.

Now Gaylon spared a brief moment for fear. He pulled Arlin from the tangle of horns and carried him to the nearest table.

"Is he gored?" Rinn demanded while the king feverishly searched through the Southerner's heavy winter clothing for wounds.

"He is not," said Arlin, dark eyes open and full of mischief. "But well tenderized." He pushed Gaylon's hands aside and groaned as he slid to his feet.

"Look at my floor," Tassic snarled, standing near the blood that pooled in the rushes beneath the deer. "A table

and three chairs broken. And customers run off." He
turned his anger on the tailor's son, who stood nearest.
"I've known you all your life, Rinn, and never thought you
a simpleton. A commoner belongs with his own kind, yet
you play the fool for noblemen. Why do you keep company with these royal braggarts and louts?"

Arlin, white-faced, reached for his dagger, but Gaylon
stopped him.

"Let him speak," the king muttered.

"I'll speak, I will—no doubt at risk of my tongue." Tassic stared boldly at Gaylon. "Wynnamyr may have been ill-
served by Lucien D'Sulang, but he was a better king than
you, Gaylon Reysson." His gaze flickered nervously to the
ring on the young man's hand, but the Sorcerer's Stone remained dark.

"Was he?" the king asked gently. His friends were silent,
aghast.

"Yes! He at least knew how his countrymen fared. You
have ruled eight long years, but you have yet to show interest in anything but drinking, hunting, and fighting. Redmond of Graymount is dead because he followed you, just
as these other young fools do. You might have lost another
here today."

"Thank you for your insights," Gaylon said before the
barkeep could continue. Redmond, the youngest of their
group, had been crushed by his mount when it fell during
one of their cross-country races some months before. A cold
ache filled the king's chest, but he refused to acknowledge
the guilt and sorrow. Instead he pulled a pouch from his
sword belt and placed it on the table where Arlin had lain.
"Take this for the damages." Gaylon turned away.

"Milord . . . *Sire*, I would ask a favor of you," Tassic
called belligerently when the group crossed to the door.

Gaylon paused. "That is?"

"Please don't come back to my tavern, any of you."

"Bastard," Arlin snapped as he stamped over the snow

to gather his reins from Karyl.

"No," the king chided. "He has the right. Tassic is a brave man. Few would have the courage to reprimand a king, let alone one with a Sorcerer's Stone." He shrugged. "Besides, there are a half-dozen other good taverns in Keeptown that still appreciate our patronage and our money."

"So far," Rinn said dryly and started to mount.

Gaylon caught his friend's arm, still troubled by the inn-keep's words. "Wait a moment. Have we misused you, Rinn?"

"Of course not, milord."

"It would hurt me to think so."

"Oh, no, Sire!"

"Well, we'll remedy the commoner problem here and now." The king smiled gently. "My second cousin, Chace of Greenwood, died last summer. Being without heirs, he left his lands to the crown." Gaylon put a hand on the young man's shoulder. "Therefore, I give them to you and name you, Rinn, First Baron of Greenwood."

The tailor's son looked startled. "I . . . cannot accept, milord."

"Don't be a dunce," Marten snorted, already mounted. Behind him, Karyl of Oakhaven tightened his lips sullenly.

"But truly, I can't," Rinn insisted.

"It's a very small barony," Gaylon told the youth as he pulled on his gloves. "And not all that wealthy. Still, it should support you and your parents and sisters well enough."

Now Rinn looked unhappy. "Milord, it's my father. I promised him I would be a tailor. I'm his only son. He's a master and a proud man."

"He might also be proud of a son who's a baron. At least let him know of my offer."

The sorrel mare swung away when the king put a boot toe in the iron stirrup, forcing him to hop on one foot after her. None of his little group bothered to offer help. Whatever else they might be, the young men rode as equals, and now Karyl chuckled with dry amusement. To hide his irritation, Gaylon gave the reins a hard, sharp jerk that made the horse stand firm, then climbed into the saddle.

"Where's my wineskin?" he demanded.

"Here!" Karyl tossed it to him.

"It's empty."

The redhead grimaced. "I was thirsty."

"I'm far too sober, so we'll have to find more," Gaylon said and glanced around him. "But the king is penniless at the moment."

"I'm not." Marten jingled his purse. "Let's go to the Yellow Dog. They've a serving wench there with eyes the color of a summer sky."

Arlin laughed. "Those aren't her only attributes, as I remember."

Gaylon was no longer listening. He studied the low gray clouds, heavy with snow, and considered what other reckless, mindless diversion he might find on this empty wintery day.

* * * * *

Tydus Dorenson, as always, was alone in the council chambers of the keep. His paperwork done, he stepped through the drapes that covered the chamber door and onto the dais in the dimly lit audience room beyond. A great oaken chair with deep blue velvet upholstery overlooked the empty hall. So far in his reign, Gaylon Reysson had sat upon this throne just once.

Dorenson slipped into the wide soft seat and dared to imagine a crown of gold encircling his white hair—a fanciful, impossible dream for a man of middle age, born to a merchant family and not to royalty. That mattered little. Tydus was far more interested in the power than the crown.

Feydir D'Sulang, the former ambassador to Xenara, had handpicked Tydus to lead King Lucien's council. Though Feydir and his vicious nephew, who had usurped the Wynnamyran throne, were long dead at Gaylon Reysson's hands, Dorenson had managed to survive the political upheaval. He'd even inherited much of the ambassador's wealth and power, here and in the rival kingdom of Xenara to the south.

For the past eight years, Tydus had ruled Wynnamyr in everything but name, for unlike his murdered father, King Reys, Gaylon Reysson had proven to be a brooding and reflective young man who seemed to care nothing for his royal station. From the beginning, he had spent little time within the keep, often disappearing into the mountains for weeks. This was all to the head councilman's advantage. So long as Gaylon paid no attention to affairs of state, Tydus had free rein. But Tydus dreamed of far greater things.

Gaylon Reysson was a sorcerer-king. The wreckage left in the dungeons the night Lucien had died attested to the young man's powers. More than this, though, it was whispered among the people that the king had taken up Orym's Legacy against his enemies—that fabled sword, Kingslayer, which had turned on its master and destroyed him nearly a millennium past.

Tydus had hoped that Gaylon Reysson would take up the terrible weapon and turn it on his neighbors as well. Through such a sorcerer-king, Dorenson hoped to gain even more power, but the king had shown no such inclinations. He had remained aloof to Tydus's kindly counsel, distant to the approaches of both King Roffo of Xenara in the south and Zorek, king of Lasony in the north.

No matter. Gaylon was young still, inexperienced, and deeply troubled. Soon he would be forced to turn to someone for help, and Tydus would be at his right hand, ready and most willing to provide it. The man smoothed his white hair and straightened his impeccable robes, then headed once more for the chamber doors. Yes, in Tydus, Gaylon would find the father he had lost so long ago, someone kind to praise and guide him.

*   *   *   *   *

Lady Gerra had fallen asleep in the wingback chair before the wide hearth in the queen's sitting room. Her snores were fitful and punctuated with sighs. Jessmyn, the young queen of Wynnamyr, put down her needlework and brought a comforter from the bedchamber to cover the elderly governess, then found a shawl for herself to add to the warmth of her long woolen gown. Despite every effort to caulk the windows and seal the stones, despite the heavy, dark tapestries that covered the walls, the queen's apartments remained drafty and cold—though no more so than the rest of the ancient keep. Beyond the leaded windowpanes, an early winter dusk had arrived, bringing an even deeper chill with it.

Twice this afternoon, servants in the blue livery of the household staff had come to inquire of her needs. Each time, Jessmyn had sent them away. The young queen, attended only by her aging governess, had as usual spent the day in her apartments, sewing. Her hands were kept busy this way, but her thoughts had free range. As always, they turned to Gaylon.

She set the needlework aside again and rose to feed the fire, then added more crushed mint and raspberry leaf to her teacup. Next, steaming water was poured from the kettle on the hearth.

A sudden tension in the air made her pause—a familiar raw energy. The king had returned to the keep, and she could feel him near. Soon enough the scuffle of many boots sounded in the corridor. Laughter echoed. Jessmyn settled in the rocker and took a sip of tea.

Without the courtesy of a knock, the heavy door to her

chamber opened, and Gaylon stood on the threshold. His russet hunting leathers were rumpled and soiled, and his close-cropped red beard dripped melting snow. Even so, her heart leaped at the sight of him.

"My lady," the king said, smiling. Yet his eyes remained bleak. There were bloody scratches on his face from the hunt and older ones, half-healed.

Behind him, Jessmyn could see his entourage, as sodden and disheveled as he. They jostled one another in the hall with elbows and knees like so many schoolboys.

"My lord," the queen said, gazing into her cup, "how went the hunt?"

"His Majesty killed a stag," Arlin offered, then remembered his manners. He bowed gracelessly and fell against the wall behind him. The others laughed.

Abruptly Gaylon stepped into the room and shut the door on his friends.

"Forgive me for coming to you this way," he murmured.

"My lord, you may come in any manner, at any time to your wife."

His eyes searched the room restlessly, but the king would not look at her. "Do you have wine?"

"No, my lord," Jessmyn lied. "I can offer you tea."

He chuckled morosely. "I doubt that will have quite the same effect."

Oh, Gaylon, she thought, her face carefully devoid of expression. What can I do to help you, to ease your pain? Instead of voicing these pleas, she kept silent.

The tall young man gazed into the fire. "May I rest a while here . . . with you?"

"Of course," Jessmyn answered. She hid her joy when Gaylon ignored the other stuffed chair to settle on the braid rug at her feet.

"She sings a merry tune," the king said with a nod toward the sleeping governess.

"She does," the young queen agreed. "I'll send her to

fetch supper for us if you like."

Gaylon was long in answering. "For me, wine only."

Jessmyn woke Lady Gerra gently. The governess, graying
and stooped, had slowed greatly over the past few years,
but the sight of their visitor startled her out of her chair.
She received her orders, then fled the chamber, obviously
unsettled by the king's presence. The room grew silent except for the crackling of the flames on the hearth.

All the nobility took quiet meals in their chambers now.
There were no longer grand dinners in the great hall. Lucien's court had been loud and gaudy, but after his death,
most of the Southern gentry had fled back to Xenara out of
fear that the new king would seek revenge. This had left
the keep nearly empty and very lonely.

Jessmyn fought the urge to lay her hand on Gaylon's
shoulder. Wise beyond her twenty-four years, she had already decided that she must accept whatever the young
man offered and never demand more. As his wife and
queen, she had spent only one night with him—the night
he had killed Lucien D'Sulang and taken his crown. He
had not come to her bed since, and rarely to her chambers.

It had taken many years for him to regain his throne, and
in that time Gaylon Reysson had lost nearly everyone he
loved: his father, the king; his mentor, Daryn, duke of
Gosney; and even the usurper Lucien, who had been a
friend once. Gaylon had taken up the burden of Kingslayer, also called Orym's Legacy, and it had changed him. Jessmyn feared for her lord, though she could never tell him.

The king had put aside the crown he'd earned at so high
a price. In a matter of months, he'd gathered around him a
half-dozen young noblemen, all of them wealthy, bored,
and wild. They became his private council, and he led
them on every insane adventure that could be found. All
Gaylon's bright energy was spent in devising ways to risk
their lives. While injury was common enough, Redmond
of Graymount had been the first true casualty of their

games, though the death hardly caused a ripple in the small pool of Wynnamyran court life. The poor young man's king and cohorts had dared to arrive drunk at the funeral, scandalizing the family and all the mourners. Afterward, Gaylon had seemed even more driven than before.

A gentle scratch at the chamber door brought Jessmyn's thoughts back to the moment.

"Come," she called.

A servant entered, eyes downcast, a loaded tray in his hands. All of the household staff were extremely nervous around the king. Lady Gerra came in behind the man. Before the fire, Gaylon didn't stir. The young queen received the food and offered her thanks, then let the servant go. She prepared a plate with her own hand for Lady Gerra, then sent her to her small bedchamber adjoining the queen's.

The king roused only when Jessmyn placed a wine cup on the hearth near his hand. She prepared a plate for him and for herself, but he wouldn't take the food. That worried her. His cheeks had hollows nowadays, and his hazel eyes were dark-shadowed. His slender height and red beard, so incongruous with the sandy-blond hair on his head, were all that he had inherited from his father. Somehow Gaylon had failed to acquire the calm, steady strength and wisdom of that great man.

The young king sneezed suddenly.

"Blessings, my lord," Jessmyn said, concerned. "Perhaps Girkin should be called to prepare a medicinal draught."

"No. It was just a whiff of smoke from the fire." Gaylon stared at the cup in his hand as if seeing it for the first time, then emptied it in one long pull. "With you I hope to find some little peace tonight. Do you mind terribly?"

"I'm glad of your company, my lord."

"Is there anything I can do for you? Anything you desire?" His gaze returned to the fire.

This rare generosity shook Jessmyn. "I miss your music," she said quietly, then feared she'd asked too much. "But if you're tired . . ."

"I think I could manage," he said and nodded. "Do you have a lute?"

"Yes." She set the untouched food aside and went to her private bedchamber. Her knees on the soft wolfskin rug, the young woman pushed aside the heavy curtains at the foot of her bed and dug through the large chest there. A battered lute was pulled free of protecting blankets. The lacquer was worn and darkened with age, and a deep scratch marred the curved wood at the back. Jessmyn remembered Gaylon walking along the riverbank on a late fall day long ago, the lute in his arms. Smiling, she carried the instrument to the sitting room.

The king took the lute by the neck and glanced up in wonder. "Where did you find this?"

"One of the servants had given it to a sweetheart in town. He thought possibly the instrument had been discarded."

"Such an ugly old thing, no wonder." Gaylon crossed his long legs on the rug and strummed a chord, then spent a while tuning the strings. "It's been some time. I hope I remember how."

The first notes were clear and sweet. He had not forgotten. The young man played a snatch of this melody and that before finding something that pleased him. Jessmyn listened and watched. The lute took on a faint echo, an eerie resonance, and she noticed the Stone in his ring glimmered blue. Finally he added his voice, a fine rich baritone.

The song was a ballad, gloomy and dark, yet somehow compelling—a tale of a young woman who had died of sorrow over her faithless lover. The lover, at last realizing the grief he had caused, killed himself out of remorse. The final melancholy note faded, and the queen closed her eyes to hold back the tears.

"I—" she managed when her voice had steadied, "I've never heard anything so beautiful and sad."

Gaylon bowed his head. "Daryn taught me that song a long time ago. He never said, but I'm certain he wrote it."

The king's Stone brightened with some strong emotion, and his sorrow washed through Jessmyn. Without a word, he laid the lute on the braid rug, then rose and strode from the room. The door closed behind him, and she heard his footsteps fade in the corridor.

His sorrow stayed with her.

* * * * *

The king didn't want to be alone, but neither did he desire the company of his friends. Weary and sore from the hunt, Gaylon found the chamberlain, a stoop-shouldered fellow in faded blue livery, near the servants' quarters and demanded hot water for a bath. The apprehension in the man's face irritated the young king, but somehow pleased him, too. At least an evil reputation brought obedience and quick service. Gaylon walked the empty candle-lit corridors back to his apartments.

The moment he closed the heavy oak door, someone knocked on it. Immediately there were five male servants with buckets of hot water milling in the room. Gaylon stood in their midst, eyes unfocused, thoughts hazy with fatigue. A fire was built on the hearth, the hinged copper tub lowered from the wall and filled. But when fingers tried to unlace his shirt, the king backhanded the man out of numb reflex. It was a thoughtless mistake, yet he couldn't apologize. Better to be seen as unpredictable than weak.

Daryn would have had plenty to say about that. . . .

Angry, Gaylon sent the servants away. They were glad to

go and didn't hide it from him. He wandered into the bed-chamber in search of a nightrobe. These had been his fa-ther's rooms, and later Lucien D'Sulang's. Now Reys's sturdy, spartan furnishings were once more in their proper places. All of Lucien's gaudy finery had been long since burned. The old familiar trappings of his childhood brought the king no comfort, though.

On the wall to the left of the platform bed, Gaylon pulled back the tapestry and touched the cold stones that covered the secret compartment. Kingslayer lay hidden there, safe. The Sorcerer's Stone on the young man's finger pulsed lightly in longing. What harm could there be to take the hilt of the sword for just a moment and stare into the black gem that glittered with fiery stars? The memory of the blade's dark song of power brought aching desire and repulsion. Gaylon snatched his hand back as if burned.

Oh, gods! He still needed Daryn to temper the anger and hatred. These were the only emotions left to him after Lucien's death, and there was no one to whom he could turn with all his internal confusion. Not even Jessmyn. *Especially not Jessmyn.* He could never burden her with the venom in his soul.

Gaylon found the nightrobe, then took the decanter from his father's cabinet and filled a cut crystal glass with golden liquor. In a worn leather camp chair before the fire, he came to regret dismissing the servants. His boots, the stockings soaked with sweat and melted snow, proved al-most impossible to remove. Surely a master sorcerer would have a handy spell for such occasions, but there were none the king could think of for so mundane a task. Cursing softly, he worried the boots loose, then peeled the socks away and stripped off the rest of his clothes.

Vapors curled from the water in the tub as he sank into it. The soap and washcloth lay on a stool close by, and these were put to good use. Memories of his last bath were vague.

The king had been careless of his person lately, as careless
with diet and rest. The cuts on his face stung when the
lather touched them. He felt for the brandy glass on the
floor with wet soapy hands and nearly dropped it.

Finally, the glass empty, Gaylon laid his head back on
the rim of the copper tub and closed his eyes, drifting without thought. There was only a vast emptiness now, a darkness that seeped slowly through him until much-needed
sleep arrived. Yet even in sleep, he could find no peace.
Dreams came, familiar nightmares filled with blood and
fire. Lost in them, he formed an unconscious wish, and his
Sorcerer's Stone answered. There was one person who had
always been kind, who possessed the understanding and
strength to offer the solace Gaylon needed. In Dreaming,
he might find comfort.

The king willed himself away, and the nightmares
slipped into the distance. A wooden floor with a high wax-
en shine appeared beneath his bare feet. He knew this
place, a simple thatch-roofed cottage in a sheltered valley
well south and west of Castlekeep. The high stone hearth
covered nearly the entire far wall of the large single-room
dwelling, and firelight danced over the remaining three
whitewashed walls with their small shuttered glass windows. Braids of onion and garlic hung from the rafters
among bundles of herbs in neat rows. The air was rich with
the scents of rosemary, horehound, and pennyroyal. A
long, rough-hewn oak table and similarly wrought benches
sat before the fireplace. In the great bed against the left
wall, blankets covered a huge sleeping man, his head buried deep in the pillows.

"Misk?" Gaylon called quietly.

Multiple shadows wavered suddenly across the flames on
the hearth, and the king heard a sad murmuring of voices.
The shadows seemed to collect themselves into one, then
Misk, a tiny woman in long patchwork skirts, appeared before Gaylon.

"Misk," he said again, but unseeing, unhearing, she walked past him to the table.

"The baby," she muttered. "I must be there for the baby."

From behind Gaylon came the same soft voice. "Jimi? Jimi?" Another Misk stood beside the bed. Her sleeping husband groaned and turned over, and this Misk faded away into nothingness.

The woman had strong unearthly powers, but her bizarre behavior was an illness peculiar only to her. She moved along the lines of time, back and forth without control, and her many possible pasts and futures often produced the multiple images that haunted the cottage. Much of the time, Misk could be clear and lucid, but at night or when tired or worried, the present moment grew indistinct, difficult for her to hold. So it seemed now.

Gaylon tried once more to capture her attention. The woman had taken a seat at the table. The king sat across from her just as he had as a boy of ten, so long ago, and searched the gentle, unlined face framed in silver hair.

"Misk?"

She continued to mutter a moment longer, then gazed suddenly into his eyes. "Beware, Gaylon Reysson. He who dies once, may die again."

"Who? What do you see?" the young man asked gently, feeling the shiver her prescience often brought. "Can you tell me?"

Now her right hand lay palm up on the table, a round, flat black stone on it.

"It's not magic," she said, "but it has power." Misk listened for a moment, smiling faintly, then, "You may deliver it for me."

She spoke to another Gaylon, though, to the boy prince, and failed to see the king before her. The adult Gaylon reached out to touch her hand, but his fingers passed through her flesh. The image of her flickered and dimmed, and Gaylon could only watch, heartsick. Voices continued to mutter in the dark corners of the cottage. He had rarely seen the madness with so strong a grip on her.

The king of Wynnamyr closed his eyes and willed himself away. Silence now, and cold stone flags lay beneath his feet. The metallic click-click-click of a ratchet sounded hollowly. He opened his eyes on darkness. Only a few faint stars glimmered through a slot in a curved ceiling high above, and Gaylon raised his ringed hand. The Stone in its gold band brightened enough to cast a soft, watery light against rock walls.

At the far side of the chamber, a little man in blue-black robes leaned over the eyepiece of a telescope, the huge cylindrical body pointed at the wide crack in the roof. "What do you want?" the fellow snapped irritably without looking up.

The king snapped back, "I want your attention, Sezran."

"Do you?" The man straightened, and his iron-gray mane fell back from his narrow forehead, from a face so like Misk's. His dark eyes widened, and he laughed mirthlessly. "Do you Dream naked now, or have you fallen asleep in the bath again?"

Gaylon glanced down at his unclothed body, awash in the blue light of his Stone. The little wizard touched his own Stone and gestured, and a bundle of cloth appeared in his hand. He tossed the bundle to his visitor.

"I know that as a Dreamer the cold doesn't affect you, but the sight of you dressed will be far less offensive."

The king dropped the material to the floor at his feet. "I worry for Misk," he said.

Sezran merely put an eye back to the telescope. "This is quite interesting—a new star forming at the center of your galaxy."

"Her sickness seems worse. Do you care nothing for your sister?"

"My meddlesome, bothersome sister?" The wizard continued his search of the heavens. "As a matter of fact, I do care. How kind of *you* to take an interest after so many years. You have only yourself to blame for her condition, you know."

Gaylon swallowed back the anger those truthful words brought. "You will help her," he ordered imperiously.

"I know only one way to help her. You must first give me Kingslayer."

"And if I did, what would you do?"

That brought Sezran upright again, interested. "With the star gem that powers the blade, I can take Misk home to our own world. There she'll receive proper care, perhaps even a cure."

"What else?"

"What do you mean?" The little wizard's gaze shifted aside.

"How else would you use the sword?"

Sezran shrugged, smiling. "I would kill you."

"As I thought," the king muttered. "But I don't understand why. You were my teacher once."

"Only at Daryn's persistence, and that was one of my gravest mistakes. I needn't worry, though. Kingslayer will destroy you. My curse cannot be denied. Two kings have fallen to it, and you'll be the third."

Gaylon gritted his teeth. "What if I never take up the sword again?"

"Ha! You can't resist its power, not forever. No sorcerer can. Kingslayer's song will draw you back, and then . . ." The wizard's smile grew broader. "But tell me, young one, how does your royal life treat you? Do you feel their hatred, do you see the fear your power provokes in those around you? Even while you Dream, one of your subjects may steal into your chambers and slit the throat of your sleeping body."

"Hold your tongue, old man," Gaylon snarled. "If you

can't help Misk, then you can return to Castlekeep and serve me."

Sezran snorted. "You have your little band of mongrel pups to scamper at your heels. Let them do you service. Now get out!" He leaned over the eyepiece once more.

The king stood a moment longer, then raised a fist. A wave of blue fire exploded from his Sorcerer's Stone. By its bright glare, he saw the metal cylinder of Sezran's telescope turn to molten slag and collapse to the stone floor.

"Gaylon!" the little wizard shrieked and leaped back to safety.

"Till another day, old man. . . ." The king closed his eyes and willed himself back to the keep.

The bathwater had turned cold, and unattended, the fire had died back to coals. Gaylon, teeth chattering, pulled himself from the tub.

Two

A sharp jolt woke Jessmyn from a deep, dreamless sleep. She lay a long moment in the dark, uncertain. Something was very, very wrong. Dimly came the sound of hurried footsteps passing in the hall. The queen found her way into the sitting room and lit a taper from the low-burning fire on the hearth. The footsteps returned as she donned her red brocade robe, and someone began to pound on her door.

"What is it?" Jessmyn demanded of Ned, the young male servant who stood on her threshold.

"The king . . . milady . . . is unwell."

His obeisance was awkward, and she knocked him off balance in her hurry to push by. Frightened, the young woman rushed down the corridor toward the king's apartments.

The boy galloped after her. "The physician is already there, Your Highness."

A small tight group of people stood motionless in the hall before Gaylon's closed door. Portly, balding Girkin, the keep physician, was there along with the young earl of the Lower Vales. Marten Pelson clutched one arm, his face drawn with pain, and Jessmyn pulled his hand loose to observe the blackened sleeve of his nightdress. The skin underneath was badly blistered.

"What have you fools done now?" she demanded.

Marten glanced down at the burn. "The king's delirious, milady. He didn't recognize me when I—"

The ground shook suddenly, and within the chambers, something heavy crashed to the floor. The queen wrenched at the doorknob.

"Milady, no!" Girkin reached for her. "It's sweating sickness, and you risk taking ill yourself."

Jessmyn slapped his hand away. "Cowards!" She turned on the chamberlain. "Temric, open this door immediately."

The man obeyed, fumbling the iron key in the lock, and the door finally opened on a room filled with thin gray smoke. The bed drapes were in flames. Marten rushed past a fallen cabinet to yank the cloth from the rods, then stamped the fire out. Wide-eyed, the queen gazed down at her husband.

Gaylon lay tangled in the quilts, his face flushed and slick with sweat, his hair plastered to his skull. She could smell the peculiar acrid odor that came with this illness. Under the king, the pillows and sheets were soaked. Now the Sorcerer's Stone on his right hand glimmered and brightened, and a cold wind whirled through the chamber.

The servants fled into the hall as tapestries fluttered on the walls and the wind found strength. Jessmyn leaned across the mattress, her face close to the king's.

"My lord," she murmured in his ear. "Beloved, tame the powers. You must, so that we may help you." The young woman stroked the sweat-soaked hair, feeling the impossible heat that radiated from him. The Stone flared, and the ground lurched again. "Gaylon! Be calm." The blue light dimmed slowly, and the king moaned and clenched his fists. So near were they, so closely tied by love, she felt his pain, the horrible aching sickness that burned unchecked in his body.

"Bring fresh linens, now!" the young woman ordered.

"And snow," Girkin added.

"No!" the queen said sharply, and the servants hovered in the doorway, confused and fearful.

The physician puffed himself up. "Please, Your Highness. Believe me, the very best treatment for this illness is to pack the patient in snow to cool the fever."

"How many patients with sweating sickness have you saved in that manner?"

"None," the fat little man admitted unhappily.

"Then we'll try another treatment," the young queen ordered, refusing to accept so grim a prognosis. She clapped her hands at the servants. "Bring linens and heated bricks, but bring them only to the door. We can't risk the spread of the illness. Hurry, all of you! Marten, will you stay? We'll need your help." The young earl nodded, his eyes on the king. Gaylon lay very still.

"There is a new treatment," Girkin muttered from the foot of the bed. "In Xenara they have begun bleeding their patients for all manner of ailments."

"Bleeding them?" Jessmyn took Gaylon's left hand, felt the fingers relax. So hot.

"It involves opening a vein in the wrist and letting the bad blood out."

"How positively brilliant," the queen said, voice low with outrage. "And how does one tell the bad blood from the good? Is it a different color?" When Girkin opened his mouth, she cut him off. "Forget your knives, physician, and go instead to the apothecary. Bring every herb and oil you think will help us fight each set of symptoms as the disease progresses."

"Yes, Your Highness." Girkin bowed. "But I beg you, leave this chamber. We're all in danger, but you most of all. You've always been frail and prone to illness."

Jessmyn ignored him, her fingers twined in Gaylon's. The sweating sickness. She closed her eyes. Each winter it claimed lives—usually the weak, the very young, and very old. Some years the disease reached epidemic proportions, striking hard at every country along the Western Sea.

The symptoms were always the same. First came burning fever that raged through the body, bringing a foul, sour sweat. Next came chills. Then the lungs filled with fluid and the skin turned blue. Sometimes death took a week or more, sometimes mere days. No, Jessmyn thought bitterly, after all we've been through, I will not let death have him. But how could she stop it? Misk or Sezran might be of help, but the fastest rider sent south would never reach the tiny woman in time, and Sezran, so cantankerous and spiteful, would as soon see Gaylon dead.

Dismissing the ideas as useless wondering, she gently set the king's fevered hand aside and tugged the blankets over him. Marten used his time to build an immense fire on the hearth, but the chill in the air would be hard to dispel. Jessmyn abandoned her anger at the young earl and his thoughtless friends. They were not to blame.

The bricks and linen arrived, and the queen helped Marten change the sheets and blankets under and around the king. Then they rolled the bricks in the quilts and laid them all along the sick man's body. More blankets were piled on the bed. Gaylon's eyes were half-open now, unseeing, but his Stone remained dark. Girkin led a pair of servants to the door finally, their arms loaded with jars of powdered herbs and essential oils. It seemed the little man had brought his entire apothecary with him. Soon, the chamber was filled with the scents of burning eucalyptus and camphor.

Jessmyn, eyes gritty and tired, stood back to let the physician work. The first light of dawn glowed gray through the king's high windows, and snow drifted past the thick, warped glass. There were no comfortable chairs in this austere room, but she let Marten lead her to a worn leather camp chair before the fire.

"Sit, milady, please." The kindness in his voice nearly brought tears.

The bricks were exchanged for hot ones, the others placed on the hearth to reheat, and the sheets, once again soaked, were also replaced. The soiled linen would be boiled, though no one was certain just how the sickness spread. At the sound of the door opening, Jessmyn turned her head. Arlin and Karyl, in nightshirts, stood on the threshold, white-faced and worried.

"Stay back," Marten warned them. "It's sweating sickness."

Arlin D'Lelan, dark and handsome, reacted almost violently. "No!" He took a long stride toward the bed, but Marten caught him and shoved him roughly into the hall. With muttered words, they spoke a moment, then the earl closed the door on his two friends. Jessmyn saw him wince when the cloth of his sleeve brushed the burn on his arm.

"Marten?"

"Yes, milady?"

"Have Girkin tend your arm."

"It's nothing, Your Highness."

Jessmyn nodded. "It will be tended. Now."

"Yes, milady."

While the physician treated and bound Marten's injury, the queen closed her eyes once more, aware of Gaylon's weak struggles beneath the heavy blankets. With almost dreamlike detachment, she remembered the night the young king had taken his throne. It had been Jessmyn then, lying helpless and near death on this very bed after accidently ingesting the poison Lucien had intended for Gaylon. Misk had saved her with a foul-tasting antidote, but more than this, the queen remembered the pain of thirst and how a mere cup of water had brought such relief from suffering.

"Girkin." She opened her eyes. "His Majesty has lost a good deal of fluids. We should give him water."

"He is unconscious, milady," the physician said gently. "He might choke."

"We'll feed it to him most carefully."

"But there's another problem. That will only increase the sweating, Your Highness. The proper method is to deny liquids until the sweating ends."

"No," she snapped. "The more he's allowed to sweat, the more poisons will be lost."

Thoughtfully Girkin stared down at his patient. "Milady may be right. . . . But let me make an infusion of blood purifiers. If we are to fight fire with fire, let's feed him hot medicinal tea." He glanced at her. "Do you agree?"

"Yes," the young woman answered and felt relief wash over her. The aging physician was finally willing to approach this sickness in a new way. Now, at last, she might trust him to do what was best for Gaylon and not what was best for Girkin's pride. Her eyes teared, and the room blurred momentarily.

Marten, unshaven and hollow-eyed, dropped to one knee beside her chair. "Don't give up hope, Highness."

"I can't," Jessmyn whispered and managed a faint smile for him.

A day and a night passed, and the king grew slowly worse. Food was delivered and left uneaten beyond the door. Every moment was spent in fighting Gaylon's sickness. Exhausted, the queen remained for long periods seated on the bed beside him. The young man raved at times, and she listened to him converse with Daryn, with his father, even with Lucien—all his ghosts of guilt come to haunt him in the fever.

Deep in the second night, Gaylon's Stone woke again. It flared suddenly, and the fire on the hearth exploded, showering them all with hot embers. To Girkin's and Marten's horror, Jessmyn caught the ringed hand of her lord and quieted the Stone.

"Take care!" the physician cried.

It was well known that a Sorcerer's Stone, touched by the naked skin of any but its master, could bring death. The queen had no fear of Gaylon's Stone, though. She had worn the ring once, in desperation, to save her lord's life. Jessmyn clutched the ringed hand and pressed the hot flesh to her forehead.

"Hear me, Gaylon Reysson," she said bitterly. "We've done all we can. You've got to fight this sickness."

The king took a sharp, rasping breath. Immediately Girkin was at his side. He uncovered Gaylon's chest and put an ear to it, then straightened slowly.

"The lungs have begun to fill."

"Then hurry." The queen stood. "The bricks are cooling. We'll—" She looked about her, dazed by fatigue.

Marten led her to the chair again. "Rest, Your Highness. Let us tend him."

Gaylon's head was propped with more pillows, a thick yellow paste spread over his chest, and the bricks replaced. Throughout, the king continued the short, labored breaths. Jessmyn watched, numb.

The room grew still. The earl had settled on a pile of clean blankets and fallen instantly asleep. Girkin sat against the wall beside the hearth, his head leaned back on the stones. His puffy, dark-circled eyes were closed. Exhausted, the queen returned to the bed to keep watch alone. Gaylon's face had grayed, and his lips were faintly blue. The skin under his nails was tinged the same color.

While she considered the closeness of death, a breath of cold ocean air somehow entered the chamber. Jessmyn felt a familiar stirring and glanced behind her. On the worn carpet at the center of the floor stood a wizened man in midnight robes. He smiled at her, amusement in his glittering black eyes.

"Have I arrived too soon for the funeral?" Sezran asked quietly.

The queen clenched her fists at such audacity, then felt a sudden desperate hope. "Will you help him, please?" she asked and hated her own pleading tone.

"Why should I?" The wizard's gaze wandered over the draped walls. "Is it here, do you think? He would keep the Legacy close at hand."

"Get out," said a husky, breathless voice, and Jessmyn turned. Gaylon's eyes were open, focused and aware. The Stone on his finger flickered to life, and the one on Sezran's chest pulsed in answer.

"No!" the queen hissed angrily.

The wizard only smiled again. "Death hovers near, Gaylon Reysson. Tell me where Kingslayer is, so that some good may come of all this. For Misk's sake."

The king, too weak to move, managed a short bubbling laugh, then whispered, "For Misk's sake, I might, but never for yours. With my death . . . the sword will be lost forever. It carries my own curse now as well as yours . . . one that not even you can undo." Sezran tensed in rage, and his Stone turned a deadly blue. Gaylon's eyes closed. "Begone, old man. I'm weary."

The little wizard's robes swept around him, and snarling, he vanished in a gust of sea air. Jessmyn buried her head in the king's damp shoulder. When she realized the fever had broken, tears of relief began to flow.

"My lord, I thought I'd lost you."

"Hush, wife," Gaylon murmured, already drifting into exhausted sleep. "I . . . will never . . . leave you."

*   *   *   *   *

The high-domed ceiling and white marble columns of the temple glinted red-gold with the light of a rising winter sun. A dozen braziers scattered across the wide expanse of floor radiated warmth, but little of it reached Roffo, king of all Xenara, where he lay prostrate on the tiles before the altar. Tek, the high priest of Mezon, intoned the blessing melodiously, on and on.

The king, his great round bulk covered only in thin sackcloth, tried to still the impious thoughts that nagged at him. For the past forty years, he'd been subject to the god's holy rites—purified to Mezon's righteous will during the winter solstice—and every year, he had dreaded the coming moment.

Tek's voice droned on in invocation, and four priests helped the king, grunting, to his knees. The predawn chill was deep in Roffo's old bones. Head bowed, he let the high priest anoint him, brow and hands, with sacred oil.

"Mezon keep and protect the faithful," Roffo sang in his cracking basso, an echo of Tek's strong tenor. "Mezon defend Xenara and its king against the faithless."

Never had those words seemed quite so significant as they had these past few years. A tiny fear blossomed in the old man's barrel chest. Gaylon Reysson was the king of a faithless nation. Wynnamyr had long ago forsaken the gods of its forebears. The people were allowed to worship whoever and whenever they pleased, or not at all.

To that blasphemous country, Roffo had once sent an infant princess, his own daughter, in an attempt to bind Wynnamyr to Xenara by blood. Eight years ago, the promised marriage had taken place, yet nothing but ill had come of it. Gaylon Reysson was a dangerous young monarch in possession of the most horrible magical weapon ever wrought—Kingslayer.

Roffo had been an unhappy witness to his daughter's marriage to the young heir of the Red Kings. He had gone to Castlekeep to see her wed Lucien D'Sulang and found the keep in an uproar, Lucien dead.

The king of Xenara had seen the mad light in Gaylon's eyes as he gained wife and throne at the same time. Worse, Roffo had recently received strong evidence that Gaylon Reysson was finally ready to take up the sword of Orym and make war on his neighbors. That thought was almost too dreadful to contemplate.

The elderly monarch felt a drag at his elbows and realized that the time of the final offering had come. Shaking slightly, he allowed the priests to help him to his feet and lead him to the gold-inlaid alabaster altar. The god's huge double-edged sword lay across the altar surface.

Tek continued to sing the litany, intoning fervently, "Through the blood of the pure and the innocent, the god accepts us. Through our sacrifices and devotions, we humble ourselves to his purpose."

The priest placed a tethered white dove in Roffo's unsteady hands. The bird's tiny black eyes glittered, and its soft feathers ruffled in the light, cold breeze that drifted through the open temple. Tek's chant ended and silence fell. The king could only stare at the creature in his grip.

"Now!" the high priest hissed.

Roffo remained frozen, his eyes on the dove. With a growl of frustration, Tek caught the king's hands in his own, used the old man's fat fingers to give the bird's neck a sudden twist, then wrenched the head free so the hot blood could be dripped along the god's blade. Revulsion filled Roffo. In the age when mad Orym ruled Wynnamyr to the north, Xenara had been a more savage place, too. Then a baby was sacrificed here each winter, on this same altar. Roffo shuddered at the thought and dropped the bird's carcass into a proffered basin.

A great woolen cloak of royal blue settled on the king's shoulders, and, grateful, he wrapped it tight around him with bloody hands. Done! Another year dedicated to the god, the hours of discomfort and humiliation over. Someone placed the heavy jewel-encrusted crown on his long black curls. Roffo followed the double line of silent white-robed priests past the marble statues of the lesser gods that graced the temple's outer vestibules. Before him, Tek's back was rigid, possibly with anger. Every year, Roffo balked at the live sacrifice, and every year the high priest was outraged.

At the moment, the king of Xenara could not have cared

less. He wanted only to return to the warmth of his palace and share a sumptuous breakfast with his multitudinous family, his many wives and offspring. But Tek followed him down the broad marble stairs and across the gardens.

Roffo's knees and lower back ached. Irritated, the old man paused, waving his kilted palace guards off a distance.

"What is it?" he snapped at the priest.

There was no anger in Tek's narrow, craggy face. He offered his king the same serene smile that always made Roffo leery.

"I wish to discuss the solstice gifts you will send to your daughter, the queen of Wynnamyr."

The old man clutched his cloak tighter, aggravated. "Not now, Tek. I'm hungry, tired, and in pain—as you and your god require. Leave me in peace."

"Majesty," the priest said gently, "this is something that must be dealt with immediately. The great god, Mezon, has given me a dream."

Roffo closed his eyes momentarily. Whenever Tek wanted something, the god always gave him a dream or some portent. Unfortunately, the high priest's judgment, whether god-given or not, was often enough correct. However much the king disliked Tek, he had to give him grudging respect. In the complex political structure of Xenara, Tek held nearly as much authority as Roffo, and together they managed to balance the power held by the merchant families. There was an uneasy, but necessary, alliance between the two men that had lasted well over a quarter of a century.

"A dream," the king muttered finally, his gaze on the guards who stood just out of earshot.

"Majesty, the solstice gifts—"

"Lady Jarath chooses all presents for our mutual children, Jessmyn included. I have forty-three sons and daughters at last count, priest. You can hardly expect me—"

"My lord is truly virile," Tek interrupted, amusement in

his voice, "but I am more concerned about the delivery of
the gifts, not their selection. I have commissioned Sedwin
D'Loran to take them north with all haste. With Mezon's
help, he may deliver us from Gaylon Reysson at the same
time."

Roffo frowned. "Sedwin's a boy."

"Young, but artful. Already a swordsman of note and
quite devious, but loyal to his king and god. He's most eager to undertake the task—for considerable reward, of
course."

"Of course." The king tugged at his mustache. "What
reward did you offer him?"

"I said he might be consort to the widowed queen of
Wynnamyr."

"And rule with her?"

"Under your good auspices."

"What if he fails?"

Tek's serene smile returned. "Ah. Sedwin is the last male
heir of the D'Loran's. One of your many princes could be
married to the eldest D'Loran daughter. She's only eight,
but . . ."

"Yes, yes." Roffo nodded. The D'Loran trade ships
would tip the scale ever so slightly in the favor of the
king—and the priesthood. Whatever the outcome, they
could only gain. "Do it."

Tek bowed deeply, his gold-edged robes fluttering in the
breeze. "It is done." He backed away, then turned and
strode toward the temple.

His stomach rumbling, the king continued through the
gardens, under the date palms, past the olive and citrus
trees. The morning light struck the red-tiled roofs of the
city that lay beyond the high palace walls. Dimly he could
hear the shouts and laughter in Zankos's teeming streets,
the bells on the ships in the harbor. The scents of the palace
kitchens reached him even on the chill air, rich with cinna-
mon and clove.

Once inside the garden patio, servants came at a run to take his cloak, wash the blood from his hands, the soot from his face, and wrap him in robes of ermine and gold—all as the king walked. The shrieks of children greeted him in the entrance to the breakfast room. A dozen or so of the youngest were on him immediately, clamoring for his attention. Joy and love swept over Roffo as he caught them up one by one and gave them hugs and kisses.

Their mothers and elder siblings sat at the long table, quiet and regal. The women watched closely, to see which child he favored most. It was always thus, the jockeying for power and prestige among them. Roffo hated the family politics, but he loved the women more, and absolutely adored his numerous children and grandchildren.

Nursemaids finally chased the youngsters back to their places. Smiling, the king pushed a small wooden horse from his chair, removed someone's dolly from his platter, and took his seat at the head of the table.

"Shall we eat?" he asked and rang the little silver bell. That simple sound chased all his worries away.

* * * * *

The children of the town of Riverbend were never allowed to play near the South Fork River. There, at the headwaters, the river ran narrow, deep, and swift, its banks dangerously steep. The small flood plain below the town that grew crops in spring and summer was their playground in winter. With a touch of longing, fifteen-year-old Davi stood behind his mother's establishment, the Fickle River Inn, and watched a group of children in the trampled snow.

Two opposing armies of boys had built ice fortresses, and, armed with snowballs, carried on a cold but happy war. Their shrieks and laughter had drawn Davi's attention, made him pause with the heavy wooden bucket in his hands. In all his young life, he had never once been allowed to join the childish fun of his peers. An innkeep's life was hard, and Davi's mother, Haddi, insisted his days be spent in labor, not play. Someday, she often said with a certain bitterness, the Fickle River Inn would belong to Davi. Then he would be grateful he'd learned life's harsh lessons early.

Davi felt anything but grateful as he carried the bucket to the well and set it on the frozen ground beside the mortared stones. He wanted to be a woodsman, not an innkeep. He wanted to work in the forests cutting down the giant redwoods and firs. That somehow seemed far more romantic, dangerous, and exciting. Unfortunately, at fifteen and a half, Davi was only of average height and much too slender of build to handle a long, two-man crosscut saw. The woodsmen, of necessity, were all large and burly.

Despite an almost fragile appearance, though, the dark-haired boy was strong and quick. He lowered the bucket on a rope into the well, heard it splash into the water. The dozen or so patrons' horses stabled in the small shed behind the inn were nearly all watered, but after that the kitchen ovens must be stoked, the wood carried in from the stack by the well. In the snowy fields below, the children continued their happy shrieks.

The water slopped over the bucket rim as Davi lugged it back to the shed. His trouser legs were already soaked from previous trips and stiffening with ice. This bucketful was for Katy, his own little blood-bay mare, given to him years ago by a young patron passing through town. She nickered from the far side of the shed, lost behind the larger horses tied to rings along the wall.

Davi stepped carefully through the dung-littered straw. The shed would have to be mucked out as soon as the ovens were stoked. The thought made him groan. Katy bobbed her head at his approach, jingling the piece of chain that hooked her halter to the ring. The fat little beast had chewed her way through a number of ropes and led Davi on many a merry chase before he'd gotten wise.

He gave her a shriveled carrot pilfered from the root cellar and unhooked the chain to let her drink. Katy dipped her head to the bucket, then backed suddenly away into the aisle. One of the patron's horses squealed in outrage as the pony charged past and out the shed door.

"Katy!"

She paid no mind—as usual—kicking up her shaggy heels in joy at this unexpected freedom. The boy followed, angry and cursing. There was no time for such foolishness, not with so many chores yet undone. His mother would say to let the mare go. Haddi would just as soon Katy ran off and never returned—one less mouth to feed—but Davi loved the little animal, contrary and nasty as she often was.

"Katy. Whoa, girl."

The pony had trotted, head high, across the yard, and now she pawed the dirty, trampled snow, her eyes on Davi. This was a game the boy knew well. Katy wanted him to chase her. Feeling contrary himself, he turned his back. But when he started toward the shed, he heard her hoof steps behind him. Then her nose bumped him hard between the shoulder blades. Davi made a fast, desperate grab for the halter, and, snorting, the mare jerked away. She halted just out of reach again.

Another carrot might entice her. Might. The boy walked slowly toward her, a mittened hand held out. Impudently, the mare spun and struck out at him with a hind foot, then raced out across the road and up into the trees on the hillside beyond. Torn, Davi watched her go.

Mountain lions had been sighted close to town, driven down from the ridgetops by the harsh weather, and despite her playfulness, Katy was well along in years. Something terrible might happen to her out in the snowy woods. With only a glance back at the inn, the boy gritted his teeth and went after her.

Three

Tydus Dorenson brought his gift hidden in the folds of a blanket. He paused to smile at the guard who stood alone in the drafty corridor just outside the royal apartment. Girkin was very strict where the king's health was concerned since this recent illness. While recuperating, His Majesty could receive no visitors other than servants and the queen. There'd been howls of protest over that by the young lords who counted themselves Gaylon Reysson's closest friends.

Of course, Girkin's restrictions did not include Tydus. The head councilman must consult with the king now and again, just as he intended to do this very moment. Tydus pushed the door open gently and peered in. Gaylon, face pale and bruised about the eyes, stared at the tapestry on the opposite wall.

"Milord?"

The young man turned his head.

"May I come in?"

"Please do," Gaylon muttered. There was still considerable weakness in his voice.

Tydus closed the door behind him. "I've brought you a present, Sire."

"Another blanket. How kind," the king said with little enthusiasm.

"Ah, this will warm you better, I think." Tydus pulled

an amber bottle from the folds of wool. "Brandy. It's Xenaran and half a century aged in oak, or so the merchant promised."

The king's eyes lighted, and now he managed a lopsided smile. "Tydus Dorenson, you are a man of true compassion. I'm sick to death of Girkin's foul herbal teas." Gaylon struggled to sit up.

"Here now, don't overdo." Tydus set the brandy down on the bedside table and helped his lord, plumping the goose down pillows behind him. Then he uncorked the bottle with a conspiratorial air. "This is strictly against your physician's orders, so we'll drink from teacups. It'll be our secret. . . ." He filled a cup for the king, then poured a small amount into another cup for himself.

Gaylon downed his too quickly and choked. Smiling indulgently, Tydus filled his cup again and set the bottle on the floor this time, should Girkin arrive unannounced.

"How can I ever repay you, Tydus?" the king murmured finally. Some color had returned to his cheeks, but the effort of holding the cup had obviously exhausted him.

"There's no need, milord. I wish only to serve."

The latch on the door clicked again, and this time, the guard pushed it inward to let another visitor pass over the threshold. The queen held a loaded tray in slender hands. Tydus bowed deeply, nudging the brandy bottle under the edge of the bedclothes nearest his foot.

"Your Highness," he murmured.

The young woman wore a rich purple gown of tightly knit lamb's wool, her long honey-colored hair bound high in a thin gold coronet as befitted a married lady of royal blood. An exceptional beauty, Tydus thought with admiration and just a little longing.

"Tydus," Jessmyn acknowledged curtly and gave the head councilman a bare nod, but her pale green eyes were on the king. "Girkin feels a bayberry tea will help to clear your lungs, my lord."

Gaylon made a face and groaned as the queen set the tray on a nightstand. She reached across the bed for the patient's teacup, then paused, nostrils flaring slightly. Tydus realized that they'd been found out. Most regrettable.

"Your Majesties," he said and bowed again in his most self-deprecating manner. "I beg your leave. So much to do." He backed his way to the door, aware of the queen's anger, and escaped into the corridor. Once past the guard, Tydus's smile returned. He may have provoked Jessmyn's ire, but he'd gained His Majesty's gratitude. A more than fair trade.

*   *   *   *   *

Katy's behavior worried Davi. The elderly pony, overweight and huffing, had led him farther and farther afield. Occasionally she stopped, as if to make certain the boy still followed. Several times, when he was about to give up in disgust, the mare waited until Davi very nearly got a hand on her halter, then she'd dash away. Frustrated, yet determined, the boy continued to trudge along in her wake.

Snow began to fall, light flakes that drifted gently down into a forest already covered in a thick white mantle, and Davi began to regret his rash decision to go after the little mare. His face and fingers and toes had long since gone numb. The course Katy followed seemed to lead in no particular direction—up treacherous mountainsides, down into narrow valleys, over ice-rimed creeks.

At first, the twisting trail hadn't bothered him. He knew he had only to follow his own deep tracks back to Riverbend. But as the snowfall grew steadily heavier, those tracks were being covered. The adventure and excitement he had craved lost all their appeal when set against the possibility of freezing to death. Night was fast approaching. The boy curled mittened hands into fists and blinked away the snowflakes that caught on his eyelashes.

As the day faded, Katy brought him at last to a gap in the steep terrain that opened out on a small, sheltered valley. There, beyond a snow-shrouded orchard, Davi saw yellow candlelight gleaming from two small windows of a cottage, and relief washed through him. The mare had at least led him somewhere he might safely spend the night.

He watched the pony disappear behind a low stone byre. Refusing to follow her any farther, Davi hiked through the fresh snow to the cottage stoop. Standing there, cold, hungry, and tired, it finally occurred to him what a terrible, thoughtless thing he'd done. His mother would be frantic with worry. The chores had been left unfinished, and in all his young life, the boy had never slept anywhere but on his own cot in his tiny room next to the inn's warm kitchen. Guilt and shame settled heavily in the pit of his empty stomach.

At the creak of hinges, Davi turned. The cottage's heavy oak door swung slowly inward, and a small dark form stood silhouetted there against the candlelight and the dancing flames of a huge fireplace. The boy stared at the shadowy figure—a child, perhaps.

"Oh, my dear, you must be so cold." The words were soft, the voice feminine, but with a gentle timbre of age.

Davi remained silent, uncertain how to respond. A hand darted up to touch his face. The fingers were hot against his icy cheek.

"Come inside, Daryn, before you catch your death."

The boy found his tongue at last. "My name isn't Daryn."

"Well, of course it's not." A tiny woman stepped back into the light. "Who said it was?"

"You just—"

"Come in, come in. Please. I'm Misk. How kind of you to visit . . . Davi. Such a long, cold journey."

Misk. The name was familiar.

"How do you know who I am?" Davi stepped inside.

When he reached for the door though, it swung shut of its own accord. The wind perhaps, only there hadn't been any wind a moment ago.

"Are you hungry?" someone whispered, and the whisper echoed around him, "Hungry . . . hungry . . . hungry."

"Ma'am?" The boy turned, confused.

The woman was gone. Davi found her before the fireplace now, at the far end of the long, wide room. His sense of misgiving grew even stronger. The flames on the hearth leaped and fluttered, throwing eerie shadows over the whitewashed walls. Even in the fire's warmth, the boy shivered.

It was a fine big cottage. The furnishings were few, but well-crafted: a large bedstead with lumpy straw mattress under one of the little windows, several shelves and cupboards, and a long table with benches. Bundles of dried herbs hung from the open rafters, and above them was the thick sturdy thatching of the roof.

The boy hovered by the threshold, uncertain, until the door flew open again. The wind was not to blame this time either. Davi looked up into the broad, pleasant face of a huge man in rough clothing.

"Jimi?"

"Aye, lad," the fellow answered.

Davi had known Jimi, a local cheesemaker, all his life. The big man came to Riverbend several times a year to sell his cheeses and buy supplies. This must be his small farm. Now the boy remembered hearing of Misk, Jimi's wife, a healer and, some said, a harmless madwoman. That thought only made him all the more nervous.

"Yer old pony's to bed," the giant rumbled.

"I—I can't stay, Jimi. My mum's gonna skin me. Could you show me the way home? I'm lost."

"Tomorrow. When the storm's past."

"My mum—"

"Got milkin'," Jimi grunted. "Rest, lad. Listen to

Misk." He turned and ambled back out into the cold night. The door closed behind him.

Slowly Davi pulled off his mittens, then his cloak. Melting snow dripped from the hem as he carried the garment over the highly polished wooden floor to the fireplace and hung it on a peg near the heat. Misk, with her back to him, used a long wooden spoon to stir the contents of a small cast iron cauldron hanging on a metal arm over the flames.

"Are you hungry?" she asked.

Davi stared at the pot she carefully stirred. There was nothing in it. A little tremor of fear rushed through him. The woman was truly mad.

Misk cocked her head. "What troubles you, child?"

"Your pot . . . It's empty."

"No." The tiny woman looked down. "It was empty yesterday, and will be again tomorrow, I think. But not tonight."

Even as she spoke, the full rich smell of venison stew filled the boy's nostrils. Now the cauldron brimmed with meat and vegetables in a thick brown gravy. Davi backed a step from the hearth, wondering if he were the mad one.

Misk smiled up at him. "You have your mother's green eyes . . . but your father's features and build."

"You knew my father?" That caught Davi's full attention. This was a subject his mother rarely spoke of.

"I knew him long ago."

"Then you know he died—a logging accident. My mother says he was crushed by a tree."

"Is that what she told you? What a bitter woman she is to have denied you your heritage all this time." Misk took a bowl from a shelf, then bent over the pot again. "Your father was Daryn Emilson, Duke of Gosney."

"No . . . His name was Davlin, and he was a simple woodsman." Davi watched as she filled the bowl.

"He was a sorcerer and a duke. In denying you your heritage, your mother has also denied the king of Wynnamyr his closest ally. The dukes of Gosney have served the Red Kings over the past millennium, and now you must take your place at Gaylon Reysson's right hand."

The boy opened his mouth to argue.

"Sit down at the table," Misk commanded. "I couldn't wait any longer for Haddi to come to her senses. Events are forming that will change the course of Wynnamyr's future, and Gaylon is incapable of facing them alone."

"My mother says Gaylon Reysson is insane," the boy stated, his eyes on the steaming bowl of stew before him.

"In a way, he is. It'll be up to you to temper those chaotic forces that drive him."

Davi shook his head. "You're mistaken, madam. I'm an innkeeper's son. Not a duke's."

"Eat," Misk said sharply and pushed a small spoon into the boy's hand.

Hunger overpowered fear. After the first hesitant bite, Davi ate with relish. Misk brought him warm, frothy milk in a pitcher and thick slices of brown bread spread with pot cheese, then sat on the bench opposite the boy.

"They came here that night," said the woman, her vision turned inward. "Daryn and his young prince. The duke had been poisoned and was very ill, but Gaylon had seen his father murdered. He was only ten, and his injuries were of the spirit. Those wounds never healed, and they filled him with a hatred and rage that rule him to this day.

"Your father, while alive, managed to hold Gaylon in check. Now you're the duke of Gosney, and this task falls to you."

"If all that's so, why has my mother never said anything?"

"Haddi never told you because she knew a duke's son would be discontent with the life of an innkeep—because she knew a Gosney would want to serve his Red King. And then she would lose you."

Except for the crackling of the fire, silence had fallen. A

faint puff of woodsmoke escaped from the chimney. Misk's eyes had unfocused, and her features grew indistinct, colors fading. Behind the boy, someone stirred, and he heard the woman whisper in a gentle voice, "You met your father once, Davi. He taught you a tune on the lute."

Davi turned quickly, hackles rising, and found the room empty behind him. When he turned back, Misk reached out suddenly and stabbed a finger to his forehead. Sharp pain blossomed behind his eyes, then color and light exploded. A lute.

Memories, bright and clear, formed in Davi's mind—of a battered string instrument in the hands of a red-bearded young man whose clothes were little more than frayed rags. He'd come to the Fickle River Inn in the company of an elderly man dressed in black robes. Davi had been seven years old then, or perhaps eight, but he remembered all of it clearly. Something about the two visitors had drawn him inexplicably.

The older man had worn long black hair and a full beard, both heavily streaked with gray. His face was aged with cares, and his left hand had somehow been mutilated, the fingers all but gone and covered with thick scar tissue. Even so, he had shown Davi how to place his own small fingertips on the lute strings, had taught him the beginnings of a song about a dappled pony named Thistledown.

The two men had stayed only one night at the inn, but before they left, the younger one had given Katy to the little innkeeper's son. Now Davi understood the sorrow in the older man's eyes . . . and remembered the warmth of his voice.

"Misk!" the boy cried and felt her touch his shoulder immediately. "How did my father lose his hand?"

From behind him, the little woman wrapped her arms across Davi's chest. "It was destroyed along with his Sorcerer's Stone and his powers when he defied the wizard, Sezran, all for the sake of the prince."

"My father was truly a sorcerer?"

"Yes."

"And he gave up his magic for Gaylon Reysson?"

Misk leaned to touch her cheek to the boy's. "And his life. But had he the chance, Gaylon would have done as much for your father. The bond between Gosney and Red King is a strong magic of its own."

"Tell me," Davi said, the visions still swirling through his head. "Tell me of my father and Gaylon and how this all came about."

"Yes," the tiny woman whispered in his ear. "I will tell you everything, Davyn Darynson."

* * * * *

It had been a dreadfully dull week, and by Arlin's reckoning, the next week would be the same. And the next, if Girkin had his way. The young Southerner glared at Karyl, who sat in a stuffed leather chair of the southeast wing's study, his freckled nose in a book, a cup of mulled wine beside him on a table. This studious side of the king's third cousin came as an irritating revelation.

Arlin was not the only one to think so.

"Karyl," snapped Marten from his own chair, "you're not paying attention." Karyl's silence only proved this true, and the earl growled in exasperation. "I'm going to die of boredom. Let's go into Keeptown."

Rinn straightened his blond lanky form on a stool beside the fireplace. Being a tailor's son, he could neither read nor write, so books held no interest for him either. "I say we find another way into the king's apartment."

"If you could reach them, you might fit through those narrow windows," Marten said glumly. "The rest of us will need a wider entrance."

"Wait!" Arlin snatched the book from Karyl's hands, making him squawk. "There is another way. A secret staircase that leads up from the dungeons."

"It's hardly a secret if you know about it." At the voice from the doorway, all four young men leaped to their feet. "Unfortunately, the dungeons aren't very safe. I've saved you the trouble in any case."

"Sire!" Arlin murmured. "Should you be up?"

Gaylon's face was pale and nearly as thin as Rinn's. He leaned on the door frame, dressed in dark broadcloth trousers, shirt, and high boots, grinning at his friends. "The king has been supine long enough."

"Well, then," Karyl laughed. "We'll get the horses and go into town to celebrate your recovery, milord."

Arlin, though, had noticed the sheen of perspiration on the king's brow. He took a clean cup from the table by the hearth and filled it with mulled wine, then carried the warm brew to Gaylon.

"Sit and rest a moment first," the Southern lord said gently.

The king took the cup and emptied it. "I'm tired of rest." He gazed at his friends. "But we won't need the horses. I thought we might try a little adventure close by."

"Where?" Marten demanded.

"Patience, Earl. More wine for your sovereign."

This time they scuffled for the honor, and Rinn won, slopping wine over the carpet as he returned. Gaylon drank the second cup as quickly as the first, then stifled a cough.

"I have brandy in my chambers," Marten offered.

"No," Arlin snapped.

"Yes," the king said. "We'll stop on the way for coats and cloaks, as well. Let's go."

He turned back to the passageway, and the others followed, laughing and joking as they always had, all but Arlin. Servants scattered at their approach. The young Southerner walked behind, worried. While Gaylon's movements were steady, they were also slow and careful, and when he coughed, the sound of it was ragged.

In his musty, cold chambers, the earl of the Lower Vales found his brandy and shared out all his spare cloaks and overshirts. Rinn had brought his own warm clothing from town, but even the king wore borrowed clothes as he led his band out through the rear courtyard and onto the castle grounds.

The morning sky held monotonous, low gray clouds, and Arlin wondered briefly if the winter would never end. The air was clear and cold, the snow deep from last night's storm. Gaylon paused to lean against an ice-covered fountain while the others trampled the snow and passed the brandy.

"Milord, use my shoulder for support," Arlin said.

The king's hazel eyes hardened with momentary irritation, then he managed a brief smile. "I have other, more subtle, means of support, thank you." The gloved fingers of his left hand touched the forefinger of his right, where his ring lay hidden by the soft kidskin.

Karyl let loose a sudden howl as Rinn poured snow down his collar. They tussled a moment, until Gaylon walked away toward the whitethorn hedge that ringed the grounds. The path led them past an armory and the weapons arena, past the rose gardens whose dormant bushes had been pruned and tightly wrapped with burlap.

"Just where are we going?" Marten demanded again, loudly. Karyl, his hands full of snow, still sought noisy revenge on Rinn.

The king spoke as he trudged through knee-deep drifts. "I want to visit an old friend." He located a break in the hedge and passed through. "And I thought we might explore death while we're at it."

Marten slowed long enough to send a troubled, questioning glance at Arlin, but the Southerner had already guessed where they were headed—to the keep's burial grounds. The woods crowded close on the hillsides, and Gaylon led them among snow-burdened evergreens and

oaks with nude branches strung with icicles. The earl of the
Lower Vales dropped back beside Arlin.

"This is the way to the tombs," Marten said, face nearly
as pale as the king's. "Why would he bring us here?"

It was Karyl who answered, having stopped to take a pull
from the brandy. "Who cares?" He passed the bottle to
Marten. "You said you were dying of boredom. Perhaps
we've come for your funeral."

Unamused, the earl tilted the brandy to his lips and
swallowed.

"Hallo!" Rinn shouted in the distance. "This way.
You're falling behind!"

Gaylon, the hood of his borrowed cloak pulled up over
his head, dropped out of sight on the slope, and the tailor's
son followed. Karyl snatched the bottle back from Marten
and galloped after the king, clumsy in the snow.

The three waited impatiently for Arlin and the earl at
the low stone fence that ringed the burial grounds. Redmond of Graymount lay here in a small solitary tomb of
imported Xenaran marble. Arlin paused to wipe the snow
from Redmond's name carved in the stone, but this was
apparently not the friend the king had come to visit.

Gaylon strode past the tomb and past the mausoleum of
the Red Kings, where his mother and father had been laid
to rest long ago. He stopped before the stone portal of an
ancient cairn dug into the hillside.

"What is this place?" Rinn asked, arriving with his companions.

Redheaded Karyl grinned, a royal cousin well versed in
royal scandal. "This is the cairn of the Dark Kings. Orym is
suppose to lie here among his incestuous relatives."

"Just so," said the king and passed out torches taken
from inside the cairn's entrance. "It's Orym's bones we
seek. A treasure hunt."

"After a thousand years," Karyl snorted, "his dust is all
we'll find."

Marten's face had gone as white as the snow. "It's wrong to disturb the shades, milord, especially the shades of sorcerer-kings."

"And queens," added Rinn happily. "There were a lot of folk, I hear, in that royal line, all put to death. They must have stacked them in the cairn like firewood at the last."

"So far," the king said with a dry smile, "we've made mischief only among the living. The dead deserve our attentions, too, don't you think?"

He pulled the glove from his right hand and gestured. The Sorcerer's Stone in his ring flared a brilliant blue for just an instant, and Rinn's torch burst into flame.

Afterward, while the others lit their torches from the first, Gaylon leaned against the stone retaining wall. Arlin could see the exhaustion in his eyes, in the pinched drawn face. This was madness for him, so soon from his sickbed. The others noticed nothing, only followed their monarch into the dark beyond the portal.

Marten balked one last time before the entrance. "This will bring nothing but ill luck," he muttered, then dipped his thumb in the urn of woodash beside the door and drew a thick sooty line across his forehead.

This was a Wynnamyran custom that Gaylon and Rinn and Karyl had disdained. Arlin had been raised with Southern gods and other traditions, but he hesitated. There were likely spirits here. The dead did not always rest easy. With a final, wary glance around, the Xenaran lord pushed his right thumb into the ashes as Marten had done and made the mark above his eyes. Only then did he take the narrow stone steps down into the cairn.

Torchlight fluttered below, and Rinn and Karyl's voices echoed up to Arlin. Their laughter seemed strained, though. The antechamber was small and dank, the cold deeper than winter. Tunnels radiated outward, dug unknown distances into the hillside, and rubble lay in the mouths of some. Marten stood alone in the center of the

floor, but his friends tagged close on the king's heels while
he checked each opening.

Arlin joined them just as Gaylon paused before the tunnel nearest the stair. The king took Rinn's torch and held it
above his head to reveal a coat of arms carved into the stone
there—a bear, rampant, with a crown in its jaws and barred
by crossed lances.

Gaylon handed the torch back to Rinn. "Arlin, with me.
The rest of you, wait here." He ducked into the low opening.

The young Southerner ducked quickly after him, bearing his own torch. The fir pitch crackled, and the flame
scorched the tunnel roof. Soon the passage curved, then
opened on a tiny chamber with two sarcophaguses. The
stone lid of one was cracked and sealed with mortar. Arlin
sidled past it and felt something crunch underfoot. The
sound sent a shudder through him, but it was only a
flower, brittle with age. A white rose.

Gaylon had stopped beside the newer coffin. Now he
leaned both hands on the lid, head bowed, and gave into a
spate of coughing.

"Do you smell it?" the king asked finally, breathlessly,
wiping his mouth with the edge of his borrowed cloak.

"What, milord?"

"A sweet scent. Violets, I think."

Arlin shifted uneasily. "No, milord. I smell only smoke
from the torch."

"Why do you follow me?" Gaylon demanded suddenly.
He looked up, eyes narrowed.

"What do you mean, Sire?"

"I mean what I say. Why do you follow me?"

Confused, Arlin answered, "Because you're the king."

"Roffo is your king, not I. Answer me truthfully."

"I follow you—" The Xenaran lord felt a chill. "We all
follow you because we . . . love you."

"Gods! That's a fool's reason." Gaylon slammed a fist

down on the coffin.

Now Arlin felt a touch of anger. "Then we are all your fools, but me most of all. Milord, you *are* my king, and I'll swear fealty if it pleases you. I would gladly die for you."

"No, for all the gods' sakes!" In the fluttering torch-light, the king's face contorted. "Promise me you won't die for me. Promise it!"

"No, Sire. That's a promise I can't make." Arlin dared a step nearer, hoping to divert the king's attention. "Whose coffin is this?"

"Another fool's," said Gaylon bitterly and turned away. He raced down the tunnel, disappearing in the dark.

The young Southerner chased after him, his torch guttering with the rush of cold air. In the antechamber, the others were already gathered around the king, who fought another bout of ragged coughing.

Arlin shoved Rinn aside. "His Majesty is tired. We should return to the keep."

To the Xenaran's surprise, Gaylon agreed. "I'm tired, indeed." He upended Marten's brandy bottle, then dashed it against the stone flags. "Much too tired to make the long journey back. But perhaps there's a shortcut." The king snatched his cousin's torch and dodged into the tunnel farthest from the stairs.

"Come on," Karyl snapped at Rinn. "We'll lose him."

"We won't," the tailor's son snapped back. "It's a game. He doesn't want to be lost." Even so, the lanky young man allowed himself to be guided into the same tunnel.

Cursing under his breath, Arlin started to follow, but Marten caught his arm.

"He's going insane, isn't he?"

"That's something we've always known. Marten, go back. You don't have to do this."

The earl laughed shortly. "Yes, I do. I just wish I'd brought more brandy. It's gods-cursed cold down here." He lowered his torch and stepped into the passageway.

*   *   *   *   *

Alone, the king moved deeper into the tunnel. Exhaustion dogged him, and his chest ached dully, but he'd been too long abed with only his thoughts for company. For a time, the others' muffled voices reached him, then a bend in the passage silenced even that. The way was strewn with slabs of porous stone that had fallen from the arched ceiling, exposing rotted timbers.

Orym lay in this direction—Gaylon had sensed faintly the same raw energy that emanated from Kingslayer and let it lead him. Now a strange dense fog came to flow around his ankles, tendrils curling, licking at his boots. There were openings here on either side of the main tunnel, small chambers with single stone coffins, unadorned and dust covered. The king checked each opening and found some of the chambers had collapsed.

"Milord!"

"Here," he called over his shoulder.

Karyl arrived with Rinn, both huffing. The pudgy redhead raised a booted foot and white fog trailed after. "What is this? I feel like I'm walking in soup." He sniffed. "Smells foul, too."

"Then don't put your nose in it, Cousin," Gaylon advised. "And stay to the center of the passage or you'll bring everything down on top of us."

"There's nothing here," Karyl grumbled. "Let's go back."

The king ignored him and headed once more down the tunnel, drawn by the heavy darkness, the hint of Orym. At last the passageway ended in a chamber far larger than any of the others. Gaylon stepped to the center, where another single sarcophagus stood. This one glittered in the torchlight. Behind him, Karyl and Rinn drew sharp breaths.

The ancient gods of Wyndland—the land that was now called Wynnamyr—had been carved into the walls and inlaid with beaten gold. On the coffin lid itself lay a wide golden crown and a scepter, each encrusted with gems. Chalices and plates of gold were stacked about the floor. Gaylon glanced at the high arch of the ceiling overhead. It had remained whole, but a crack, in the shape of jagged lightning, spread up from the entrance.

"Such wealth," Karyl whispered, voice husky with awe. "Here all this time and never touched."

"It's cursed," Marten said from where he stood with Arlin on the threshold.

Rinn, silent until now, muttered, "My father says all gold is cursed."

"That's because he hasn't any," Karyl snorted.

Gaylon pushed a shoulder against the coffin's stone lid and found himself too weak to move it.

"Milord, no!"

Marten's cry was disregarded. The king tried to draw on his Sorcerer's Stone's power, but it answered only dimly. That simple act of lighting the torch earlier had drained him.

"Help me," he demanded of the others.

They were slow to respond. In the chill air, Gaylon's face grew slick with sweat as, together, the young men slid the top aside, stone grating over stone. Orym's rage swept suddenly through the king, but it was the impotent rage of the dead.

Karyl had been wrong—the sorcerer-king's bones, white and smooth and one thousand years old, had not turned to dust.

"They're broken," Arlin said. "Every bone has been broken. Why?"

Gaylon clung to the edge of the coffin for support. "That much I remember from my history lessons. The people feared his dark sorcerer's powers. By breaking the bones, they believed they could prevent Orym from creating himself new flesh to cover them."

"Apparently it worked," Karyl observed. "Marten?"

The earl had backed suddenly away from the sarcophagus. "I saw something move."

"It's the unsteady light from the torches," Arlin told him.

"No. I saw movement."

"Marten!" Gaylon snapped.

The earl bumped into the wall beside the entrance, not hard, but hard enough. A sudden, inhuman groan filled the chamber, and the crack in the ceiling widened, tiny fractures racing in all directions.

"Sire!" Arlin shouted. He flung himself against the king and bore him to the floor just as the roof fell. The groan turned to muted thunder. The hillside gave way and stone rained down on them, followed by timbers and damp earth.

The rumbling died away finally. Gaylon lay with Arlin's weight on his back and his face trapped against the floor in that thick, rank fog. The torchlight was gone, everything lost in pitch dark.

The Xenaran stirred. "Milord? Are you all right?"

"If you move your elbow, I think I'll survive," the king grunted. When the Southerner shifted aside, Gaylon levered himself into a sitting position, tangled in his cloak. "Marten! Rinn! Karyl!"

They answered, all but Marten.

"Are you hurt?" Gaylon asked, and listened to his cousin's grumbled complaints, Rinn's vivid curses. With effort, the king managed to wake his Stone and send a faint, cold blue light into the cluttered chamber.

Marten had last been near the tunnel mouth. Gaylon worked his way over the debris in that direction, Arlin stumbling beside him.

"Here, Sire," the Southern lord said urgently. He leaned across one end of a large beam wedged at an angle close to the threshold.

Gaylon crouched to brush dirt from the earl's face. "Marten . . ."

A long moment passed before the man roused, then he drew a hissing breath and his eyes flew open.

"Easy," the king murmured. "Don't try to move. Your leg's caught. We'll have you freed straightaway, but I'm afraid I owe you a new cloak. This one's a bit worse for wear."

Eyes filled with pain, Marten licked his lips. "Orym wants you dead. He wants to trap you here forever with him. Can't you feel it?"

"I feel him, but his bones are broken, Earl. He has no power over me . . . over any of us." Gaylon glanced up. Rinn and Karyl hovered with Arlin. "You'll have to move the beam."

Karyl shook his head. "It's propping the wall. If we move the timber, he'll be crushed."

Orym was most certainly here. The king could sense the spirit's joy. Any death would please that dark lingering essence, but what drew him most was the flickering energy of the Sorcerer's Stone. Gaylon sat among the fallen stones and gave in once more to the spasms in his chest. The cough was growing steadily worse, as was the weariness.

There was a spell, one he'd studied in the *Book of Stones*, that might aid them. He had seen it performed once, partially, by Ambassador Feydir long ago. Then the spell had been a deadly trap set to snare young Prince Gaylon, and he had barely escaped it.

The king pushed himself heavily to his feet. "There's a thing I can do with my Stone. Be ready to pull him to safety, but you'll have to do it in darkness."

"Sire." Arlin touched his shoulder.

"Don't distract me," Gaylon said irritably, shrugging him away. "Just be ready."

The threshold to the chamber had held well enough in the first upheaval. The king positioned himself under it,

finding support against the mortared stones. He tried to
envision a page with tiny runic symbols in unbroken lines.
His Stone's glow faded and died. From somewhere deep
inside, Gaylon sought the necessary strength to tap.

"Blue light attend me," he murmured, remembering.
"Blue powers ascending. Thy bitter cold fire is mine."

The Sorcerer's Stone brightened, an intense internal
light with which the king drew the first glowing beryl
thread in the dark air before him.

"As I invoke thee,
Thou must obey me,
By the trace of each glowing line."

With his Stone, he drew an intricate pattern that floated
before him. "Go," Gaylon whispered and sent the web of
light against the unseen wall to shore it momentarily. Already, though, his control was slipping. "Do it. Now!" he
cried to his comrades. His Stone winked suddenly out, but
the glowing net held a short time more. The king could
hear the others, stumbling about in the dark. Marten cried
out with pain.

The pattern dissolved then, and the wall, unseen, collapsed. Had it held long enough? Exhausted, the king felt
a sudden, dizzying weightlessness, then a face appeared
before him, black-bearded and pale.

"Daryn?" But the eyes were wrong, filled with hatred
and triumph. Arms opened wide to receive the young
king. Helpless, Gaylon floated into their embrace.

Four

She was with him, her love and concern even more tangible than Orym's sick rage had been. Cool fingers touched his forehead, and Gaylon struggled toward consciousness. A feather mattress supported his body and blankets lay heavy over him.

"I'm absolutely amazed that the fever hasn't returned," someone said in hushed tones. "There's still a chance of relapse, though."

The king opened his eyes on the all-too-familiar tapestried walls of his own apartments. Girkin stood beside the bed, but Jessmyn sat close on the quilts, her lovely face devoid of expression.

"Finally," she said, voice as neutral as her expression. "I am so angry with you, Gaylon Reysson."

Such a gentle reproach brought a momentary ache of regret. The king glanced down at his hands. "The others. How are they?"

"Well enough, milord—" the portly physician began.

Jessmyn cut him off. "Marten Pelson's leg is broken, so he won't be a party to any more of your pranks in the near future. And your brainless cousin had to have his head sewn up." The queen folded her hands in her lap. "Rinn and Arlin are only bruised top to toe. Our young Xenaran lord, I'm told, carried you from the cairn on his shoulder."

"I've always suspected," Gaylon said with forced levity,

"that Arlin has a heroic nature. How should we reward such valor, do you think? A medal, perhaps? A plot of land?"

That small attempt at humor went unappreciated. Jessmyn lifted her chin and narrowed her jade eyes. "You might send him home to Zankos where he'll be safe."

Despite himself, Gaylon laughed. Her timing and delivery were perfect. The teeming streets of Zankos were well known for being anything but safe. A fit of coughing quickly followed the laughter, making him doubly aware of his weakness. The queen stood and motioned to Girkin.

"A pennyroyal and horehound tea will be brought," she said to Gaylon. "You will drink it. Rest well, my lord."

"Yes, my lady," the king muttered and watched the physician usher Jessmyn from the bedchamber.

He was alone again, staring at faded tapestries where lean deerhounds harried stags, and aristocrats followed on well-bred steeds, all frozen in midstep forever. Gaylon pushed his head back into the pillows and twisted the gold ring on his forefinger, taking some comfort in the rough surface of the small gray Sorcerer's Stone. Then something stirred on the edge of his vision, a glimpse of red, and the king looked toward the door.

"Your Highness?"

"Tydus. Enter, please . . ."

The elderly man smiled, then bowed awkwardly in his crimson robes of office before stepping into the chamber. His arms were full.

"Another gift?" the king asked hopefully.

Tydus's smile faded. "Milord, I'm afraid my ears still sting from your lady's scolding over the last gift I brought you. So these are far more sensible items."

"I prefer the insensible," Gaylon sighed.

"Sire . . ." The head councilman unloaded his arms onto the blankets on the far side of the king's wide bed. "Allow me to help, if I may. I've considered the problem most carefully and have come to the conclusion that you are a man who abhors captivity. Therefore the wisest course of action is to make that captivity as short as possible."

Gaylon eyed the cloth bags and leather satchel doubtfully. In his own way, Tydus Dorenson could be as pompous as Girkin, and just as long winded.

"May I be blunt and to the point, Your Highness?"

"Please," the king said without much hope.

"Your complete recovery depends entirely on you, milord. This morning's little escapade has only set you back. Let me advise you. It is, after all, my most important function in the Wynnamyran court, and sadly, you have so far refused my counsel." The man paused long enough to look duly hurt and put upon. "Will you accept it now?"

Gaylon began to twist the ring again. "Of course."

"Thank you, Sire." Tydus positively beamed, then grew serious. "You have been a most recalcitrant patient. I advise you to take any and all medication our good physician prescribes . . . without complaint. To these I shall add my own dear departed mother's remedies." He poured the contents of one sack onto the blankets. "Fresh fruit—apples, winter pears. Girkin says your appetite is poor, but you must force yourself to eat—small amounts all through the day—and you must drink lots of water. According to my mother, this is most important." The leather satchel was opened. "And since your body must rest, I've brought things with which you may occupy your mind. I've arranged my busy schedule so that I'll have more time to spend at your side."

Gaylon groaned mentally while Tydus pulled a familiar hinged wooden case from the satchel and laid it open on the covers. A feirie board with leather dice cups and wooden discs of brown and black.

"Games of strategy, milord. A kingly endeavor."

"No!" the king snapped. "Not feirie."

The head councilman blinked. "Oh. Of course not.

How silly of me—a child's game." The board was closed and set aside. "Rastik, then."

"Rastik?" Intrigued, Gaylon stared at the handful of tiny carved ivory figures Tydus removed from the bag.

"It's all the rage in Xenara now," said the white-haired man happily. "Brought from one of the eastern nations. Rastik means challenge in the Berbiri tongue—an intricate game of aggression and defense. One you will, without doubt, excel at, Sire. Please allow me to show you how the game is played . . . though a simpleton like myself will present little challenge to the brilliant and most clever king of Wynnamyr."

Gaylon sighed once more. Tydus was obviously playing other games here, and the man was anything but a simpleton. Under his stewardship, the country had continued to survive well enough, despite a neglectful and reticent monarch. A rigid checkered board was placed on the tray beside the bed, and the head councilman began to set up the black and white pieces in neat rows on opposite ends.

He glanced up from his work, and Gaylon caught the man's gaze.

"Whatever else you may do, milord councilman, you had better play to win," warned the king with a small, dry smile.

* * * * *

The morning after his arrival at the cottage, Davi woke just before first light on his pallet near the hearth. Jimi, already dressed, crouched to rebuild the fire, stacking the wood carefully over the coals. Then the man rose and left by the front door. Davi threw on his own clothing and hurried after, stepping in the giant's deep, snowy footsteps all the way to the byre. The boy was tired still. Misk had told him fantastic stories late into the night, and most of the tales had only confused and frightened him. Looking back now, he could no longer decide what might be truth and what might be an old woman's whimsy.

The dawn was bitter cold, but the snowfall had ended. Davi wrapped his cloak tight before pushing the stable door open. Six shaggy, dun-colored cows lined the left wall, their heads caught in stanchions, their mouths full of hay. Over the munching, the youngster could hear the rhythmic hiss of milk hitting the bottom of a pail. The air was close and warm here, and pungent from souring milk and dung.

"Jimi?"

"Aye, lad."

The boy followed the voice to the farthest cow in the row and found Jimi squatted on the animal's right side, his hands lost under the beast. Katy stood in the corner, eating her own breakfast. She didn't bother to look up.

"I have to get home," Davi said. "My mum's gonna be worried."

Jimi shook his head. "Misk says you've more to learn." When Davi opened his mouth, the big man stopped him. "Grab a pail and help me milk."

"I've never milked before."

"'Tis easy. Watch how I do."

Davi hunkered down, took a teat in his right hand as Jimi instructed, squeezed thumb and forefinger at the top of the nipple, and rolled his other fingers down. The milk shot out in the wrong direction, soaking the knee of his breeches. With a chuckle, the giant gave him a short sawn log to use as a stool and let him choose a cow. All went well enough for a short while, until the animal noticed Davi wasn't Jimi and put a back hoof in the bucket. Jimi had to finish for him.

The next cow the boy tried kept her feet perfectly still, but not her tail. Every so often, the manure-coated tip would snap through the air and catch him hard on the ear or the side of his face. At least the work left him little time to fret. Afterward, he helped Jimi pour the milk into tall wooden vats to separate. Next they took care of the chickens and calves. Covered in muck, Davi returned to the cottage with Jimi.

Misk had breakfast ready. She wrinkled her nose at her young guest's appearance and handed him a basin of warm water and soap before placing two bowls of porridge on the table. Some of Davi's uneasiness returned as he cleaned his face and hands. The woman seemed far less mysterious in the light of day, though she still flittered around the room with moves almost too fast to follow, never in the same place if Davi so much as blinked.

"Have you eaten?" he asked politely, taking his seat on the bench.

"Yes." Misk paused with a teapot in her hands, then her brow furrowed. "I think so. No, I'm quite certain . . ." She didn't look certain in the least.

Jimi pushed a small pot of honey across the tabletop to the boy. A pitcher of cream stood beside it, but Davi shook his head at both. His mother, Haddi, was a frugal woman, saving her pennies for harder times ahead, and he had always eaten his morning cereal plain.

"I have to go home today," the boy said gently. "I can't leave my mum without help."

Misk poured him tea. "Does she never hire help?"

"Sometimes, when the inn's real crowded, Coby Sandorson comes to work the day."

"Well, then, she can spare her son a while longer."

"But you don't understand," Davi muttered, his mouth full of porridge. "Coby gets paid, and we can't afford it."

"A duke could afford all the help he wants, I imagine."

That made the boy shiver momentarily. "Misk, even if what you say is true, no one will ever believe it. There's no proof."

"But there is," Misk said. "The duke gave your mother a paper, claiming you as his heir. And even if he hadn't, the king of Wynnamyr will know the truth of what I've told you. One look at you is all the proof he'll ever need."

"No," Davi muttered. "I don't want to hear any more."

"Why?" Misk demanded.

Jimi served himself more oatmeal. "The lad's afraid."

"Of what?"

"Of you," the boy said vehemently. "Of sorcerers and kings." In all his young life, he'd never dealt with magic of any kind—or royalty.

"Child." Misk touched his face. "You *can* go home and be an innkeep's son. Life would be far simpler. But you were born to greater things. The blood of the Dark Kings ran in Daryn's veins, and from your father you've also inherited the potential for magic."

"Orym . . ." Davi shrank back. This was even worse. The Dark Kings had been great sorcerers and murderous madmen. "I've never . . . felt anything magical."

"You only have the potential," the woman continued. "You may never find a Sorcerer's Stone of your own. Realize though, that a Stone is only a bridge that helps to connect you with your special abilities. It enhances what power you already have." Misk watched the boy, eyes bright. "There are ways to tap that magic without one."

"Can you teach me?" Davi asked, shocked by his own question.

"I could, but I won't. The future holds danger enough for you. You must go to Castlekeep and take your place beside the Red King."

The boy glanced down at his bowl. "My mum will never allow it."

"You're near grown—old enough to make your own choices now."

Those words had a curious hollow sound to them, a faint echo. Davi looked up. Misk faded as she had the night before, until she was only a bare outline. Afraid, he reached out to take her hand, and his fingers found nothing substantial. The vague form sparkled a moment, then vanished completely. Sorcery. Fear turned to abject terror, and Davi fled the table, headed for the cottage door and the winter reality beyond it.

Jimi caught him in the middle of the floor. A huge arm wrapped around the boy's waist, dragging him back.

"Easy, lad, easy."

"I want to go home!" To his shame, Davi felt hot tears on his cheeks.

The giant's brown eyes filled with pity. "All right."

*   *   *   *   *

Baron Sedwin D'Loran rode into Castlekeep's snow-packed stableyard late in the afternoon with two mounted escorts and three packhorses. His men and animals were exhausted, for the baron was an impatient young man and never dallied when there was a task to perform. All things were done with typical D'Loran alacrity and flair. Stepping from the saddle, he tossed the reins of his black Majeran stallion to one of the three liveried stableboys and turned to the horsemaster.

"Find quarters for my retainers," Sedwin ordered imperiously and pushed back the wide hood of his heavy cloak from long chestnut hair. "And inform His Majesty of the arrival of Baron Sedwin D'Loran with solstice gifts from the court of King Roffo. I am expected."

At a nod from the gray-haired master, one of the youngsters headed at a run through the outer courtyard and into the keep. Sedwin followed the same well-worn path in the snow with a faint smile on his full lips.

Little over a fortnight past, he'd accepted his orders from Tek, the Mezon high priest in Zankos. Later, he'd kissed King Roffo's fat-fingered hand, dutifully accepting another, conflicting, set of orders. It hardly mattered. Sedwin could, as always, do things in his own manner and still satisfy both king and priest. And himself.

The high double doors swung open to admit him to the entrance hall. Servants rushed to take cloak and gloves and thick woolen overshirt, to offer hot refreshment—a cup of mulled wine. The stone walls were coarse, the hall cold and drafty, the servants more than a bit untidy. This was nothing like one would find in the king of Xenara's great palace, but D'Loran had expected as much. Wynnamyr was well known for its rustic, and somewhat crude, charm. He doubted very much that even the king had running water in his quarters. Not a pleasant way to live. Sedwin glanced around. Of course, renovations could always be made.

Figures appeared from a dim corridor on the far side of the hall, and the baron froze, breath caught in his throat. The young woman on the left could only be Jessmyn. Her mother, Queen Jarath, had passed her delicate beauty and red-gold hair to this daughter. But the queen of Wynnamyr wore a gown only marginally finer than that of the elderly lady-in-waiting who walked beside her.

"Milord . . ." Her Majesty said.

Closer now, Sedwin saw that Jessmyn far surpassed her mother's radiance. With reverence, he caught her hand, bowing to kiss it.

"Your Highness."

The queen's face took color, and her light green eyes looked aside. "How kind of you to observe the solstice with us, Baron D'Loran."

"Cousin," the man said in Xenaran, his attention fully on her. "Your beauty devastates me."

The old woman frowned, but Jessmyn blushed even more deeply.

"You seem . . . familiar somehow," the queen murmured, but in Wynnamyran, "though I'm certain we've never met."

"Perhaps you remember my elder brother, Roric, who was baron before me?"

"No."

Sedwin did not press her with details. It would not be a pleasant memory—of a guest who had died of poison in Lucien's court many years before.

"It matters not," the baron said and kissed the hand again, feeling the most exquisite ache of desire.

"My lord king," Jessmyn managed, flustered, "has been ill. The physician says we may visit him, later, so long as we don't tire him overmuch."

D'Loran smiled warmly. "Of course."

From the young woman's tone, she did not seem worried for her husband. Not a dire illness, then. More's the pity. But any illness might be used to the baron's advantage. This task might just prove a lot easier to perform than he'd first thought. Regretfully, Sedwin released the queen's hand and bowed deeply, then allowed the servants to lead him away in another direction.

*   *   *   *   *

The ride home had taken longer with so much fresh snow. Katy trailed behind them, tugged along by the reins, and Davi could see the little mare was exhausted. When at last Jimi brought them to the shed behind the inn, the daylight was fading.

"You better stay the night with us," Davi said.

The giant shrugged his broad shoulders. "I know my way well enough, lad." He handed the boy down to the trampled snow. "Come visit, if you've a mind."

Never, thought Davi as he watched man and horse move away slowly. Katy pulled at his arm. She wanted her warm spot in the shed, her dinner. He led her inside, past the rumps of the patron's horses—perhaps a half-dozen—and unbridled her. Then he slipped the leather halter over her head. While she ate, Davi unsaddled and curried her. The shed was clean, freshly mucked out by Coby, no doubt.

The inevitable could not be put off any longer. The boy climbed the one step to the kitchen entrance and pulled the door open on the small enclosed porch where the wood lay stacked for the ovens. Coby had seen to that, as well. A clatter and harsh laughter found its way into the kitchen from the common room beyond. The double-hinged door swung open, and Haddi came through, a grim smile on her lips, her hands laden with dirty wooden plates. Her long black hair, touched with gray at the temples and caught up in a silver clasp, had escaped around her damp forehead.

She halted at the sight of Davi, green cat's eyes gone wide with relief. Then her eyes darkened with anger. The woman went past her son to drop the dishes into a bucket of soapy water on the counter.

"The log on the main hearth needs turnin'," she snapped. "And bring more water for the kitchen before it grows too dark to fetch it."

"Mum, I'm sorry—"

"We'll discuss this tonight, after I've closed the common room. Get to work."

Dismissed, Davi did as he was told, but felt a strange discontent with the routine chores. There were few patrons tonight; several woodsmen from the logging camp south of town, four soldiers—mercenaries—who pinched the young serving wench and spilled their ale on the floor. Those that had rented rooms for the night thumped up the stairs early, and Davi followed soon after while his mother finished in the kitchen.

Not once in his life had the boy ever entered his mother's small room without being invited. This evening, he only hesitated briefly, then turned the latch. The room was dark, but the light from the oil lamp in the hall threw a fitful flickering glow past the door. Haddi's furnishings were spare, austere: a narrow bed, a chest of drawers, and a table beside the window. Under the bed, he knew, was a wooden box in which were kept the deed to the inn and other papers his mother deemed important.

Davi, on his knees, reached beneath the fall of blankets and pulled the box out. The pages it held were oddly shaped, some folded, some torn. They dealt mostly with the payment of supplies for the Fickle River, but at the very bottom, he found a crumpled roll of yellowed paper tied with a bit of string. Then warm lamplight filled the room.

"Couldn't you wait?"

The boy turned at his mother's voice, ashamed. "Mum, I'm sorry, but I had to know."

"You would have learned the truth after my death, but go on, open it."

Fingers trembling, Davi slipped the string off and unrolled the paper. He held the brittle page to the light. The ink had faded, but the neatly written words were clear enough, simply phrased and beyond doubt.

"I *am* a duke's son."

"No. You are a duke now," Haddi said softly. "But you're my son, as well."

He'd been afraid of her anger. The quiet sorrow on her face was far worse.

"Mum, this means land and wealth. You'll never want for anything."

"You were all I ever wanted, Davi. And we have everything we need here. Don't go. . . . Don't leave me."

The boy clutched the paper. "A Gosney is born to serve the Red Kings—"

"You have nothing to offer Gaylon Reysson but your life." Bitterness crept into her voice. "How can I stop you? How can I keep you here?"

Davi stared at his hands, at the long fingers, the angle of bone and flesh. They were not a man's hands, but no longer a child's. The thought of leaving Riverbend both frightened him and filled him with an odd elation.

He looked up at his mother. "You can't."

* * * * *

The baron's evening meal was served in his chambers.
This didn't please him. The room was chill, the food cold,
and the chimney drafted so poorly that the closer he sat to
the fire, the smokier his clothing and hair got. Used to
warmer climes, Sedwin did not find winter in Wynnamyr
the least appealing. The queen of Wynnamyr was another
matter altogether.

D'Loran sipped his wine and watched the dancing
flames on the hearth. Married nearly eight years now, Jessmyn had produced no children, no heirs to the throne. She
might be barren, which would be unfortunate; then again,
perhaps she hadn't been bedded by the right man.

Sedwin had studied the Wynnamyran succession most
carefully. There were no close claims to the crown other
than cousins many times removed. So long as Jessmyn
lived, their claims could be contested. The marriage con-
tract made it clear that she was not just the king's wife, but
a joint ruler. Through her, D'Loran could have the powers
of a monarch, if not the title.

His belongings had been delivered to the chamber earlier, and now he pulled a rectangular metal box from the
floor to his lap and opened it. The contents were few: a pair
of soft kidskin riding gloves and a quirt—a short whip of
braided leather strips with a loop for the wrist. At the end
of the quirt, three lengths of the leather had been left un-
braided and capped with beaten silver tips.

A horse struck with such a whip would certainly feel the
sting, but this was not meant for use on an animal. The
high priest had presented Sedwin with the quirt along with
his orders in Zankos. Uneasily, the baron remembered that
encounter. Tek, in his gold-edged white linen robes had
met him alone in the inner temple. D'Loran was not a man
given to worshiping gods, but that place had made him
extremely nervous with its blood-stained altar and heavily

incensed air.

"You must strike the king of Wynnamyr three times with the whip," the priest had said. "Blood must be drawn. The spell cannot work any other way."

That sounded like poison, not magic. Sedwin had refused to take the vile thing from Tek's outstretched hand.

"I am well versed in many forms of assassination, Reverence. Poison offers no satisfaction, and certainly no honor."

The priest laughed. "A knife in the back brings honor? Young fool, this is not poison and will have no effect on anyone but a magician. You may use your knife or any other device that pleases you, but first you must render the king helpless. Otherwise he'll kill you. Take it!"

Unwillingly the baron had accepted the quirt, and Tek had nodded, satisfied. "Strike three times, no more, no less. Then you must kill quickly. The spell lasts only moments, but will sever Gaylon Reysson from his Sorcerer's Stone completely."

A scratch at the door jerked Sedwin from his thoughts, and hurriedly the box was closed.

"Come."

The youngster that entered gave an awkward bow, then straightened and tugged at his overlarge blue uniform, the front of which was spotted with his dinner. "The queen asks you attend her, sir."

"Certainly." The baron stood gracefully. He had donned a pair of rich green silk breeks and matching long vest in which to greet King Gaylon. Even with his heaviest white lawn shirt, though, the cold air raised goosebumps. To counter the chill, he swung a hooded hunters' cloak over his shoulders before following the servant into the hall.

It could be useful to question the boy, but Sedwin resisted the urge. The Wynnamyran court might be provincial, but its servants would be as gossipy as any other, maybe more so. They passed the great hall on the way, silent and empty, cobwebs draped on the furnishings. What a dread-

ful, dreary place. Where was the music and dancing, the
giddy laughter, the cheerful devious plotting? Jessmyn
must be so very lonely.

Down a long dank corridor the servant led him and finally to a heavy oak door. The youngster scratched once
more, then pushed it open so the baron could enter the
chamber beyond. The queen sat alone in a rocking chair,
unattended even by the doddering lady-in-waiting. Smiling, D'Loran closed the door on the servant, then dropped
to one knee beside the woman.

"Your Highness."

"Baron." Her eyes were downcast. "The king awaits our
visit."

"Please, grant me a moment more alone with you,
Cousin," he answered, again in his own tongue, which was
hers by birth. "We *are* distant cousins on your father's
side."

Despite the blush, Jessmyn laughed. "On my father's
side I am related to half of Xenara," she said in that tongue
also, only prettily accented.

The queen wore one of her finer gowns on this
occasion—blue velvet, with a high brocade bodice edged in
satin ribbon. The style was years out of date in Zankos, but
on Jessmyn the gown seemed ageless.

"Forgive me, Highness," the baron murmured, watch-
ing the young woman's face. "You are anxious to see your
husband. It must be difficult for you—to spend these
nights away from him during his illness."

Her look told him everything he wanted to know. With a
mixture of embarrassment and faint longing, she revealed
that the royal couple did not share a common bed. What a
fool was Gaylon Reysson, but in Wynnamyr, the men
equated strength with an ability to overcome their natural
instincts, their physical desires. Not so in Xenara. Quite
the opposite, in fact. And Jessmyn, in every sensuous move
she made, proved her Southern heritage.

Sedwin took her hand as he had at their first meeting, only this time he turned it over and kissed her palm lingeringly. She trembled under the touch of his lips. At last he rose, pulling her to her feet with him.

"Come," the baron said. "Take me to your lord . . . to your sorcerer-king."

Jessmyn allowed Baron D'Loran to place her cloak over her shoulders. His hands slid down her arms, and he took an elbow through the cloth and led her to the door. His behavior was most unseemly, yet somehow she couldn't take offense. Everything about him brought confusion. He was darkly handsome, but smooth-faced—clean shaven like Arlin D'Lelan, while many of the men at the keep were bearded. A large ruby stud in the lobe of his left ear sparkled with each move of his head.

His every look, every word, disturbed her, and his hand on her elbow as they walked the passageway only made the shivers worse. At the king's apartment, Jessmyn tried to pull her arm from his grasp, but he tightened his grip. With the other hand, he knocked on the chamber door.

When Gaylon answered from within, the baron opened the door and guided the queen through first. Jessmyn found the bed deserted, though. The king was seated on the leather camp chair by the hearth, fully dressed and in riding boots.

"My lord," she said, alarmed. "You should not be up."

Gaylon smiled. "I try not to make a habit of receiving emissaries in my nightgown."

"Your Highness," said the baron with a deep bow, "seems to make a habit of receiving Xenaran emissaries not at all."

A momentary silence followed, then the king's smile broadened. "Indeed. Mostly they're packed off to Tydus Dorenson. But since you bear gifts instead of political complaints, we'll make an exception. Brandy?"

Jessmyn threw her husband a sharp glance, but D'Loran

bowed again.

"Thank you, milord. If you will allow me to serve you."

"No need."

But the baron had already stepped across the worn carpet. Without comment, he began to pour the liquor into three of the short goblets on the hearth near Gaylon.

"My lady queen drinks only wine," the king advised their guest. "And very little of that."

"Your queen will have brandy, thank you," Jessmyn said curtly. Feeling a sudden urge to spite him, she accepted the cup Sedwin brought her, then took a seat on a wooden chair.

By the fireplace, Gaylon frowned over his drink. The queen took a sip and found the taste nasty, the heat in her throat unpleasant.

"So," said the king. "How was your journey, Baron?"

"Without incident, but cold," D'Loran answered readily. "I hope you'll forgive me, Highness, but I do bring one complaint from my lord king, Roffo." At Gaylon's annoyed look, the baron went on. "It's not political, but simply the unhappiness of a father who misses his daughter. When my duties here are done, King Roffo has asked that I escort Her Majesty back to Xenara for a visit with her family."

That announcement brought a flutter to Jessmyn's stomach, and not just over the thought of traveling in the company of the handsome Southerner. She had been brought as an infant to the court of Wynnamyr and had no memories of Xenara. But Lady Gerra had filled her with colorful stories of that land, of the royal palace at Zankos.

Eight years ago, the young queen had met her parents for a brief, confusing time. They had traveled north for her marriage to Lucien—only to find Gaylon as the groom. But to see them again . . . Jessmyn watched the expression on her husband's thin, drawn face now. The baron's request did not please him.

"Rastik." Sedwin D'Loran had paused to study the board beside the bed with high interest.

"Do you play?" the king asked.

"Play? No. . . . Games I play, and rastik is anything but a game. It's bloodless combat—most times."

"Perhaps we could . . ."

The baron inclined his head. "Certainly, when Your Highness is sufficiently rested." He looked up. "But be forewarned, I give no quarter, not even to royalty."

"Good!" Gaylon's eyes had brightened despite the dark circles under them. "Tomorrow, then."

"Tomorrow is winter solstice, milord," D'Loran said. "There will be celebrations, feasting. Your energies will be needed for things besides rastik."

Jessmyn took another sip of the brandy. "There are no celebrations . . . not here. In town, but not within the castle."

"Well." The baron raised a dark brow. "However the solstice is observed in the Wynnamyran court, I've brought two pack horses weighed down with the most wonderful gifts from the king and queen of Xenara to their daughter and good son. That should bring some cheer."

Gaylon only poured himself more brandy and glared into the cup.

Five

The king's apartment was cluttered with bits of brightly colored cloth, satins and silks, and the yarn that had tied the material over the solstice presents. A thin winter light beamed in through the narrow arched windows, but candles and lamps added their yellow glow to dispel the chamber's dusky gloom. Jessmyn had left a short while before with Lady Gerra and another servant loaded down with gifts.

Baron D'Loran studied the rastik board before him and remembered the childlike delight on the queen's face as she opened the packages. There had been a golden hand mirror in one, and jars of kohl and lip rouge in another, material for dresses, a boar-bristle hairbrush with an ivory handle, jewelry, and a clever Deragi music box. The queen's laughter when she lifted the lid and heard the tune had made Sedwin's heart miss a beat.

The king, after long consideration, now moved one of his tiny ivory soldiers up one square on the board. His gifts had been opened and discarded on the blankets of the bed—a jeweled hunting knife, a snuff box, gloves, and much more. They held no interest for him. D'Loran wondered just what it might take to truly catch the interest of such a man.

When Gaylon Reysson had first donned his crown, the entire civilized world had shuddered in terror of this new sorcerer-king who supposedly wielded Orym's Legacy. But he had done nothing aggressive in all these years. The baron had been sent to dispatch a dangerous madman and found instead a quiet, thoughtful young lord who apparently appreciated his brandy more than his kingdom and his queen.

Sedwin made the countermove with one of his own black rastik soldiers. "She seems very lonely, milord. . . ."

"Who?" Gaylon said distractedly, his fingers hovering over the white ivory priest at his end of the field.

"The queen, your wife." D'Loran refilled the king's cup with amber liquor. "She has no friends, nothing to occupy her time. I mean no offense, Your Highness, but Castlekeep is a cold and melancholy place."

"I like it that way." The king pushed one of his cavalry pieces into the fray, then winced when Sedwin snapped it up with a lowly foot soldier.

"Of course you like it, milord. These cold climes are yours by birth, but Her Majesty is born of milder lands. Have you never visited Zankos, Highness?"

"No."

"This time of year, the nights are long and the days cool, but the air is still sweet with flowers. The citrus trees are heavy with fruit, and ships arrive in the harbor daily filled with marvelous trade goods. It's a truly wondrous place."

"I am well aware, Baron D'Loran," Gaylon snapped testily, "of how great Xenara is, and that, with your fleet of trade ships, you are far wealthier than the king of this minor realm—"

"Milord, that's not what I meant."

"Then by the black beard of Orym, let's get on with the game."

"Yes, milord. It's your move."

After long deliberation and more brandy, the king sent another soldier forward, farther away from the white emperor and empress sitting at his edge of the board. Sedwin slipped past with his black priest and took Gaylon's other cavalry piece. The Xenaran emissary found His Majesty easily distracted and hardly a challenge.

The king took a long drink from his cup and growled, "I think I'll appreciate Tydus, here on out."

"Your Highness does quite well for having little experience with rastik."

Gaylon only growled again, then bumped Sedwin's priest from the board with one of his own. The baron frowned. Perhaps he'd been a little too confident. His next move was far more careful.

"Milord," he said, shifting a horseman out of danger, "will you permit me to escort Her Majesty south to Zankos?"

"No."

"Majesty, King Roffo has bid me not return without his daughter."

"Then I suppose you'll grow to love this cold and melancholy keep, in time." Gaylon pounced on the baron's other cavalry piece.

"Milord, excuse me, but that was an illegal move."

The king grinned. "I wanted to see if you were paying attention." He replaced the two game pieces. "Are you acquainted with the D'Lelan family, Baron?"

Sedwin kept his face neutral. "We have been business rivals, lord, for several centuries."

"Arlin D'Lelan says you arrived on a fine black horse—a purebred Majeran stallion."

"Yes, milord. My family breeds them."

"They're a small animal, but known for endurance and speed."

"Yes, milord," Sedwin repeated, charged with a sudden sense of anticipation.

"My companions and I occasionally engage in crosscountry horse races." Gaylon looked up from the board. "It's obvious I'm not going to beat you at rastik. Perhaps you'll allow me the chance to beat you in the field."

"It would hardly be fair, Your Highness. Against a Majeran, your animals would have little chance."

"Don't count your winnings yet. I've got a sorrel mare who's swift as the wind, and we're far more experienced on snowy terrain. There'll be prize money of course, but you and I should have a small private wager, as well. What would you deem fair?"

Now D'Loran allowed himself a tiny smile. "There's only one thing for which I will race, milord."

"What?"

"Queen Jessmyn's company south in a fortnight."

For the first time, the baron felt a hint of danger. Gaylon's face stiffened, and the small gray stone on his ring flickered blue. Then the moment passed.

"Agreed," the king said. "But the final choice will be my wife's."

"Of course," murmured Sedwin and gestured at the board. "Your move, milord."

* * * * *

"My lord," Jessmyn said, trying to hide her irritation. "You wished to see me?"

The king sat alone in his bedchamber, his head bowed over the rastik board set up beside the hearth. The empty dishes on his dinner tray proved he'd at least had some appetite tonight.

"Yes, my lady." Gaylon turned toward her finally.

The queen frowned. "What did you do?"

"I had the beard shaved . . ." Gaylon rubbed a hand along his jaw. "It's been a long time."

A very long time. The smooth face made him boyish again, made her remember her childhood, made her remember color, light, and laughter.

"It's . . . becoming," Jessmyn said softly.

"All the Southern ladies seem to think the same, or so the baron tells me." Gaylon pushed himself up from the chair and moved across the chamber to her. "You're quite taken with D'Loran."

Uneasy, the queen took a small step back toward the door. "He's very charming."

"Jessmyn . . . it hasn't been easy for you here." Gaylon came close. "I haven't . . . been much of a husband. Perhaps I could change that."

His fingers reached out to brush her cheek, and a jolt of panic rushed through her. She had felt his love always, but not his touch, no overt affection from him in all this time, even though she'd longed for it. Now, somehow, his nearness frightened and angered her.

"Would you spend this night with me?" the king whispered and leaned to kiss her lips, the liquor strong on his breath. He hadn't asked so sweetly the first time, the only time. Then he'd taken what he wanted and left her alone.

There were reasons for his behavior, she knew. No doubt the dashing baron had something to do with this amorous change of heart. Her own bitterness surprised her.

"No." Jessmyn turned her face from his kiss.

"No?"

"I am your wife, my lord, but it'll take more wooing than this to make me your lover." She refused to look at him. "Besides, you'll need your rest if you're to win the race." The queen retreated to the door, then paused, a hand on the knob. "I've already decided, though. . . . Should D'Loran win, I will accompany him to Zankos."

Gaylon said nothing, and Jessmyn passed into the corridor, closing the door on her husband.

* * * * *

The king had been in a foul temper the past two days. His companions had steered clear as much as possible.

Arlin watched His Majesty now in the aisle of the long stable, pacing in the scattered straw and haranguing the horsemaster, Luka.

"She should have been re-shod a week ago," Gaylon growled. "If she comes up lame, so help me . . ."

The master grimaced, revealing teeth that had been filed sharp once and were now worn. "Why not ride the dapple, Sire. He's a strong one."

"And clumsy as an ox. I want the sorrel. Have new shoes fitted. Immediately."

"Yes, milord." Luka bowed deeply, his gnarled hands tucked to his belly after the fashion of his people. "I'll oversee the work myself so she ain't trimmed too short."

But Gaylon had already strode from the stable.

"It's all right, Luka," Arlin said gently.

"She ain't even got a name, that sorrel," the elderly gray-haired man muttered, his words heavily accented. He was a Noro tribesman, taken as a slave long ago by Xenaran mercenaries and abandoned to the Wynnamyran court after Lucien's death. "Pardon, lord, but the king don't care for nothing but her speed."

"True enough."

"His Majesty's been ill. I had no way a knowin' there'd be a race so soon." The master took a halter from the wall and stepped into the red mare's stall. "But she'll be ready, poor thing. Aye, you can count on that."

Arlin offered him a conspiratorial smile over the stall door. "Take heart, Luka. She's kicked him twice and thrown him once that I know of."

"The king?" The old man's eyes lit, and he patted the sorrel's neck. "Well, the lass has spirit."

The young Southerner stepped back to let man and horse through. Luka led the mare down the aisle toward the wide double doors that let out on the exercise yard. The horse sidled suddenly to the left, and Arlin heard a high squeal, then a series of crashes coming from the far stall.

"Here!" the horsemaster shouted. "Ge' back, ya fool!"

The Majeran stud pressed his nose to the iron bars, nostrils fluttering, ears pricked, and the mare danced a step and lashed her tail seductively. Luka chided her with a jerk on the lead rope, then pushed one door open and headed across the snow toward the blacksmith's shop.

Arlin paused before the stallion's enclosure, a respectful and safe step away. The animal eyed him suspiciously through the bars that lined the upper half of the wall. He was a fabulous creature with a thick-muscled neck and blue-black coat. The body, too, was stocky and heavily muscled, but the legs were slender, almost delicate, with long, feathery fetlocks that draped over wide and sturdy hoofs.

"He's an ugly bastard," Karyl said from behind the Southerner, having come unnoticed into the stable.

"No, he's not." Arlin turned. "And he's worth his weight in gold."

The king's redheaded cousin snorted. "Not to me. I don't fancy running against him, either. He doesn't have to be fast. He'll just kill anything that tries to pass him."

"Majeran stallions are more savage than most," D'Lelan admitted. "But under saddle and bridle, they're easily handled."

"So I've heard," Karyl grunted. "They're also used in battle, as deadly as their masters' swords."

The stud decided he didn't care much for Karyl either, and spun about, laying both hind heels against the boards with a thundering crash. The two men retreated down the aisle.

"You don't have to ride if that's how you feel," Arlin told the redhead. "In Xenara, we connive and scheme and plot against one another, but never without good reason. There's a strange honor of sorts involved." He shrugged. "Personally, I find the D'Lorans a loathsome clan of back-stabbers, but there's nothing for Sedwin to gain here. Revenge on me is useless since I've been disinherited."

Karyl clapped an arm across his friend's shoulders. "You were disinherited because you make a rotten Xenaran, Arlin. You just don't have a devious enough mind." The king's cousin elbowed Arlin hard in the ribs, then sauntered to the exit. "The baron's here to deliver more than solstice gifts, mark my words. Come on. Gaylon wants to lay out the course for tomorrow's competition."

The Southern lord followed, disturbed.

* * * * *

The sun chose this morning to rise in a clear sky, but its light was winter feeble and distant, without warmth. On the road below the keep, five riders gathered. The horses danced with a high, nervous energy—all but the baron's stallion. Gaylon nodded at the others.

"Remember, once past the town you take the coach road north to the first league marker, then go west, up the mountainside to the ridgetop. Circle the shepherd's summer hut and head back. No cheating, gentlemen, on your honor."

"Does cheating include magic, Your Highness?" Baron D'Loran asked, resplendent in scarlet-dyed leather. A short leather quirt with silver tips dangled from a loop on one wrist, and under him, the black stallion stood perfectly still, chin tucked, arched neck lathered.

The king felt a surge of irritation at this petty Xenaran, but forced a smile. "Do you mean the spell that gives my horse wings? Have no fear. Much of the run will be under the trees where wings of the necessary size will do me no good. I've never gotten the horse feathers right anyway."

Rinn snickered, but Karyl guffawed and slapped his horse's neck. The king's cousin had chosen the clumsy dapple gelding as his mount, and they were well suited to one another—all elbows and knees.

Sedwin's jaw tightened, and he gathered his four reins through the fingers of both hands. For better control over the Majeran stud, he used a double-bitted bridle—a thin snaffle of twisted wire, plus a short-shanked bit with a barbed curb chain that ran under the animal's chin.

The baron turned a cool eye on Rinn. "I object to a commoner running with us. Look at his animal, for the gods' sakes. It should be pulling a plow."

Rinn's long, good-natured face reddened, but the king only winked at him.

"The horse in question," said His Majesty, "has actually won its fair share of the competitions. And Rinn, being a master tailor's son, had no use for the barony I offered him. Commoner or not, he rides with us."

"Suit yourselves." Sedwin D'Loran's voice was mild, his expression faintly amused. "But steer clear of me, tailor's son."

The wind blew a gust up from the river, bitter cold, and Gaylon found he regretted the loss of his beard. They were all lightly clad in leather this day, without heavy cloaks to tangle and snag on branches. Arlin, black hair tied back like the baron's, leaned to adjust a stirrup leather under his thigh. His bay gelding, feeling the shift in weight, tried to lunge forward, but the young Southerner brought the horse under control with gentle hands and soft words. He glanced over at the king, a brow raised.

Yes. It was time to start. "One last thing, milords," Gaylon said. "We will, if at all possible, avoid running down the good folk of Keeptown. They've been warned, but an addle-brained gawker or two may wander onto the main street. Take care."

On the narrow roadway there was hardly room enough to line up abreast. The king put the fractious sorrel mare on the opposite end from the Majeran. Karyl found himself next to the stallion, which pleased him not at all.

"When the stone strikes the ground," Gaylon shouted,

pulling the fist-sized rock from a pocket.

It arced high above their heads, then dropped to the earth close by. The sorrel reared and leaped forward a split moment after the rest. The cold winter air held no sound but the muted thunder of hoofs on the packed snow while the horses jostled and shouldered for position. Rinn's rawboned black gelding broke in front, its heels flinging ice in the others' faces.

Under Gaylon, the mare scrambled for footing. She loved to run and hated to be anywhere but in front. They descended into Keeptown at breakneck speed, Rinn still in the lead, the baron close behind. The king pushed the sorrel past Karyl and saw, briefly, an intent scowl on his cousin's face.

Arlin had the bay held in, pacing his animal as he always did. For the young Southerner the horse meant more than the race, but he'd won many a time by coaxing a hidden burst of speed from his mount at the last. He had only to stay close on the leaders' tails and wait for them to tire.

Cheeks numb with cold, Gaylon felt a heady rush of joy as the group fled into town. There were gawkers, all right, clustered on the walkways. Some cheered, some jeered. Up ahead, Gaylon saw one man on the edge of a small crowd toss a red bonnet under the feet of Arlin's bay. The animal shied left suddenly, nearly unseating the rider, but the young Southerner righted himself and sent the gelding on.

The king, in the midst of the mad dash, still managed to focus on his Sorcerer's Stone and release the tiniest nudge of power. A heavy load of snow from the roof above dropped onto the miscreant and his friends. Laughing, Gaylon raced past to overtake Arlin on the icy bridge.

That small taste of power brought a black temptation, though. It would be so easy to upset the baron and leave him in a snowdrift while his fine steed finished the course alone. Then Jessmyn would stay. No, he decided, somehow this race must be won honestly or not at all.

There were now two competitors ahead and two behind
the king. Where town road met coach road, the tailor's son
led them right. That would be the ultimate disgrace for
Sedwin D'Loran to be beaten by Rinn on his plow horse.
The thought made Gaylon laugh again, breath turned to
white vapor, streaming back.

Under his knees, he could feel the sorrel draw great lung-
fuls of air with every forward leap. She was a mystery to
him, unruly and headstrong, but with more heart than any
horse he'd ever ridden. If he only asked, she would run
herself to death for him. That realization made him ease
back on the reins gently in an attempt to slow her.

The baron had slowed his stallion as well, most likely in
preparation of the long climb yet to come. Rinn's gelding
galloped merrily on. Gaylon glanced behind him. Arlin
closed once more, this time with a riderless dapple gray on
his heels. The king drew up sharply, and his mount fought
him for the reins.

Arlin D'Lelan waved, shouting, "Go on! Karyl's all
right. He fell off again."

They found the league marker, a small obelisk of gray
stone jutting up through the snow. The tailor's son turned
his mount west up the mountainside and into the trees.
Now the riders could go as they pleased, though the snow
lay deeper here. What looked to be a faster route might
spell disaster if a horse stepped into some hidden depres-
sion or collided with an unseen obstacle. Best to do as
Rinn, keep to the trail they had made the day before when
laying out the course.

The Majeran stallion followed almost effortlessly. The
baron was unmistakable, a bright red form against the
winter white. Gaylon let the mare choose her own way at
her own pace under the oak and fir and myrtle. This would
be the hardest leg of the run, but the sorrel never faltered,
ears cocked forward, determined to gain on the leaders.

The trail led back and forth across the slope, zigzagging

upward, sometimes steep, other times almost level. Occasionally Rinn's hoots could be heard high above, encouraging his leggy black horse to greater effort. From Sedwin D'Loran there was nothing, not a sound, only an occasional flash of black and red through the trees.

"Don't count the race won, you jack-a-dandies!" came a cry from below. It was Arlin, no doubt hoping to force the lead riders to quicken their pace.

The sorrel broke from the shadowed dusk of the forest and onto the ridgetop meadows. The glare of the late morning sun off the snow made Gaylon's eyes tear. Rinn thumped by on his way back down, his unhandsome gelding all sweated and wheezing. The baron came next, the Majeran stallion held at a slow, graceful lope.

"Your Highness," he said with a polite dip of his head, but the smile was confident and insolent.

Gaylon put the spurs to the mare for the first time, and she responded with little energy. White fields rolled into the distance, broken by the occasional copse of aspen and oak. The shepherd's hut was a small dark shape against the snow. Squinting into the reflected light, the king pushed the sorrel past it and back around. Arlin, still headed upslope, met him on the path. The bay had plenty of wind left.

"Don't get too far behind," Gaylon snapped. "Or you'll never have time to catch up."

D'Lelan grinned and called over his shoulder. "Milord has some catching up of his own to do."

The king jabbed the red mare in the ribs again, sent her at a leaden gallop down the long winding trail and once more into the forest. The downhill run was far harder on man and animal, throwing both gait and balance off. A stumble now could mean broken legs and broken necks. On the steepest grade, Gaylon rode leaning back, the stirrups high on his horse's shoulders.

The mare's hocks were skinned and bloody by the time

they found the coach road, but with spurs the king drove her on at a run. Rinn appeared ahead, moving slow, his big gelding spent. He whooped at Gaylon as the mare passed by, cheering the king on. At the next curve in the road, both Sedwin D'Loran and the bridge came into view.

Gaylon tucked himself in close to his mount's neck. This race must be won. Jessmyn was angry at him and with so many good reasons. Petty jealousies did not become a king. He would beat D'Loran and still allow the queen to travel south to see her family.

The thought that she might choose not to return to Castlekeep brought an ache, but what, in all this time, had he done to deserve her love and patience? Nothing. Gaylon had given himself two rules to live by since his ascension to the throne of Wynnamyr: never get close to those he cared about, and never care about those he was closest to. Death and destruction came to the ones nearest a sorcerer-king. Only with Jessmyn and Arlin he'd broken those rules, however slightly, and that frightened him.

Ahead, another rider sat motionless in the middle of the road, just where it forked left toward Keeptown. He wasn't one of the competitors—the horse was too small, near pony size. The rider, wrapped in a rough cloak, had the cowl pulled up around his face as he watched the approach of the two lead horses.

"Get out of the way!" Gaylon cried, and at last drew abreast with the baron. The unknown rider moved off just as the two galloped past.

D'Loran's stallion showed the strain now, and white foam spilled from the double bit to fleck the animal's broad black chest and shoulders. Side by side, the two men raced onto the icy planks of the bridge. Somewhere near the center of the wooden structure, the Majeran stud suddenly squealed. His head snaked down and under, and jaws wide, the creature sank long teeth in the mare's throat.

"Here!" Gaylon shouted and saw the baron swing the

quirt to separate the animals.

Instead, the whip swung quickly at the king's face, and Gaylon felt a sting along one cheek. Three times in lightning succession the quirt struck him. The stallion slammed the smaller mare sideways into the railing, and her knees buckled under her. Sunlight glittered briefly on a dagger blade in D'Loran's hand, then Gaylon hit the wooden rail and rolled over it, flinging out a hand to catch himself.

The world had dulled around him, left his mind somehow detached from his body. Confused, he tried to focus on his Sorcerer's Stone, tried to find the rage that such an attack would surely bring. But he could connect with nothing—not even fear.

An angry shouting began, muted yet familiar. Arlin. The Southerner had arrived on the bridge.

Help me, Gaylon thought, unable to form the words.

The river flowed black and slushy beneath the king's feet, and one gloved hand was all that kept him from it. The baron's stallion wheeled and drove both hind heels into Arlin's bay gelding.

Helplessly, Gaylon watched his friend thrown into the opposite rail, watched man and horse pushed up and over by another vicious kick. They dropped out of sight, and immediately there came a splash. No, Gaylon moaned wordlessly and glanced down in time to see the current sweep them downriver. No.

Sedwin nudged the stallion closer to the king, the knife bright in his fingers. Yet the odd mental numbness had lessened, replaced finally by outrage and hatred. Gaylon caught a post with his left hand and made a fist of the right. All control was lost though, and the blue fire that erupted from his Sorcerer's Stone engulfed both the baron and his stallion.

A wave of heat washed over the king, bringing the strong smells of scorched hair and burning flesh. In silent agony, the Majeran stud staggered several steps, then collapsed.

Sedwin D'Loran was no longer recognizable, only a small blackened shape fused to the larger.

Gaylon got both hands around the railing post and dragged himself over the fallen mare. She struggled feebly in a widening pool of dark blood, dying, but the king had no time for regret. He fled on foot across the bridge, slipped and slid down the roadbed to the bank of the river.

"Arlin!" he screamed and blundered through the snow-topped boulders.

A voice answered. "Here, sir! Hurry!"

A stand of young evergreens crowded close to the water. Gaylon fought his way past them and found a little blood bay pony standing alone on the stony bank. The rider, the one who had blocked the road earlier, had somehow crawled out over the river on a downed fir bole. Legs wrapped tight around the small tree, he clung precariously to a bundle of sodden leather.

The king started into the water, but the shock of the icy flow drove him back, numb to the waist instantly. He was forced to slide along the fallen tree toward the cowled stranger. Together, they pulled Arlin D'Lelan's still form from the river and dragged him over to the bank. Gaylon gathered his friend up in shaking arms. The young Southerner's lips were blue, his face an ashen gray.

"I was too late," the stranger muttered, forlorn. His features were lost under the folds of the cowl, but his voice was youthful.

"No," Gaylon said sharply, refusing to accept that truth. He started back into the trees, awkward with his burden.

"Milord! Take my pony." The stranger came after him, the little horse towed along behind.

Gently the king laid D'Lelan across the saddle and took the reins. Something about the pony nudged at his memory, but the urgency of the situation allowed no time for contemplation.

Rinn met them at the road, face white. "Sire! What's

happened?" He dismounted, his eyes on Arlin lying limp across the pony's back. Behind him, blue-black smoke smudged the winter sky, still drifting up from the bridge.

"Hand him to me," the king commanded and climbed into the exhausted gelding's saddle.

The tailor's son pulled D'Lelan from the pony and looked up, tears on his cheeks. "He's dead, milord."

"Hand him up!"

Arlin was laid across Gaylon's lap. The king reined the sweated black gelding around and gave him a vicious rake with the spurs. The animal went at a tired gallop over the bridge toward the keep.

Six

The king refused to let anyone touch Arlin, not the horsemaster or the grooms, but carried his friend's body in his own arms across the snow-blanketed bailey to the innermost courtyard. There Gaylon kicked on the door with a wet boot until it was finally opened. The young male servant on the threshold stepped back, eyes wide, but the maid behind him wailed and began to sob noisily. D'Lelan was well loved by the women of the keep.

"Shut up!" the king snarled, refusing the manservant's help. "Get Girkin. Now! Tell him there's been a drowning. He's to meet me at his quarters."

"He is with the queen, milord."

"Run, then! Tell him to wait there. I'll go straight to my lady's chambers."

It mattered little what Jessmyn might think or say, her anger or sorrow, so long as Girkin was found quickly. The heartbroken wails began anew the moment Gaylon started toward the southeast wing. He left a dark trail of river water and melting snow along the stone flags. Feeling had come back into his legs finally, but with it came a burning pain. His hands and feet were still numb.

The king hugged Arlin's cold, wet form against his chest, unmindful of the weight or his own exhaustion. It wasn't too late. It couldn't be too late. A spark of life, however weak, must still burn somewhere within the young Xenaran. Gaylon refused to believe anything else.

"Sire!" Girkin waddled down the passageway as fast as his pudgy legs could bring him. "Oh, no! Oh, dear me." He halted beside Gaylon, found one of Arlin's wrists, and pressed his fat fingers to it. Brow furrowed, the physician shook his head, then placed the fingers next on the Southerner's throat. The hand was withdrawn slowly. "Dead, milord. I'm very sorry."

Gaylon fought the urge to rage and felt the stir of his Stone. "Perhaps I need a new physician, old man."

"A thousand physicians would tell you the same, Sire." Girkin's face held sadness and understanding. "Arlin D'Lelan was a fine young man, but he's gone, milord. This is a sad loss for us all." Now he studied Gaylon carefully. "Best I tend the living. You need warm, dry clothes and a hot herbal tea or you'll find yourself another week in bed."

Cursing, the king turned his back on the useless physician and headed with his burden to the library. He would not give Arlin up to death without a fight. Among the pages of the *Book of Stones* an answer had to be found.

Alone in the library and behind its locked door, Gaylon laid Arlin gently on a table. Dislodged books and scrolls fell unnoticed to the threadbare carpet. A bitter memory came then, of that day in the Stagg when he'd placed his friend on another table, fearing the worst. This time, though, Arlin failed to open his eyes.

The chill, damp air carried the musty scent of aging paper, glue and ink, and all around, crowded bookcases formed high walls. Carefully the king stacked billets of wood in the cold ashes on the hearth, then thought better of it. Best not to heat the chamber, not yet.

He stripped off his soaked gloves and took a seat finally on the stool before an enormous tome bound in leather and wood—Feydir D'Sulang's copy of the *Book of Stones*. The barest thought lit the fat candle on the small desk. It flickered fitfully in a draft.

The wet clothing dragged at his limbs, but Gaylon opened the book and tried to focus his attention on the task. Every bit of space on every page was filled with tiny runes in unbroken lines, unrelieved by punctuation. The rows blurred before the king's tired eyes. Somewhere within these endless pages was the spell he sought, but the volume had a life of its own. Unless it deigned to gift him with what he needed, he might spend days, even weeks, in the search. By then, it would be far too late.

Twice during the king's search, Karyl came to the locked door to beg admittance, and even Rinn, another time, but Gaylon refused to answer their pleas. He continued to turn pages with cold, stiff fingers. His Sorcerer's Stone glimmered in its golden ring, aiding him in the comprehension of the runes, but a hopelessness slowly filled his heart.

In bitter desperation, he buried his face in his hands and murmured, "Please, I beg you, give me what I need."

"Perhaps this will help."

The familiar melodic voice startled him, and the pages in the *Book of Stones* ruffled suddenly as if windblown. Brittle sheets of paper turned, one after the other, then lay still. His eyes were caught by a single line in the midst of all the others.

To dispel death . . .

Cold fear came to replace the hopelessness, and Gaylon turned on the stool. A fair, slender man in russet leather garb stood beside Arlin's body. No . . . not a man, but something far different, a spirit Gaylon had met long ago when he'd first found his Sorcerer's Stone. The creature tried to trap the king's gaze now with its fathomless blue eyes, but Gaylon glanced aside.

"Will you not look at me?" the spirit asked gently.

"No."

"What do you fear? You've grown strong—become a great sorcerer. The power of the Stone is yours . . . and so am I. Ask of me anything. I must obey."

Whatever the creature's pledge, Daryn had once warned
young Gaylon that any dealings with it would be fraught
with danger. The king focused instead on Arlin, who lay
unknowing and lost in death. River water puddled on the
rug beneath the table.

Ask of me anything. I must obey.

"Give him back to me," the king said without further
thought.

"I can and will do this," the spirit murmured, voice as
liquid as birdsong. "But know this, milord. There is a balance in life and death, and all such magic carries a price."

"What price?" Fear nudged Gaylon again.

"One that any king must be prepared to pay. To bring
this loved one back, you must choose another to take his
place. Read it there upon the page. . . ."

"No," the king said sharply. "Tell me."

The spirit bowed gracefully. "You must, by your own
hand, sacrifice another life. Someone as dear to you as this
one, whether it be tomorrow or the next day or the one
after, so long as the death occurs by summer solstice. But
the longer you wait, the more difficult the task will grow."

"There must be some other way."

"None, milord."

"And if I can't choose?" Gaylon asked, dread and fear
goading him.

"Then the sacrifice will be chosen for you—a far greater
sacrifice than just one life. Best, milord, to abandon this
course. In seeking to defy nature, you open yourself and
your world to the most dire of consequences."

"Whatever the price, I'll have him back. Just show me
how to begin."

The creature smiled and sang, "I must obey. You have
only to look into my eyes."

Against his will, Gaylon met the spirit's gaze.

*   *   *   *   *

Davi trudged up the steep road, Katy behind him, dragging back on the reins. Death and destruction had greeted his arrival here. And sorcery. The blackened, charred bodies on the bridge attested to that. Even the citizens of Keeptown had shuttered their windows and locked their doors in fear.

The road grew steeper still, the woods thicker. Over a final rise, the keep came into view—high walls of lichen-covered stones crudely stacked and mortared, but fashioned well enough to stand one upon the other for more than one thousand years. Snow capped the battlements, and behind them craggy mountains rose sharply into the winter blue sky. A king's abode, yet somehow dark and despairing.

No one challenged his approach. The only witness was a youngster in a faded blue uniform leading two horses across the stableyard. There were other buildings scattered over the grounds, all of them showing neglect and decay. Katy tugged on the boy's arm, drawn in the direction of the stable, to the sounds of other animals and the smell of sweet hay. She was hungry and tired, and had lost her roly-poly look over the past few days.

"Hello," Davi called to the youngster with the horses. "Could you take care of my mare?"

"Got any money?" the stableboy asked with just a hint of insolence.

"A little."

"Then bring her here."

They dickered there in the snow, and the transaction cost Davi a ten-penny copper. Finally, his leather bag thrown over a shoulder, he headed through the trampled, dirty snow of a courtyard. Wide oak doors in a windowless castle wall greeted him. In time, his knocks were answered by another older servant in faded blue.

"Whatcha want?" the man demanded, taking quick

note of Davi's shabby attire.

"I've come to see the king."

"Go away."

The door began to swing closed, but Davi dodged past it.

"Here, boy! You can't do that."

Davi pushed the cowl back from his face and stood his ground belligerently. "I must see the king."

"Let him come," someone called from the far side of the reception hall. It was the tailor's son, Rinn, who Davi had met by the bridge.

Grumbling, the servant barred the door and turned away.

There was far more activity inside the keep than out. Davi glanced around. Servants, male and female, young and old, hurried through the cold, dusky chamber. Their distress was obvious, and some of the women were in tears. Beside an ancient stone slab table, the tailor's son stood with a young redheaded man and a stately white-haired fellow in expensive velvet robes of scarlet.

"Arlin D'Lelan is dead," the elder one said harshly. "And the king has locked himself in the library with the body. He refuses to listen to me. Perhaps he'll listen to one of you."

Rinn shook his head. "We've tried. Best to leave him be, milord Tydus. Let him mourn in peace."

"In peace?" Tydus growled, his handsome face flushed with anger. "How many of your circle have to die before the rest of you come to your senses? You're all to blame for this, aiding and abetting the king on every hand, in every foolhardy scheme." His harsh gaze came to rest on Davi. "Who are you?"

The boy fought to hold his own gaze steady. "Davyn Darynson, milord. I've come to serve the Red King."

"We've servants enough," Tydus snapped.

"Darynson?" the redheaded man echoed with a glance

at Rinn, who only looked confused. "Daryn, duke of Gosney?"

"He was my father," Davi said. The words felt strange on his tongue.

"Absurd!" The older man adjusted his heavy robes. "Gosney left no heir."

"I have a paper. He—"

"A worthless forgery, no doubt."

Davi straightened, jaw tight. "Let me see the king. He'll know I speak the truth."

"Take your papers and your lies and leave here, young brigand," Tydus said angrily, his face darkening, "or you'll find yourself in a prison cell instead of a duke's rich chambers."

"Wait," the redhead murmured, a hand on the older man's sleeve. "If the boy's a Gosney, he may be the one capable of reasoning with Gaylon Reysson."

"Ridiculous!" the elder man snarled.

"It won't hurt anything to let him try."

Tydus's angry expression altered, then became thoughtful. "All right, Karyl. But have him bathed first, and properly clothed, then bring him to my quarters."

"Properly clothed?" Karyl frowned. "His Majesty won't mind how the boy's dressed."

"I mind," Tydus said and swept off toward a dim passageway across the hall.

About his own business, the head councilman went first to Sedwin D'Loran's chambers. There might be, among the baron's papers, something to shed light on this ghastly incident. Anger and excitement wormed their way through his gut. No one lived who could explain what had happened on that bridge today—except Gaylon Reysson—but Tydus had his suspicions. No, it had not been an accident.

He found the chamber door already unlocked and ajar. The white-haired man pushed against the wood gently. Alone on a chair within, the Wynnamyran queen sat unmoving. A single candle lit the page in her hand, and a packet of letters lay in her lap. She looked up, face stricken and pale.

"What does this mean?" the young woman asked, holding the folded sheet of paper out.

Tydus accepted it with misgiving and scanned the fine Southern script. The last line caught his eye. *And with the execution of these favors and the death of Gaylon Reysson, we do award Baron Sedwin D'Loran governorship of Wynnamyr and, as consort, the widowed queen, our daughter Jessmyn.* It was signed, Roffo, master of the house of Gerric and king of all Xenara. The ornate royal seal had been pressed into the red wax below.

"Tell me what it means," Jessmyn demanded.

"The intent is clear, milady." The head councilman paused to clear his throat. "Baron D'Loran was sent to assassinate the king."

"And to court the newly widowed wife," the woman responded with anger. "How could my father do such a thing? Why?"

"The logic of politics is not readily explained, Your Highness. You mustn't despise your father, though, for acts of expediency."

"Acts of greed, you mean," Jessmyn said bitterly. "My father has long coveted Wynnamyr's timber and water, but we've continued to share our resources generously. Why murder my husband?"

Tydus forced a warm, sympathetic smile. Her Majesty understood the politics far better than he had anticipated. "Milady, your father fears Kingslayer and the sorcerer-king who might wield it."

"That makes no sense. Gaylon's done nothing in all these years—" The queen fell silent momentarily, eyes unfocused. "But once he finds out what my father has done . . ." She glanced down. "This document must be destroyed. All the baron's correspondence must be burned immediately."

Tydus felt a tiny panic. All that he desired could be brought about with this one damning bit of evidence. "Milady, His Majesty's life may still be in danger. He should know the truth."

"No! We'll protect him, you and I, but Gaylon must never know of this. He must never have reason to take up Kingslayer again."

"Yes, Your Highness," Tydus murmured, his disappointment carefully hidden. "Only, please allow me the honor of carrying out your wishes. Let me dispose of the papers."

The young woman held out a slender hand to him. "Thank you, but I shall tend to them myself."

She allowed the head councilman to help her from the chair, then see her to her chambers at the end of the long, drafty corridor. There, Tydus left her with the papers still clutched in her fingers. Then he returned to his own rooms.

Once inside his chambers, the head councilman let go of the useless frustration. There were too many other things that required his attention at the moment. He paused before the hearth in his sitting room. The fire had died back to coals, and already the air grew chill. His personal servants had strict orders to keep the fire stoked, and Arlin D'Lelan's death was no excuse for irresponsible behavior.

Angry, Tydus turned back to the chamber door just as someone in the passageway knocked gently on the oak panels.

"Come!" he snarled, expression stormy.

Two servants entered—a girl with a dinner tray in her hands, and Raf, a sturdy young man whose foremost duty was to tend the fire. He carried billets of wood, and, with a muttered apology, went immediately to the hearth.

Tydus opened his mouth, scathing words of rebuke on the tip of his tongue, then noticed the boy, Davi, standing just inside the door. Excellent. Raf's trespasses forgotten, the head councilman beckoned this new arrival into his chambers.

"You. Come here," he ordered, then turned away to take his seat near the hearth. The girl placed the food tray beside him on a small table, curtsied, and left immediately, but Raf continued to fuss with the firewood. Impatient, Tydus snapped his fingers, and the manservant also took his leave. Davi had not moved.

"I said, come here!"

The boy came unwillingly, hostility on his handsome young face. Karyl had dressed him in castoff clothing: breeks and doublet of a noisome mustard-colored velvet, several sizes too large. Even so, with the cloak gone and the thick black hair neatly combed, the youth's aristocratic blood was clearly evident. Tydus could see it in the boy's slender, long-fingered hands, the wide-set eyes, and high cheekbones.

"So you would have us think you are a Gosney," the head councilman said pleasantly enough. He took a thick slice of buttered bread and dipped it into his soup. Davi said nothing, only watched the food travel to Tydus's mouth. "Let me see this paper you have," the man growled while he chewed.

The boy shook his head. "I'll show it to the king."

"You will give it to me. Now!"

Slowly Davi brought a yellowed, much crumpled page from under the doublet. Tydus snatched it from him. The quality of the paper was so poor that the ink had seeped through the fibers, and the words had blurred. Still and all, the intent was clear enough—a dukedom had been handed down from father to son.

"A bastard son is better than none, I suppose." Smiling, Tydus tossed the document into the fireplace, and it was engulfed in flames before the boy could react.

"How dare you!" Davi cried, face flushed with rage.

"Be quiet, boy." Tydus took another huge bite, enjoying Davi's angry confusion. "I am the king's personal councilor, and I may advise him that your claim is valid, despite the unfortunate accident that befell your paper. . . . But in exchange you must first make certain promises to me." He paused to spoon more soup into his mouth.

"What promises?" Suspicion edged the youth's words.

"What promises, *milord*. You will show proper courtesy to your betters." Some of the anger returned to those startling green eyes, but Tydus ignored it. In time, the boy would learn who was master. "As head councilman, it will fall to me to see to your education. A duke has many duties, and you will work long before you're worthy of the station. But put all dreams of quick wealth out of your head.

"The Gosney lands and holdings were parcelled out by Lucien D'Sulang during his reign, sold or given as favors to political allies. Much of this will be returned to you eventually, but in the meantime you'll be living on the king's largess—and mine."

Davi's jaw tightened, and Tydus went on. "If the Gosney legend holds true, you will have the Red King's ear as no other could. That's a dangerous power in a youngster's hands, but I will guide you. Therefore, in return for all my kindnesses, you'll carry certain petitions of mine to His Majesty and present them as your own. Also, I expect from you complete reports on the king's conversations and activities, as well as—"

"I'll do no such thing. I don't want your kindnesses," the boy snapped. "And I owe you nothing. Even without my father's paper, the king will know me." He turned and stalked away to the door.

Not so easily led, this young one, but Tydus wasn't beaten by this unexpected show of strength. "Then it isn't true. . . . The Gosneys don't love their Red Kings more than life."

Davi hesitated, a hand on the door latch.

"Do you think my motives wicked? Not so, Davi, duke of Gosney. *I* do love the king and want only to protect and help him," the head councilman murmured soothingly. "Gaylon Reysson, in these past years, has lost the will to rule. He's grown reckless of his life. I fear for him . . . as do we all. He needs purpose and hope. These are things you might provide—if you knew how to go about it."

He had snared the boy. Slowly Davi turned back.

"That's why I've come," the young duke said.

"Just so! Let's not work at cross purposes, then. We both desire the same goal."

Davi's chin came up again. "I won't be treated rudely by you or anyone."

"Forgive me, young lord," Tydus murmured, though the words nearly strangled him. "But after what's happened today, I must be certain to let no one near the king who might wish him harm." When Davi opened his mouth, the older man cut him off. "Yes, I see now that your intentions are pure, and I welcome you to Castlekeep on behalf of His Majesty. I'll have the servants ready the Gosney apartments for you. For now, return to Karyl with my blessing. He'll take you to the library, but don't be discouraged if Gaylon Reysson won't receive you immediately. This is a sad time for us all."

* * * * *

The Stone's blue glow enfolded the king, and he found himself trapped within its bubble of luminescence. All around him, the spirit sang, but without words. He felt safe, comforted. Then the beryl light winked out.

Dark emptiness rushed in, complete and absolute, and Gaylon cried out soundlessly.

Be calm, his guide whispered in his mind.

With difficulty, the king formed his own words in the

same manner. *What is this place?*

This is no place, unfound in Dreaming, existing beyond that which is known—even to sorcerers.

Something appeared in the void, a softly luminous globe that bobbed past. Gaylon sensed a faint energy pulsing within. Another drifted toward him from another direction—though direction meant nothing here. More arrived and floated away.

What are these things? the king asked.

Souls, milord, each trapped in their own tiny existences, in joy or sorrow as was their wont in life.

Why are there so few?

These are but newly dead. They'll find their way in time.

To where?

Musical laughter followed that question. *That, even I do not know. I know only that once beyond this plane, they can never be brought back. So call to him, milord, the one you would have returned, before it's too late.*

That same awful dread swept through Gaylon, increased a thousandfold. To pay such a price . . . He remembered the young Southern lord on the bridge, bent on saving the life of his king and losing his own instead. No, somehow payment for this magic would be deferred. He had lost Daryn forever, but that made him all the more determined to hold onto Arlin D'Lelan.

Arlin! he shouted voicelessly into the emptiness. *Arlin!*

The globes continued to float in random patterns, never touching, always in slow, stately motion, while the king called his friend's name over and over. At last, a globe hesitated, then drifted toward Gaylon.

He is yours once more, the spirit of the Stone sang. *Take him home.*

The Stone's blue glow wrapped around the king again, and with its soft embrace came the gentle tug of gravity beneath him. He opened his eyes and found himself sprawled across the *Book of Stones.* A quick glance around

proved the chamber empty. The spirit had gone, and
Arlin's still form lay on the table. Gaylon almost believed
he had dreamed everything, but the chill in the room
seemed deeper and there was a faint tang of lightning in
the air. Then someone moaned softly.

His legs refusing to cooperate, the king stumbled over
the floor toward Arlin. Every part of him ached with the
cold. He fell against the heavy table, and it shuddered under his added weight. The young Southerner coughed suddenly, and river water gushed from his mouth. Gaylon
caught his friend's arm in a tight grip and pulled him over
until the convulsions ceased. Swiftly he swung his ringed
hand toward the hearth. His Stone flashed, and the fire
that erupted there threw sparks to smolder on the faded
rug.

He turned back to Arlin. The young lord's brow furrowed, and his brown eyes grew troubled. Lips blue with
cold and lack of oxygen, he struggled to form words. Finally, in horror, he whispered, "What have you done?"

Seven

Distracted and silent, redheaded Karyl led Davi down yet another dimly lit passageway. The boy, still in baggy yellow velvet, tried to keep all the turns and junctures straight, but it was proving hopeless. The castle seemed a labyrinth of chill, musty tunnels. Despite all the tales he'd been told as a child about the royal splendor of kings and queens, this place might as well have been a miser's tomb.

They stopped at last before a wooden door that looked no different than the dozens they had already passed. Only this one swung suddenly wide of its own accord, revealing a huge fire on the hearth within.

"Milord!" Karyl cried as a shadow blocked the entrance.

"Find Girkin, immediately," the king said harshly as he stepped into the corridor, his arms burdened once more with the drowned man from the river. "Send him to Arlin's chambers."

Arlin D'Lelan, drowned or not, brought a hand weakly to his mouth to cover a spate of coughing. Davi watched the king's cousin back away to the opposite wall, saw the color drain completely from his round face.

"Bring blankets, mulled wine, and heated bricks," the king growled, headed away down the passage with his burden. "Hurry!"

"Dear gods," Karyl breathed, still frozen.

The boy stood a moment, divided, then turned and

raced after the Red King. The tall man continued to walk, but his steps were heavy and slightly unsteady, and he failed to notice Davi behind him. The whole time, Gaylon spoke in murmured tones to his friend.

The king halted finally before a closed door, and Davi ducked past him to take the latch and push it open. Darkness greeted them, but an eerie blue light followed Gaylon Reysson inside. Awed and more than a little frightened, the boy trailed the pair across the chamber where the king placed Arlin gently on the unmade bed. The three nearest candles lit themselves.

"You," Gaylon said brusquely without turning Davi's way. "Stack wood on the hearth." He piled blankets over the ill man. "Rest, Arlin. Girkin will be here soon." That said, the tall man sank wearily into a chair by the bed, then turned his attention on the boy. "That's not nearly enough wood. Stack it higher."

Davi obeyed, then stood away as he was told. A minuscule blue sun rose with the king's right hand, and the wood on the hearth burst into flames, throwing out a heat so intense it drove the boy even farther back. Along with the fear came a sudden elation. Magic. The dank, shadowed room was charged with it. Fingertips tingling, Davi felt an unreasonable longing for such power. Misk had said he held the potential, and now that he had tasted actual magic, even secondhand, he wanted more. Much more.

"Who are you?" the king demanded from his chair, voice rough with exhaustion.

The boy looked up. "Davi, sir."

"Davi . . . Yes, I remember you." His face haggard with spent grief, Gaylon Reysson appeared far older than the young man Davi had met years ago. "You are very like him."

"I've come to serve you," Davi blurted.

"Go back to the inn, lad. Return to your mother. I know you didn't leave with her blessing. Whatever she's told you about me is no less than the truth, and I can't bear anymore sacrifices for my sake."

"Misk told me to stay. She says I'm the only one who can help you."

Gaylon shook his head. "I've more help than I can stand. Arlin helped me, and see where it's gotten him? Your father helped me. . . ." He gazed long at the still man on the bed. Arlin's eyes were closed. He looked more than ever like a corpse.

Before Davi could respond to the king's words, Karyl and a short balding man in voluminous broadcloth robes arrived. Behind them came servants carrying blankets and heated bricks.

"Girkin." Gaylon rose with difficulty.

"Milord," the little man responded, but his eyes were already on the bed's occupant. "Karyl brings me wild tales of Arlin—"

"All true. He lives, physician."

"Sire, you're distraught, and so is your poor cousin. Sometimes a body moves after death, out of reflex. Arlin D'Lelan is drowned. There was no heartbeat, and the lungs were filled with water." Girkin wrapped fat fingers around Arlin's wrist. "The flesh is like ice, milord."

Gaylon's sudden laughter startled them all. "That's why you're here, you old fool. He still has trouble breathing, and he complains of numbness in the limbs." The king bent to take his friend's shoulder and shake it gently. "Arlin! Your king commands you to wake from the dead once again."

Face and lips still blue-tinged, D'Lelan slowly opened his eyes. That brought an immediate squeal of terror from one young servant, and all the household staff dropped their things and fled out the door. Girkin remained frozen beside the bed, but Karyl had nearly rushed from the room with the others. He hovered near the threshold, body tense, eyes huge.

Even the physician's expression was less than calm. "Necromancy," he said, his revulsion clear.

"Yes!" the king snarled. "Necromancy, black sorcery. Call it what you like, but Arlin lives and needs your expert care. Now!"

Girkin finally stirred and stripped away the covers. "Come, you two," he snapped at Davi and Karyl. "Help me remove these wet garments, then lay the bricks and blankets. We've got to restore the circulation."

Davi found himself pressed into service with Karyl, while Gaylon Reysson crossed to the hearth and piled more wood on his small inferno. Smoke escaped the flue to drift in wisps on the warming air. On the bed, Arlin endured their ministrations, though it grew apparent to Davi as he massaged an arm that the young lord was in great pain.

Girkin also noticed, for he drew the king aside. "I must go to the apothecary if we're to ease his suffering. But, Sire, you must understand that my arts are of a mundane nature. I know nothing of sorcery. Is Arlin truly alive, or have you merely reanimated his dead body?"

"He lives," Gaylon said through clenched teeth.

"Yes . . ." The physician looked at the stone flags beneath his feet. "There appears to be some crippling, milord, and possibly frostbite, in which case, there's also danger of gangrene. D'Lelan could lose fingers and toes . . . or worse."

Davi had listened closely to their murmured conversation and now saw a brief agony on the king's face before the man turned away.

"Do what you can for him," Gaylon said softly as he found the chair once more. "And have no fear, physician. The blame in this rests entirely on me."

"Your Highness," Girkin said with obvious relief. He managed a stately bow despite his wide girth and left the chamber.

On the bed, Arlin stirred. One quick glance down at

that young man's bloodless face and desolate brown eyes was enough to unsettle Davi.

"Bring more bricks," the royal cousin ordered tonelessly, and gladly the boy deserted the sickbed.

Using the tongs to pull bricks from the coals nearly got Davi's eyebrows singed. Panting, he carted them, one after another, to the bed, then carted the cool ones back to the fireplace. Somewhere about the fourth trip, the boy noticed someone standing in the open doorway—a slender young woman in a purple woolen gown. Her delicate, fine-boned face was framed in loose waves of honey-gold hair, and firelight glinted from eyes a much paler green than his own.

Stunned by her beauty, Davi paused over the hot, heavy brick. She took a timid step into the chamber, her gaze first on Arlin, then on the king.

"My lord," the woman said gently.

Gaylon had nodded off in his chair. At her voice, he woke with a start and came clumsily to his feet. "Jessmyn."

"You're wet . . . and chilled, my lord," she chided. "How can so great a sorcerer bring the dead to life and still not take the simplest care of himself?" Before the king could answer, the queen turned to the boy. "You must be Davi Darynson."

She reached her hands out to him, and Davi dropped his tongs and brick in order to clasp the proffered fingers. Her smile grew wistful. "Welcome to Castlekeep, milord, though I would it had been under pleasanter circumstances. By now, you must realize that service to this Red King will be anything but easy."

The mustard velvet embarrassed him suddenly. Still, even without any formal training in court etiquette, the boy knew enough to bow, however awkwardly. Jessmyn nodded in return, then went directly to the sickbed, where she bent to kiss Arlin's damp forehead.

*   *   *   *   *

It had been unseasonably warm over the past fortnight. The potted dwarf citrus trees had been fooled into blooming, and their rich fragrance drifted with the evening air. In that early winter dusk, Roffo, king of all Xenara, lounged alone on the patio of his favorite terraced garden. High to the north came a scattering of first stars, and from benighted Zankos on the hillsides below, a first flickering of street lanterns.

While the king thrived on the pandemonium created by a dozen wives and forty-odd children, these rare solitary moments brought a profound pleasure. Roffo settled deeper in the cushions. Somewhere in the shadows, a soldier's armor-clad elbow jostled a sword hilt.

Well . . . nearly solitary. He had not survived these many decades by being careless of his safety. In a court as wealthy and huge as Xenara's, poisonings and assassinations were commonplace. Palace intrigue was to be expected, and the antics of the aristocracy, their bids for power and position, provided the king with many happy diversions. Some unhappy ones, as well.

It had been nearly a dozen years, and the memories haunted him still. A king must often make bitter decisions, but that was little consolation. Dear Jarath, his first wife and queen, had given him nine beautiful daughters, but no male heir. His second wife, Calmia, though, had given him three fine sons. Roffo felt a tiny shiver run through him. Three sons who had very nearly sent their father into Mezon's realm.

In the presence of the entire royal family, the king had ordered the slaughter of the co-conspirators—the plotting wife, the deceitful, murderous sons. A cruel lesson, but necessary. Now, Kanin might someday wear the Xenaran crown. Unfortunately, the youth was nearly as dull-witted as his mother, Roffo's third wife, Allysa.

At the far end of the long compound, the king noticed an eerie green glow against the thickening night. The priests called it godfire—a minor bit of sorcery. Mezon had gifted his devout with certain holy powers, some more spectacular than others and some, more deadly.

Roffo, being a wise man, knew that illusion was also much employed by the priests in their rituals, but beneath the simple trickery they performed for worshipers lay the dark magic of a cold and cruel warrior god. Truth be told, the king of Xenara did not follow Mezon out of love, but out of a respect born of fear.

The ethereal green light grew stronger as it drew near and finally separated into two distinct clouds floating above the heads of three white-robed priests and two laymen. Even at this distance, Roffo recognized Tek's tall, angular form and wondered what would bring the high priest from his temple so late. The godfire followed the little group through the spindly olive trees and up the broad terraced slope to the king's patio.

"Your Majesty," Tek said, breathless from the climb. As one, his companions all bowed. The sickly green light gave them a ghoulish look.

"Tek," Roffo grunted, still ensconced in his satin pillows. "Whatever the problem, it had better not keep me from my bed."

He glanced at the laymen, who, with the two lesser priests, had stopped at a respectful distance. Still, the old king's ears detected the quiet scuffle of the half-dozen guards behind him and was comforted.

"Highness," the gaunt priest continued. "These are the men who accompanied Baron D'Loran to Wynnamyr."

Interest pricked, Roffo leaned toward Tek, his voice held low. "Is my daughter a widow then, priest?"

"No, milord. Best you hear the tale these two carry."

"Well, bring them here," the king snapped. "And let me have some decent light. Your god's fire makes the lot of you look too many days dead."

With a thin smile, Tek snapped his fingers, and a young priest trotted away, his green cloud following. The baron's men came forward hesitantly, making deep obeisances.

"Speak!" the king commanded, irritated. "What has transpired?"

The smaller one began, words rushed. "Highness, our lord and baron is dead by the hand of the sorcerer-king, Gaylon Reysson."

"Yet, *you* return home alive," Roffo said, outraged. "Explain this failure to protect your lord . . . if you can."

By the light of the lanterns that had just arrived, Roffo could see the two men's wide, frightened eyes and weary faces.

"Highness," the high priest said gently. "Hear them out. It is imperative."

"Continue, then."

Again the smaller one spoke. "There was a competition, a horse race among the lords. We were not allowed to attend, though we begged to. Later, while we waited at the stables, the Wynnamyran king returned, carrying the body of a drowned man. Our kind and good lord, we were told later, had died most horribly . . . burned to death—"

"Did you not seek revenge?" Roffo asked, curious.

The man's head bowed. "No, Highness, though it was our intention, but what happened after the baron's death proved so much more terrible that we rode home straightaway, as quickly as we could."

The king cocked a brow at Tek, but the man's thin smile had turned enigmatic.

"Well?"

"Highness," the second man answered. "While we didn't see our lord's death, at the stables later we learned of foul sorcery. The Wynnamyran king, defying the gods and nature, restored the drowned man to life."

Roffo rocked back in his cushions, at first not clear as to

what he had heard.

Tek clapped his hands abruptly at the priests. "Return to the temple. Tend to these men's needs. Food and wine and rest for them." As his group started back down the terraces, the high priest glanced across at Roffo. "Highness, best dismiss the guards."

"Why?" the king demanded.

"Because what we must discuss now should be heard by no others."

Reluctantly Roffo sent the soldiers to their barracks, then made himself comfortable once more. "Those two are mistaken, of course," the king noted flatly. "This drowned man could not have been dead."

"Necromancy is an ancient art, milord."

"Yes, yes. But long lost . . . a thing of legend and fable."

"Perhaps, but the god has sent me a dream."

Roffo groaned before he could stop himself, and, somewhat annoyed, the high priest went on, "Gaylon Reysson has offended Mezon. He has deigned to wield powers to which no mortal has a claim, and his punishment has fallen to us. He must die."

"I believe that's exactly what we've been trying to accomplish. However badly."

The elderly priest dared to pull some pillows for himself and settled beside the king. "Assassination would be ideal, but it is impractical at this juncture. Our quarry is a powerful young wizard, and now he'll also be wary. No. He's played into our hands with this black miracle of his. Every nation will be outraged and terrified. They believe he commands Kingslayer, but now he raises the dead, as well. Imagine if he raises a great army of lifeless soldiers that can't be killed."

Roffo plucked worriedly at his mustache. "Is this possible?"

"Hardly. But our neighbors will still panic at the rumor. They'll gather here with their own armies, all pledged to you, of course. Together we'll have the means to destroy Gaylon Reysson once and for all."

"As you said, he has Kingslayer," Roffo pointed out.

"And we have Mezon. In my dream, the god promised me the sorcerer-king's death. He's promised to gift his priests with a magic strong enough to overcome Orym's Legacy. It's been many years since Mezon's followers girded themselves for war, but as a warrior sect, our skills have always been kept honed." Tek smiled again. "You, Majesty, will command such an army as this world has never seen."

Roffo sighed, his attention on a mockingbird that warbled somewhere among the olive trees below. The night air tasted sweet. In fact, all of life was sweet, and the king of Xenara was not at all certain that he wanted the dubious honor of commanding an army. More than twenty years had passed since his last military endeavors against his neighbor to the north. He'd failed to conquer Wynnamyr even then. The old man remembered bitterly his beautiful queen's tears when her infant daughter was taken from her and placed in King Reys's hands—a future bride for Gaylon and a trade for the natural resources Xenara had not been able to take by force.

"How shall we go about this?" Roffo asked finally.

Tek plucked a bit of down from a pillow. "First, we will make certain that word of Reysson's necromancy is known in every land. Then we'll invite statesmen to Xenara to discuss our common problem. By spring thaw, the northern and eastern realms will have joined us, and we'll begin to build our army."

"You forget. Lasony and the far north has long been allied with Wynnamyr. . . ."

"Zorak was allied to the father, not the son. Gaylon Reysson has done little to endear himself with his neighbors. Black sorcery has few friends, Highness. Have no fear. When war is declared, Wynnamyr will find itself very much alone."

*   *   *   *   *

At first he slept for long periods of time, unknowing, uncaring. There seemed little connection between body and mind. The awful burning pain hadn't lasted long, and it occurred to Arlin vaguely that he should be grateful to the fat little physician for his medicines and gentle care. Voicing those thoughts had proven impossible at first.

Dreamlike wanderings took his mind to distant places, sometimes home to his father's huge manse at Zankos, where he watched his family engaged in their idle, selfish, and useless lives—all but Markim, his eldest brother who had joined Roffo's palace guard. Arlin's love for each of them had not diminished, but he realized how little he'd lost by leaving that life behind.

Other dreams let him wander unnoticed through the corridors of Castlekeep. A great fear and anxiety had touched the occupants, servant and lord alike, and the young Southerner knew the reasons. Even his companions, Marten, Rinn, and Karyl, appeared to have succumbed to the wild tales of necromancy and demons. Convinced that the Arlin they had known was truly dead, the young men refused to deal with the situation in any way, and Gaylon, driven by guilt and sorrow, retreated even farther from those who loved him. So many things became clear to Arlin in these dreamlike meanderings—a deeper understanding of the necessity of death and the purpose of his own restored life.

In the soft darkness now, he heard stirrings around him.

"D'Lelan's a most fortunate man, Sire. No infection has set in."

"What of the crippling?"

"He's shown some use of the limbs, but little control. I'm not certain why, milord. Perhaps with time . . ."

The voices faded in and out, and Arlin struggled toward wakefulness. When at last his eyes opened, he found only the king beside his bed, unsmiling. A half-grown beard shadowed Gaylon's gaunt cheeks.

Arlin cleared his throat and murmured weakly, "Shall we exchange places, milord? You look more in need of this bed than I."

"Forgive me," the king said as if he hadn't heard. "I've done a terrible and foolish thing." His intent expression hadn't changed, but his hazel eyes glittered with candle-light. "Once I held another man to life, because I thought my needs were more important than his free-dom. Arlin, I can't be so cruel again. Only tell me, and I'll let you go. . . ."

The blankets were heavy, the room chill despite the crackling fire on the hearth. Arlin mulled his lord's words over carefully.

"Go where?" the Southerner asked at last, mystified.

Gaylon frowned. "Do you remember any of what hap-pened?"

"More than I care to. I remember the baron attacked you, and I fell into the river—" A shudder rippled through him. "I remember being lost, and you came to find me in a place where no living creature may go. That was a foolish thing to do, but not so terrible."

"How can you say that," the king demanded, "when you may be crippled?"

A sobering thought. Arlin tried to raise an arm. Much of the numbness had gone, but shoulder, elbow, and wrist seemed to have lives of their own. For one frightening in-stant, the Southerner considered the worst, then gritted his teeth and forced the muscles to obey. The right hand came up from the blankets, formed a weak fist, and collapsed. So small an act had thoroughly exhausted him, but he grinned triumphantly at the king.

"See? Nothing to it."

Instead of being relieved, Gaylon only looked sorrowful, and that angered the Southerner for some reason.

"Don't mourn me," he snapped. "I'm alive. And hungry, for that matter."

"Good. Food it shall be," the king said, finally smiling. "Is there anything else your lordship desires?"

Yes, but how to ask? Tired, Arlin closed his eyes and searched for the words. "Your indulgence, Sire. Death has made me far more aware of life, yours as well as mine. You've no time left for wild games, no time for regrets or sorrow over things that once were and are no more. Be a king, milord—and a husband—before it's too late."

In the silence that followed, the chamber door slammed, and Arlin knew without looking that Gaylon was gone. The young king had left a faint scent of thunderstorm in his wake, just a hint of magical fury on the cold air. The Southerner drew a weary breath and let it out, all the more aware of his hunger. Dinner, though, might be a long time in coming.

Eight

"Ow!" Davi squawked and suddenly jerked free of the tailor's ungentle grasp. The newly pinned sleeve tore loose in the old man's hand.

Despite every effort, Jessmyn laughed while the two dodged around her sitting chamber, the boy just out of reach, the tailor crying foul and flapping his sleeve like a banner.

"Felser!" she called just above their clamor. "Felser!"

"Your Highness," Rinn's father panted. He was stooped with age, and Jessmyn worried for him after such exertion. "This is unseemly behavior for a young duke."

The queen forced the smile from her lips. "Certainly, but he's only just come into his title. I think he's sat long enough for this fitting."

"I was commissioned for four suits, milady. . . ."

"We'll do the last another day."

"As you wish, Your Highness."

Felser bowed stiffly and, with a glare at Davi, gathered his bolts of cloth himself, then his basket of chalk, scissors, and pins. He had come alone to the keep this morning, apologizing for his apprentices' poor health, but Jessmyn knew why no one had accompanied him. They were afraid.

Davi stood beside the hearth now, angry and glowering, until the queen raised a questioning brow and sent him to open the door for the old man.

"Come and sit," she directed as soon as they were alone. "We have some time to work on the future tenses before Tydus arrives."

The boy's shoulders sagged, and Jessmyn smiled again. He had a definite gift for languages and already spoke a fluent gutter Xenaran that he'd learned in Riverbend. That would hardly be suitable in the company of kings, though.

"I'd rather play you the new tune Marten taught me," the young duke said slyly from his upholstered chair.

He had a gift for music, as well, and though Davi had come fairly late in life to this formal education, he'd proven a more than apt student in all the disciplines . . . except perhaps in courtly manners. That might come in time, but somehow Jessmyn doubted it. Daryn, himself, had held little use for court life.

When the queen failed to answer, Davi picked up the battered old lute from beside his chair and began to pick a melody on the strings. Maybe not so neat and precise as Gaylon's playing, or so sweet as Jessmyn remembered Daryn's, but with a certain grace and style. The youth played the melody through a couple of times, then added the chords and his own voice, which was uncannily like his father's.

These similarities were the very reason Gaylon refused to allow the boy around him. The king spent nearly every moment alone in his library in the company of his *Book of Stones*. The queen wondered briefly just what her husband sought in that ancient tome, then her attention returned to the black-haired youth seated before her.

If Davi's looks and voice had been inherited from his father, the similarities ended there. While Daryn had been a dark and brooding force, the son had brought light and laughter to this crumbling old castle. Davi had come to serve the Red King, and being denied that these past few weeks, he simply pursued other interests, content to wait.

Behind the youth's song, Jessmyn heard a knock at the door. It would be Tydus, not a servant. Since Arlin had been restored to life, the household staff had diminished somewhat, though most had stayed on, despite the undercurrent of fear that pervaded the castle. Many of the staff had never lived anywhere else, being descendants of servants who had attended the first Red King, centuries ago.

The knock came again, and the queen called, "Enter."

Tydus Dorenson stepped into the room and bowed. This day he wore robes of white linen, edged in fine gold thread. With the thick white hair to top it all, he reminded Jessmyn of a handsome snowman. Davi's song faded to silence.

"It's time for the young master's history lesson," the head councilman said gently.

The boy set the instrument aside. "I want to study the last Xenaran conflict today. Karyl says his father fought in it."

"We've yet to get through the reign of Pernin, the third Red King." Tydus gave the queen a polite smile, but his irritation was obvious. "No, young man, time starts at the beginning and finishes at the end, and so will we."

Davi stood up, grumbling. Tydus was not a tall man, and they were nearly the same height.

"What do we say?" the head councilman demanded.

"I don't know what you say," the boy snapped. "But I say Pernin was an old bore and should have stuck with herding cattle."

Tydus's face reddened slightly. "What do we say when we leave the queen's presence?"

"Oh." Davi performed a careful obeisance for Jessmyn. "By your leave, Highness?"

The queen gave her permission with a small nod, then accepted Tydus's bow as well. The older man paused near the door.

"He's a bit stubborn, milady, but learns quickly," the

head councilmen said quietly. "With my considerable help, I think he'll make a fine duke one day."

"Thank you, Tydus. I never doubted it."

*   *   *   *   *

"If the Wynnamyran crown trades water and timber rights to Xenara, what does it receive in return? Where are the revenues?"

Irritated, Tydus gazed across the table at his student, who was trying to divert the topic again. "We're discussing King Pernin and the social and political impact of his first trade agreement with Lasony."

"I know . . ." Davi flicked his stylus thoughtfully. "The countries benefitted mutually from that agreement. But what has Wynnamyr gotten from its present arrangement with Xenara?"

"That's hardly your concern at the moment," the head councilman said. "And I doubt very much that you'd understand the intricacies of foreign policy at this point." Tydus tapped a finger on the boy's page in an attempt to deflect his attention. "Read."

Davi's green eyes narrowed. "What I *do* understand is that you wear robes of finer quality than the queen's, this castle is falling to ruin, and the people of Keeptown seem little better off than beggars."

This young duke was far too sharp and obviously wouldn't be shaken from this train of thought. Tydus considered his reply carefully, sitting there among his expensive, imported tapestries and furniture. Best to tell the truth, at least in part.

"All right. I'll answer as simply as I can." The disgust on Davi's face amused him. "While Lucien D'Sulang and his uncle ruled this realm, they made an open trade agreement with Xenara. On the one hand, they brought great wealth to Wynnamyr, and on the other, they took it away.

"There were mercenaries to pay, Xenaran officials to buy. A good deal of the collected money was invested in their family businesses in Zankos and Katay. Before their deaths, the D'Sulangs had put Wynnamyr so deeply in debt that it will be many years yet before there are profits to be made. A few Wynnamyran merchants who were clever enough, were able to disguise their wealth and keep some of it—"

"As you did?" the youth asked, expression benign.

"Certainly. I admit to superior intelligence." Tydus smoothed a wrinkle from one impeccable sleeve. "It was hardly the Red King's fault, though, that when he came to power, he found every bit of wealth drained away—much like the Gosney monies and lands had vanished. The poor commoners had been so severely taxed over the years that they had no more to give. And—" the head councilman lifted his chin "—while it is unfortunate, it is true that His Majesty has shown little inclination in improving his court or the lot of his people."

He'd made the duke angry with that last statement. The boy's nostrils flared. How curious that this young Gosney lord, ignored by his Red King, would still be so willing to defend him. Tydus would give him no chance, though. He snapped his fingers.

"I've answered your question. Now kindly attend to your history lesson."

Jaw tight, Davi turned the pages of the book before him.

* * * * *

When the chamber door creaked open, Arlin had been staring fixedly at it from his bed, willing it to do just that. Amazed, he saw a crop of black hair, not unlike his own, and under that, a pale young face and bright green eyes. The face disappeared, and the door began to close.

"Wait! Don't go!"

The visitor hesitated, then peered around the frame once more. "I don't want to disturb you."

"For all the gods' sakes, disturb me. Please."

That plea brought the youngster into the room. Arlin considered him wonderingly, well-dressed in blue woolen riding breeks with matching vest and coat over a white lawn shirt—all obviously new, down to the knee-high boots.

"I've never seen you before," the Southerner said.

"I was told I couldn't come here."

"I'm surprised that you'd want to. No one else seems so inclined . . . except Girkin, of course, but he only brings me my meals and empties the chamber pot, and he's always rather in a hurry. Do you suppose death is catching?"

"Sometimes," the boy replied ingenuously. "No one visits you?"

Arlin shrugged. "The queen has. She's very kind. By the way, who are you?"

"Davi Darynson, duke of Gosney."

"A duke. I'm impressed. As for me, I was once, and am again, Arlin D'Lelan. How do you do?"

"Very well, thanks." Davi paused beside the hearth. "Your fire's gone out."

"It tends to do that with no one about. The chamber stays awfully cold anyway—even with a fire."

"So why don't you just get up and leave?"

That question brought a small ache of despair. The Southern lord looked away. "Aside from a slight coordination problem, I really don't think I'd be very welcome outside of this room. Do you?"

"Does it hurt to be dead?"

"No." Arlin could only laugh at that. "It hurts more to be alive. Can you tell me of the others? I know the king has returned to his library, but do you know of redheaded Karyl or Marten Pelson or even Rinn, the tailor's son?"

Davi wandered to the bed. "Rinn hasn't returned to the keep since . . . that day. Marten wears a splint on his leg,

but gets around fairly well. He's teaching me music and
ciphering. The king's cousin is helping me with weaponr
and horsemanship."

"You poor thing," the Southern lord commiserated
"Karyl's a fair hand with sword and bow, but hasn't ye
found a horse he can ride."

"He does fall off a lot," Davi admitted with a quick grin

Silence followed, and Arlin could sense the lad growing
restive. "Before you leave, tell me one last thing. Is i
winter still? I've lost track somehow, and there're no win
dows here, as you can see."

The boy-duke of Gosney nodded. "It's winter still, bu
you should go look for yourself."

"Maybe I will," Arlin said softly. "Maybe I will. . . ."

* * * * *

It had been many years since she'd left this peaceful littl
valley and the close comfort of her cottage, but things tha
must happen were in danger of never happening. Wit
one foolish, impetuous act, Gaylon Reysson had disrupte
a thousand thousand futures.

Misk pushed a few items of clothing into a leather bag
aware of her husband's gentle brown eyes on every mov
she made.

"Let me go with you," he begged one more time. "Th
weather's no good, woman. You'll freeze."

"Ah, Haryld Jackson Jimison, my love." She reached u
to stroke his cheek. His hair was streaked with silver, hi
face deeply lined, but he appeared so strong and vital. "I'
take you if I could. Stay and bide." Misk stared into hi
brown eyes. "You'll remember what I asked?"

Troubled, he pursed his lips. "Aye. Tomorrow night, I'
turn the cows and calves together out into the orchard an
open the coop. But why? It don't make sense, Misk. Th
owls'll get the chickens, and how will I make cheese with

out milk?"

"No questions, darling. You'll understand in time. . . ."
The tiny woman gathered her heaviest cloak from the bed.
"Is the gelding ready?"

Jimi nodded and followed her outside into the cold
morning air. The snow lay deep, and thick icicles edged the
thatched eaves of the cottage. As though she were a child,
he lifted her onto the horse's bare back and helped her arrange her long patchwork skirts comfortably.

"You'll send for me, and I'll come to Castlekeep soon,"
Jimi promised.

"Yes, dearest. Soon. I will love you always." Misk kissed
him lingeringly on the lips, determined to hold the memory of the kiss and him forever, then turned the gelding
north through the orchard.

He would understand. Tomorrow night, her husband
would turn the animals out to fend for themselves. By
morning, he'd be dead. So the lines of time had shown
her, over and over. Another Misk, along another timeline,
would stay at the cottage with him. She would save the life
of her husband, find a way with an extract of foxglove to
regulate that huge faulty heart, but leave him suffering,
helpless, and aged far beyond his years. No. Better for him
one sharp moment of pain and then peaceful oblivion.

Alone, Misk had to go to Castlekeep, where there was
still small hope for the future. She had wanted to be there
for the baby. Now the baby might never be conceived. But
it was still within her power to redirect and mold some
events. For a short while yet.

After centuries, after so many twists of fate, Misk had
found that moment in time where her vision ended. She
could see this world vaguely beyond that point, but neither
she nor her brother, Sezran, existed in it. Their own lives
were finally coming to an end.

* * * * *

The winter castle, dark and chill, had become home over the past month. Its passageways no longer confused him, and the faces met along the way were familiar and most often friendly. This afternoon, Marten waited for Davi in the huge kitchen area. The earl of the Lower Vales had told him that warmth and light were necessary in the pursuit of music, that stiff cold fingers could never stroke the strings of a lute properly. Or stroke a woman either.

But the young duke of Gosney had divined other reasons for taking his lessons in the kitchen. Tidbits of food were always forthcoming, and the harried kitchen staff was an appreciative audience—one pretty lass in particular, who Marten seemed to have his eye on. In the rest of the keep, the servants still moved timidly, though the king was rarely about. Among the ovens and flour boards, the common folk worked and gossiped and laughed.

Oddly Davi had never once felt homesick for the Fickle River Inn. He knew that he had changed somehow and wondered at those changes. It had to do with more than age—another five months must pass before his sixteenth birthday. It was more than his newfound nobility, too. Certainly a duke wore better clothes, wasn't expected to muck out horse stalls, and servants treated him with deference, but Davi, duke of Gosney, was still the son of Haddi.

No, the real changes had come in his perception of the world around him. That world seemed to have gotten many times larger in these past weeks, and whatever the outward trappings of dukedom, Davi had discovered that knowledge and education were true wealth.

His mother had taught him to read and do simple ciphering. These were necessary skills for an innkeep, but Davi had never read much beyond a supply list or added up more than a patron's bill. And there had never been time for music. Now he had books filled with fascinating mysteries and tutors to explain them.

Only one thing in all this might make him happier, but
that had been denied him so far. The king had refused all
further contact with his young duke. With anyone, for that
matter. Gaylon Reysson had remained sequestered in his
library for over three weeks, taking only food and wine,
and very little of those.

The boy became aware of heat and lamplight. Day-
dreaming, he had come into the hot, moist air of the bus-
tling kitchen. Two young women with loaded dinner trays
dropped curtseys and dodged around the boy. Venison siz-
zled and turned on one spit, and a half-dozen chickens on
another. Eryn, an older woman with heavily muscled arms,
kneaded a small mountain of dough on a wide counter.

"Milord!" Marten called from a stool near—but not too
near—the ovens. "Are you ready for another lesson in the
commonalities of music and mathematics?"

Davi held up the lute, sad and battered, and the earl
laughed. Pretty the instrument might not be, but its sound
was undeniably sweet, and the queen had insisted Davi
keep it. Sometimes, when he practiced alone in his chambers, he'd be haunted by a snatch of melody, by a momentary sense of loss and sorrow, but never for long.

"Mulled wine for the duke!" Marten had his splinted
left leg propped on a stack of flour sacks and his right hand
wrapped around a full cup. Now, he noticed his pupil fa-
voring a leg. "I'm the one with the broken bone. Why are
you limping?"

Davi found a bit of lint to pick from his sleeve, then
mumbled, "I fell off the dun this morning."

"Oh, gods!" the earl roared with delight. "That's the
one thing you weren't suppose to learn from Karyl."

"Karyl told me," the boy said in his own defense, "that
a man who says he's never fallen from a horse has never
ridden one."

"Well, Karyl should know," Marten said solemnly and
covered his amusement with a drink of wine. "Horseman-

ship aside, how are you doing with the sword?"

This was another touchy subject for Davi. "I'm still very clumsy with it."

"I'll tell you a secret, lad." The earl slipped a cup in the boy's hand. "We're all clumsy until that moment we face the enemy. Don't let it worry you."

The kitchen girl, Cally, brought a heaping plate and set it on the table next to Marten. With his light brown hair and eyes, and angular face, the earl was not a particularly handsome young man, but the women of the keep seemed to find him more than attractive.

"What's this?" he asked her sweetly.

"What ya always says ya like, milord," Cally answered just as sweetly. "Tender white breasts." Then her cheeks colored, and she scurried away.

Davi reached for a piece of the roast chicken and got his hand slapped.

"None for you," Marten said with his mouth full. "You've music to play. Give us the Inland Isle's bawdy, the one about the cross-eyed tavern wench. It always makes Eryn laugh and Cally blush an even lovelier shade of red."

The duke positioned his fingertips carefully on the strings and strummed the first chord. He found it hard to concentrate, though. He liked these young lords, the king's cohorts, and had heard of their exploits from just about everyone in the keep. What troubled him was Arlin, alone in his chambers, deserted by those who had called him friend.

* * * * *

Seward Castle stood lonely watch upon wide green meadows that overlooked a cold and restless sea. The unending surge of the ocean and the gathering of storms on the distant western horizon had brought the old wizard solace over the past millennium. Even deep within the castle walls, Sezran felt a part of the ocean's ebb and flow, a part of the shifting weather patterns high above the vast waters.

This day, he sat silent in the great hall, content with darkness all around. Seward's many levels and chambers had been built over the centuries for no other reason than to please its master, to while away the monotonous days and nights of exile. With tedious exactitude, Sezran had placed each stone, then set his sorcerous Shadows to guard the castle.

No creature had ever passed through Seward's Shadows and survived, except one . . . Gaylon Reysson. Even now the old man's bitter hatred of the young sorcerer-king brought an angry blue glare from the Stone at his breast. Daryn, who had once been the old man's student, had died for the Red King's sake, and that only deepened Sezran's hatred. Never mind that he, himself, had twice tried to kill Daryn, had crippled him and destroyed his magic.

Gaylon dared to possess Kingslayer, dared to keep what was not rightfully his. Far worse, the Wynnamyran king's powers were greater than Sezran's, and this was intolerable. The old man's Sorcerer's Stone flared brighter still on its golden chain, and hard blue radiance chased the writhing, living night from the great hall for just an instant. That sudden release of energy calmed him. Soft darkness closed in around his chair once again.

"Sezran!"

A shout boomed on the empty air, then a faint nimbus formed in the center of the chamber. The young sorcerer, Gaylon, was artless, his magic strong but crude. He appeared in the center of the hall. The old man straightened in his seat and tried to deny the quickening of his pulse.

Gaylon, blind without visible light, held his ringed hand high, then turned slowly, his Stone aglow. "There you are." He sounded almost amiable.

"What is it, now?" Sezran asked and let his voice roll like thunder through the chamber.

The king let the echoes fade. "I've come as your humble pupil, once again." There was nothing humble in his stance, though, nor in the pale, arrogant face.

"You've come to torment me."

"Please. No one else can help me."

The wizard chuckled. "Then all shall pity you, Gaylon Reysson."

"Sezran, listen to me. I called the spirit of the Stone. With its aid, I brought a comrade back from death. . . ." Gaylon clenched his hands into fists. "I knew the price. Now I need your help to avoid payment."

"Why should I help you?" In the silence that followed, the old man waited his answer.

The sorcerer-king's gaze shifted aside. "Because I'll give you Kingslayer in return."

A tiny joy filled Sezran, but that died abruptly. "Liar. Do you think me a fool? You offer me what's mine in exchange for an answer that doesn't exist. Go home, boy. When the time comes, you'll do what you must."

"No! I've searched the *Book of Stones*, day and night, until I'm near blind. There must be a way out."

"The only way out is death. It's always been thus. Without death, there could be no life. That's why necromancy carries so dear a price. Perhaps you should simply undo what was done."

"I can't. Arlin has suffered enough."

"Ah, then all is lost." The wizard leaned forward, smiling. "This brings me great happiness. Even if I could help you, I wouldn't. I wish you only misery and misfortune. I wish you neverending sorrow. Now, young sorcerer, you'll know there are things beyond even your powers."

The king had stiffened, and his Stone brightened. "Shall I share my misfortune, then? Shall I level Seward, old man?"

"If that makes you feel less impotent, then do so. Stones are only stones, however they're stacked." Sezran settled back in his highbacked chair, moved to laughter despite the danger.

Gaylon's fury made the castle lurch violently beneath their feet. Blue lightning arced in all directions from his ring, then he was gone. A small amount of dust drifted in the darkness, but Seward stood fast. The wizard only laughed harder.

* * * * *

Arlin hadn't expected the boy-duke to return. There was little Arlin expected anymore, therefore he could not be disappointed. At least the tall clock candle, with its dark rings marked for midnight and noon, proved that time did pass. This was replaced now and again by Girkin, who remained kind, but distant, bringing meals and medication. When asked for news of the keep, the physician's answers were gruff, even evasive.

Davi had been right though—to join the rest of the world, Arlin need only leave his bed and chambers. Fingertips and toes remained oddly numb, but with concentration, the limbs obeyed. Alone, the Southerner took his first steps, using the bed to steady himself. This awkward, stumbling body had served him well before, and so it would again.

It took six long days before he could dress himself and move about the chamber for short periods of time. Exhaustion left him stupefied, though, and Arlin finally realized that much of his tiredness was due to the concoctions Girkin brought him. After that, the young lord refused to take the drinks. The physician protested very little and noticed nothing, not even that the fire now miraculously stoked itself or that his patient no longer needed help to feed himself.

The last barrier proved to be the worst, though. After working so hard to prepare himself, Arlin found he couldn't cross the threshold, couldn't open the unlocked door of his prison. What lay beyond was unknown and therefore terrifying. For four more interminable days, he struggled with the fear, then finally gathered enough courage to bath and dress himself and try again.

The door creaked as it always did upon opening. The passageway beyond was chill and dimly lit, but familiar. The Southerner took a candle lantern with him and started the long walk toward the great hall. The first servant to come across him fled. The second, a chambermaid, squeaked in terror, then ran as well.

"Perhaps I should drag chains behind me," Arlin muttered to himself. "And moan now and then."

A third person appeared well down the corridor, carrying his own light and moving quickly toward Arlin.

"Good day," this person said politely as he hurried past. "Davi!"

The youth stopped and turned back, grinning. "You've joined the living."

"Don't jump to conclusions, milord. The living have yet to join me. Where are you going in so great a hurry?"

"I'm on a treasure hunt," Davi answered.

"Treasure? What kind?"

"The kind that king's have. Or are supposed to have. Want to help?"

Arlin nodded, though his knees were weak and already trembling. "All right . . . so long as there's a convenient wall for me to lean on every once in a while."

The young duke started out, headed away from the great hall. His pace had slowed considerably. "Can you tell me what's at the end of this northwest wing?" Davi asked.

"The nursery, but the only things being raised there now are baby spiders. Certainly there's no treasure."

"How do you all live?" Davi asked, brow furrowed. "Financially."

That was a highly personal and impolite question, but

Arlin couldn't take offense.

"Karyl and I have no family income. We receive small pensions from the king. Marten inherited the Lower Vales and has his own money from that. Rinn, of course, works for a living."

Davi frowned. "I get an allowance. But where does the king get his gold?"

"From Tydus Dorenson."

"That's an odd arrangement," the duke said.

"Not really. Lucien D'Sulang was a squanderer and left the court penniless. Tydus has done what he could to straighten things out. Besides, Gaylon hardly cares where the money comes from, so long as he has enough for the taverns."

"After eight years, it seems to me that things are worse, not better." Davi gestured around him. "The keep, the grounds, are all in disrepair. The servants wear rags. My clothes are the newest of anyone's, by far. I know very little about the aristocracy, but I always imagined they lived better than this."

"Then go south to Zankos," Arlin advised and paused to rest. "As far as opulence goes, Roffo's court puts all others to shame."

"I'll probably go south, someday," Davi said with a shrug. "But at the moment, I think there's hidden treasure somewhere within this castle. Or at least ledgers and books to explain where the treasure's gone."

"Have you asked the queen?"

"Not yet."

"What of Tydus? Certainly, he could tell you."

"No. Can't you rest a little faster?" the duke asked impatiently.

Arlin let go of his wall, and they walked on together. The Southern lord had some questions of his own about Davi, and how he'd come to Castlekeep. The boy answered readily enough, and if he'd been raised a commoner, it was

no longer apparent. Every unconscious step and movement, every spoken word, proved him a duke. In the years
to come, Arlin believed Davi Darynson would be a formidable presence in the court of Wynnamyr.

The youth turned right at the next corridor. "Since the
nursery has only baby spiders, let's visit the queen instead."

Via a circuitous route, Davi led them back toward the
keep's southeast wing. Arlin continued to startle the
household staff that met him in the halls. When at last he
reached the queen's chambers, the Southerner wanted
nothing more than to find his bed and crawl back into it.
He settled, instead, for an overstuffed chair before Jessmyn's hearth.

The queen, herself, served him a steaming cup of tea.
"Should you be up so soon, Lord Arlin?" She smiled, but
there was worry in her eyes.

"Obviously not," Arlin quipped as he fumbled the cup
with clumsy fingers and dumped hot liquid on the arm of
the chair. "I'm really sorry . . ."

"No matter." The young woman poured him more tea.
"I'm so glad you're feeling better."

Davi had pulled a wooden stool up to the fireplace and
sat with his own cup, listening.

Amenities over, he said with deference, "Highness,
where would the ledgers be kept?"

"What ledgers?"

"Any books dealing with the keep . . . how supplies are
ordered and paid for, servants' wages. That sort of thing."

"Have you asked Tydus?"

"Yes, but he feels it's not my concern."

"He's probably right," Her Majesty observed, smiling.
When Davi pursed his lips, she went on. "The likeliest
place would be the council chamber behind the throne.
The council meets rarely now, since the king refuses to hold
audiences." Jessmyn turned back to Arlin. "Have you seen
the king?"

Arlin shook his head. "Girkin says he's still in the library, milady."

"No longer. He's deserted the *Book of Stones* finally." She sipped her tea. "I believe His Majesty is at the stables, organizing another drunken hunt."

Her tone was mild, her demeanor calm as always. Yet somehow Arlin was, for the first time, aware of the pain behind her smile. He'd seen that pain behind so many of her smiles over the years and never truly noticed before.

"I think you've suffered enough, milady," he said gently and saw her confusion. The Southerner set his cup aside, spilling the tea again, and stood up. "Your leave, Majesty?"

"Of course . . ."

"Wait." Davi rose to his feet hurriedly. "Where are you going?"

"To join the hunt one last time," Arlin told him.

Nine

A thin layer of fresh snow blanketed the castle grounds, and the afternoon sun was hidden behind thick gray clouds. Arlin insisted on taking Davi out through the keep's gardens and approaching the stableyard from the opposite direction—a roundabout way that seemed senseless to the young duke, especially with the Southerner's slow pace.

"This is taking too long," the boy complained when Arlin halted once again, this time to lean against the low stone wall that circled the weapons yard.

"Then go on ahead," the nobleman muttered breathlessly. Despite the cold, his dark hair clung to his sweated brow.

"No." Davi tried to quell his impatience. "This is foolish, anyway. We're not properly dressed for a hunt. I wasn't even invited, and you—how are you going to stay on a horse?"

"I'll manage," Arlin grunted and propelled himself from the wall to start out again on rickety legs.

A pair of ancient grandfather oaks spread their bare branches over the snow-covered roof at the rear of the stable. As the two of them approached, Davi heard coarse laughter and the jingling of tack, the stamp of hooves. He pulled one side of the rear double doors open and let Arlin enter first. The front doors were already wide. In the yard beyond, the boy could see Karyl's bright hair poking out from underneath a knit cap.

The king, doubled in size by a huge bearskin coat, had a bow and quiver slung over his shoulder and a filled wineskin in one hand. Two grooms checked saddle girths and headstalls, while the horsemaster handed Marten Pelson awkwardly up onto a tall, dapple gray mount, then lowered a stirrup to accommodate the earl's splinted leg. A scattering of snowflakes began to drift earthward.

"Idiots," Arlin snapped under his breath and made his way down the long aisle between the stalls.

Rinn was there, too, ruddy-cheeked and laughing, already seated on his ugly black gelding. The wineskin made the rounds and came back again to the king.

"You weren't thinking of going without me?" D'Lelan asked loudly from beside the open doors.

Everyone turned at the voice, but their reactions to the speaker were mixed. The grooms stood frozen, eyes huge, while Karyl blanched visibly. Marten and Rinn's faces were touched with fear.

"Arlin!" the king shouted joyfully, the word gently slurred with drink. "Find him a mount! Hurry!"

"Find two mounts," the Southerner said. "I've invited the duke of Gosney to ride with us."

Gaylon's focus shifted to Davi, and he frowned. "The ride'll be too difficult for a boy. . . ."

"But not for a man with a broken leg?" Arlin wondered aloud. "Or for a man newly risen from the dead? Highness, this is your Gosney, as willing as any of us to follow you happily to his death. You can't deny him that honor." In the chill silence that followed, the young Southern lord stepped out into the yard, smiling. "Look at me. I'm even willing to die twice in your service, milord. Only give me a horse and a long drink of brandy."

Davi watched and listened, aghast. D'Lelan's words were sharp-edged and cruel, even when spoken so gently.

Instead of royal outrage though, the king stared fixedly at Arlin. "By the gods, you won't let go, will you?"

"No, milord. I'm determined to serve you better with this life than I did with the last."

"Easy enough for you to tell me to be a king and a husband," Gaylon said, suddenly morose, "when I'm not sure how to be either."

"It'll come to you," Arlin promised. Then his weak leg gave way, and he sat heavily in the slush.

The king cast bow and quiver aside and gathered his friend, once more, in his arms. "This is getting to be a habit with you," he growled and stood, glaring at the others. "We'll hunt another day. Bring the brandy."

Karyl and Rinn dismounted, as did Marten, with a little help from a groom. The king's comrades seemed to share a common confusion over what had just happened. Arlin insisted on carrying his own weight now, and Karyl offered a shoulder for him to lean on. After a slight hesitation, Rinn offered his own shoulder on the opposite side.

The grooms led the horses into the stable to be unsaddled. Davi remained alone in the yard, uncertain, but as the group of men walked toward the bailey, the king stopped abruptly and turned.

"Gosney," he snapped. "Don't lag behind."

*   *   *   *   *

Davi sat and listened from his seat on the edge of the hearthstones while the king and his companions talked. The royal apartments were thinly furnished, and that furniture had seen far better days. This main chamber felt dark and gloomy, despite a dozen candles and the fire. Dust lay thick on every surface. Supper dishes had been added to the general disorder, scattered over tables and floor. Poorly aimed chicken bones that had missed the flames littered the hearth.

Early on, Gaylon had settled in an ancient camp chair with leather bindings that creaked and groaned under his weight. His booted feet, crossed at the ankles, were stretched out on the hearth next to Davi, and much of the time the king stared intently at the young duke, his face empty of expression. The boy couldn't quite find the courage to meet his gaze, but was content just to be in the Red King's presence.

"Give the boy some brandy," Karyl insisted from his seat on a much-scuffed armoire chest that he'd dragged close to the fire.

"It'll make him sick," Marten said while refilling his own cup with amber liquid from the cut glass decanter.

"So? He's old enough to suffer with the rest of us."

"But is he foolish enough?" Marten set his drink aside and heaved himself to his feet. "Stand up," he ordered, and when Davi complied, the earl glanced at Karyl. "Well?"

"Near as tall as you," the royal cousin said pleasantly. "We won't be calling him boy much longer." Then he nudged Rinn in the chair beside him. "Arlin's gone to sleep on us again."

The young Southerner had been given the one soft seat in the room—an armchair with tattered upholstery. Pale and drawn, he slept with one of Gaylon's cloaks across his lap.

"Let him rest," the king muttered. His Majesty had spoken little over the course of the night, but he'd also drunk less. Now, with eyes once more on Davi, Gaylon said, "I'd very much appreciate the moral support of my friends tomorrow, when I hold my first audience."

"You're really going to do it?" Karyl asked. "You're going to sit on your throne?"

Gaylon frowned. "That's part of it, I believe—as well as considering petitions and making judgments."

"No one will come," Rinn told them, his attention on

the sleeping Arlin.

"Sure they will," the royal cousin argued, "if only to
gawk at a real live king upon a throne."

The tailor's son shook his head. "No. I've heard the talk
in town. The people are all convinced that their king has
conjured a demon to inhabit D'Lelan's body. Orym was al
so a necromancer, and Wynnamyr has lived with the mem
ory of the Dark King's reign for too long. They've always
been afraid of sorcery. Now they're absolutely terrified."

"It's true," Marten said. "The keep servants believe the
same. Perhaps it would be best for Arlin to return to
Zankos and his family."

"No." Gaylon's jaw tightened. "We're his family. The
only way to prove to the townsfolk that they're wrong is to
let them see Arlin, speak to him." The king glanced
around at his friends. "And to me. If they won't come to
my audience, then we'll go to them, but not drunk and
rowdy as we've always done."

Karyl chuckled. "Next you'll want dinner served in the
great hall, and fancy dress balls."

"Excellent idea, Cousin," said the king. "I want you to
send invitations to our mutual relatives and invite them to
the keep for an extended visit."

"What will you feed them?" Karyl demanded.

"We'll worry about minor details later."

"Do I have to invite Grand-aunt Elsith?" The royal
cousin rolled his eyes. "Her beard's longer than yours . .
and she's been in such a foul temper these last twenty
years."

"Be nice," Marten advised, "and you may inherit some
thing."

Karyl winced. "With my luck it'll be her beard."

"So how can I help?" the tailor's son demanded.

"You can bring me a problem to solve," Gaylon answered. "I know there're a few level-headed people in
Keeptown—your father for one. Get them to come to me

and the rest will follow. Davi!"

The young duke, caught up in the conversations, jumped. "Yes, milord?"

"Is your handwriting legible?"

Davi nodded. "Yes, milord."

"Good. Karyl's isn't. You write the invitations. Ask my lady queen about the wording."

Debating the issues, they settled back in their seats. The room seemed charged now, almost as Arlin's chamber had been that first night Davi had spent in the keep. This magic came from a shared purpose, though. The boy looked across at the Southern lord and found him looking back, very much awake. They exchanged conspiratorial smiles, and Davi felt happiness for the king. Whatever his reasons, his sorrows and fears, Gaylon Reysson had set them aside and was about to take up his crown.

*   *   *   *   *

Late in the day, Jessmyn experienced the most wonderful sense of anticipation. With it came sudden, bright flashes of childhood memories: the scent of roses, the angle of the summer sunlight on a leaded window pane, the bleating of the gardener's sheep on green lawns. The thoughts were both wonderful and disturbing. She found herself smiling at her needlework, at the fire on the hearth.

The light beyond her windows faded, and supper arrived. Even that simple fare tasted more delicious than usual. Lady Gerra, somehow prompted by this mysterious force, rocked in her chair and called Jessmyn her sweet princess again. For the first time in many years, the elderly woman was moved to spin tales of Zankos and the royal palace there, of ships and sailors and brightly plumed birds.

When the silver-haired governess retired late to her bedchamber, the queen sat alone, oddly happy and at peace.

"It's begun. . . ."

The whisper came from behind her, but she recognized
the speaker immediately. "Nanny . . . Misk?" A look back
revealed only candlelight and shadow among the shabby
furnishings.

"Where is he?" the voice murmured clearly. "I would
speak to the boy."

Jessmyn saw a vague shape, an outline of a tiny woman
on the windowseat. Only her dark eyes had substance,
glinting with an inner light. She gazed at the queen intently, and smiling, faded into empty air.

Jessmyn's sense of anticipation intensified, and, happy,
she drew a deep breath. These small hauntings could mean
only one thing—Misk would soon arrive. Before midnight,
the young queen took herself to bed.

Her dreams were sweet that night, and sad. They
roamed together in the rose gardens—Daryn, Gaylon, and
Jess. The keep grounds, aglow in a diffused golden light,
had seemed so big when she was so very small. The duke of
Gosney carried the little princess trapped against his chest,
safe and secure. They seemed to float together over the
sward. She twined her fingers in the thick black hair at the
nape of his neck and begged him to sing her a song. Then
Gaylon's father appeared in the dream—King Reys, tall
and handsome, his face stern, but his eyes kind.

The vivid images faded at dawn, and the queen woke in
tears over their loss.

"Don't cry, dear child," a voice said gently.

Jessmyn opened her eyes. Morning light haloed the tiny
woman bending over the bed, and a hand, flesh solid and
substantial, brushed the queen's cheek. She was truly here.

"Oh, Misk, dreams are so cruel."

"Why should you think that?" the woman chided.
"You've never truly lost someone, if you can find them in
dreams. There are creatures in this universe who have no
tears to vent their sorrow and no sleep in which to dream.

Pity them, not yourself." She bent to kiss Jessmyn's forehead. "Get dressed, my dear. It's begun."

"What has?"

"The world is not as you left it last night." Misk skated to the chest of drawers and began pulling items of clothing out. "No, not at all. You'll see. . . ."

The queen donned the petticoats and pale green gown that Misk had chosen, a frock that had lain in the bottom drawer, unworn, for years. It smelled of tansy and rose petal. "When did you arrive, Misk?"

"Tomorrow," the silver-haired woman said mischievously and led the queen into the sitting room. Before the windowseat, she paused, head cocked, brows knitted. "Have you seen Davi? I would speak to the boy."

Both of them turned at a scratch on the door. Cally entered with a breakfast tray, Davi on her heels. The duke of Gosney had a crumpled sheet of paper clutched in one hand. At sight of Misk, his bright green eyes lit.

"When did you get here? Where's Jimi?"

Jessmyn thought she saw a momentary sorrow on the tiny woman's face, then Misk shook her head.

"You've better questions for the queen, I hope, Davyn Darynson."

The boy blinked tired eyes. "Oh, yes. His Majesty is inviting relatives to Castlekeep for an extended visit." He waved the page. "Karyl made a list, and there are sixty-two names. Marten says they won't all come, but I have to do the invitations. The king said you would tell me what to write."

Jessmyn sank into the chair beside her breakfast, thoroughly bewildered. "Visitors? Sixty-two . . . How will we feed them all? What sort of madness has struck Gaylon now? This has to be another foolish game."

"No, dear," Misk said. "Your husband is quite serious. As for how you'll feed so many guests, Davi can solve that problem."

"I can?"

The elderly woman smiled. "Certainly. Leave the list with us. We'll write the invitations, while you continue your hunt for treasure. You don't want to be late to your history lesson, either."

It took a moment for the young duke to sort all that out, then he solemnly handed his list to Jessmyn and bowed. "You're staying with us, aren't you?" Davi said to Misk. "I mean . . . I'll see you later, won't I?"

"Of course. There's much to do."

* * * * *

Tydus Dorenson noticed heavier than usual servant traffic in the passages that morning, but he paid it little thought. Such increased activity most often meant the king had perpetrated some spectacular new outrage or another. By mid-morning though, the scuffling in the corridor had failed to lessen. The head councilman stood a while longer in front of the full-length mirror that had been imported at great expense from Katay. His reflection, as always, pleased him. The robes were perfect, a deep shade of plum, not quite royal, but almost.

All of Tydus's clothing was tailored in Katay during his yearly sojourn south. He'd long ago found that a quasi-military cut was the most prepossessing; hence his wardrobe tended toward dramatic colors with plenty of gold braid. With a final stroke of the comb through his perfect white hair, the head councilman left his chambers.

The door stood open on the empty apartments nearest his own. He paused to look in on a harried chambermaid making the bed.

"Here, you. What's going on?"

Eyes wide, the young woman curtsied. "His Majesty's ordered all the rooms made up, milord—even upstairs."

"Whatever for?"

"Don't know, milord."

Disturbed, Tydus went on toward the great hall. There, a half-dozen men with buckets, mops, and brooms cleaned the long sections of the trestle table and swept cobwebs from high corners, but a far more disturbing sight awaited him in the throne room. Gaylon Reysson, in slightly frayed royal-blue velvet, was seated on the massive oak throne, chin in hand. A thin gold band encircled his brow. Otherwise, the chamber was empty.

"Sire," the head councilman said, much worried, and stepped out onto the freshly washed floor. "Are you well?"

"Ah, Tydus!" The king beamed at him. "Do you by any chance have a petition? Some important business that needs my . . . *our* most regal attention?"

"No, Sire."

Gaylon sighed, then reached out with one blue satin slipper and stamped on the stone flagging before him. He looked up. "Did you know we have cockroaches?"

"Yes, milord."

"I've never noticed them before. Is there any way to rid a castle of such vermin? Never mind, I'll look for a spell in the *Book of Stones* later."

"Sire . . ."

The king nodded. "You have my leave, sir. Don't worry. I expected business to be slow the first day."

Tydus bowed and backed into the corridor, thoroughly shaken. He'd grown accustomed to mad and unreasonable behavior from his monarch, but this was too much. Perhaps Girkin should be informed. Then again, perhaps it would be best to return to his chambers and let the insanity run its course.

The kitchens lay just beyond the great hall. The head councilman stopped there on his way back to the southeast wing and informed the kitchen mistress that he would have rabbit for dinner. The heavy-set woman, well dusted with flour, gave him a curt nod. Behind her, seated in a warm

corner near the ovens, were Marten Pelson and Arlin D'Lelan. D'Lelan offered Tydus a tight smile, then returned to
his conversation, and the head councilman's heart gave a
sick lurch. Dark sorcery and madness on every hand.

He fled back to his apartments. In time, dinner arrived,
but his stomach was most unhappy and nothing appealed,
not even the succulent roast rabbit. Davi would arrive soon
for his history lesson, and Tydus spent a while setting out
the books and scrolls. Finally, there was a knock on the
door.

"Come," he said and took his seat at the table as the boy
entered. "You're late, young duke."

"I've had a busy morning," Davi answered. He had arrived dressed in leather, cheeks flushed with cold, and
there was snow on his boots. There was also a subtle new
authority in his stance.

"What have you got there?" Tydus asked.

The duke pulled a thin volume from under his arm. "I
found this in the council chambers earlier, hidden in the
bottom of a cabinet. It was one of Feydir D'Sulang's ledgers, but all the latest entries are yours, I think."

Davi sat in the chair across the table and opened the
book. Tydus stared at the pages, at his own beautiful and
uniquely ornate script. Every column of numbers was exact, every penny meticulously accounted for.

"What did you do with the Southern gold mentioned
here, that the ambassador had set aside to pay his mercenaries?"

"It's all safe, my young lord," the head councilman said,
tapping the book. "I've kept what I could for the king,
hidden, so that when the time comes, he'll be able to build
his armies."

The boy looked perplexed. "What makes you think the
king needs armies?"

"Because he has many enemies. But more than this,
with Orym's Legacy and a great army, our Red King has the

power to bring all nations under him, to bring peace and prosperity to the entire world." Tydus smiled. "Of course, our king isn't aware of his own potential, just yet. He needs to mature, and he needs my gentle guidance as well as yours, Gosney. I couldn't let him know about the gold or any of the wealth the D'Sulangs left behind. He would have squandered the fortune, just as Lucien did."

Tydus had mixed enough truth with the lies to convince the boy-duke of his sincerity, for Davi glanced down at the pages.

"No matter your motives, milord," the boy said evenly, "you must return to the king what is rightly his."

"I agree." The head councilman dared to lay his hand over the young duke's. "With your astute help, His Majesty is ready to assume his financial responsibilities. Some of the gold is hidden in the dungeons below the keep. There are precious gems, as well, and much jewelry. I'll tell you where, but I would ask one favor. Let this be your own happy and accidental discovery. I would not want the king to think me a fool."

Or worse, Tydus thought bitterly.

*   *   *   *   *

Karyl stood in the wine cellar, poised at the top of a long, winding stairway that dropped at an alarmingly steep angle into the depths of the castle. When he pried the door loose from its jam, the dungeon exhaled an icy breath touched with a faint whiff of old death.

"Are you sure we have to do this?" the royal cousin demanded.

Davi nodded, mute, eyes trapped by the dark stairwell. The torch in his hand fluttered wildly with the very first step past the entrance.

"I'm really not all that interested in treasure," Karyl muttered as they started down. "The foundation is in so

bad a state that the masons refused to even start repairs—
for fear the weight of the keep would bring it all down on
them. We've got to be insane to go digging around in the
mess."

The duke of Gosney ignored the nervous chatter, so
Karyl continued. "Nearly three hundred prisoners were
lost in the cave in. All we're going to find are their bones.
That's not my idea of treasure."

The stairs twisted and turned in their descent. The light
from the cellar above was soon lost, but the narrow steps
carved of stone continued down and down. The royal cousin almost preferred Orym's icy cairn to this. Almost. Now
there were noises—a scrabbling of tiny claws, intermittent
squeaks of rodent ardor or outrage. It took every bit of
courage Karyl could muster to manage the last dozen steps.

They paused on the broken floor. The torch threw a wavering, fitful circle of light, but beyond that lay pitch darkness. The foul, sweetish stench was stronger here, mixed
with the musky scent of fungus. Karyl trembled and
prayed the young duke wouldn't notice his fear.

Davi glanced side to side, then pointed the torch out
ahead. "There's an old fire pit somewhere in the center.
That's where we need to look."

"How do you know all this?"

"I told you. I found some of the ambassador's old papers."

"Right. We're wasting our time, Davi. And risking our
lives."

"Come on." The boy moved with calm assurance over
the rubble-strewn floor.

They found the fire pit easily, a wide hole chiseled
through the stone flags. Davi handed Karyl the torch and
stepped down into the dead ashes that covered the bottom.
He crouched to scoop them away.

"Find me something to pry with," the boy commanded.

Karyl bit back a protest, then made a halfhearted survey

around him. There was rubble and more rubble, none of it suited to their purpose, but the master of the dungeon had left the tools of his torture trade behind to rust. The royal cousin picked through the pile, his lip curled in distaste, and found a thick iron rod he carried back to Davi.

"Will this do?"

"It might." The boy hefted the piece before wedging the end along a lip of stone near his feet. "Grab on."

Together, grunting and groaning, they levered a thin stone slab free of its bed, got the thing on edge, and let it topple clear of the pit. Karyl pushed his torch over the hole. Four wooden boxes, each an arm's length in size, sat tightly arranged in the hidden space.

"Won't be anything in 'em," the royal cousin insisted, though excitement tugged at him.

Davi jammed the rod into the latch on one box and broke it loose, then lifted the lid. The torchlight put sudden fire to the gold within. Coins, each a small blazing sun, dazzled their eyes.

"Well," the duke said as he took hold of the torch. "Do you think we can feed all your royal relatives with this?"

"For at least a fortnight," Karyl joked, then grabbed the boy's shoulders and shook him like a rag doll, but the ecstasy faded with realization. "Oh gods, how are we going to get these all the way back up those blasted stairs?"

Ten

"Lord D'Lelan!"

At the bellow, Arlin froze. Lady Elsith swept toward him along the passageway, elegant yellow silk billowing around her. Her small entourage of servants and family tripped along behind. Despite her great age and formidable size, the lady was irrefuted matriarch of the Oakhaven clan, having outlived her own generation and a good deal of the next. The sight of her rolling down the hall would inspire awe in anyone, and no little panic.

She arrived, hooking a thick arm in Arlin's elbow, and wheeled him about. "My dear boy, we don't want to be late for dinner."

Gods forbid. "I'd lost track of the time, milady," the young Southerner murmured. Mentally he added, otherwise you'd never have caught me so easily. He forced a smile and chided himself for such uncharitable thoughts.

"Plenty of food and exercise has kept me well these eighty-one years. They'll do the same for you, young man."

Resigned, Arlin let himself be dragged back toward the great hall and dinner. Karyl had been right in one thing—his grand-aunt Elsith was indeed lightly bearded, sporting numerous coarse hairs on her well-fleshed chin, but her temper, while imperious, was not entirely foul.

She, along with all of the Red King's kinsmen, had tak-

en Castlekeep by storm. They had come from every part of
the snowscaped countryside without hesitation, more enthralled with the king's sorcery than afraid. Gaylon was
family, after all, and they had waited long for this invita-
tion. Arlin had found them, as a whole, intelligent,
learned, and extremely sensible. It was a pleasant surprise.

At first it had been strange to hear so many voices in the
corridors, so much friendly laughter, or to be seated at a
table with over sixty noisy diners after being so long seclud-
ed in this murky old keep. Arlin, of course, had been raised
in a court far larger, but Xenaran aristocrats were cold and
calculating, and far more given to intrigue than these
good-natured folk.

D'Lelan had let his thoughts wander, and he took a sudden clumsy step, ending up tangled in his own feet on the
hard, cold floor. The kindly entourage rushed to his assistance, but Lady Elsith, being closest, caught him in an iron
grip and hoisted him upright on uncooperative legs.

"There, there, my boy," she cooed. "After dying, you've
simply come back newborn. Any baby takes time to learn
to walk."

Arlin tried to accept this well-intentioned sympathy
with grace. The kinfolk had not reacted to Gaylon's necromancy as the townsfolk had. Not at all. To Grand-aunt
Elsith and the rest, Arlin was a curiosity, a phenomenon to
be explored, not reviled. But all the kindness and concern
was somehow worse. The Southerner had no answers to
their questions, no understanding of what had happened
to him, and the king would not speak of sorcery at all. Having no real memory of the experience, death remained a
dark mystery that Arlin could not explain.

A wave of heat and sound washed over Lady Elsith and
her group as they entered the teeming hall. Seating order
at the trestle table rearranged itself constantly all through
the meals. Enormous amounts of food and wine were consumed, and wandering diners made it more difficult for

the servants to deliver their heaping platters. Along with
the servants the guests had brought, the household staff
had been further enlarged over the past few weeks, and
their uniforms were new.

Karyl's grand-aunt towed Arlin down the row to a spot
hastily cleared for them. Clean plates and utensils appeared immediately. The keep servants had quickly learned
not to incur the old lady's wrath. Davi waved a turkey leg at
the Southern lord from his seat near the head of the table.
Gaylon, splendidly dressed in slashed red satin with a jeweled crown upon his head, looked slightly uneasy.

Communal meals tended to affect him this way, and he
drank more heavily during them. Beside him, the queen
picked delicately at her dinner. She, too, was crowned and
royally attired in a gown of the same red satin. Still, husband and wife had little, if anything, to say to one another.
There seemed to be a rift between them, despite the fact
that Gaylon had made so many positive changes in so short
a time.

"D'Lelan!"

A well-chewed chicken bone landed in Arlin's empty
dish. He glanced along the table and found Karyl and Marten grinning at him. The bone, neatly returned, caught the
earl on the cheek. Before Arlin could retaliate again, Lady
Elsith turned to him.

"Milord," she scolded, "you must eat to keep up your
strength." With that she began to pile roast turkey and cur-
rant stuffing before him. Next came yams, lamb, and curried eggs.

When the lady began to pour a clotted venison gravy
overall, Arlin cried, "Enough! Please . . ."

Unoffended, she picked up a spoon, placed it in his
palm, and curled his fingers about the handle. "Eat."

After a quick glare at his two highly amused friends,
Arlin obeyed.

* * * * *

On a dark, chill night some weeks later, Lady Gerra passed gently away in her sleep. The old governess had been Jessmyn's only true link to her childhood and to her royal family in Xenara. The queen was devastated. In a quiet ceremony, they laid the lady to rest in the frozen earth of the burial grounds.

Winter lost its grip on the land soon after. Spring rains banished the last of the snow, and warm sunlight and longer days coaxed the first tender green blades of grass from the earth. Wood iris and lilies bloomed, and new redleafed growth appeared on the roses in the castle gardens.

Despite her mourning for the Lady Gerra, these marvels of nature were not lost on Jessmyn. Even more wonderful were the sounds of children at play on the keep grounds and in the nursery—a great flock of healthy, happy, and very often redheaded children with freckled faces. All of them carried some visible characteristic of their mutual familial bloodline, these young descendants of the Red Kings. None of the children were Jessmyn's.

One rambunctious toddler in particular had stolen her heart, though, a nephew of Karyl's. Misk had just gone to fetch him from the nursery, and the queen sat on the windowseat with morning light streaming in through the glass. The children's games on the lawns held her attention until Misk returned with Tari. He saw the queen and galloped stiff-legged toward her.

"Jeth-myn," the boy squeaked.

Jessmyn leaned to hug him, then glanced at the wet stain on his britches. "What happened?"

"Don't know." He offered her wide, innocent blue eyes under a forelock of fine blond hair.

"Did you sit in a puddle on the way?"

The toddler nodded solemnly, evoking delighted laughter from Misk as she brought a blanket for the queen's lap.

Tari held his arms out, and Jessmyn took him up.

"I have something for you, my fine little fellow," she said.

He tilted his head back and peered at her, owl-eyed. "What?"

The lid of the cedar box was hinged and tightly fitted. The queen opened it in front of the toddler.

"These were Gaylon's when he was a little boy. Sometimes he let me play with them. I saved them for him, but he was all grown up by the time he came home to be king." Jessmyn watched Tari pull one small wooden soldier from the rest. "Their uniforms could use a fresh coat of paint, I suppose. Look. Some have swords, and some are bowmen, and some even have horses to ride." The queen set the child back on the floor with his box. "You can play with them here on the carpet."

Tari didn't respond. He was already in that miniature world, commanding his armies. It had always amazed Jessmyn how quickly the littlest of boys took to the concepts of war, almost as if they were born valiant.

Misk laid a hand gently on her arm, and the queen looked up.

"Is there nothing you want of the king?" the tiny woman asked.

The question startled her, but Jessmyn answered, "He's given me all I could want."

"Has he?" Misk set a cup of hot tea on the windowseat beside the queen. "I've watched the two of you, rarely speaking, never touching. I've never seen so chaste a marriage in all my days—which are far too many to count. What I can't understand is why."

"Ask His Majesty," the young woman said, irritated, and put her attention on a group of children racing over the grass below.

"No. Far better that you ask him."

"I couldn't." The thought of even speaking with Gaylon

made Jessmyn's heart race.

Misk's eyes were dark, unfathomable, but her smooth, ageless face held a vague sorrow. "You must, dear heart, if something of Gaylon is to live on. . . ."

"What have you seen?" the queen asked, suddenly afraid.

"Endless possibilities, child, always. I'm more concerned for your immediate happiness."

Beside them on the carpet, Tari had arranged his men in haphazard rows. Now, with obvious joy, he laid waste to the army, toppling them all.

"I kilt 'em," the toddler said with pride and tugged at Jessmyn's skirts. "See?"

"Yes, darling." The queen smiled. "I see."

*   *   *   *   *

Gaylon held audiences only one day out of the week, for which Davi was extremely grateful. The king had placed a low table to serve as desk at the right and behind his throne, but the young duke rarely had the chance to sit there. One of his many duties took him out among the petitioners, as he was now, deciding which problems needed more immediate attention.

Spring flooding near the mouth of the Great River was just such a case. Those who had waited longest resented Davi's interruptions, but stood back all the same to let the young nobleman bring this latest petitioner to the fore.

"Sire, this is Kalep Demson, mayor of Teely Creek."

The long, thin man in rough clothing bowed deeply, and Gaylon straightened on his throne.

"Speak, sir."

"Your Majesty. The river has taken our town. We've lost a dozen souls and have near a hundred homeless and hungry." Demson twisted an old felt cap in his hands. "I was told that a man may come before you seeking aid, and that this aid might be granted if you deem the purpose worthy."

The king signaled Davi to his stool. "So many suffering
is more than worthy, Mayor. Milord Gosney . . ." The
young duke found his stylus and dipped it in the ink.
"Granted to Kalep Demson, one hundred gold decos. He
may collect the money in the morning from my clerk. Make
a note to send Jaret to help the mayor find his supplies and
hire wagons and drivers to haul them. We may have to send
to other towns to meet his people's needs. Is this to your
satisfaction, sir?"

Kalep Demson's mouth worked a moment before he
found his voice. "Sire, it is well beyond my hopes. My
gratitude—"

"Your gratitude is not necessary, Mayor. Only remember
us at tax time, once your town has fully recovered. There
could be future hardships in store for others."

"Yes, Sire." The mayor bowed and backed away.

In the crowded chamber, appreciative murmurs were
heard. However Gaylon may have alienated his subjects in
years past, word had quickly spread that a just and compas-
sionate monarch now sat upon the Wynnamyran throne.
Davi felt a touch of pride, mixed with fatigue. In matters
of dispute, the king relied much on his duke. Gaylon tended to react to disagreements on an intuitive and emotional
level, while Davi held to logic, sifting through testimony
carefully until every fact was unearthed.

The king made no judgments in these cases without the
duke of Gosney's counsel. There might be some among the
petitioners who took exception to a boy advising a king.
Most saw only a bright and confident young nobleman at-
tending his lord.

Davi looked out over the room full of people. Soon, they
would need to set two days a week aside for audiences. As it
was, meals consisted of fruit, cheese, and wine that could
be taken while they worked. Gaylon turned no one in true
need away, and often, audiences were held late into the

night. His Majesty ingested far more wine than perhaps he should during these long days, but never appeared drunk.

"Milord duke?" The king lifted a brow.

With a weary smile, the boy left his desk and descended the dais stairs in search of the next worthy petition.

* * * * *

Music and light and the muted sounds of voices led Jessmyn to the great hall's open doors. Even this late at night a few couples still danced in the center of the floor. She observed the graceful steps, the hands that met and held, the faces of the dancers, old and young, and felt an emptiness. Robe wrapped tightly over her nightgown, the queen moved on into the candlelit passageway.

This path would take her to the king's apartment. What she would do there, or say, was unclear, but something would come to her. Before his door, Jessmyn paused, afraid, then knocked so lightly that it surprised her when the door opened.

"Milady?" Byler, a new manservant assigned to the king, bowed and moved to let her pass. "His Majesty hasn't returned from his audience, yet. Would you care to wait?"

The queen stood undecided, but the servant's friendly, open manner gave her the courage to step into the chamber. "Thank you, I will wait . . . but alone, Byler. Please."

"Of course, Your Highness." He gave her a respectful, but curious glance. "Perhaps some wine to make the wait a pleasant one?"

"No . . . Yes, please."

Byler led her to a couch before the hearth, then brought the wine. "Will there be anything else?"

"No."

"Very good, milady."

The knowing smile irritated her, but she returned it

pleasantly enough as the servant let himself into the passage. Alone, Her Majesty admired the chamber. Nothing fancy, of course: several gaudy tapestries and thick rugs, and the few bits of furniture were new, commissioned and bought in Keeptown. There were grease stains on the couch already, and she vowed to mention the advantages of slipcovers to Byler. All that remained of the old furniture was King Reys's camp chair, banished to a corner.

The fire needed tending, and Jessmyn fed billets from the nearby stack into the small blaze. It would be midsummer before the inhabitants of Castlekeep could appreciate their cold damp chambers. Feeling just a touch nervous, she finished her wine and served herself more, then settled on the couch again to stare into the hypnotic flames.

Several times there were footsteps in the corridor, heard briefly as they passed the door—but not his footsteps. Much later, the sharp sound of hard-soled boots on the flags brought her upright on the couch. The door swung open.

"Byler!" Gaylon already had the voluminous ceremonial robes pulled halfway over his head. Something clanged against the floor. "Blast!" A slender gold crown rolled toward the queen, then fell over ringing. She smiled at her floundering husband. Under the gorgeous rich robes of state, he'd worn a favorite old shirt, frayed breeks and his new riding boots, already considerably scuffed. "Byler! For the gods' sake, help me." The words came muffled.

Jessmyn went to his aid, tugging royal blue velvet first one direction, then another. The wine had eased the nervousness, and the king's antics amused her. Gaylon pulled free finally, sandy blond hair on end.

"Were you trying to smother me?" he said irritably and froze. "My lady—"

"I'm sorry. You had everything so tangled, though."

The king glanced around. "Where's Byler?"

"In bed, I should think, this late at night."

"Then I'll see you to your chambers, myself."

"My lord . . ."

Gaylon chucked the robes onto the couch and scooped up the fallen crown. "I'm really very tired. We can talk tomorrow."

"No," Jessmyn said to her own amazement. "What I want to say should have been said long ago. May I pour you some wine?" She didn't wait for his answer, instead filling two cups brimming from the bottle on the small table. "Drink with me, if nothing else. Come sit. I know you're tired." She sat once more on the couch, pushing the blue robes aside.

Hazel eyes troubled, the king took his wine and himself to the camp chair in its corner. Jessmyn refused the hurt that caused, found instead a little anger.

"What would you have done?" she mused with just a touch of sarcasm. "That night, when you thought to divert my attention from Baron Sedwin . . . what would you have done if I'd said yes to sharing your bed?"

Gaylon took a long pull from his cup, stubbornly silent.

"You knew I'd decline. You counted on that." The queen looked into her own cup. "I have never doubted your love, my lord. I've felt it every moment of every day. How then can you both love and abhor me?"

"Don't speak nonsense," the king said sharply.

"Tell me what I've done to deserve such treatment."

"It's a matter of what *I* deserve . . . or *don't* deserve." Gaylon shifted nervously. "If anything, you must abhor me."

His face held intense self-reproach, and his eyes were bleak now. Why? Jessmyn thought, why should I abhor you? Deep down, the bitter answer came.

"The night you destroyed Lucien," she said, "and took up Kingslayer, your power and rage terrified me at first—"

"Don't, please," Gaylon begged, and the misery in his tone proved her assumptions right.

"My lord, listen." The queen put her wine aside and went to face him in his corner. Trapped there, he stiffened as she spoke. "You were brutal, almost cruel, and driven by forces beyond you. Even so, I have never regretted that night with you, only regretted the lonely nights that followed. I've been such a fool, all this time. I should have told you. . . ."

Gaylon swept a hand before him in despair. "I knew you didn't blame me, but that only made what I did all the more loathsome. This!" He showed her his Stone, glinting blue with his distress. "This still rules me. If I give in to desire, there's no telling what might happen."

"You forget, Gaylon," Jessmyn said gently, "that your Stone accepted me long ago. Neither it nor you would ever harm me." Before the king could stop her, she took his ringed hand and brought the Sorcerer's Stone against her cheek.

Heat and ice came with the touch, and a burst of the king's sorrow, his longing. She turned the hand and pressed her lips to the palm. Gaylon flinched, but Jessmyn held tight.

"You mustn't," he muttered huskily.

The queen answered by seating herself across his lap and wrapping arms around his neck. She initiated the kiss, but he responded almost immediately with breathless urgency. The camp chair creaked under the added weight, then broke apart beneath them, shocking them both into laughter.

"Oh, gods," the king growled from his seat on the floor. "I told you disaster would strike."

In his lap still, Jessmyn smiled and cocked her head. "Perhaps the bed is more sturdily built?"

"Let's find out." Gaylon struggled to his feet, the young queen held firmly to his chest. In this manner, they finally found their way into the bedchamber.

Eleven

While Wynnamyr welcomed the first signs of spring, Kenara, far to the south, already felt the promises of summer. On hot, windless days such as this, the trade ships were forced to leave the Inland Sea under the power of oars. The still air rose shimmering from the city's streets, and clouds of biting flies descended on the populace.

The fine mesh netting draped over the litter kept the worst of the insects away, but did nothing for the stench of Zankos. The heat and filth and noise were appalling. Tek pressed a perfumed handkerchief to his offended nostrils and inhaled deeply, reminding himself that, with the return of a stiff salt breeze, he'd look more kindly on the city again.

Under the priest's directions, the acolyte bearers turned off the avenue of the usurers and onto one of the many food vendors' streets. Unfortunately, the most direct route back to the palace and Mezon's temple was down this teeming, clamorous thoroughfare. People of every hue and nationality crowded the cobbles—slave and merchant, sailor and soldier. Mingling with the varied citizenry were a few of royal blood, highly visible in their rich garments while they pushed through the crowds in search of excitement. Let them venture into one of the narrow, shadowed alleys, and they'd have cut throats instead.

As he passed, Tek paid particular attention to the sol-

diers milling in the press. Many wore the brightly kilted
uniforms of the eastern countries—Benjiri and Turvia—
that had now allied themselves with Xenara against their
common threat to the north. These few men were the har-
bingers of what was to come. On the Xenara Plain there
soon would be one great encampment, an army so vast that
not even Kingslayer could defeat it.

This army would be under Roffo's command, and since
Roffo was under Mezon's command, Tek would actually
have most of the power. The high priest thanked Mezon for
his blessings, for this chance to prove the warrior god's su-
premacy in battle. A sudden warm zephyr brought flies in
thick swarms, and with them, the scent of death from the
slaughterhouses on the eastern edge of the city. Tek held
the perfumed handkerchief to his nose again and cursed
the ill wind.

His bearers took another turn and slowed. The street had
narrowed, and the cobbles led steeply downhill, twisting
and curving as it went. Tall buildings with tiny wrought-
iron balconies at their windows rose to either side. The
stucco surfaces of their walls were cracked and broken away
in places.

Ahead lay the becalmed Inland Sea, shining in the midday sun. Ships with naked masts moved lazily across the
glassy water. Tek's eye, though, was on the cool marble
columns of the temple and the palace beyond them. Only
rarely did he venture into the city on errands, but the king
had need of funds to feed his army, and the high priest
could best accomplish this himself. Having the warrior
god's displeasure as a bargaining point had facilitated matters with the usurers and insured a better lending rate.

He and Roffo had carefully invited only the wealthier
nations to participate in this war. It would not do to have
Xenara stripped bare by a huge and hungry military popu-
lation, however temporary. Twenty years ago, such an army
would have been an impossibility, considering the amount

of water it would require. The Xenaran aqueducts that had
been built to divert water from the Gray Mountains of
Wynnamyr would supply their needs easily now.

Those same aqueducts had helped to nearly double the
size of Zankos over the last two decades, but this much heat
so early in the spring could mean a long dry summer in an
already arid land. The price of water would rise, of course,
but since water was King Roffo's most profitable source of
income, it hardly mattered.

The lumbering downhill movement of the litter
annoyed Tek, and he closed his eyes against the glare of the
sun off the water. Almost immediately a soft, golden light
filled his head, and his irritation was gone. The noise and
the stink of the city faded away, leaving him alone in a
dream-state.

A vision of the inner temple formed, the pillars and
sculptures all touched with diffuse illumination. Something moved. Mezon, as cold and white and perfect as his
marble statue, strode across the wide expanse of floor. Only
somehow it was Tek who stood on the stone pedestal watch-
ing while the god laid a young man upon the blood-stained
altar.

Mezon held out the hilt of a golden sword to his priest.
Tek grasped the heavy weapon and raised it over the breast
of the god's sacrifice. Unmoving, the man watched Tek.
This was a just and proper punishment for the crime of
necromancy. The high priest stabbed with all his might,
then ripped the chest open.

Hot blood poured from the heart and seeped upward
along the blade to Tek's hands. As the man died, a great
joy swept through the priest, but the sacrifice was not yet
complete. He swung the weapon over his head and
brought it hard against the altar. The blade snapped, and
red fire gushed from the hilt, spreading swiftly over the
flagstones. A river of flame covered the body and melted
flesh from bone, then turned suddenly and flowed back

toward the priest.

Tek jerked awake with a gasp, his skin burning, but it was only the heat of the sun. A long moment passed while he struggled to calm himself. In all the high priest's years of service, the god had never given him so clear a portent. With this dream, Mezon had promised in exquisite, vivid detail, the death of Gaylon Reysson and destruction of the sword of Orym.

*   *   *   *   *

"There, dear one. It's all right."

Misk stroked the queen's hair and tried to console her. The poor child cried brokenly over a rose that Gaylon had left on her pillow this morning. The flower had wilted. Such sorrow struck as often as glowing joy these past couple of weeks. The female human body had to deal with many physical and emotional changes when first preparing for the miracle of birth.

"I should have put it in water," Jessmyn sobbed.

"Think how much longer you'll have the rose if you press it in the pages of a book," Misk pointed out.

The sobs dwindled to sniffles. "I could, couldn't I?"

"Why don't you do just that, darling. There's bound to be a nice thick volume in the library."

"All right." Eyes still brimming, the young woman smiled. "I could use the *Book of Stones*. It's far bigger than any of the others."

"No, no," Misk said hastily. "I doubt very much Gaylon would appreciate that." Then she saw by the mischievous glint in her eye that the queen had been teasing. "Go on. But don't climb any ladders or lift anything too heavy. This early, we want to make sure the baby stays snug."

"I promise not to even look at a ladder." The tears were over, the bright, cheerful Jessmyn restored. Soft plum skirts swirled around her ankles, and her slippered feet hardly touched the ground as she left the chamber with the wilted rose.

Misk sank into the cushions on the windowseat. Jessmyn's beautiful needlepoint and lace decorated the pillows, and late spring sunlight poured through the leaded panes. It was easier here in the castle to hold on to the moment, especially now that the corridors were filled with life. Still, an uneasiness prevailed. More and more, the tiny woman's future sight dimmed, while the many pasts haunted her till she could no longer recall which had actually come to pass.

This small moment in the here and now, though, Misk had set aside for a visitor. That much of the near future she remembered. Very soon there came a darkening of the air at the center of the room and, with it, the rich scent of the ocean storm her brother so liked to tame. Winds swirled and miniature lightning strobed the solidifying clouds.

Sezran stepped forth, a tight smile on his thin lips. His midnight robes settled about him, and the whirlwind died.

"Sister," he said—a deceptively genial greeting.

"You seem well pleased, Brother." Misk let her attention wander to the games on the castle lawns below, though she knew that would irritate him.

"I am that, and you know why."

"Do I?"

The sorcerer's tone turned sly. "Certainly. There's a great war brewing that will utterly destroy this happy little domestic setting you've created for Gaylon. Soon he'll be forced to make a deadly choice." Sezran smiled. "If he takes up Kingslayer, he'll die. If he refuses to, he'll die at the hands of his enemies."

Misk hated the glee in his voice. "Don't count overmuch on your so-called curse, Brother. Gaylon may be the one human capable of truly mastering Orym's Legacy."

"No!" Sezran snarled, his excitement quickly turned to anger. "Not even your meddling can save him. But you've seen the future and know the truth of what I say. That's why you still practice husbandry. You hope to save the bloodline. Which will it be, son or daughter?"

"A son." Misk watched the children below, and an odd sorrow came over her.

"They won't let the child live." The old wizard's pleasure was obvious. "Not the son of a powerful sorcerer, a necromancer. As in Orym's day, the people will hunt down and destroy all those related to the Red Kings or anyone with magical inclinations. Or those just suspected of them. You'll be fortunate to save the queen."

Misk looked at him. "Return to your castle, Brother, where you can gloat in private. By your ignorance and ambition you've twice brought this world to the brink of destruction. You may succeed this time, but I'll do everything in my power to prevent it."

The little sorcerer's robes began to flutter as Misk spoke. The winds of his rage filled the chamber, gathering force.

"Ignorance?" he stormed. "You think me ignorant? This world is populated by creatures only barely sentient. They're toys for my pleasure. And you! You've played the game all along. How dare you judge me?"

"I only speak the truth." But Sezran and his winds had already faded from the chamber.

*   *   *   *   *

Tydus Dorenson was not by inclination an early riser, but this morning, he got himself up and about at first light. Today the court had planned a hunt—not the drunken debauchery of months past, but an outing that included ladies on side saddles and lords in fine leather. The affair would take most of the day, with a picnic lunch at some prearranged site along the way. The head councilman was determined to speak to the king first.

Gaylon, in rusted suede, was found in the busy, crowded

kitchens, making certain the meal would be perfect. Dorenson stood back respectfully until the tall young man had finished, then followed him along the corridor.

"Sire, could I have a private word with you?"

"I'm running behind schedule," the king said distractedly. "Can it wait till this evening? Or perhaps tomorrow?"

"No, milord. You seldom have time to spare for your head councilman these days, and this is of the gravest importance."

Gaylon gave him a sidelong glance. "All right. The library's closest."

This didn't please Tydus much. The library held the *Book of Stones* and had been the site of necromancy, but he dutifully followed His Majesty along the passage and into the chamber. The door was left open in case Tydus felt a sudden urge to leave this place of dark sorcery. Unhappily Gaylon sat them at the very table where Arlin D'Lelan had lain in death. The head councilman brought his packet from a wide pocket of his robes and placed it on the table.

"Milord, I must tell you, Wynnamyr will very soon find itself at war."

Uncertain, Gaylon blinked. "What?"

"I have in these papers all the information, duly corroborated by my people in Zankos." Tydus watched the king's incredulous expression fade. "Xenara, along with six other nations from the east and south, have begun to amass an army, which my sources inform me will number over a hundred thousand men."

"Wait . . . wait. There must be some mistake. Our countrymen still trade with Xenara. Surely they would have heard something of this."

"It's been a most carefully guarded secret. They hoped to catch you completely unawares and undefended."

"But why, for the gods' sakes? We've done nothing for them to justify such an act of aggression."

"The warrior-priests of Mezon have named you necromancer and heretic. They say that their god demands your death and the destruction of Kingslayer."

Gaylon, troubled, laid his hand on the packet. "Then we'll treat with them . . . anything to avoid war. Tell them I'll destroy the sword. I should have done it long ago."

"No," Tydus said sharply, then steadied his voice. "Sire, they'll never be satisfied with that. You have offended their god. The priests will never tolerate so powerful a sorcerer-king. Your death is all they'll accept. The Mezon high priest sent Baron Sedwin D'Loran to assassinate you."

There were hurried bootsteps in the hall, and Arlin appeared at the open door.

"Sire," he said breathlessly. "The riders are mounted. We await only you."

"I'm afraid I can't join the hunt today." The king's eyes remained on Tydus.

"Milord, why?"

"Go on without me," said Gaylon, irritated.

The young Southerner still hesitated. "Shall I stay, as well?"

"No, Arlin. I'll speak with you after. Go on. Close the door, please."

D'Lelan pulled the door after him. They heard his footsteps fade.

"What shall I do?" the king asked.

Tydus felt joy. Finally Gaylon Reysson would need his wise counsel. "Sire, there's only one thing you can do. Prepare for war."

"Against one hundred thousand? I doubt we have a tenth of that to serve in all of Wynnamyr."

"With Kingslayer, you have no need of a large army, milord."

The king shook his head. "I won't take up Orym's Legacy."

"You must."

Gaylon slapped a hand to the tabletop. "No! This simply can't be happening. I've only just begun to rule Wynnamyr. And there's my child." He opened the dispatches and scanned the pages, then closed his eyes. "I've dealt with these men. Gern D'Siler, Baronet D'Haldrick . . . They're not given to tales."

"No, Sire. This is not a tale, and there is no mistake. You will have to deal with all the consequences of your sorcery."

"How long before Xenara has readied her forces?" Gaylon opened his eyes again, and they were filled with pain.

"Two months, no more."

The king clutched the papers in his hands tightly. "Around the summer solstice. Of course. I truly have offended the gods, and this is my punishment for necromancy."

"Not a punishment, Sire," Tydus said gently. "This is a gift, a reason for you to explore your vast powers. With Kingslayer you can bring the world to its knees, bring every nation under your command. I'll advise you. I can make you the greatest king to ever live."

Gaylon's gaze became speculative. "You think to advise me in war?"

"And in the peace that follows. It's a reasonable assumption, and my duty. After all, milord, you can't possibly expect a fifteen-year-old duke to guide you through problems of this magnitude. Let me prove myself worthy of your trust."

"Tydus, I'm grateful for this information," the king said, his attention now on the Stone in his ring, "and I do trust you, but if war is inevitable—and I'll still need more proof of that—I'll have to choose my own advisers. You greatly underestimate Lord Gosney. I doubt I'll find a clearer or more concise mind in the kingdom."

"Milord, I must protest." All that Tydus had hoped for seemed to be slipping suddenly through his grasp. "I'm an experienced statesman. I have so much more to offer—"

"You do. That's why you'll remain here—should the worst come about—and hold the country safe for my return." Gaylon folded the papers, then managed a distant smile. "Of course, I have no firsthand experience, but my father once told me that war is a nasty, dirty business. We wouldn't want you to soil your handsome robes."

The king rose, and Tydus got hastily to his feet.

"I'm sure my head councilman has much to attend to," Gaylon said, his tone curt. "As do I. Call a council meeting for this afternoon. . . . No. Make it for tomorrow morning. I want Arlin and Davi to attend."

"D'Lelan is Xenaran, Sire. That would be most unwise."

"Nevertheless, you'll do as I command."

Tydus Dorenson bowed deeply. Inside, he seethed with outrage. "Yes, Sire."

Gaylon let himself out into the passage. This time, his faithful lord did not follow so quickly.

* * * * *

Once, with Kingslayer in hand, he'd thought of war—a war that would not only conquer this world, but others as well. Even now, the memory of the sword's power and Orym's evil influence made Gaylon's chest tighten with anxiety. He had released the weapon that night long ago, only because another, greater need had driven him. He had taken his hands from Orym's Legacy and laid them on Jessmyn.

Afterward, filled with shame, Gaylon had forbidden himself both—Kingslayer and his queen. Each required access to his soul, and to that dark, ugly region, none must be allowed to go. He'd opened himself finally to Jessmyn, and it appeared as if he might be forced to take up the Legacy, as well. The thought brought a pall over the happiness the king had found these last few weeks.

The keep was quiet so early in the day, especially with

most of the lords and ladies on the hunt. Jessmyn would be lying warm and asleep in the king's bed. She slept much more of late, but Misk said this was to be expected so early in pregnancy. A child . . . a tiny daughter with red-gold hair like her mother's, or a son . . . It was difficult to imagine. What would he leave an heir? A devastated world—at peace, because there was no one left to break it?

At the door to his apartments, Gaylon paused. The queen might wake, but he felt more at ease Dreaming within his own chambers. A quick peek into the bedchamber showed him Jessmyn buried among the blankets and pillows. Sweet, undisturbed slumber. He envied her, yet knew that soon her joy might be in ruins as well.

The couch before the hearth would serve in this. A faint blue glow had already touched the Stone on his finger, and Gaylon draped himself as comfortably as possible, long legs dangling over one end of the couch, head propped against the other. Though there were a thousand places he'd rather go in Dreaming, the king dredged up a distant memory of Daryn beside a campfire. The duke had related a visit to the capital city of Xenara that night.

In Zankos, Daryn had once visited the temple of Mezon. While religions had held little interest for him, the structural beauty of the temple and the taste of ceremonial magic that permeated the atmosphere had kept him spellbound. So Gaylon now tried to envision something he had never seen and Dream himself to that temple as he had so often dreamed of strange new worlds under Sezran's tutelage.

The Stone's blue glow spread over him, bringing a sense of tranquility that the tension in his body opposed. The gentle pull of gravity rearranged itself under his feet once more, and the king opened his eyes on soft daylight through distant columns and smelled warm, perfumed air. Burning oil lamps hung suspended from long chains that reached into a high ceiling lost in darkness. On one side stood an altar, curiously and beautifully wrought, yet ominous.

What took his breath, though, was a white marble statue of the god, Mezon, that towered well over the height of a man. Kilted and girded for battle, the god gripped a real two-edged sword of steel—not unlike Kingslayer—in both hands. His otherworldly face was the most disturbing. A master sculptor, enraptured by his work, had somehow given Mezon's face human expressions blended with the attributes of the god—compassion and dispassion, love and rage.

The eyes of stone had been carved to mesmerize and horrify, and Gaylon felt locked in that cold gaze. Somewhere a gong sounded, reverberating through the empty temple. Immediately after came numerous quiet footsteps. The king of Wynnamyr faded back into the statue's shadows. His visit would be anything but welcome, whether the priests knew him or not, but he would watch and listen for a while, in hopes of learning something.

Sandaled, white-robed men filed across the wide expanse of polished stone floor and began to kneel before the altar in neat rows. Gaylon counted over one hundred. A single priest near the fore began to sing in a high fluting voice. The others joined him with impossibly sweet tones. They were castratos, one and all. So Daryn had told him. Mezon required emasculation of his priests, and yet the order was renowned for having the finest, fiercest warriors.

The voices softened, and another man, tall and gray-haired, arrived at the altar. His white robes were edged with gold thread heavy enough to weight the hems. For the first time, Gaylon felt a hint of danger. Before the others, this high priest made a sudden violent gesture.

"Quiet! Eyes down!" he snapped in Xenaran.

Instantly the song died, and every man bowed his head. The elderly priest turned his back on them, facing the statue—or the shadows beyond it. In the warm lamplight, his expression seemed almost kindly, but his eyes were the god's eyes, cold and arrogant.

"Your effrontery astounds me," he said in heavily accented Wynnamyran. "Or have you come to beg the god's forgiveness and accept his judgment?"

Gaylon stepped into the light. "I've come only to verify a rumor of war."

"It is not a rumor, though it would have pleased the god for you to remain ignorant a while longer."

"Why? Are war and madness both godsent?" the king demanded. "War will destroy us all. I don't want your death on my hands, or the deaths of a hundred thousand. You must stop this now."

The priest only smiled. "Mezon demands."

"Then he is a cruel and callous god to demand so great a sacrifice." Gaylon saw the high priest's smile fade. "In what realm does he dwell, this Mezon? I've never destroyed a god, but I'm willing to try."

"Fool! Necromancer! Every breath you take offends him."

"Let him come and tell me so himself. Better yet, if the god is so powerful, let him strike me now." This was a taunt worthy of his childhood, and the king regretted the words as they left his tongue.

The old priest's face turned to stone. "Your death alone will no longer suffice. We must have the sword." He brought up a graceful arm. "But attend, young sorcerer. Attend and learn." Then he cried in his own tongue, "Obey me, children of Mezon!"

As one, bowed heads lifted and five score mouths opened. This time, the priests' song was anything but sweet. A wordless shout rose, spiraling upward, threatening eardrums. Gaylon staggered back under the onslaught of sound, his hands clamped to his ears. Desperate, he tried to will himself away, but some powerful force dragged at his limbs. The high priest stepped before him, his lips moving.

In the king's head, words formed. *You will remember the truth of this dream.*

He woke with a start in his chambers, feeling a sharp, aching pain deep in his ears. Something warm touched his upper lip through the mustache, and he tasted blood. More of it leaked hotly from each ear. Cursing, Gaylon got his feet under him, then leaned forward, struck by an over-whelming dizziness. Dimly, from far away, he heard a voice.

"My lord?" Jessmyn's hands touched his shoulders.

"Find Misk," he managed. "Please."

*   *   *   *   *

By late afternoon, Gaylon's ears still rang persistently, but the pain and dizziness had eased. Misk sat with him throughout, every little while dripping a warm, soothing oil in his ears. He lay in his own bed and knew that the queen had been sent, protesting, to nap in hers.

"Can you hear me?" Misk asked finally.

Gaylon nodded and felt a twinge of pain. "Yes, though your voice seems distorted. My own sounds even worse."

"You're lucky you didn't lose your hearing altogether."

Her disapproval was obvious. The king brought a slightly shaking hand to his face.

"I guess I should have asked *you* whether Tydus's rumors of war were true."

The tiny woman frowned. "I'm afraid I wouldn't have remembered . . . yet."

"I've never had any faith in gods, Misk. Do they even exist?"

"As long as there are followers, there'll be gods. What we believe strongly enough, we create . . . make tangible even." Misk gazed at her patient. "Mezon exists and is a very real danger to you."

"Then there will be war? There's nothing I can do to prevent it?" The thought brought a sickness to the pit of Gaylon's stomach.

"There will be war."

The dread grew stronger. Almost afraid of the answer, the king asked, "Do you . . . can you see the outcome?"

"War is inevitable, the outcome is not."

"You won't tell me," he accused.

Eyes peaceful, Misk shook her head. "Be grateful, young man, that you're blind to the future."

"I won't take up Kingslayer. I can't."

"You are a most obstinate king, Gaylon Reysson, but you *will* be forced to take up the sword." The tiny woman settled on the edge of the bed. "Listen to me. In peacetime, the world has little impetus to change, but in war, man's great ingenuity is put to use." She stroked his hair. "Those things he invents to further aggression can also further civilization later, when peace returns. Orym nearly destroyed your world, but you—" her finger tapped his forehead gently "are not a madman."

Gaylon groaned, and the feeling of sickness spread over his entire body. "Dear gods, Misk, we're both mad. And a madman leads us. Orym may be dead, but the sword absorbed his essence. When I held Kingslayer, I wanted what he wanted—total obliteration of every living thing."

"Why didn't you do it?" the woman demanded.

"Because I wanted Jessmyn even more." Shame made the king close his eyes.

"You had the strength to let go. You had power over yourself and over the sword."

In disbelief, Gaylon laughed. "I had nothing more than animal lust." His laughter died abruptly. "What of the curse on Orym's Legacy? What of Jessmyn and the baby?"

"No more questions," Misk said and studied her hands resting in her lap. "Fate is rarely kind. You'll do what you must."

Twelve

With summer solstice fast approaching, the four defunct armories at Castlekeep were called back to duty. The clanging of hammers on anvils continued day and night, and the tang of hot metal flavored the air. If an army could be mustered, it had to be armed with lances, swords, and arrows. Those who could find them dug rusting hauberks from ancient trunks; those who couldn't commissioned chain mail to cover whatever parts of their anatomy their finances allowed. Leathercrafters produced less expensive cuirasses and shields guaranteed to deflect arrows from the short bow, if not the long.

Crops were left to be tended by elderly fathers, wives, and children, while the farmers, along with tradesmen and noblemen, made their way to the keep. The barracks there, tripled in number during Lucien's reign and then allowed to fall to ruin, had been rebuilt. Even so, they could hold no more than three hundred men. The latecomers were encamped on the bluff above the South Fork River, near Keeptown. Other sites were scouted out for even later arrivals.

Aristocrats commanded the men they brought with them, while lower-ranking officers were picked by age, ability with arms, and potential to give and take orders. This was probably not an altogether wise approach, but the best Gaylon could come up with on so short notice. In this,

e also relied heavily on his duke—much to the annoyance
f some would-be captains.

What appeared to be an economic boon for some would
rove to be hardship on far more. An army must be provid-
d for. The king had quickly depleted his resources, and,
enniless once more, found himself reduced to begging
elp from the merchants of Keeptown. Those kinfolk that
ad stayed on at the keep had gladly offered what succor
ey could. Sadly, the high life of the court had been short
ut sweet.

On this particular afternoon, the sun set the sky afire for
time as it slipped below the ridgetops of the coastal
nge. The early summer heat continued to radiate from
e earth, and Gaylon's mount stamped constantly against
e bite of flies. Beside him, Davi leaned to pat his bay
are's neck, gazing out over the trampled meadows, where
umerous campfires had begun to glow with the dusk. The
ry, still air carried the sounds of numerous voices and the
nells of woodsmoke and the middens dug around the pe-
meter.

Much had been accomplished in the past two months,
ut time grew short. Only a week before, the king had sent
rlin D'Lelan south with Marten Pelson to view the situa-
on firsthand. Karyl had been sent north with Rinn nearly
fortnight ago in hopes of making Zorek of Lasony an ally.
he king's cousin had wanted to take Davi as well as Rinn,
nce the Gosneys had always been the Red Kings' arbiters
ith Lasony, but Gaylon had convinced himself that he
eeded the boy more. While that was true enough, herein
y a problem.

In Davi, the king had found much of Daryn, enough to
ase the emptiness he'd felt since his mentor's death. The
oy worked hard with his weaponry and could more than
old his own with a sword. He was ready to fight, deter-
ined to, but when Wynnamyr's small army finally
arched, it would be without the young duke of Gosney.

Gaylon wanted Davi safe with Jessmyn, safe with the poss[ible] heir of the Red Kings. Telling the boy his decisio[n] would be the hardest task of all.

"How many men?" the king asked to take his min[d] from the problem.

Davi responded immediately. "Fifteen hundred twenty[-]three in this camp. Nine hundred eighty-six on the bluf[f] and another five hundred sixteen at the barracks and in th[e] keep. Three thousand and twenty-five all told." He turne[d] his eyes on Gaylon. "I've never seen so many men in m[y] life."

"Hmmm," the king grunted. His hearing was sti[ll] slightly impaired, but he'd heard the pride in the boy['s] voice well enough. "Imagine them thirty fold if you car[e] my duke. That's what we'll be facing."

"We have Kingslayer on our side."

That brought a shiver, even in this heat. "What we hav[e] is a narrow, defensible pass in the Gray Mountains wher[e] that range runs into the Western Sea. We have rugged te[r]rain and men who've lived on it all their lives, some [of] whom have even fought the Xenarans at one time or an[other. We'll wage this war as my father did, and his fathe[r] before him—almost entirely on the defensive."

"What of Claw Pass to the east?"

"It's high and narrow and much more easily held," Gay[lon said, pleased by the boy's question. "We'll send a sin[gle troop to guard it, but since that's the long way 'round, [I] doubt the enemy'll waste their time. No. The Xenara[n] forces hope to overrun us by sheer numbers."

"Well, their ships won't do them any good, either,[" Davi added, again with a touch of pride. "The coast's to[o] rugged, and the mouth of Full Moon Bay is chained."

The king envied the boy his optimism and decided n[ot] to mention that the aforementioned chain, while massive[,] had lain over a century rusting in sea water. Roffo woul[d] save his trade ships for trade, though, and put his faith i[n] the army that was massing even now on the Xenara Plain.

"Let's get back before the light's completely gone," Gaylon muttered.

In the dusk and shadows, the duke of Gosney nodded and reined the mare around. The way he sat his horse, moved his head, even the quick flash of a grin, all nudged at Gaylon's memories of Daryn. How could so much of the man be born again in the child? Would it be the same for his own child? the king wondered fleetingly.

Davi spurred his mount into a reckless canter under the oaks and called, "Come on!" then slowed when Gaylon only followed at a walk. "What's wrong?"

"Tired."

"Well, no one's asking you to gallop. Let the horse do it."

"He's tired, too."

The boy pulled a face that was entirely his own invention and none of his father's. "It must be terrible getting old." He kicked the mare once more and sent her all the faster toward the keep.

This time Gaylon spurred his dapple gray gelding after the impudent youngster. In the long summer gloaming, they thundered down to the river and then up toward the stables on the other side. Not a race exactly, but certainly competitive. The king arrived first, though he thought Davi might have pulled his mount back, at the last. Grooms rushed to take the sweated animals' heads, while king and duke dismounted.

"Roast venison," observed Gaylon as they crossed the deserted bailey. "Smells good."

"It's from the cookfires at the barracks," Davi told him. "We're having mutton . . . again."

The king turned his nose in the direction indicated and sniffed. "Guess it's only fair that the soldiers eat better than royalty."

"They've been complaining about venison at every meal."

"Let's arrange an exchange of provisions, then." Gaylon pushed the tall door to the entry hall open before his duke had the chance. "Why must I always think of these things?"

"Because you're the king?"

Cool air greeted them, sweet and musty and somewhat drier than in winter. The keep had quieted over the past weeks, despite the fact that it was crowded with officers and their aides—who would now be at supper in the great hall. The thought of war had put a damper on aristocrat and servant alike. Oddly, Gaylon found he missed the noisy children most. They'd been packed off to their homes immediately.

The king had already arranged for Jessmyn and Davi to stay with Grand-aunt Elsith at Oakhaven Manor, which lay inland from Gosney in the north. Should the worst occur, they would be taken into Lasony. Karyl had been ordered to make certain of the queen's sanctuary with Zorek above all else.

In the passages of the northwest wing, Gaylon managed to snag a young chambermaid. He ordered up supper for both him and the duke, to be delivered to the audience chamber. Davi had a broad smile for the girl and watched her progress down the hall.

"She likes my singing," the youth said when he noticed the king's speculative gaze.

"And she's pretty," Gaylon added for him.

Davi's smile twisted a little. "She is."

No, not a boy much longer, the king reminded himself. "Come on, we've still work to do before we can rest."

Unpleasant work. Tonight they must make judgments on military matters. With so many men kept in close quarters, disputes naturally arose. Add to that the pressures of coming war, and some of those disputes grew violent. Minor problems were dealt with by commanding officers—theft, cheating, disorderly conduct. All else was brought before the king.

Thankfully supper arrived before the complaints. The king had already found his way to the throne, and Davi received both trays from the kitchen girl, Laur. She paused long enough to whisper in his ear, then left in a great hurry.

"What was that about?" Gaylon demanded.

The boy reddened slightly. "Nothing." He set one tray down on a dais step and carried the other up to the throne, picking a bite from each portion and popping it in his mouth as he went.

"Is that mine you're eating?"

"I only took a little."

"Seems to me you've been taking a little of my meals a lot lately," the king said. He grabbed the tray with one hand and caught Davi's wrist with the other. "If you're trying to make certain I'm not poisoned, be a bit more circumspect. Dirty fingers in someone's food can be poisonous all on their own. Use a spoon, if you must."

The boy looked at his dusty boot toes. "I'm sorry."

"Jessmyn put you up to this?"

Davi nodded reluctantly.

"And she forgot to tell you to wash your hands? This isn't the Xenaran court, my young duke. Poisons have never been popular here. If they were, I'd want someone less important than you doing the tasting." Gaylon stared at the mutton stew heaped on his plate and remembered poison had been a favorite of Lucien's. He glanced at the boy. "Thank you, anyway. Is the wine safe, do you suppose?"

The duke of Gosney brought his king a cupful, untasted, but the agony of doubt on the boy's face made Gaylon give him a short nod of permission. After taking a slow sip, Davi passed the cup over. This only made the king all the more aware of the wine bottles that had sat unattended in the audience chamber since yesterday.

There were worries enough without such added aggravation. Supper was taken in silence, and Davi seemed more

subdued than usual, seated on his step. They were both
tired and facing a long late night ahead. Soon someone
knocked on one of the tall double doors to the chamber,
and the duke went to answer it. The petitioners filed onto
the floor in orderly rows. Davi brought the first two forward.

Lyle, the grizzled captain of the king's first lancers, stood
beside a younger man in irons—the first brought before
Gaylon in this manner.

"Speak," the king said, uneasy.

"Sire, I beg yer judgment." Lyle bowed. "This here's
Dobs Renson, who cut the throat of another lancer while
the poor lad slept."

Gaylon frowned. "Did you do this, Renson?"

"Aye," the fellow answered simply, chin lifted, gaze direct.

"Why?"

Now Dobs looked down. "He insulted me."

The king searched the room for some easy solution. Every man in the small crowd was shabbily dressed. Most
couldn't afford uniforms, and a troop's coat-of-arms had to
be painted on their shields so they could find one another
in battle. No matter how ragged his army, these soldiers all
stood with their eyes on the king, who was also their general, expecting justice of some sort. Gaylon felt a touch of
panic.

"The dead man. What of his family?"

Lyle answered, "Wylem 'twere only a boy, Sire. Never
spoke of no family."

"Do you regret what you've done, Renson?" the king
asked and watched the man closely.

Renson's chin came back up, belligerence in his eyes.
"The foul-mouthed little bastard deserved what I done—"

"Do you have anything to say in your defense, then?"

"Only that you should know I have a family," the prisoner said quickly. "A wife and four little ones to care for."

Gaylon looked out over the rest. "Nevertheless, there's only one judgment I can pass. Our small army can ill afford the loss of even one soldier, but Dobs Renson has caused us to lose two. Captain, you will hang this man tomorrow morning without ceremony."

On the edge of the group, Davi turned toward the king, eyes wide, but Gaylon kept all emotion from his face and voice.

"Come forward with the next complaint."

Renson suddenly balked in his captain's grip. Perhaps the realization had finally gotten through that haughty exterior.

"No!" he snarled. "You can't do this. What of my children?" At the king's dispassionate gaze, Dobs cried, "I can outfight any one of the lancers. You need me. I deserve to die in battle, Sire, defending you."

"Wylem deserved as much," the king said tonelessly, "but you do not. Have no fear for your children. They'll be cared for. See to that, Lyle."

Davi, face ashen, stood aside as Dobs was led from the room. For the rest of the evening the young duke refused to meet Gaylon's eyes.

* * * * *

Tydus Dorenson spent much of his time lately in his splendid chambers, but the joy of his possessions—his jewels and fine clothing—had faded. His years of careful machination had come to nothing. He had gained the wealth, but not fame and power. Without those, wealth really meant very little—especially considering that most of his holdings lay out of reach in Xenara.

Tonight, as every night now, the head councilman drank wine alone and considered his failures with deepening despair. Elbows planted among the scattered papers on the desk, he stared unseeing into the flickering candle flame.

At some point during this particular session of maudlin self-pity, a notion occurred to him . . . but to carry out such a notion would require a strength and resolve that truly frightened him. Tydus, for all his intriguing, was still Wynnamyran and a peaceable man, unsuited to war or assassination. The thought of harming another living creature without provocation brought a curious pain, but the wine brought determination.

The head councilman of the court of Wynnamyr might join his vast wealth in Xenara, though, by simply murdering Gaylon Reysson. In doing so, he would save the world from a sorcerous madman, and also bring about his much-desired fame and power. A magnificent plan, but with obvious pitfalls. After all, the good Baron Sedwin had attempted just such a thing, and died most horribly for the effort.

No. With careful planning and clear thought, a man could achieve anything—even the death of a sorcerer-king. Tydus poured more wine into his cup and searched for inspiration in the candle flame.

* * * * *

"Haven't you seen enough?" Marten Pelson demanded. "Let's get down from here before they start using us for archery practice."

He and Arlin had found a stone outcropping high on the mountainside that gave them a tremendous view. The Southerner stood motionless, awed by the gathering military force on the Xenara Plain far below. Millennia before, the sea had shallowly covered that vast plateau. Now the sun glared off white, salty dirt and forced D'Lelan to squint. Tents of various sizes were scattered over the land, their materials fluttering in the wind, and everywhere tiny figures marched or moved about or practiced with weapons. Well in the distance, the Inland Sea glittered.

"How do you suppose they manage down there?" Arlin asked distractedly. "It must be hot enough to roast meat without an oven."

Despite that heat, the great arid plain was dotted with smoke rising from hundreds, maybe thousands of cookfires, creating a dirty brown pall that lay trapped against the base of the Gray Mountains. Well down the steep slopes from Arlin and Marten, details of men cut trees for firewood. Their shouts and the fall of timber could be heard when the wind shifted.

The young earl of the Lower Vales shrugged. "Who cares how they manage? We're the ones in danger here."

"The finest long bow couldn't send an arrow this far," the Southern lord argued.

"I've heard the Mezon priests have some nasty sorcery to add to their bows and swords. Let's get back out of sight."

Arlin refused to budge from his rocky perch. "My father once tried to convince me to join the priesthood. Perhaps he felt my branch of the family should end." He glanced at his friend, amused. "Relax. Mezon and his lot are mostly full of hot air."

The words had hardly left his lips when he heard the sharp buzz of fletching. A white arrow shaft flashed between the pair and buried itself in the earth under the evergreens.

"I told you!" Marten Pelson growled as they scrambled back to safety. "Look at your hand."

Arlin glanced down. Across the back of his left hand, a deep score dripped blood.

"That was too close, by the gods!" the earl said. "But you deserved it, you idiot. Does it smart?"

"A little."

In fact there was no pain at all. While D'Lelan's coordination had steadily improved, the numbness in his fingertips and toes had been slowly spreading. He wrapped a clean handkerchief tight around his palm.

"Can we leave now?" Marten asked. "We've ill tidings
aplenty for the king." He turned and began the long climb
back to the horses.

After a last, brief glance over the plain, Arlin started after him. They wore only sleeveless leather jerkins and knee
breeches against the summer heat. Even at so high an alti-
tude, the sun felt uncomfortably hot, and the thin air had
them panting long before the two had crested the ridge.

The horses were tethered deep in a hazelnut thicket, well
down the north-facing slope, and they had stripped the
closest branches of leaves for their lunch. Arlin led his
brown colt into the open and let him drink from a brook
that bubbled out from under the fat, gnarled roots of a
mountain alder.

Marten led his black mare to the same spot. "We'll stop
at Arbor House to exchange horses and have that hand
looked after."

Arlin nodded. Arbor House was Marten's country manse
and only a short distance north. They tightened their saddle girths and mounted, heading the animals west out of
the forest and along a narrow, stony path, then down to the
floor of the Sea Pass. Here shadows reigned, and a cold
wind whipped hard through the natural channel in the
high rock formations, moaning as it went. At a muted
shout, both men looked up and waved to the eight guards-
men positioned high on the rock walls of the pass.

Marten had long known the men who watched and waited in this lonely spot with only small stone huts on narrow
ledges for their homes. With fire and smoke, the guardians
could signal that an enemy approached. They could very
ably defend the pass until help arrived, as well.

Arlin and Marten turned their mounts north, riding
down off the mountains and though the foothills to the
sunny Lower Vales. There, on every side were rolling vineyards in neat rows, lush and green. Clusters of ripening
purple grapes lay partially hidden behind the wide leaves.

Below the vineyards, fields of wheat, barley, and oats were enclosed by low stone fences. They spread into the distance, all across this valley floor, and the next valley, and the one beyond that. The vales, irrigated by the mountain springs that also fed the headwaters of the Great River were Wynnamyr's richest, most productive lands, and all of them belonged to Marten Pelson, earl of these Lower Vales, the fourteenth in his line.

As soon as they cleared the roughest terrain, the two men pushed the horses into fast gallops along the old coach road. Time was essential, and they could spare neither the mounts nor themselves. Marten took them down another road that cut east through the fields toward Arbor House.

His pretty widowed mother met them in the shaded yard with servants to take their mounts and a half-dozen younger brothers and sisters to swarm over Marten. Arlin stood back respectfully while the family milled about, trading hugs and kisses. There was also fear, though, an almost tangible energy on the air. Those who lived closest to the Sea Pass were always the most vulnerable to invaders. The young Southerner gazed out over this, the largest of the vales, and saw that many tenant farms still had laborers in their fields.

Tradition had the residents remain here to defend the pass if necessary, until the king could arrive with his troops. But a farmer's life was hard and left little time for anything but work. With no experience in weaponry, they were often the first casualties of any war.

Lady Vyla held out a gracious hand to Arlin. "Milord D'Lelan, we have food and drink within. Won't you join us?"

"Mum, we can stay only long enough for the new horses to be saddled and Arlin's hand to be tended." Marten tried to quiet the lamenting youngsters. "I'm sorry, but we must be back to Castlekeep as quickly as possible."

A shy young sister took Arlin's uninjured hand and led

him through the wide entry hall of the manse.

The earl gave his friend a wry smile. "I just realized something. You're the first wounded in the line of duty. I hope that turns out to be the worst you suffer, Arlin D'Lelan."

"Thank you," Arlin replied and felt a tiny shiver ripple through him. "I hope *you* suffer not at all, my friend."

*   *   *   *   *

Misk came and went as she pleased, though no one ever saw her actually enter or leave the keep. At this particular moment, Gaylon couldn't find her anywhere. He had left the sleeping queen in their shared bed, and wandered the dim passageways alone, dressed only in breeches. Sleep was rare to him these long nights. His mind refused to let go of the day's problems.

At last the king had sought out the *Book of Stones*, though there would be no solace found among its brittle pages. Sometimes, with his hands upon the tome, a faint presence touched him—as now. Not a madness like Orym's, but a sly cruelty, an evil that might be perhaps another previous owner's. Gaylon knew that darkness all too well; he had fought those impulses his entire life.

Often of late, the hatred and rage would swell without reason, threatening to drown him in burning choler. It took every bit of strength within him to subdue the destructive urges, to hide them from Jess and Davi and the others. Those brief weeks of happiness with the queen had only served to make his misery more complete—now that he knew what he might lose. A black despair descended on Gaylon.

The *Book of Stones* continued to tingle under his fingertips, and the Stone in his ring woke, shedding blue light over the library. Something stirred among the bookshelves—a rustle of cloth, a scent of herbs—and the king knew instinctively who stood there. He had searched, and she had found him.

"Child," Misk murmured, and the word was echoed by a dozen faint images of the tiny woman, all moving toward him, toward this one moment in time. "What is it that troubles you?"

To be called a child disconcerted him, but in her reckoning of age, he was and always would be.

"Better to ask what doesn't trouble me," the king answered and felt her hand against his ear.

"They've healed?"

"Well enough." He leaned his head into her touch, comforted by it. "Look again into the future, and tell me what you see."

Misk's dark eyes clouded, and she pulled her hand back. "There's no sense in that."

"You've seen my death, haven't you?" The act of finally voicing those words brought an odd peace. Gaylon smiled. "You've seen my death, just as you once saw Daryn's."

"All life ends, child. Even mine."

"That's answer enough, I suppose. Would you tell me of the baby?"

The woman glanced away. "Jessmyn will bear a son, an heir to the Red Kings . . . though there'll be—"

"Thank you," Gaylon said softly and put a finger to her lips. "I think I can sleep now."

Thirteen

Marten and Arlin changed horses over a dozen times on the journey back. The mounts were varied—some handsome and sleek chargers, others raw-boned nags borrowed from farms along the way—but from each animal, the two men coaxed every bit of power and speed. Neither did they spare themselves, making what might have been a leisurely three-week passage in only seven days.

At eventide of that seventh day, Marten, with the Southerner close behind, sent his final horse, winded and staggering, into the stableyard of Castlekeep. His own legs were no more steady when he dismounted, and Arlin's limbs seemed to obey him not at all. The grooms quickly stripped the saddles from both animals and led them away to be cooled.

"You look awful," D'Lelan muttered to his companion.

The earl grunted. "You should talk. I'd give my right arm for a bath, though . . . and something cool to drink."

"You'll need that arm to defend the king," said Davi from behind them, grinning when they turned. "The sentries signaled your approach, and I thought you'd have a thirst. There's cool wine here, but His Majesty wants your report before you bathe."

He'd brought the drink in deep pewter mugs, which was well. Arlin's hands shook so badly, he could hardly find his mouth. With the red liquid spilling over his chin, the

Southern lord was reduced to exhausted laughter.

Davi caught his elbow, concerned. "Perhaps you should sit for a moment."

"Oh gods, no! I've spent the last two days standing in the stirrups to avoid just that." Now Marten laughed, and Arlin threw him a rueful look. "I can't sit, and I doubt I can walk. Any suggestions?"

"Try the horizontal," the earl offered. "Rest, and I'll give the king our news."

"He's asked to see you both," said Davi.

D'Lelan pushed sweat-damp hair from his filthy, sun-burned face and nodded. "We've made a round trip of two hundred and fifty leagues in little more than a fortnight. I suppose I can survive a few steps more."

Under a darkening sky, they crossed the bailey. Torches, their flames fluttering, lined the keep's high walls. A hot summer breeze brought woodsmoke to sting the eye, and from all around came the shouts of men and the clang of the armories. Marten offered Arlin a shoulder, though every muscle in his own body ached.

To stand before the king in travel-stained clothes that stank of horse and unwashed body went against the earl's meticulous grain. He scratched at a burgeoning beard and tried to focus on the placement of each foot. The young duke of Gosney moved ahead to open doors, the empty pewter mugs clacking together in one hand.

In the relatively short time they'd spent on the road, Davi had changed again, though exactly how was hard to pin down. Perhaps his movements had a certain maturity to them, and the green eyes now held a touch of melancholy. He wore a new tabard of burgundy velvet with the Gosney coat-of-arms emblazoned on the front—rampant bear with a crown in its jaws—and a sword on a wide belt that crossed from waist to hip. The unlined, unbearded face was still that of a boy.

Davi led them past the great hall where the king's guard

and officers already gathered for supper. The smell of roast meat was maddening, and Marten's stomach clenched.

"His Majesty has ordered our meals served in the council chambers," the duke said when the two lords hesitated under the arch.

They found the throne room empty, but muted voices could be heard beyond the dais. Davi climbed the stair and parted the wall drapes for them. The door behind was already open. Gaylon stood beside the long, candlelit table, eyes on a sheaf of papers, and three of the four other men that shared the room with him were arguing intently. Only one was seated, a dark-haired young fellow with a stylus in his hand, poised over a tanned sheepskin. Marten recognized the three others as landed gentlemen with whom he had a nodding acquaintance.

"No-no," the middle-aged lord of Alderdale snapped at the rest. "You're wrong. Hunter's Point is much farther east of the Sea Pass. This small canyon runs deeper into the mountains between here and here." He jabbed at the map with a stiff finger and smeared the still-wet ink, much to the cartographer's dismay.

Marten glanced at the sheepskin. "Milord has an excellent memory. There is indeed a small canyon, though it angles slightly more southeast than you have it drawn."

Now the artist seemed positively annoyed.

The king looked up, hazel eyes glittering. He, too, wore a tabard, snowy white with an eagle in gold across the chest, its empty claws outstretched as if reaching for prey. Gaylon rounded the table to embrace the earl, grimy clothes and all. Next he caught Arlin, then held him back for a good look before releasing him.

"I know you're both in dire need of rest, so we won't keep you any longer than necessary. There's bread and cheese and wine until our supper arrives." The king motioned to the table. "Come, sit down."

D'Lelan gave him a lopsided grin. "Only if there's a pillow handy."

Once again, Davi had anticipated their needs. He brought thick cushions to line the seats of two chairs. Marten settled into one gratefully and accepted the crusty bread and sharp yellow cheese the boy brought.

"What of Karyl?" the earl asked. "Has he returned?"

"Not as yet." Gaylon sat in the head councilman's chair. "We expect him at any time. But what have you found out?"

Marten answered with his mouth full. "If I hadn't seen it with my own eyes, I could never have believed such a thing might exist—an army, Sire, spread across the whole of the Xenara Plain."

"How many men?" Lord Alderdale demanded.

"I couldn't even hazard a guess. . . ."

"There were eight individual camps," Arlin said, paying far more attention to his wine than the food. "I recognized the markings on some of the tents—Shalta and Turvia from the south, and Benjir from the east. Then Roffo's lot, of course, and a good-sized encampment of mercenaries. The other three were unknown to me."

The Southerner let Davi refill his cup, sipped, and continued. "Just from counting the tents, I'd guess there's close to ten thousand in each group, a little less with the mercenaries. They seem to be waiting for more arrivals though—there were several vacant areas left among the camps. The one closest to the pass is no doubt being held for the priests of Mezon."

Marten stared at his companion with a new respect. The earl could never have remembered such detail. He hadn't even thought to try.

"All of those nations I recognized are peopled by fearless warriors," Arlin added, "but the Benjiri are a cruel, merciless lot. Even more so than the Xenarans or the Noro tribesmen. It's said that their foes will often take their own lives rather than face Benjiri torture."

Balser of Graymount was the uncle of Redmond, the youth who had died in the king's reckless games so many months past. He gazed down on the Southern lord with unconcealed disdain. "You speak of Xenarans as though you aren't one."

"He's not!" the earl snapped, tired and easily angered. "And he's a better Wynnamyran than some—"

"Stop it." Gaylon smacked a hand on the tabletop and gave Graymount a sharp look. "We've no time to bicker among ourselves. Arlin D'Lelan has my complete faith, and he'd better have yours, milords."

"Sire," Balser muttered and bowed his head.

"What of the vales, Marten?" the king asked, the incident already forgotten.

"They'll be ready for our arrival, Highness. The past few years' harvests have been good. The loss of this year's crops won't bring that much hardship."

"Three thousand men trampling your fields and eating everything in sight will," Gaylon said, unhappy. "I wish it could be otherwise. . . ."

"Sire, the Lower Vales have hosted many a Red King with many an army over the centuries. It'd be far worse if we were left undefended."

The king forced a smile. "Somehow we'll make restitution. I promise." He eyed Arlin, who was nodding off, bristly chin in hand. "I doubt the two of you will make it through supper, so let me ask one more question. I've never ridden the coach road that far south. How long do you suppose it'll take our little army to make the journey to the vales?"

"You might send a horse battalion on ahead," Marten said after a moment's thought, "if you think it necessary. The foot soldiers and supplies will probably take four weeks. If it doesn't rain and muddy the road—which, by the way, has not been tended in a long while and will need repairs if we're to get wagons through."

The king stared at the papers under his hands. "Then I suppose we had better get on with it quickly."

*   *   *   *   *

Roffo lounged in the shade of a small kiosk within the high-walled yard of Mezon's temple. Tek stood beside him on this hot afternoon, and, together, they watched as nearly two hundred priests performed an intricate series of movements. Sunlight gleamed on short white tunics and on golden tanned arms and legs that were slender, yet muscular. This was the first time the king had been privileged to watch one of Mezon's inner temple rituals. While it was graceful, even beautiful, Roffo could see no earthly reason for the priests' exacting, twisting hand gestures or their exaggerated, slow steps.

"Why are they dancing?" the king demanded finally. "Do you expect the enemy to die of boredom? Or laughter?"

Tek's smile remained benign. "This *dance*, Sire, is an exercise in perfect control over mind, body, and soul, all of which are the god's weapons. The priests of Mezon are as deadly with empty hands as with the sword or bow."

"Hummph," Roffo grunted and eased his great bulk more evenly over the cushions. "Faster," he told the young servant with the palm frond fan, then frowned at Tek. "Can't you have your men do something more interesting? Something slightly more dramatic?"

The high priest clapped his hands, and Mezon's followers dropped instantly to their knees, foreheads pressed to the red tiles.

"Your Highness," Tek said with infinite disapproval, "we are here for the god's pleasure, not yours."

"Oh, please," the king said brusquely. "Mezon knows I meant no disrespect. You've told me often enough that the god enjoys putting on a little show now and then. Then why not for me?" He smiled up into the old priest's stern face. "I would dearly have loved to have been there when you put the young sorcerer, Gaylon Reysson, to rout."

That memory made Tek's thin lips curl slightly. "A painful experience, I'm sure. All right, milord . . . a small display of the god's strength will not offend him." Once more he clapped his hands. "Children of Mezon, call down his wrath."

The priests remained prostrate, but a low, resonant hum started in the ranks, almost below hearing. Roffo settled deeper in his pillows. This was more like it. Above the faithful something sparkled on the afternoon air. A writhing, roiling shape appeared, translucent, tinged faintly green in such bright sunlight. It hovered, growing. Within the kiosk, the king could feel an intense radiant heat—not at all comfortable.

Tek watched, oblivious. Just as Roffo's doubt turned to outright fear, Mezon's priests raised their heads and shouted as one, a sharp instant of sound. In the silence that followed, the fiery cloud over them erupted into tongues of emerald flame that flashed suddenly upward toward the clear blue dome of the sky, then vanished.

Roffo mopped sweat from his face with a handkerchief and fluttered his fingers at the boy with the fan. The god's powers were great, and Mezon had promised much. Anticipation filled His Majesty. Soon a sorcerer-king would fall, Mezon would have his retribution, and Roffo would have Wynnamyr, a land rich in resources for which his forefathers had yearned and had never been able to take.

There would be new aqueducts to carry even more clear mountain water to the coast of the Inland Sea, even more forests to strip for new cities and ships. All this would mean unprecedented growth for Xenara, and Roffo might name himself emperor then, not just king. Tek had hinted as much. Ah, life was so very, very good.

* * * * *

Karyl and Rinn made camp that last evening along the banks of the Great River. At this time of year, the term "great" was a misnomer. Wynnamyr's largest river wound docilely and shallowly over sun-heated rocks that were bearded with long-trailing water mosses. It had not always been thus. The king's cousin remembered how rafts had once floated downriver to Moon Bay all summer long—but no more, not since Roffo's aqueducts had diverted so much of the river's southern headwaters.

The ride home hadn't been a hard one. The Lasony border was a mere sixty leagues from Castlekeep, yet Karyl refused to hurry their return. While the king was in need of his cousin's reports, Karyl had no great desire to deliver them. No, far better to sit next to the smoky campfire and stare into the flames, remembering a distant, happy childhood at Oakhaven. This he did until sleep finally found him.

Next morning, he and Rinn rose at first light in an effort to avoid the worst heat of the day during the last, short leg of their journey. They reached Keeptown by midmorning, and there, Rinn stopped to visit a while with his family. Karyl went on alone toward the castle. The army's river camp had grown in his absence, and the stench and the noise had grown along with it. A small troop drilled with weapons under the strident orders of their captain. Through the clouds of dust, one could almost mistake them for soldiers instead of farmers.

Luka, the horsemaster, met him in the stableyard and whistled up a groom, then sent Karyl and his dispatch pouch directly to the throne room where the king held audience. Even then the royal cousin's footsteps dragged. Unaware of the activity around him, he made his way to the chambers. Orderly chaos reigned within, merchants and artisans all vying politely for attention, their bills for services and goods clutched in hand. Davi spoke alone to an elderly man beside the entrance.

Seated on the throne, Gaylon spied Karyl immediately. "Sirs," he called over the quiet rumble of conversation. "I beg your pardons for the moment, but there's a matter of state that needs our private attention." The king rose from the huge oak chair and signaled Karyl to follow him into the council chambers behind the dais. Davi also followed, bringing the royal cousin a cup of wine.

"Thank you," Karyl murmured and watched the boy move to stand in silence behind the king's seat at the long council table.

"Welcome home, Cousin," Gaylon said, smiling. "Where's Rinn?"

"With his father in town."

"Good. Tell me, how fares fair Lasony?"

"Very well, Sire," Karyl responded solemnly. "It's a beautiful land. Almost as fair as Wynnamyr."

"What answer do you bring?" The king's worry and impatience were equally obvious.

His redheaded cousin pulled a small scroll from his pouch and held it out.

"Read the missive," Gaylon ordered.

Karyl stripped the yellow ribbon off and unrolled the parchment. "To our brother in royal blood, Gaylon Reysson, Red King of Wynnamyr, greetings from Zorek of the house of Nele, king of all Lasony and—"

The king waved a hand, annoyed. "I'd forgotten what a wordy old bastard Zorek is. What's the gist? Will he send us troops?"

"No, Highness. Your petition was denied, though I begged, badgered, and beseeched for a fortnight. He's afraid. He promises not to raise arms against us, but that's all." The royal cousin's gaze faltered. "The king of all Lasony also denies the queen sanctuary." Karyl glanced at

Davi. "Nor will he take the duke of Gosney."

At mention of his title, the boy's expression altered slightly, and he turned his eyes from Karyl to the king.

Gaylon was suffused with a frustrated anger. "My brother in royal blood would turn away a boy and a woman with child? What can he possibly fear of them?"

"Milord, Zorek wishes to remain neutral so as not to bring the wrath of Mezon upon his people. He says—" Karyl glanced down. "He says that, with your death, a pogrom will begin as it did in Orym's day. Should any kin of yours be kept in Lasony, the priests of the warrior god will bring destruction to that northern realm as well as Wynnamyr."

"Then where?" The king's hands tightened on the arms of his chair. "Where can I send them to be safe?"

The duke of Gosney stepped away from the chair. "I go where you go, Sire," he said, voice tight.

"You go where I command," Gaylon snarled. "What makes you think I'd want a clumsy youngster beside me in battle? Davyn!"

The boy had strode away to the door and disappeared beyond the drapes. All the tension drained suddenly from Gaylon's body. "I've made a royal mess of things now."

"You have," Karyl agreed wearily.

"Thank you so much. . . ."

"Davi's been training hard for war, and now you tell him he can't fight. You even called him clumsy. But then, Cousin, you've always been quick to be cruel."

"Thank you, once again. Don't you have something better to do than chastise your sovereign lord?"

Karyl scratched at his chin. "I could bathe and eat and rest, all of which I richly deserve."

"Do so, please. Only don't plan on resting long. The army moves out tomorrow before light, and you'll be with it."

This news hardly pleased him, but Karyl of Oakhaven

bowed his red head and turned away.

"Oh, and, Cousin," Gaylon called after him, his voice mild. "Answer me one more small question. . . ."

The royal cousin paused. "Yes, milord?"

"Did you manage to stay on your horse the whole journey?"

Too tired for embarrassment or even anger, Karyl only laughed and exited the chamber.

* * * * *

These past few weeks had been frustrating for Tydus. Having been a clever and resourceful man all his life, he found himself somehow inadequate for so simple a task as murder. The king was rarely alone these days and even shared his bed with the queen at night. Poison had proved out of the question. Davi and Jessmyn both tasted the king's food and drink, mostly without His Majesty's knowledge, and the head councilman was not willing to take the innocent lives around Gaylon in order to achieve his goal.

Worse yet, the army would leave this very next morning. Tydus Dorenson must assassinate the king tonight or not at all. Excitement and fear nagging at him, the elderly man stalked his quarry the entire day through the passages and chambers of the keep. No one took notice of a useless old councilman in the turmoil. No one cared for his advice or sought his counsel.

For a man with no sorcerous powers of his own, the only way to destroy a sorcerer would be to catch him unawares, hopefully asleep. Determined, Tydus waited outside the audience chamber and listened to the merchants pleading for payment of goods the army had received. The red-headed cousin, Karyl, returned with news of Lasony, and went alone with king and duke to the council chambers. Before long, Davi left them. Stone-faced, the boy also took his leave of the throne room, perhaps on an errand. Karyl followed soon after, as ignorant as the others of the watchful Tydus.

Gaylon Reysson continued his audience, offering special consideration to those merchants and artisans who would wait on the payment of their bills. With careful dickering and eloquent appeals for patriotism, the impoverished king managed to assuage his creditors' fears. By evening, the last of the petitioners had filed from the chamber.

The head councilman stood in the now-empty corridor and pushed one of the doors open just wide enough to peer through the crack. Gaylon, setting his crown aside, worked a while longer with ink and stylus at the duke's little desk near the throne. Then, obviously weary, he laid his forehead on his arms. Alone. At last, His Majesty was alone. But for how long?

Fingers tight around the hilt of his dagger, Tydus gathered courage. The door swung open silently under his touch. Soft brocade slippers made no sound on the flags. The king lay still, unknowing. This was a deed best done quickly, then Dorenson could lay the weapon aside and race down the passageways, a poor hysterical old man crying for someone to aid his murdered lord. No one would suspect a thing.

Breath held, he took the stairs slowly, noiselessly. Gaylon didn't stir. Tydus stepped carefully behind him, where back and shoulders were exposed. Blood would ruin the beautiful white tabard, but that couldn't be helped. With this man's death would come the death of one dream for Tydus and the birth of another. He brought the dagger up, and all his anger and fear brought an inhuman strength to his arm.

Hands seized his wrist in a sudden, tight grip. The shout that followed brought a momentary confusion. Vaguely, he realized it was Davi who had arrived to stop him, but that only made him all the more desperate. The head councilman wrenched free and stabbed. Even as the king turned,

Davi threw himself between them. The blade found flesh; horrified, Tydus saw it sink into the young duke's neck.

Gaylon, just as shocked and horrified, caught the boy as he fell. With a wail of despair, Dorenson flung the knife across the floor. He went to his knees at the king's feet, sobbing. A mere thought would bring fiery retribution from his lord's Sorcerer's Stone, but none came. Instead, Gaylon's fingers were pressed to the wound in an effort to staunch the flow of blood.

"Get help," he said urgently, eyes wide with distress.

"Milord," Tydus moaned. "What have I done?"

"Go! Find Girkin or Misk, only hurry. Do this, and I swear you will leave here unharmed, a free man. Please!"

Dorenson fled the chamber and out into the hall—a poor hysterical old man shrieking for help.

*   *   *   *   *

Bright crimson blood flowed through Gaylon's fingers no matter how he clasped the wound. The young duke's eyelids fluttered, but refused to open no matter how the king coaxed or cajoled. Helpless, Gaylon crouched on the floor with Davi held tightly. They were equally covered in gore now. Rage and sorrow came and went, and the moments stretched on endlessly.

Whatever Tydus's motives, Gaylon cared little. Davi, duke of Gosney, had taken the blow meant for his Red King. This was the kind of devotion and sacrifice Gaylon had tried so hard to refuse, but such nobility and selflessness could not be denied. With his free hand, he brushed dark hair from the boy's colorless face.

"Don't die. Please don't die," Gaylon murmured, then remembered saying those words to another duke, long ago. "Misk! Why didn't you see this? Why aren't you here?"

"I am here," the tiny woman whispered from behind him. Her voice grew stronger, nearer. "What I see, I cannot always act on. Sometimes events must happen as they will."

"Just tell me, does he live?" the king demanded as she
came to kneel beside the boy.

"There is a chance, if we work quickly."

Misk set a piece of waxed cloth on the floor and unrolled
it, revealing a set of tiny curved needles with bits of thread
and several small, scissorlike tools. Humming a quiet tune,
she pressed a thumb to Davi's forehead. Almost immediately the flow of blood through Gaylon's fingers lessened.

"Place your thumb as I have," the woman said, "and use
your Stone. Will the boy's heart to slow."

"His heart's already beating far too slowly," the king
said, afraid. "It might stop altogether."

"You have no time for useless worries. Do as I say, or
he'll certainly die."

Gaylon obeyed and watched Misk work, her hands moving far too quickly to follow. The wound was opened while
she sewed small severed blood vessels back together with
one of her tiny needles, then tied even tinier knots in the
thread.

Girkin and the still-sobbing Tydus entered the throne
room, accompanied by two guards.

"What does she do?" the physician asked in a hushed
voice, when they had climbed the dais stair. "Is this magic?"

Misk answered him. "No, not magic. Your brethren will
have knowledge of this in later years . . . if Gaylon Reysson
finally fulfills his part in the destiny of your world." She
picked a small paper packet from among her tools. "Gold-
enseal. Some natural things with healing power endure forever." A yellowish powder was dusted into the yet-open
wound. "It's impossible to have a sterile field here in which
to work, but there are other ways to stave off infection."

"What is a sterile field?" Girkin had leaned close to better see. "And what of the thread you leave deep in the
flesh?"

"That will dissolve in time. It's made from the intestines of a cat." The woman stitched the lips of the cut together.

"You use lute strings for thread?" The physician grunted and shook his head. "That alone will cause the wound to fester."

Misk tapped the king's shoulder with bloody fingers. "You may release him."

Gaylon took his thumb away, then drew a deep breath. His own heart had slowed while Misk worked, and now it beat erratically for a moment. Davi remained pale and unknowing.

"He'll be weak for a time from blood loss," the tiny woman said gently. "You must let him sleep and keep him warm. I'll prepare an herbal draught. . . ."

"Sire." One of guards stepped forward, a hand on Tydus's arm. "Lord Dorenson has confessed everything. What are your wishes?"

"Let him go," the king said heavily.

"Milord?"

"Let him go." Gaylon turned his gaze on the head councilman. "The duke lives, and I'll keep my word. Take what belongings you can carry and leave Wynnamyr. But our mercy has limits. Should we meet again, this will be your reward for treason." He made a fist of his right hand, and the Stone in his ring flared a deadly blue.

Tydus, eyes swollen and red, cheeks wet with tears, shrank back.

"Escort Lord Dorenson to his chambers," the king ordered the guards. "Help him collect his things, but do not mistreat him."

Fourteen

All in all, the pain was tolerable, merely annoying in consideration of other events. Davi sat bolstered by half a dozen down pillows, head tilted to the side, while Girkin examined the wound in his neck. Late morning sunlight poured through the bedchamber windows, which meant the army had long since left for the Lower Vales with Gaylon at its lead. And without the duke of Gosney.

"You're an extremely fortunate young fellow," the physician grunted, fat fingers prodding the stitches.

Davi hissed and pushed the man's hand away. "I don't feel fortunate."

"Just think if Tydus had cut your throat. Misk and all her fancy sewing wouldn't have saved you then. I really should bandage this."

"Misk said not to." Again the duke fended off Girkin's fingers. "She said the air would help it heal."

That only made the physician growl in irritation. "Well, don't blame me when the wound festers. I did my best. I tried—"

"Girkin," Davi said as gently as possible. "Get out. Please."

Offended, the portly little man gathered his things from the bedside table. "Certainly, milord. Whatever you say." He left the chamber, double chins held high.

The duke of Gosney, arms crossed, glared at the windows

and the hot summer day beyond them. A week, Misk had said. He must stay abed for an entire week, and under no circumstances was he to scratch at the wound or the stitches. Of course that thought alone made the wound itch maddeningly—a far more acute sensation than the ache of traumatized muscle and flesh. This was only one more misery added to all the rest.

His Red King had rejected him once more, and why not? What could a green youth have to offer a king in pitched battle? There was more to it than that. Should Gaylon fail to survive this war, he intended for his child, the heir to the Red Kings, to be raised by a Gosney, as Davi's father had raised Gaylon. Understanding the logic behind the king's actions still failed to lessen the hurt.

A scratch at the door went unanswered, but the loud knock that followed forced him from his sullen reverie.

"Come," Davi growled, mood foul, expecting a servant with an unwanted dinner tray.

"His lordship is cheerful, I see," said Gaylon from the entrance. "Should I come back later?"

"No," the boy answered quickly. "Sire . . ."

The king was plainly dressed this day in a sleeveless leather jerkin and corded trousers, no better than the roughest peasant in his kingdom might wear. In his hands, he carried a long object wrapped in coarse burlap.

"You're not quite so pale as you were last night." Gaylon smiled as he came to the bed, but his eyes were haggard and dark-circled. "How are you doing?"

"Much better than a moment ago." The boy stared at the heavy package that had been laid on the blankets, then glanced up. "Why are you still here? What of the army?"

"It left this morning as planned. Marten leads the troops with Arlin's, Karyl's, and Rinn's assistance. I'll catch up with them later."

Davi drew a noisy breath. "And me?"

"No, lad. Nothing's changed. I can't risk you in battle."

"Marten says I'm near as good as any with a sword," the boy began to argue. "I'm old enough. Burnic, the grocer's son, is only sixteen, and he's an archer. And there are others as young. I'll be sixteen on the summer solstice."

Gaylon frowned. "Are you so eager for blood?"

"No, milord," the duke answered quickly. "Only to keep yours from being shed."

"I'm not sure I can take any more of your heroics, Davi—not after last night."

"It's my duty to protect you."

"And mine to protect you. . . ." The king shook his head. "We'll discuss that later. You have another duty as a Gosney. I want you to keep this for me."

He tugged at the brown cloth, and an ancient two-edged sword rolled out against Davi's blanketed knee. The boy stared at the cracked leather scabbard feeling a sudden, strong aversion. Just the weight of the weapon made him shiver.

"My father," said Gaylon, "gave this to your father to pass down to me. Now the sword's keeping falls to you. You'll give it to my son one day."

Understanding and fear washed through Davi. "This is Kingslayer."

"Yes."

The duke of Gosney, pulled now by another unknown force, reached out to grasp the ugly lacquered hilt. Immediately his hand tingled, and fire and ice raced up his arm. Blurred images danced behind his eyes, and dim emotions nagged at his consciousness—rage, hatred, desire. He saw an endless night with bright, colored stars caught deep within it.

"Davi!"

The sword glimmered golden and began to sing some distant melody of power. Then Gaylon tore the weapon from the boy's iron grip. Davi felt emptied suddenly. His head, heavy now, lolled back, and the ache in his neck sharpened.

"Dear gods," the king whispered. "You've inherited more from your father than I ever would have guessed. Do you, perhaps, have a Sorcerer's Stone that you've failed to mention?"

"No." There was a vague sorrow in that word. The boy found the strength to raise himself on the pillows again.

"Yet, somehow you woke the sword." Mystified, Gaylon furrowed his brow. "Or very nearly. And that's something I can't do without my Stone." He stared at the boy. "Daryn had the blood of the Dark Kings in him, and so do you. Perhaps Kingslayer recognizes that. What did you feel when you took the hilt?"

Another shiver rippled through Davi. "A murderous fury, a madness—only . . . the feelings seemed very far away, disconnected from my own."

"Be grateful, my young duke. I only wish it were the same for me." The king stroked the scabbard almost lovingly. "When the sword wakes in my hand, I feel an irresistible lust for death and destruction. Whatever the weapon might have been once, Orym's dark powers have tainted it forever . . . and will corrupt any who seek to use it."

"That's why you refuse to take up the Legacy?"

Gaylon nodded distractedly. "Now that I see how it affects you, I'm not so certain you should keep the sword."

"I have to," the boy said hurriedly, afraid to lose contact with what small magic he possessed.

"All right," the king muttered, doubt edging his words, "but you've got to promise to be careful. Keep the thing tightly wrapped and handle only the scabbard. As soon as you're recovered, you must hide the sword. Hide it well, even from me. The closer we come to war, the weaker my resolve."

"Sire." The duke of Gosney pulled himself more upright on the bed. "Orym's Legacy must go south with you. How can you possibly defeat the enemy without it?"

"No," Gaylon said angrily. "We don't have to defeat the enemy, only hold them at the Sea Pass until the first winter snows. We've managed to survive a millennium that way. Xenara can't hope to feed so great an army for very long. Eventually Roffo's allies will grow tired of waiting and go home."

"But . . . Arlin says they'll overrun us. He says we can't possibly stand against so many, that only Kingslayer can save us."

"Does he?" Gaylon grunted. "Listen to me, Davi. Kingslayer has no friends, only enemies. It has one purpose . . . to kill. No one would be safe—not our soldiers or Roffo's. Do you understand?"

The duke stared long at the decrepit weapon lying at his feet, then glanced up at the king. "I understand why you're afraid." Before him, Gaylon's jaw tightened. "But I also believe Arlin's right, and there'll be slaughter one way or another. Take Kingslayer with you into battle, Sire, and use the blade if all your defenses fail."

"Ye gods! I've a fifteen-year-old duke who would command his monarch," the king snapped. "Your father was just as determined that I take up Orym's Legacy. And so is Misk."

"Then perhaps you should. The sword has waited one thousand years for the Red King who might finally master it. We've all read the legend in the history books, of a Red King who would undo all the evil Orym perpetrated with his weapon."

"More likely I'll perpetrate some vast new evil of my own." Gaylon's smile turned grim. "Or become a fleshless pile of bones as the Dark King did . . . as Lucien did. The sword is justly named. Or had you forgotten that part of the legend?"

The boy's excitement drained away as his lord spoke.

"Even so, my duke, you've won your argument. The

Legacy goes south to Xenara."

"And me?"

"I've already given you my answer on that."

Davi felt a surge of frustrated anger. "Sire, if you leave me behind, I swear I'll follow somehow."

The Stone in Gaylon's ring flickered blue, then died abruptly. Instead of outrage, the duke saw only sorrow on the man's face.

"Your father was just as hardheaded," the king muttered. "All right. Come if you must."

Davi listened to the resignation in Gaylon's voice, and a cold dread formed in the pit of his stomach.

*   *   *   *   *

Seated before the polished bronze mirror at the dressing table, she drew the soft-bristled brush through her long hair, counting the strokes silently, automatically, her mind on other things. The king would stay another fortnight while Davi recovered. A reprieve of sorts. And yet, this would only prolong her suffering. Jessmyn had already said her goodbyes and now would be forced to say them all over again.

Something fluttered deep within her, and she pressed a hand against her slightly rounded stomach, below and to the right of her naval. The flutter came again. Eryn, mistress of the kitchen and a mother five times over, said it was much too early to feel the baby kick, but the queen knew without a doubt that a tiny foot or fist had just now struck against her womb. Joy and sorrow mingled equally, and a single tear slid down Jessmyn's cheek.

A callused hand came to rest on her bare shoulder, and she tilted her head back to look up into the king's face. He'd come silently into her apartments. With a fingertip, Gaylon caught the tear and carried it to his mouth, then bent to kiss her forehead lightly.

"My lady," he murmured and knelt on the carpet beside her chair. "Now that the army has gone, I find myself with much spare time. Would you consider spending it with me?"

"We would be honored, my lord." Jessmyn took his right hand and held the palm to her stomach.

The baby struggled again in its soft prison, and Gaylon inhaled sharply. His face filled with wonder. Then, for one brief instant, she saw the old bleakness pass behind his eyes. There were ways to make him forget though. The queen pressed her mouth against his, and in the midst of that sweet kiss, his hand found a tender, swollen breast and cupped it through the nightgown.

"I will always love you," the king whispered as he gathered her up in his arms.

* * * * *

Rinn arrived at the head of the column late in the morning, his pale hair and shoulders covered in dust, his face smudged with sweat and dirt. Even his bony black gelding's flanks were coated with the fine ocher grit from the road. Arlin tried not to notice, but lost the battle to an amused smile.

"You try riding behind an army that's spread two leagues back along these dales," the tailor's son grumbled and let his mount slow enough to walk alongside the others.

"How are the wagons doing?" Marten asked. He had a sheepskin map spread across the pommel of his saddle and began to roll it up as they talked.

"Loyl's broke an axle in a bad rut. He'll catch up as soon as they've got a new one on."

"He'd better," Arlin said. Loyl carried the bulk of their arrows in his huge triple-axle rig. "So what's ahead?" he asked Marten. "Anyplace we can put up camp?"

"Another five leagues and we should come to a couple of good-sized glens. It'll be a tight squeeze, but we'll manage." The earl glanced at Rinn. "Ride back and find me at least two dozen volunteers—mounted archers, bow and crossbow. We need a couple of hunting parties to go on ahead if there's to be enough to eat tonight."

"Why can't you send Arlin?" the tailor's son groused. "Or Karyl? Where *is* the royal cousin?"

"Gone ahead to scout our way," Marten answered. "Now do as I ask or hear about it from the king later."

Rinn reined the gelding around and, thumping his heels to the animal's ribs, sent it at a ponderous lope toward the rear. The ragged line of foot soldiers stretched into the distance. As yet, there was laughter and camaraderie in the ranks. The men were tired, but still swept up in the adventure. Later the doubts and fears would come.

Arlin tilted his head to look up into the blue summer sky above. Wooded ridgetops crowded close, and water rushed bubbling down streambeds and creeks. Without the shady trees or the cool, moisture-laden breezes, this passage would be far worse than dusty. Beside him, Marten pulled the map out again. He studied the lines for long periods of time, as if something helpful might have been missed, as if some hitherto unfound plan of action might make itself known.

Yet with each passing day, the hopelessness of the situation came clearer and clearer. Arlin and Marten each knew that the greater number of these brave men marched to their deaths. Kingslayer might be their only chance of survival, but the king had been adamant: Orym's Legacy would not be used under any circumstances, no matter how dire. The soldiers had been made privy to none of this. Their faith in the king must never falter.

"Perhaps," Marten said quietly, his eyes still tracing the map's lines while his mount plodded on, "you should consider another reversal of loyalties." He glanced over at

Arlin. "You might die anyway, but why not be on the winning side and at least make your family proud?"

The Southerner rubbed a thumb across numb fingertips and shrugged. "If winning mattered, I might."

"You'd rather be on the rightful side?"

"So far as I can tell, history always records the victor as being just and right."

"Then why?" the earl asked.

"First tell me why *you* continue with this doomed task, milord," Arlin pressed.

"For the king . . . No, for Gaylon Reysson."

Marten realized he had answered for them both, then offered his friend a wry smile.

*   *   *   *   *

The tents of the Mezon priests were a brilliant white under the harsh glare of the summer sun. King Roffo had shed his sweltering light armor and lounged in the shade of Tek's open-fronted pavilion, his eyes on the wide, barren slopes that led up into the Sea Pass of the Gray Mountains. At least a stiff wind continued to blow, snapping the silk and keeping the insects at bay. The grit and dust were a trial, though.

Iced wine was brought by a young boy in acolyte robes, and the king accepted a cup gratefully. How the priests managed ice in this heat was a wonder, but not one to be questioned. Roffo sipped, listening to the tramp of feet and the clash of steel beyond the thin walls. As old as he was and as long ago as his last war had been, the sights and sounds of this great encampment still stirred Roffo's blood.

Tek entered finally, long robes fluttering about him. The priest bowed, then found a folding camp chair to sit in. Wine arrived immediately.

"How much longer must we wait?" the king asked.

After a slow sip from his cup, the high priest replied,

"The god has shown me our enemy's army. They are traveling south. Another week and they will reach us, I believe."

"Why not take the pass now?" Roffo grumbled. "We're more than ready. We could bring Wynnamyr to its knees before their troops even arrive."

"Mezon has other plans, and we'll obey his will without question." Tek took another sip of wine. "Better first, don't you think, to make war in the pass than on the fecund earth of the Lower Vales?"

The king tugged at his mustache. "I've found that blood is an excellent fertilizer."

"Even when it's your own?" Roffo's reaction moved the elderly priest to gentle laughter. "Be patient, Sire. The god will provide."

* * * * *

A fortnight passed while Davi healed. In that short time, Castlekeep's lawns went wild again, then withered with the summer heat. The gardener and his staff had joined the king's lancers and were well south by now. In the gardens, rosebushes were busy making rose hips since their blooms had gone uncut. Even so, the flowering hollyhocks and calendula offered bright colors, high and low, in the tangled growth around the fountains.

Gaylon looked out over the grounds, trapping the memory of his home bathed in the early morning light and the young woman standing near his horse. There were tears in the queen's eyes, but she smiled through them. Misk, beside her, held up a leather satchel for Gaylon.

"These herbs are for Davi," she said, "but you might use the teas as well. They'll help you rest. Take care, Gaylon Reysson. Listen to your own heart and not to my brother. When Sezran finally comes to join your army, it'll be to serve himself, not you." Misk turned abruptly and walked away.

The king leaned down from the saddle to kiss his queen, but Jessmyn averted her face.

"Do you suppose," she asked, "here and in the countries of our enemies, that all the wives kissed all their soldier husbands goodbye?"

"Most likely, my lady."

"And as they kissed, were they aware that it might be for the very last time?"

To that, Gaylon could find no answer. Under him, the bay mare shifted her weight.

"When I was two-years-old," the young woman continued, her gaze trapping the king's, "you used to lead me out to the center of the sward and then run away."

"Was I already a monster at that young an age?" Gaylon chuckled. "Your memory is long, wife."

"I only remember because it frightened me so. I was terrified you would never come back." The queen reached up to wrap arms tightly around his neck and pull him even closer. "Promise me you won't die. Promise me you'll come back."

His face against hers, Gaylon felt warm tears. "I promise, my lady," he murmured into her ear, "that I will be with you, now and forever."

"Let's go!" someone called from behind them.

The king pulled Jessmyn's arms gently free and straightened.

Their single pack animal led on a rope, Davi sent his own mount at a trot across the dry grass. An ancient two-edged sword hung from the wide belt at his waist. He halted beside them, grinning, then noticed the queen's wet cheeks.

"Don't fear, milady," the boy told her. "I'll keep him safe for you."

"I know you will." Jessmyn beckoned him to lean closer, then kissed him full on the lips.

The duke of Gosney's wan face went suddenly scarlet, and Gaylon laughed, which only made things worse.

"What of my kiss?" the king demanded.

"Yours, my lord," the young woman said with a faint smile, "will wait until you return."

"Then I had best make haste." Gaylon reined the mare around in order to hide the ache that his wife's words had brought.

The clop of Davi's horses followed him past the stables and onto the road toward town. Already the heat of the day was building over the quiet, empty land. The chirr of cicadas had replaced the shouts of men in training. War and death seemed distant, though, in fact, they lay only one hundred and twenty-five leagues to the south.

Fifteen

The king and young duke stopped in Riverbend on the way south, though not for long. The streets of the town were crowded with women, children, and only the most elderly of men. Davi, uneasy, rode his bay gelding into the yard of the Fickle River Inn and into the shade of the old black oak near the entrance. Under the hot sun, the building looked little changed with its flaking whitewash and sagging shutters. How strange to see the place again after so many changes in his own life.

Gaylon halted his mare beside the boy. "We could stay for a while, if you'd like."

"No," Davi said, having second thoughts. "Let's just go on."

The door opened, and a shape appeared from the shadowed interior. Haddi paused on the stoop, her green eyes on her son, then joy transformed her face.

"Davi!"

His mother had never been given to shows of strong emotion. To see her so happy unnerved the boy, but he leaned to embrace her and accept her kiss.

"Come inside." She glanced at the king, and much of her joy faded. "Both of you."

"We ride to join our army in the Lower Vales, mum. I'm sorry, there's no time for a visit. . . ."

"Of course, I understand." Haddi managed a smile.

"You've grown, Davi—I can see that. And dressed as a duke and a soldier, I hardly recognized you. I was certain that two fine gentlemen had ridden into my yard."

Embarrassed, Davi stared down at the reins in his hands. "Have you been well, mum? Is everything all right?"

"Nothing can be right when a son rides off to war." The woman looked again at Gaylon, this time with an odd intensity. "Please, milord. Keep him safe. He's still only a boy."

The desperation in her voice gave the young duke of Gosney pause, but the king's answer was even more disturbing.

"Madam, whatever you might think, I hold Davi's life more precious than my own. I lost the father; I'm determined not to lose the son."

Haddi bowed her head. "I wished you ill once, Gaylon Reysson, and I have very little love for you now. For Davi's sake and Wynnamyr's, I'll pray that the Red King triumphs."

"Then let's hope there's a Wynnamyran god to hear you." The king nodded at Davi. "I'll ride on, if you want a moment alone."

"No, it's time to go," the boy said quickly. "Farewell, mum."

Beside Davi's horse, Haddi started to raise her hands to him, then lowered them again as he turned his mount away. All the way down the road, Davi felt her eyes on him.

*   *   *   *   *

The Wynnamyran army arrived in the Lower Vales a little behind schedule, road repair being the primary reason. With a great deal of disorganization and a moderate amount of confusion, the men pitched tents and made camp. Crops were quickly trampled underfoot, but that had been expected. The tenant farmers, with little left to farm, joined the ranks of the soldiers, swelling their forces to nearly four thousand.

At least the odds have gotten a tiny bit better, Marten decided. He stood with his tent flap held aside, viewing the orderly chaos of the vales under a heavy gray sky. So near the coast, early morning fog came as a blessing and a bane. Even now a chill ocean mist turned the rich black earth to a sticky goo that clung to boots and hoofs and caused wagons to slide into irrigation ditches.

Behind the earl, Arlin D'Lelan still slept on his bedroll. The young Southerner had seemed more prone to exhaustion of late, and his appetite was poor. Stress affected men in various ways though. Marten, himself, had trouble sleeping and actually envied Arlin that peace. In the distance, his family mansion stood on a tree-shrouded knoll, empty. Lady Vyla and the children had been sent north to Riverbend along with the families of the farmers.

Very soon the king would arrive, and the business of war would begin. In the south, spread across a great white plain, a vast enemy waited. Marten smiled grimly. With two local men to guide them east, the earl had sent Karyl and Rinn to the aqueducts in hopes of giving the enemy some small amount of aggravation. Or even a large amount, if luck was with them.

* * * * *

"Stay down," Rinn cautioned loudly when the royal cousin stood up to peer through their thin cover of dogwood. Sweet white blooms were scattered among the plant's sparse leaves.

Karyl sat down heavily in the damp soil, just missing his crossbow. "What does Marten expect us to do, for the gods' sakes?"

There was no need to keep their voices down. The clank and clatter of the windmills covered any sound. Add to

that the thunder of the water course and the gusts of wind
that blew constantly up this small canyon, and a man could
have a throbbing headache in no time. The tailor's son
stared in wonder at Roffo's mills.

The four enormous structures were higher than the tall-
est building Rinn had ever seen. Wide, canvas-covered
vanes acted as sails to harness the wind and pump water
through man-high masonry pipes that ran almost vertically
up the mountainside. Rinn's father had told him once that
a thousand Xenaran slaves had labored over a decade to cut
through the living rock of the mountain. Now the precious
water of Wynnamyr flowed through the tunnel to the aqueducts on the southern slope, and then to Zankos and Katay.

"What does he expect us to do?" Karyl demanded
again, even more loudly in case his comrade had failed to
hear him the first time.

"I think," the tailor's son said with some sadness, "that
Marten wants us to ruin these marvelous machines."

"But how? Look at the size of them."

Rinn pulled at his blond-stubbled chin thoughtfully,
then glanced back at the two young farmers squatted in the
bushes behind them. "They're probably geared somewhat
like a flour mill or a lumber mill."

"Only much bigger," the royal cousin pointed out.

"And far more complicated. But the size might actually
be used against them. What we need is a closer look."

"What we need is more than four men," Karyl groused.
"I've counted ten Xenaran soldiers—"

"Twelve. You missed the ones hidden around the mouth
of the tunnel." Rinn pointed high above them on the
right. "And you didn't count the two Mezon priests that
are seated beyond the mills."

"Where?"

"There. See the curves in the shadows on the far side of
the flume. Elbows and knees. They haven't moved a mus-

cle since we got here."

Karyl used some of his most colorful profanity. "I don't want to die in this place," he snarled. "I don't really want to die, but I suppose it has to happen. Only not here, not now."

"Shut up and let me think. And quit shuffling around. If we can see the priests, they just might be able to see us."

The king's cousin sat very still while Rinn thought. The guardians would have to be killed, all of them. The tailor's son picked up his crossbow and considered it. The weapon was deadly and accurate, but had a limited range. The soldiers at the tunnel would have to be dealt with by the farmers and their longbows. Marten had chosen them because they were superior archers, and Rinn hoped fervently that the earl was not mistaken. The rest of the soldiers would have to be somehow lured out into the open, all at the same moment. That left only the priests.

Only the priests . . . Those two sexless creatures were probably the whole reason why the windmills were so lightly guarded. Rinn did a little mental cursing himself, but tried not to worry about their chances of succeeding.

"I want you to fall off your horse." The tailor's son shook Karyl's shoulder to get his attention.

"What?"

"You have to fall off your horse. Down there."

"Are you crazy? They'll kill me."

"Not if they think you're already dead. You use an arrow. Like this." Rinn grabbed a shaft from one of the farmer's quivers and pushed it under the royal cousin's arm. "Keep this on the downhill side, and it'll look like you've been shot through."

"You do it."

"Karyl, I'm better with a crossbow than you. And you've had so much more practice falling off."

The redhead's face grew stormy. "Marten said we could go back for help if the aqueducts were too well guarded."

"Bringing a whole troop in here will lose us our element of surprise and we'll end up with a lot more dead." Karyl looked unconvinced, so Rinn rushed on. "Think of the glory, then. Think of the ballads we'll inspire. The earl will probably write one himself."

"And we'll never know, unless he comes to sing it on our graves."

The tailor's son sighed. "All right. I'll do the falling. Use both crossbows and keep the bolts beside your hand so you can reload as quickly as possible. Our farmer friends will take the two guards at the tunnel mouth. You take the priests soon as possible . . . that's important. Then the three of you—"

"Here," Karyl growled and shoved his crossbow at Rinn. "You could never fall off a horse convincingly, you're too good a rider. . . . And I don't have your sharp eyes or perfect aim."

"You'll be a hero." Rinn thumped the king's cousin on the back.

"I'll be dead."

The young farmer with a scar over one eye volunteered to go back for Karyl's mount. Rinn had already forgotten the names of their guides, except one had a scar and one had buck teeth. That was how he told the two brown-haired brothers apart.

The royal cousin, morose and gloomy, sat in the bushes, contemplating cruel fate, until Rinn tapped his shoulder and led him back to his horse.

"Lean over this side of the animal's neck," the tailor's son advised. "That way they'll only see the arrow shaft sticking out. When you fall, keep the same arm under you, and for the gods' sakes lie still. Leave the rest to us." Rinn looked at the farmers. "Keep your eyes on the tunnel. You've got to kill the two guards there quickly. They'll have the clearest shot at us. Choose your targets first and don't waste both arrows on the same man."

The scarred farmer pointed to himself. "Right."

The other nodded. "Left."

"Fine," Rinn said. "Use the same method on the rest of the soldiers that'll be rushing from the windmills. I'll have already gotten at least two by then."

"What of the priests?" the buck-toothed man asked, a touch of uneasiness in his voice.

"I'll take care of them." Rinn glanced at his redheaded friend.

"Well, don't expect anything from me," Karyl announced sourly. "I'll be dead."

"We'd better get on with it."

Muttering, the king's cousin climbed onto his horse and positioned the arrow. But when he leaned forward, the point pricked the gelding's shoulder and made it jump. Karyl very nearly fell off too soon.

"Easy!" Rinn snapped, frustration and fear taking their toll. He led the horse forward through the undergrowth, then waved the farmers into position. "Go," the tailor's son hissed.

Karyl nudged his mount with his heels, and the gelding started down the gentle slope and into the clearing. Instantly there came a shout from the tunnel above, and the two soldiers stepped from their sheltering rocks, arrows nocked and bows drawn. They hesitated though when the royal cousin slid slowly from the horse's back to land in a boneless heap on the leaf mold. Unfortunately his arrow had shifted angles, but the enemy didn't seemed to notice.

Rinn afforded his comrade one quick glimpse, then sighted on a kilted soldier who had emerged from the base of the nearest mill, calling to the men above.

"Now!" the tailor's son cried.

Two arrows and a quarrel were released at exactly the same moment and found their marks an instant later. One soldier at the mouth of the tunnel tumbled from the mountainside, the other fell back. Rinn grabbed the sec-

ond crossbow and launched its bolt at the man who had
caught his fallen comrade beside the windmill. They died
together.

Fletching sang near Rinn's right ear as the brothers drew
and released again. The tailor's son, crouched in the brush,
jammed the nose of one crossbow, then the other, into the
dirt. He used a boot toe to hold each secure while he
dragged the strings back and secured them. The quarrels
were quickly loaded in the slots. His eyes were on the
priests as he worked. They had moved into the light, their
hands empty and weaponless, their faces serene.

The young tailor's next shot glanced off a priest's white
painted cuirass and skittered away into the trees. A tumul-
tuous melody had reached his ears. Above the glade, sparkling green light appeared, and Rinn gazed into it,
momentarily mesmerized. The light roiled and grew, and
an impossible heat formed within, felt even from this distance. Karyl, shouting soundlessly against Mezon's song,
leaped to his feet and scrambled toward his comrades.

The emerald fire formed a ball in the treetops high
above the priests' heads. A sudden internal fear shattered
the hypnotic effect, and Rinn dragged his eyes from the
cloud, grabbing the second loaded crossbow just as the royal cousin arrived. Fir limbs crackled and caught fire, then
the gaseous orb sped toward Rinn and his companions,
long tongues of flame fluttering in its wake.

With the crossbow steadied against his knees, the tailor's
son took quick but careful aim and loosed the bolt. One
priest spun sideways, his left eye socket having sprouted a
short, feathered shaft. The fireball slammed into the dogwood, and Karyl shrieked and flung his arms up before his
face. Rinn could only close his eyes.

Silence fell. Even the great windmills seemed to pause.
His senses told the tailor's son that he was still alive. Heat
and fire and song had vanished with the priest's death, but
that brief quiet was shattered by a Xenaran officer's harsh

shout of command. The farmers resumed their archery, and
Rinn shoved a crossbow into Karyl's shaking hands.

A short time later, the four men found themselves without targets. Dead and dying foes lay scattered throughout
the area. Wordlessly, the two brothers moved down into the
clearing, dirks in hand, and began to slit the throats of the
wounded survivors.

"Not a scratch on us," the king's cousin said, wonder in
his voice. "Look at what we've done . . . and not a scratch
on us."

Rinn looked and felt sick. They could not care for the
wounded or even take them back to the vales for help, so
what the brothers did was more a kindness than anything
else. Then why did it make Rinn ill? The scarred brother
returned first, his face revealing neither joy nor sorrow.

"All are dead, but one," the man reported. "The other
priest is not among these."

Escaped. Somewhere in the woods that remaining
warrior-priest made his way to find help of his own.

"Shall we go after him?"

"No," the tailor's son said sharply. "There's no time to
waste." He headed for the first of the windmills, skirting
the flume that led from the holding pond. A body blocked
the entrance of the first structure, and Rinn stepped over it
and the blood that slicked the stones. From within, the
rumbling of huge gears shook the wooden walkway beneath his feet.

"Incredible!" Karyl shouted above the racket, his head
tilted back to better see into the high interior from which a
great metal shaft descended.

More than incredible. The shaft, rotating laboriously,
was as big around as a young redwood tree and just as
straight. To forge such a continuous piece of iron was impossible by Wynnamyran standards. The gears at the base
were larger than the largest wagon wheels that Rinn had
ever seen.

"Bring me the spanner," he called to the buck-toothed brother. "There. The big metal tool with open jaws."

The huge wrench was brought and, after careful consideration, the tailor's son cinched it down over a giant nut that held two gears of differing sizes side by side. No amount of jerking or leaning on the long handle, though, loosened the nut. His comrades watched from a respectful distance.

"I need some help here," Rinn shouted. "We have to break this free."

Karyl leaned his own weight on the spanner. "How come you know so much about windmills?" he called.

"I worked in a lumber mill at Moon Bay when I was twelve. Same principles, only with water for power." All the shouting made Rinn hoarse, so the rest of the answer he kept to himself. At twelve, the tailor's son had decided he didn't want to be a tailor. His father had wisely found him work at the mill to the north; only one summer of hard labor at Moon Bay had changed the boy's mind.

One of the brothers added his weight to the handle, and at last, the nut broke loose with a rusty shriek. Rinn swung the spanner until the nut dropped free and rolled away. Next, the tailor's son found a big wooden mallet and used it to dislodge the larger gear from the end of the spindle. Shoulders and arms ached by the time he'd accomplished this. The instant the cogs came clear of the reduction gears beneath, the machinery ground to a halt—all but the main shaft, which began to turn more quickly. High overhead, the clatter of the wind vanes increased.

"All right," the royal cousin whooped.

Rinn shook his head. "This isn't good enough. They'll just put them back together."

"What's that?" the scarred brother asked, head cocked. Another deeper rumbling had begun, and again the mill shuddered. Beneath their walkway, gears began to turn, this time in reverse.

"Hurry!" Rinn cried and got his hands under the cogged wheel he'd knocked loose. "It's the water uphill running back down into the pump. If we throw this gear into the mechanism while its moving, the whole works will bind."

Together, they dragged the wheel to the edge of the walk and pushed it over. The collision below sent explosions of sparks high into the air, while the rending and chattering hurt their ears. With a last screech of despair, the machinery seized. Water flooded into the base of the huge windmill.

"Uh-oh." Karyl grinned with obvious pleasure. "Now we've done it."

"And now we have to do it again," Rinn told him wearily. "Three more times."

The buck-toothed brother peered out through a tiny window, then turned an expressionless face to them.

"If we don't hurry," he said, "we'll have to swim out of here."

Everyone had to look for themselves, then. Sure enough, the water meant to be pumped through the mountain by this particular mill now spread over the clearing. Karyl's mount, well trained and none too bright, stood obediently where he'd been left, already up to his fetlocks in the flood.

The royal cousin resorted to profanity again. "If we don't hurry," he snarled, "my horse will drown."

They hurried.

*　　*　　*　　*　　*

Arlin and Marten sent their mounts at a gallop through the foothills toward the Sea Pass. The morning fog finally began to burn away under the relentless summer sun, drifting above them in wisps and snatches. Even the horses seemed to enjoy this chance to stretch their legs. Marten's gray gelding lashed its tail and managed a small, joyful buck every now and again.

When the army had first arrived, the earl had immediately sent a detachment of soldiers to reinforce the guards at the pass, but this was the first time he'd felt he had time enough to spare for one more personal look at the enemy.

Actually, this venture was more for Arlin's sake. The restless young Southerner had needed some form of distraction, and while Marten, restless himself, would have rather waited for the arrival of the king or the return of Karyl and Rinn, he'd decided this was a practical excursion. The earl had insisted they don light armor—helms and cuirasses along with swords and crossbows—before riding out.

The rolling grassy foothills gave way to the craggy formations of the Gray Mountains. Here, those mountains marched down into the ocean to become tiny, uninhabited islands off the coast. Near the Western Sea, the peaks were far more weathered and worn than those that continued north and created the spine of Wynnamyr. Seabirds cried, swooping through the last of the mist to dive into the cold gray-green waters that appeared briefly to the right and far below the two riders.

Marten slowed the gelding on the stony ground, and Arlin followed suit. No one challenged their approach from this direction, and they paused at the small camp while the earl chastised the elderly captain of the detachment. While no enemy had ever found a back way to bring troops through these mountains, there could be a first time.

"Hallo, Marti!" The shout from a ledge above echoed through the pass, and the earl waved at the guard, then headed on.

"Let's go back to the same outcropping," Arlin suggested from beside him. "It's got a grand view."

Marten shook his head. "There's a spot up ahead that'll serve. Not so grand maybe, but better protected."

At the far end of the narrow, rocky channel, they dismounted and secured the horses to a spindly evergreen that had somehow found enough soil to root. The earl led them along a worn footpath that ran the edge of the eastern wall and then down a steep slope that ended in a jumble of boulders. The point of land jutted out a ways and afforded a more than decent view.

"Dear gods," Marten muttered, attention trapped by the tableau to the south.

As far as the eye could see, King Roffo's army spread over the plain, much larger than it had been a month past. The tents were pitched tighter together now—all but the precise white pavilions that filled the area nearest the Sea Pass. Everywhere, tiny antlike figures swarmed over the sterile, salty ground.

Arlin gazed fixedly on the movement below. "Do you think Karyl and Rinn will succeed?"

"We can't count on it, but a thirsty army just might be easier to beat."

"We should have gone with them."

"Maybe," Marten admitted, regret coloring his words. "But you and I had other things to accomplish first. Besides, if they need help, they'll come back for it."

"Not our brave, reckless friends."

Marten mulled Arlin's statement over and tried to let go of the guilt. The fourteenth earl of the Lower Vales had been born and bred to command men. This came as naturally as breathing to him, but an inherited title, Marten knew, didn't necessarily make him a good leader. Young and inexperienced, only time and history would prove the worth of Marten Pelson.

A shrill, warbling whistle floated up from the plain below. Arlin stood suddenly and answered it with a similar whistle of his own.

"What are you doing?" the earl demanded, catching his comrade's arm in a tight grip. "Get back down."

The dark-haired Southern lord pulled free. "That's my

brother!" He pointed into the tents below, where a small
form swung a white banner on a pole back and forth as it
advanced toward them.

"Markim," Arlin shouted and whistled again.

"Brother!" the soldier shouted back. He'd crossed
through the god's white pavilions and stood alone at the
base of the mountain. "Come down!"

"No," the earl said sharply when the Southerner studied
the slope in search of a way.

"He's my brother."

"He's the enemy. Don't be a fool!"

"No one will harm you," Markim called. "I promise safe
passage. Bring your friend if you like. I've food and ale and
stories of home. Father's dead, Arlin. Let's make our peace,
you and I, before we must face one another in battle."

"I'm coming," the young lord cried. Ignoring Marten's
angry pleas, he stepped out into the open.

"Follow the mountainside to your right, Arlin," his
brother called. "Then use the road to come down. That's
easiest."

"No," Marten Pelson said clearly.

The young Southerner hesitated, then glanced back. "I
have to speak with him, but I'll be back. Wait for me . . .
please."

The hot, dry wind, the glitter of the Inland Sea, and
Markim's voice had all stirred a homesickness in Arlin that
he'd never realized existed. The earl must understand.
Within the D'Lelan clan, there'd always been bickering,
but love and trust had outweighed all other considerations.
If Markim said he had safe passage, then Arlin was safe.

He followed the side of the mountain with his brother
matching his movements on the plain below. At some
point the terrain forced him to climb again, and he lost
sight of Markim, but westward travel brought him at last to
the coach road. The way had been carved into the gray
stone in long loops that cut back and forth across the face of

the mountain—otherwise, teams of horses could have never brought loaded coaches up so steep a grade. Or down it, for that matter.

Somewhere along the way, doubts finally surfaced. To Xenara, Arlin D'Lelan would be a traitor, anathema, and a brother might be condemned by association.

"Arlin!"

Markim appeared from around a bend, trudging up the road toward him, hands weaponless, arms open. All worries vanished with the man's joyous smile. Arlin went to him and accepted the strong embrace. Physically, they were very dissimilar. Markim, ten years Arlin's senior, had taken after their mother's side of the family, which produced shorter, heavy-torsoed men of great strength and quick tempers. Even so, Arlin had always looked up to him.

"Little brother," Markim muttered and pulled away. "By Mezon, it's good to see you."

The young Southerner smiled and removed his helm. "I never thought we would meet again. Not in this life."

"Well, life is full of surprises. Nothing is so important at the moment but that we find my tent and talk." Markim started them back down the road. "And eat. I've got sesame cakes and fresh sweet dates. Bet you haven't tasted those in a while."

"Not in eight long years," the younger brother laughed, then sobered. "Father's dead?"

Markim looked out over the great plateau with its plumes of windswept dust. "Aye. But he died with your name on his lips. I wanted you to know that."

In the silence that followed, Arlin felt a tiny ache of loss, a sorrow over that last angry parting of father and youngest son. Sorrow served no purpose, though, and the Southerner put his attention on the land ahead. The two men had descended finally to the plain, and the flat, dry earth rolled away in all directions. The white tents of the Mezon priests fluttered and flapped, but the area was empty of life. Be-

yond them, though, was the Xenaran encampment.
There, what few soldiers stood idle watched the two brothers' progress across the field.

Unconsciously Arlin touched the hilt of his sword, aware
of the sweat prickling his skin under the cuirass. Markim
wore nothing but kilt, sandals, and sleeveless vest.

"Here we are," his brother said grandly and pulled back
the door flap on a round fringed tent of fine silk with a
high peak at the center. Inside, rich carpets covered the
dirt, and satin brocade pillows were scattered about. A
long, low table seemed to be the only real furnishing.
Weapons, armor, and a bedroll lay neatly off to one side.

A robed boy servant entered behind them, eyes downcast. "Milord?"

"Food and drink, Rys . . . immediately."

"You live well, Markim," Arlin said, his eyes on his
brother's few but lavish belongings.

"I have my own command, Brother. A thousand soldiers
under me." Markim gestured toward the table. "Sit. Re-
freshments will arrive shortly."

Arlin unhooked the scabbard from his belt and sat, laying the sword on the cushions beside him, then unbuckled
his cuirass and set it aside with his helm. Markim D'Lelan
had prospered over his past years of military service to King
Roffo. He'd also inherited the house of Lelan.

"I can't stay long," the young Southerner said, remembering Marten, all alone, overlooking the plain.

Markim grinned. "Well, forgive me if I try to change
your mind."

He poured water from a small ewer into a bowl, and they
washed their hands. The food and drink arrived, brought
by a pair of servants who were shooed away afterward. The
elder brother served the meal himself. Hot curried lamb
wrapped in steamed grape leaves was heaped on both their
plates, along with the promised sesame cakes and full tank-
ards of sweet ale.

Arlin had somehow forgotten the pleasures of eating with his fingers, but the heavy cloying tastes seemed strange now. His brother watched intently.

"The food is not to your liking?" Markim asked.

"The food is fine . . . wonderful. It's just that I haven't had much of an appetite lately."

"And who could eat that bland Wynnamyran fare for very long without losing his appetite?" the elder brother demanded with just a hint of irritation. "Why *did* you leave us to live in the north, Arlin? Mother has suffered so much from your desertion."

The meal turned bitter in that moment, and Arlin set a half-eaten cake back down. "I thought you asked me here out of love, but I see you want me to defend my actions instead."

"No. That's not why you're here," Markim said heavily, but his gaze shifted away.

"I was wild and irresponsible," Arlin admitted, "and I embarrassed the family at court. For that I'm truly sorry, but it was Father who made it clear that I couldn't return home. How could I stay in Zankos, Markim? There was no future for me there. I didn't have your discipline, your warrior's frame of mind."

"You seem to have found it well enough now. You'd take arms against your own people . . . your own family. You follow a Red King and bring shame on us all."

"I follow a friend. He's a sorcerer-king as well, but above all else, he's a man who I think destiny has touched. Wynnamyr is my home now, its people my family. We didn't ask for this war. You've forced it on us. There's the shame, and it's all yours."

"Enough," his brother snapped and took up his tankard. "Let's not quarrel in the little time left to us. Eat."

Arlin stared at his plate. His thumbs slid lightly over numb fingertips the while, and somehow an emotional exhaustion had overtaken him. "How did Father die?"

"At the hands of the Mezon priests."

That caused a small shock. "But why? He was faithful. Always. He loved the god."

"He did, but he also refused to do as the high priest demanded." Markim drank deeply from his mug. "I, on the other hand, willingly obeyed."

Arlin frowned. "I don't understand."

"You will. Father died calling for you. Not for me . . . for you. Eat, Brother. It grows late."

The young Southerner took another halfhearted bite, and finally noticed that Markim had touched nothing on his plate. Across from them, the door flap opened, and a tall ascetic man in high priest's robes entered. Arlin remembered his name with a sudden apprehension. Tek. Close behind the priest came another man, silver-haired and handsome. Tydus Dorenson. The sight of the head councilman brought anger and confusion.

"He's eaten very little," Markim said from beside Arlin.

"But enough to suit our purposes, I think," the priest answered. "The drug should make him compliant enough."

Tydus spoke next. "Do you believe me now, Markim D'Lelan?"

"Yes." That single word held both sorrow and rage. "My brother is dead. This creature is clever and has much of his memories, but it can only be a demon. For such black sorcery, Gaylon Reysson will pay, I swear by Mezon."

Thoughts in turmoil, Arlin listened to their exchange. Drugs, black sorcery. "What have you done?" he demanded of his elder brother, and found his tongue thick and sluggish. "You promised me safe passage."

"Demons are deceitful, and so a man may deal with them deceitfully."

"No, Markim. It's Tydus who deceives you. I'm your brother, not a demon."

"Stop your lies," Dorenson said, a thin smile on his lips.

"I was there. I saw it all."

"You saw nothing, you traitorous old man." Arlin looked at the priest. "Trust him, and you'll find a knife in your back one day."

"I trust no one but the god," Tek sneered and clapped his hands.

Two more priests entered the tent. These wore kilts and armor, and carried bared swords. The young Southerner fumbled for the hilt of his own, then jerked it clumsily from the scabbard. Markim caught his wrist in a hard grip.

"Give me this one small chance," Arlin begged him, "before I die."

"They don't want you dead. You're no good to them dead."

His brother twisted the weapon from Arlin's numb fingers, and Arlin, his arm heavy, still managed to slam a fist into the man's face hard enough to knock him back into the pillows. The warrior-priests darted forward.

Fear and outrage overcame the effects of Tek's drug. The Southerner snatched up his sword again, then turned on his knees and stabbed it into the tent's back wall. The blade ripped an opening through which he half-dived, half-fell. Hot sunlight glared off the salt-encrusted dirt and stung his eyes, and in every direction were canvas walls and clusters of Xenaran soldiers.

"Capture him!" Tek shouted. "I want him alive!"

Arlin scrambled to get his legs under him, then dodged to the right through the crowded tents. The ground seemed to roll slowly beneath his feet, the horizon tilting. A kilted man stepped in his path, long blade flashing silver. The Southerner drove his sword into an unprotected stomach before the soldier could raise his weapon. The dying man's scream turned every eye in Arlin's direction.

The jagged outline of the Grey Mountains beyond the Xenaran camp offered safety and freedom. Marten waited there, but here in the clouds of choking dust an entire army blocked the Southerner's way. He gazed along the rows of men that closed on him, and with mild regret, threw himself at the nearest.

His slashing sword very nearly forged a path. Yet the enemy had crowded too tightly, and those in the fore suffered most before Arlin's wrists were finally trapped. The weapon gone, he used teeth and feet until they bore him to the ground, and even then he fought. His hands were tightly bound behind him and his ankles as well, but, limbs numb, he felt nothing except the pressure of the ropes.

Bleeding from nose and mouth, Arlin D'Lelan was carried to the god's white pavilions and tied to a pole in the open front of one large tent. They left him there, alone with the heat and the dust and the shame. At last the poison took hold, weighing him down until his eyes closed. That drugged sleep spared him the anxiety and dread of what the future might bring.

* * * * *

Marten waited and watched. He witnessed the grand commotion in the afternoon sun, saw the crowds of soldiers, heard the distant angry shouts, but couldn't make out the cause. The day faded into dusk, and still the earl waited. By now, he had reasoned that Arlin D'Lelan had been the cause of the uproar in the enemy camp.

With just enough light left to find his way, Marten finally deserted his watch. He mounted his horse and headed back to his own camp, leading Arlin's animal. Self-recrimination helped very little. A true friend would never have let the Southerner go; a true friend would have gone with him. Helpless and miserable, the earl rode alone.

Sixteen

Karyl and Rinn arrived at the camp a short while after Marten. The pair was coated with mud from head to toe, bruised and bloody, but exuberant. They entered the earl's tent laughing and made a point of sharing the filth with their friend, giving him muddy claps on the shoulders.

"Ask us!" the royal cousin commanded. "Go on."

Marten found a camp chair and sat wearily, unaffected by their happiness. "All right. What happened?"

"We did it!" Karyl crowed. "We destroyed the windmills."

"Old Roffo's going to wake up with a terrible thirst tomorrow," Rinn added.

"Wait, wait, wait." The king's cousin danced a little jig under the oil lamps. "This is the stuff of legends. Four against twenty—"

"Fourteen," the tailor's son corrected him.

"But two were warrior-priests. They count for three apiece, at least. We were magnificent, Marten. I rode out with an arrow in me . . . well, it looked like I had one in me. And I fell off my horse—on purpose this time—and they all came out to see. That's when we got them. There was this ball of green fire, though—"

Rinn, his eyes on the earl, put a hand out to motion for silence. "What's wrong, Marten?"

The fourteenth earl of the Lower Vales closed his eyes.

"Arlin's gone. . . ."

"Where?" Karyl demanded.

"He disappeared out on the plain this afternoon."
Rinn found a seat. "You mean he's returned to
Xenara?"

"Not exactly. His brother called him down off the
mountain. The man promised Arlin safe passage to visit his
tent, and Arlin believed him. He never came back."

"Why didn't you stop him?" Karyl asked.

"I tried. . . ."

The royal cousin clenched his teeth. "Obviously not very
hard."

"Leave him alone," Rinn snapped. "Dear gods, what
can we do? How can we rescue him?"

"We can't," Marten muttered and buried his face in his
hands. "He's likely already dead."

"Who's going to tell the king?" Karyl groaned. "Not
me."

"Milord earl, I'm afraid there's another smaller problem." The tailor's son put a sympathetic hand on Marten's
shoulder.

"What now?"

"The water that was meant for Roffo's aqueducts had to
find somewhere else to go." The earl glanced up, eyes
wide, and Rinn continued. "There's seepage in the bottom
fields already, and it could get worse. I think the king's
lancers may have to move to higher ground."

Karyl looked forlorn. "I suppose this means no one's going to feel like putting our exploits to music."

His companions only glared at him.

* * * * *

"Hardly looks demonic to me," someone said. The familiar gravelly voice disturbed Arlin's stuporous slumber,
and a hand cupped his chin, pulling his head up. "If he

were a demon, could he be so easily caught or kept?"

"Does it matter what he is or is not?" the high priest asked testily. "The god has use for him."

Arlin opened heavy eyelids and tried to focus on the blurred image before him. Beyond the crouching figure was darkness, a dry windy night. Roffo, king of all Xenara, peered at the captive closely, smiling.

"You thought to be a traitor to Xenara. It's only fitting that you betray the Red King, instead." The old king pushed D'Lelan's face away roughly for emphasis, then straightened, knee joints creaking from weight and age. "I'm hungry, priest. Where is this wonderful feast you promised us?"

The king moved out of Arlin's line of vision. Behind the young Southerner, someone clapped their hands. A gong sounded, reverberating a great distance through the encampment. Servants appeared from out of the night to bring platters into the well-lit tent. The scent of food made the prisoner's stomach lurch, made him aware of a great thirst.

Others arrived to partake of the meal, some on foot, some on horseback—all men in the uniforms of high commanders within the Xenaran military and those in the equally gaudy dress of other nations. Most ignored Arlin's presence, even Markim, who arrived late, dressed in a rich tunic of dark blue silk.

Tied so he could see only the night beyond the pavilion, the Southerner dozed fitfully. Occasional bursts of laughter or angry shouts startled him awake.

"How sweet he sleeps." This time the voice that woke him was feminine, speaking in slightly broken and thickly accented Xenaran. Fingers stroked his cheek, though he felt nothing but the pressure against that senseless flesh.

Another voice, male, chided in another tongue. Arlin opened his eyes finally on a dark-skinned woman in nomadic garb squatting before him. The fur-clad woman offered him a feral smile that revealed teeth filed into sharp points. A Noro warrior-woman. So . . . even the eastern tribes had taken up arms against Wynnamyr.

She glanced up at her male companion. "This one is pretty. I will make trade for him."

"Too thin, no meat," the man said in Xenaran.

Arlin licked his lips with a dry tongue. This was their crude notion of a jape, and so they spoke in words he'd understand. He answered with the only phrase in the Noro language he knew—learned from Luka, the horsemaster— which graphically disparaged their mating rituals. The woman spat on him, but her companion drove a hardened bare foot into the Southerner's side. Pain blossomed, bright and sharp, but the two tormentors were gone when next Arlin opened his eyes.

The feast continued, the servants bringing platter after platter of exotic delicacies. Arlin listened to the exchange of battle tactics, the interpreters translating strategy. This was a victory feast before the war was even fought. Arlin concentrated as best he could on the conversations; it helped to keep his mind off the pain and thirst. Such information might aid the Red King . . . but, no, it would never be delivered. He pulled at the cords on his wrists. They were far too tight, and no amount of work would loosen them.

Sometime later a pair of muscular brown legs moved in front of him. The Southerner tilted his head back as best he could in order to better see.

"Little brother," Markim muttered, the consonants gently slurred. The wine and ale had been flowing freely at this meal. He squatted there near Arlin and spoke, voice kept low. "Understand, if they wish to name you demon, that's not for me to gainsay. I obey my superiors, as I must. Here." He held a cup of cool water to his brother's lips and let him drink.

"Thank you." Arlin trapped the man's eyes with his

own. "Tek says the god has use of me. How so?"

"It's best you don't know. . . ."

"If they think to use me somehow to destroy Gaylon Reysson, I'll stop them."

"How can you?" growled Markim.

"With your help. Please," the younger brother implored. "Cut these ropes and give me your dagger."

"So you can do what? There's nowhere for you to run."

"I don't intend to run," the Southerner whispered, desperate, and his brother's gaze at last faltered.

In the darkness beyond the tent, they could hear the beat of a horse's hoofs, the animal hard-ridden and approaching from the east. A cloud of dust arrived before it, driven on a gust of wind.

"Markim," Arlin pleaded in an low tone, but the man gave a bare shake of his head and rose. A Xenaran soldier shoved his way roughly past a group of servants who had paused in the wide entrance.

"Your Highness!"

The diners quieted, and the king snapped in ill-humor, "What brings you to disrupt our meal so rudely?"

"Lord Kedry has sent me, Sire. He says the water has failed. The aqueducts are dry and the windmills beyond repair."

Roffo cursed bitterly for a moment, and Arlin felt a touch of pride in his brave comrades, but that was short lived.

"Tell Lord Kedry," the elderly monarch said in a grand tone, "that his diligence is appreciated and will be rewarded. Now go away, and let us eat in peace."

The soldier returned to his horse with only a cursory glance at the prisoner as he passed. Within the tent, the feast resumed. Markim had disappeared. Arlin contemplated this strange unconcern for the rider's report. An army of this size without water in the heat of summer should be reason enough for panic. Unless they counted the war already won.

Heavy footsteps paused off to the left, and the Southerner craned his head to see Tek and Roffo standing just outside the fall of the light from the lanterns, perhaps in search of quieter, cooler air.

"A plague on the filthy Wynnamyrans," the king rumbled. "Did they have to destroy my mills?"

Tek stared out into the night. "The mills mean nothing."

"To you, perhaps. They took years to design and build, not to mention a great deal of money. What of my water income?"

"In your wisdom," the high priest said, his attention on the observant Arlin, "I'm certain you'll find a way to repair at least one mill with parts from the others. And as for income, when water is scarce, its profitability grows proportionate. True?"

The old king grunted. "Aye."

"Go back to your guests, Sire. Entertain and advise them. Make certain that each nation knows its part in the whole. Tomorrow will find us finally at war."

Tek didn't follow Roffo, but came instead to stand over his captive. Arlin, head aching dully, let his chin drop once more to his chest.

"Do you know what happens to a man's hands if his wrists are tied too tightly for too long?" The priest's robes fluttered around his ankles in a stiff ground breeze. When the young man at his feet refused to respond, Tek continued. "The hands blacken and die, literally rot. The suffering is long and terrible and ends in death unless the limbs are amputated. But you mustn't worry. Mezon is merciful—in his own way.

"If you must blame anyone for your misfortune, blame the king of Wynnamyr. A man by nature is mortal and granted only one life. Your second life is an abomination to the god, and you'll live only so long as you serve him."

"Then kill me now," Arlin said, jaw tight. "Because I'll never serve Mezon."

The high priest laughed, a sweet, gentle sound that belied his words. "You're serving him at this moment, D'Lelan. And tomorrow, with the dawn, after a night spent fighting the waters that flood the Lower Vales, the Wynnamyran army will find itself beset by an invincible force." He nudged Arlin's leg with the toe of a sandal. "You'll witness, firsthand, the death of the sorcerer-king, Gaylon Reysson. Then I'll personally sacrifice you to the god so that your soul may serve him for all eternity."

Fear made the Southerner's heart thud hard in his chest. He closed his eyes and forced himself to let go of the anguish. Bound and helpless, there was nothing else to do. As Tek moved away, an odd peace settled over Arlin and he looked up.

"You've planned everything so well, priest," he said, actually smiling. "But better to ask again for your god's protection. Tomorrow, it may be *you* serving him for all eternity."

Perhaps it was the wavering shadows from the lanterns or a trick of his tired mind, but D'Lelan thought he saw a momentary doubt flicker across the old priest's face.

*   *   *   *   *

They had ridden all day, and Gaylon was suddenly anxious to reach the Lower Vales. By nightfall, there were but three leagues to cover in order to reach the encampment. A fat slice of moon had risen early. With its light to show them the road, the king and his young duke continued on. Their meal, taken on horseback, consisted of stale bread and dried fruit.

The northern valleys were uninhabited, the farm dwellings along the coach road dark and deserted. Gaylon led them through a narrow gap in the coastal mountains that opened finally on the third and largest vale. Here things were anything but peaceful. Distant shouted orders came to them on the night wind, and swinging lanterns showed movement out among the fields—too much movement.

It took a moment before the king realized that the lantern light was being reflected back up from the ground.

"There's water all over," Davi said, confusion in his voice. "The field's are flooded. What happened?"

"Let's find out," Gaylon growled and kicked his mare into a gallop along the rutted road.

Davi followed as quickly as possible, hindered by the pack horse that tried to lag behind. In several places their mounts sloshed through puddles where the flooding had found access to the higher roadbed. The two travelers went unnoticed and unchallenged all the way through the huge camp until their way was blocked by a team of horses struggling to drag a loaded wagon onto the narrow highway.

"You there!" the king called.

The driver ignored him, but the soaked and mud-splattered man at the team's head paused to look up.

"Sire!" he cried, and managed a clumsy obeisance with one hand tangled in the harness.

"Where's all this water coming from?" Gaylon demanded.

"The aqueducts, milord. The earl had the enemy's water supply cut off, but none realized this would happen."

Behind the king, Davi laughed until both Gaylon and the soldier turned to stare at him.

"Is there some way to stop the flooding?" the king asked.

"No one knows. There ain't been time to find out."

"Then point me in the direction of the earl's tent."

"That way, Sire." The fellow stabbed a thumb over his shoulder. "His tent was on high ground to begin with, so he ain't had to move."

Gaylon nodded, then led the duke down into the water

and past the mired wagon. Marten Pelson had found a tree-shaded knoll on which to pitch his tent. From this small vantage, the young earl might watch over the entire encampment. Davi secured the horses to one of the lower limbs of an alder tree while the king went into the lighted tent.

Sheepskin maps lay scattered on a low, crudely made table and on the hard-packed soil that served as the floor. Weapons and bedrolls were stacked against a canvas wall at the rear, everything viewed in the unsteady glow of a single hanging oil lamp. Other than a preferred location, the earl and his tent-mate, Arlin, lived as thriftily as common soldiers. Davi came through the door flap, a set of heavy saddlebags over his shoulder.

"It's too late to set up our own gear, right?" The young duke grinned. "Even if we could find someplace dry . . ."

"There's hardly room for four of us in here, but we'll manage," Gaylon agreed, and his gaze snagged on the ancient two-edged sword that hung at the boy's wide belt.

To see the weapon always so close at hand, to see it within Davi's easy reach, had worried the king at first, but the duke continued to handle Kingslayer respectfully. All these years, Gaylon had fought the urge to take Orym's Legacy in hand and feel that rush of incredible power, but an odd relief had come when he'd given the weapon into Davi's keeping. Kingslayer no longer had so strong a hold over the Red King.

"How tired are you, lad?" Gaylon asked and sat down on a rickety camp chair.

"Not very."

The king smiled at that earnest lie. "Find me Marten Pelson, then. Or Arlin. We'll have to figure a solution to our problems soon or put our army in boats. Best leave the sword or you could sink out there in the fields."

"Milord, please," Davi said quickly, a vague alarm in his voice. "I don't feel the weight. Really. Honestly."

"All right, go on. Make it quick."

But at that moment Marten ducked in through the flap, face red with exertion, breeches soaked and muddied to the knees.

"Milord," he said breathlessly and bowed. "I heard you had arrived."

"Marten," Gaylon laughed. "What have you done?"

"A stupid miscalculation, Sire. The blame lies directly with me in this."

"Yes, but still, there's far more merit than blame, I think. Given a few dry days, our foe may be forced to pack up their mighty army and leave—not to mention the hardship you'll have caused Zankos and Katay." The king raised a brow. "Now, tell me. Have you found a way to save our own army from the floods?"

The earl nodded, expression abject. "The Xenaran slaves, when the aqueducts were first constructed, redirected the headwaters of the South Fork in order to supply the windmill pumps. I've sent Karyl and Rinn back to the mills with enough men to undo much of the rest of Roffo's handiwork, but it'll take most of the night." He sank down onto a nearby chair. "It was complete idiocy on my part to fail to recognize the consequences of my earlier orders."

"No matter." Gaylon leaned forward to pound a fist gently on his friend's wet knee. "You may have diverted a war, and for that I'll forgive almost anything. Where's Arlin? Has he gone digging with our comrades?"

Marten's reaction brought a sudden cold fear to the king's chest. The earl stared at the dirt beneath his chair, and all color had drained from his face.

"Sire . . . Arlin went into the Xenaran camp this afternoon and never returned. I fear he's dead."

Gaylon had risen to his feet without realizing it. Blue light filled the tent, but he hardly noticed.

"Milord, no!" Despite the danger, the earl had blocked His Majesty's path, even dared to brace a shoulder against the taller man.

The king struck him violently, a forearm across Marten's ear. The blow propelled the earl sideways into a soft canvas wall. Davi appeared, shouting. His hands clutched Gaylon's right wrist, but the king flung him off easily. Clear thought seemed impossible for Gaylon. He found his horse beside the tree, then was somehow mounted, already headed at a dangerous gallop toward the Sea Pass.

Arlin lost. Arlin dead. And all the while, the king lamented, I was aware of nothing except my own aching body and travel exhaustion. No, it wasn't possible for D'Lelan to pass again from this life without feeling that loss instantly. Under Gaylon, the tired mare began to wheeze, but he pushed her on recklessly, even over the rocky floor of the pass.

"Halt and identify yourself!" someone shouted from above. "Halt!"

Heedless, Gaylon went on, but another shouted from behind: "Don't fire! It's the king! The king!" Davi, unwanted and unneeded, had followed.

A thin fog drifted in off the ocean, and the cold, moist air cleared Gaylon's head minutely, enough for him to realize that he'd started down the rocky slopes where the coach road led out onto the plain. The mare had had her head too long and fought his pull on the reins, but he got her under control and headed back up the mountain.

The duke of Gosney waited at the top of the grade, barely visible in the faint starlight. All around the pair, the fog thickened. Wordlessly Gaylon paused beside the boy and listened to the harsh breathing of the winded horses. There must be something a sorcerer-king could do—to save a friend, to win a war.

"Do you see?" Davi said suddenly, his voice strange in the wet air.

Gaylon followed the silhouette of one arm pointed north and west. In the black sky, a rich blue glow soared toward them, then winked out.

"What was it?" the boy asked, awed. "A falling star?"

The king dismounted and walked along a vaguely worn path, down a steep slope, caring little if Davi trailed behind. On a rocky outcropping, Gaylon stopped. The Xenara Plain spread out below, and the lights of fires and lanterns were scattered more thickly than the stars above. A stiff wind arrived out of nowhere to buffet him, but he knew its source already.

The churning air stilled at last, and Sezran stepped out of the shadows, chuckling.

"You've chosen an excellent vantage point. And your enemy is impressive, to say the least."

"Go away, old man."

"Don't be rude. I've come to help you conquer the world, as you once asked me to do."

"I have no desire to conquer this or any other world."

"With Kingslayer in hand, you'll change your mind."

Gaylon opened his mouth to deny that, but realized his resolve was slipping again. He looked back over the plain. "They've taken him. The priests of Mezon have Arlin."

"The one you restored to life? Then perhaps your sacrifice will not be necessary after all. Tomorrow is the summer solstice."

"What sacrifice?" Davi demanded from the rocks above them. He paused at the sight of Sezran. "Who's that with you, milord?"

"Keep quiet, old man," the king warned, irritated by the sorcerer's amused laughter. "Go back to the horses, Davi, and wait."

The boy kept on, stumbling over loose stones in the darkness. As soon as Davi halted, only steps away, Sezran's eyes grew huge and his Stone took on a deep blue glitter.

"What's that on your belt, child?" When the duke drew back a little, the wizard turned a sly smile on Gaylon. "You gave the sword to a boy to carry? You're a greater fool than I thought, Gaylon Reysson. Give it to me, child. Now!"

Davi backed farther up the slope, the weapon on his hip held away from Sezran.

"Stop, lad," the king commanded. "Hand him the sword."

"Sire!"

"Do it."

Careful as always, the young duke unhooked the blade from his belt, fingers only on the scabbard. Cackling, the old sorcerer grabbed the hilt. Blue-gold light flared brilliantly, and Sezran shrieked. Kingslayer struck the stones, still an ugly, ancient two-edged sword.

"I told you, I ensorceled the weapon." Gaylon laughed sourly. "My powers are far greater than yours, old man."

"Not so great as Mezon's, I think." Furious, the wizard stood nursing his hand. "But I'll be kind, yet. At dawn, the enemy attacks. They've stockpiled water to last them long enough to defeat you, which won't be long with your army exhausted from lack of rest. That much I could learn, though the secrets of the priests are well kept." He glared at Davi, who crept forward to claim the sword. "If Arlin D'Lelan is dead, your debt is paid. If he is not, he'll be used against you, and you'll still be forced to make the sacrifice."

"I'll Dream myself into their camp and find Arlin," the king said, his eyes once more on the lights below.

"Yes. Do that. The priests are hoping for just such foolishness on your part. Listen to me, Red King. Their magic is different from ours, drawn from a different source, but all the more dangerous for our lack of understanding." The winds began to roil again, and Sezran's black robes fluttered against the black of the night.

"You asked my help," the wizard said, "and I have given it, though only to please myself. I'll be here tomorrow to watch you suffer, to see you bring death and destruction to everything you love. Finally, when Kingslayer melts the flesh from your bones, I'll claim what is rightfully mine."

"You'll have no—" Gaylon snapped, but Sezran was gone. "You'll have no use of it!" the young man shouted into the dark sky.

Davi sat huddled against the rocks, the sword caught snug against his body by his raised knees. He looked up. "What sacrifice, milord?"

"That's none of your concern," the king snarled and stepped around him to climb the slope. "Come on. If war comes with first light, then we'd best be ready."

* * * * *

When at last the feast had ended, the guests dispersed and the lights doused, Arlin began a serious attempt at freeing himself. The task proved impossible. He found the knots at his wrist, but without the sense of touch to guide him, he couldn't decide if they were loosening. His hands grew ominously slick. Sweat, he told himself, and knew different. This was blood, though no pain had warned him. Finally, weak and exhausted, the young Southerner gave up the fight and slept again.

An unknown while later, the priests, four of them in short white tunics, came to awaken him with lanterns and soft touches. They cut the ropes that bound him to the pole, then the ones at his wrists and ankles. When they caught him at shoulders and legs and lifted him, Arlin struggled feebly.

"I'll walk on my own, you bastards."

They ignored him, bearing him to another pavilion with light glowing faintly through the white material. Within, Arlin saw rich, thick carpets and low tables and chairs of finely wrought hardwoods. The priests of Mezon began to sing, a low, wordless harmony of such beauty that it brought a strange peaceful lethargy to their captive. They bathed him in cool water like an infant, first stripping off his clothes and laying him on a table. Even his hair was washed. He slapped at the soapy sponges for a time, but his hands were caught in firm grips while the blood and dirt were cleaned away.

The tattered, raw flesh of his wrists was anointed with a yellowish unguent. All the while the priests' song continued sweetly. The Southerner glanced down at his body and saw the spreading purple blotch across the left side of his ribs from the Noro tribesman's kick. The pain had diminished to a dull ache.

Long white robes of sackcloth were brought. Once more, Arlin resisted, but to no avail. He was forcibly dressed in the garb of an acolyte priest.

"So the god likes his sacrifices clean and tidy," the prisoner observed disdainfully. At least his tongue wasn't numb. "You dung-eating geldings will find *yourselves* the sacrifices if Gaylon Reysson takes up Kingslayer."

Gently the four priests carried him to a wooden platform—a litter of sorts, only without a chair—that sat in the shadows near the back wall. His wrists and ankles were once more lashed, but to the four corners of the litter. The lights went out, and the song ended as his captors left the tent. Alone, Arlin stared into the darkness above him, furious at his own stupidity and helplessness.

*   *   *   *   *

Within Castlekeep, Jessmyn woke at first light from a terrible dream of Gaylon engulfed in flames under a summer sky. The queen's desolate sobs brought Misk to the bedside, but the vision had been so vivid, so real, that not even the tiny woman could console her.

Seventeen

Even before the first pale glow of dawn, the Xenaran army and their allies were in motion. They had waited months for this moment, and while the night had been spent in celebration, morning found every man in his proper place, armed and ready for battle. Standing at the entrance to his pavilion, Tek watched the orderly chaos and listened to the tramp of hoof and boot over the plain.

They came by lots of one thousand, each led by an over-captain. Squadrons of Turvians and Xenarans stood at the fore, Benjirans and Shaltish next, then, in lesser numbers, the mercenaries, Noro warriors, and the three smallest nations of Reegar, Felwyn, and Tesik. The priests of Mezon had gathered near their pavilions, awaiting Tek's command.

The wind had died earlier, yet a great cloud of dust now rose on the morning air, fired a deep pink by the rising sun. Tek smiled benignly at the foot soldiers as they marched in orderly columns past his encampment. Such a beautiful summer day as this could only bring victory and glory to Mezon.

A strange murmur rumbled through the troops massing near the coach road. The high priest turned his gaze to the narrow gap at the top of the mountain's steep grade. There, in a ragged silhouette against the deeper shadows of the Sea Pass, stood a line of Wynnamyran soldiers, bristling with pikes. So . . . the element of surprise had somehow been lost.

Tek didn't let that trouble him overmuch. He regarded the enemy perched high above and felt a delicious anticipation. Let them try to block the pass, nowise could they hold back the Xenaran horde for long.

Near the center of his vast army, Roffo, round body packed into gaudy armor, sat astride a white horse. The huge, docile animal was led by two handlers. Two flag bearers, also on horses, rode to either side—as much to deflect any blows aimed at His Majesty as to hold the colors high and signal the over-captains. Tydus Dorenson, resplendent in red robes, sat an excellent gray steed just behind Roffo.

The king of Xenara threw his head back and bellowed a challenge to the enemy soldiers above. The flag bearers pointed their banners toward the pass, and with a roar, the first battalion of soldiers moved forward as one, eager for blood.

And the blood came . . . all too soon. From the Wynnamyran army there was an answering shout. Then a multitude of arrows arced into the sky, flashing in the early sunlight. A deadly hail of feathered shafts descended on Roffo's forces. The screams told the king and the high priest just how accurate was the enemy's aim. Men and horses both went down thrashing as volley after volley was launched from above.

Roffo signaled his own archers, but most of their arrows fell well short of the mark. Tek saw the futility of their efforts and at last shouted to his warrior-priests. Voices raised, they began a song of power, calling the god's fire. The gaseous green mass drifted above the Xenaran army and into the path of the enemy arrows. The next volley fell through Mezon's emerald fire, turning to bright sparks that died before ever they struck the ground.

The Wynnamyran archers adjusted their aim thereafter,

some firing high, some low, with almost as deadly effect as before. Angry, Tek called to his priests, and their song altered, grew strident. Now the godfire drifted toward the pass. The enemy stood fast until almost the last fatal moment, then broke and ran deeper into the narrow channel of stone.

With a great cry of rage, the Xenaran horde swarmed up the slopes, climbing swiftly past each loop of the coach road. The high priest directed the singers to follow the army's first wave up the mountain, then motioned to his eight attendants to bring the litters from the pavilion.

Arlin D'Lelan, bound to the platform of one, blinked in the light and turned his head. The dead and dying lay scattered over the salty ground, too numerous to count. Wynnamyr's arrows had taken mostly the horses and the unarmored squires, but the damage was done. The pale young Southerner laughed, a harsh almost hysterical amusement that infuriated Tek. He grabbed the man's lower jaw, and the laughter died.

"Count the moments of your life precious, D'Lelan. There're very few of them left." The high priest had gained his captive's full attention with these words. "And death will not bring freedom. Not this time. For you there'll be an eternity of suffering and servitude to a just, if cruel, god."

Arlin stared at him with sober, dark eyes. "Perhaps I should pray for Mezon's forgiveness, then." His lips quirked. "But I won't. Look around you, priest. Your god of the dung heap doesn't care for you, only for the death you reap in his name. He uses you, and when he's done, your fate will be no better than mine."

Tek's fingers clenched tighter, a slow rage burning in his gut. His other hand found the dagger at his belt, and without thinking, he raised the blade. D'Lelan's eyes widened slightly, and he grinned. That gave the old priest pause.

"You dare not do it," the young man taunted, "high

priest of offal, who serves a carrion god."

"Clever," Tek muttered and watched Arlin's grin fade.
"You've been consecrated to Mezon, but your sacrifice will
come at his command, not my whim."

The high priest climbed into his shaded chair nearby and
snapped his fingers at the attendants. They moved out
with both litters, well behind the other priests. There were
many litters on the field now, the injured being gathered
for removal to the hospital tents, the dead gathered for the
funeral pyres.

Shouts of rage continued in the pass above, while the
song of the priests grew muted with distance. Overhead,
the sun gained strength. In other encampments, the second Xenaran legion waited impatiently, convinced that
their predecessors would have the war won all too soon.
They would join the conflict at midday, whether needed or
not, with the third and fourth legions to back them up if
necessary.

Tydus Dorenson had related all he knew about the Wynnamyran forces to Tek—their strengths and weaknesses, as
well as a fairly accurate count of the soldiers. How long
could it take to overcome a mere three or four thousand
men and corner Gaylon Reysson, Sorcerer's Stone or no?
Kingslayer or no? That young monarch had already felt
Mezon's wrath once, but there was far worse in store. Far
worse.

*   *   *   *   *

Gaylon Reysson, in chain mail and half armor, watched
the progress of the godfire from horseback. Around him,
Wynnamyran soldiers fled to safety.

"Milord!" Davi shouted above the madness, his mount
already turned for flight. He, too, wore chain mail, cuirass,
and helm.

In the turmoil, those men who stumbled or failed to

move quickly were swallowed by the glistening green cloud, their screams of agony cut swiftly short. Charred bodies littered the stone floor of the pass and the ledges above. Gaylon, desperate, stared into his Sorcerer's Stone, and it answered with blue fire of its own. Fire to fight fire, then. This would still bring death to those that stood between, though. Must a few die in order to save many?

The king dismounted suddenly and fought his way against the crush of men and horses. Behind him, the duke of Gosney called out, panic in his voice.

"Sire, wait! Sire!"

"Stay back," Gaylon cried. "Get clear!"

The godfire rolled mindlessly over the rocks, and the king drew a deep breath, then held it as the searing heat enveloped him. Instantaneously, the Stone on his finger erupted with its own blue wave of fire that swept through and consumed the green until nothing of either remained. The sun had not yet cleared the high stone wall, but in the milky, smoky shadows, Gaylon looked out across the blackened remains of his men and saw a tide of Xenaran infantry flooding into the mouth of the pass.

Standing alone, he raised both fists above his head and tapped the seething rage within that he'd so long despised. When his Stone answered again, the king of Wynnamyr threw open his hands. A small blue sun exploded into existence and flashed toward the enemy. He heard the priests' song rise above the uproar, and, just as his fire had negated the god's, so the god's now negated his. Furious, Gaylon tried again and again, each time thwarted by Mezon's roiling green flames. Then a well-sent arrow struck his iron cuirass and another skinned the side of a greave.

"To the king! To the king!" The shout echoed off rock walls.

Davi arrived with Gaylon's horse, followed closely by Karyl's swordsmen and Marten's mounted lancers. The boy had his own sword drawn, Kingslayer fastened tightly over the pommel of his saddle. The mare stood trembling while the king mounted and drew his own weapon.

Midpoint in the pass, the armies finally clashed. Gaylon turned on the duke as the struggle crowded close around them.

"Get back to Rinn. Stay with the archers."

"No, milord," Davi said and, lightning quick, chopped at the exposed neck of an enemy soldier who had just run a vale peasant through. The boy's blade opened the man's flesh to the bone, but the soldier only clamped a mailed hand to the blood that pumped freely. With his dying strength, he swung his sword at the duke. Gaylon finished Davi's work for him with a stroke that severed head from shoulders. Blood gouted and splattered them both as the body fell.

"Obey me," the king snarled through his teeth. "Get back!"

"Only if you come with me." Davi swung his blade up suddenly and cried, "Behind you, Sire!"

Peripheral vision impaired by his helm, Gaylon caught only a glimpse of an enemy pike stabbing in low from the side, it's point sharp enough to open the mail that covered his lower back. Frantic, the duke charged to his lord's aid, but his gelding swung suddenly sideways into the king's mare, who in turn backed into and over the pike wielder. Two Wynnamyran swordsmen were swept off their feet, as well.

Marten appeared on a tall red horse, a bloody lance in hand.

"Sire, leave the field!" the earl cried. "You mustn't remain in harm's way."

A fierce grin lit Davi's face to hear his king so rebuked, and Gaylon gritted his teeth. "I'll leave when this battle's won," he shouted back. "Not before."

Angry, Marten Pelson turned and drove his mount into a little group of Xenarans that was advancing on the king.

Gaylon flung up his shield to ward off a sword stroke from the left. This was madness—to fight in such close quarters with so little room to move or breath, or even time to think. The tightly packed phalanxes of men battled to gain ground, and for a while, neither did. Beside the king, Davi fought with youthful energy and uncanny skill. To send the boy behind the lines was impossible now, even if he would agree to go. The northern troops had closed in around their monarch in an attempt to protect him, but had cut off any retreat, as well.

The king found he had no desire for retreat, only for revenge. Xenara had taken Arlin, so they would pay. The blood and gore released a lifetime's inner rage, and Gaylon welcomed it. He'd always felt a shameless joy in destruction and death, even as a boy.

Here in the pass, locked in this struggle, the razor-sharp sword became an extension of his arm and hand, with its own heightened sense of touch. Each kill brought an ecstasy; each taste of blood only made him crave more. This was the reason he must refuse Kingslayer and why he longed to take it in hand. Such murderous abandon would only bring destruction on them all.

His mount tight against Gaylon's, but facing the opposite direction, the duke of Gosney brought his own fair share of death to the enemy and seemed to enjoy the carnage no less than his king. This troubled Gaylon, though there was little time for contemplation. Whenever he could spare a glance, the king searched the melee for some sign of the priests of Mezon and found none. Neither had he heard their song. This troubled him also.

The sun climbed toward midday, beaming directly down into the pass. Soon the heat became a bane to the armored men. The king, drenched in sweat, caught sight of his cousin, on foot and helmless, his carroty hair visible briefly in the throng. A sudden trumpet blast from the south heralded some change, one that would most likely not benefit

he Wynnamyrans. Every warrior on the field paused a
beat, then returned to the grim task of survival.

The cries of anger, of pain and despair, were suddenly
drowned beneath another collective shout. On horseback
and on foot, a new Xenaran force poured up into the
mouth of the pass. The northerners tried to stand fast, but
the press of bodies drove them back. Gaylon, fighting to
control the mare under him, lost track of the enemy until
almost too late.

A heavy metal-shanked pike drove at him from the fore.
Without thought, the king jerked back on the reins, and
his mount reared. The pike took her deep in the chest, and
the poor animal came down hard, striking the enemy sol-
lier. Groaning, she staggered a step, then her knees bucked. The king fought clear as the mare collapsed.

When a weaponless hand reached out to him, Gaylon
very nearly swung his blade, only to realize it belonged to
Davi. The boy shouted something, unheard in the uproar.
All around them, the king's men were in rout. Gaylon
sheathed his bloody sword and, locking his mailed fingers
together, took the duke's proffered arm, dragging himself
onto the back of Davi's horse. The boy put the spurs to his
animal.

The foe, in overpowering numbers, began a systematic
slaughter of the forward guard. Nothing could stop them.
The battle very nearly lost, the Wynnamyran army ran for
the vales, their dead and many of the badly wounded left
behind. Gaylon Reysson and the duke of Gosney led the
retreat.

*   *   *   *   *

The tailor's son had not been idle. Many of his archers
were as handy with a sword as a bow, and these had joined
the king in the pass. The rest, nearly five hundred men,
were stationed in the wooded foothills on either side of the

coach road. Rinn had exceptional foresight as well as eye-
sight. All through the morning, his archers fretted at their
posts, but in this tightly fought battle, their skills were useless.

From his well-placed position above the northern mouth
of the pass, the tailor's son could see a little of the battle
within, but it was impossible to tell which army was winning. He saw the king once, the red scarf on his helm
bright in the sunlight, until the crush of men carried him
from sight.

Noon brought the disaster Rinn so dreaded. The pierc-
ing call of a trumpet came first, then another division of
Roffo's army swarmed into the pass to force the Wynnamyrans to withdraw.

A tiny reed whistle had earlier been tied to one of his
arrows, and this he shot into the air. Its scream alerted the
archers hidden among the rocks and trees. They watched,
heartsick, as friends and neighbors ran or staggered past,
exhausted, only steps ahead of the enemy. The king and
Davi shared a horse and rode the doubly laden animal at a
run along the road. Karyl and Marten came after them. For
the survival of his friends, Rinn spent a brief moment in
thanksgiving.

As the first of the Xenarans cleared the stone walls of the
pass, the Wynnamyran archers opened fire, glad for revenge. At dawn they had killed thousands in this manner,
and so it was again. Cruelty could not be a consideration
here. The men shot down the horses, the riders, and the
foot soldiers, all caught in the crossfire. This slaughter far
surpassed the one on the Xenara Plain. Five hundred determined archers firing from hidden positions in the foothills
above turned the tide—at least for a time. From the priests
of Mezon there came no rebuke.

With the enemy held at bay, Rinn trotted on foot back to
the vale. Their camp had been moved to higher ground
among the trees during the night, and, while water no

longer stood in the fields, they were still thick with mud. The roadbed was scattered with bodies. Many men had died along the way without ever reaching the tents, and the tailor's son tried to shrug off the sorrow. Better to number the living than the dead.

He found Marten crouched beside the road, his sweated horse standing nearby. The earl's face was bloody from a long gash over an eye, and he'd discarded his weapons to crouch near a fallen man. The young lancer had lost an arm and still managed somehow to make his way this far. The greenish-white luster of the man's skin made Rinn certain of his fate.

The earl glanced up. "Find a surgeon. Hurry."

It was already too late. The lancer slipped quietly into death. Cursing, Marten stood.

"He was a farmer, not a soldier. I grew up with him."

"You should rest, milord," the tailor's son said, "while you have the chance."

"Where's the king?"

"I haven't found him yet."

The earl pressed a weary hand to Rinn's shoulder. "We've got to talk him out of fighting. He's mad to put himself at risk."

"And inspirational. You won't find old Roffo leading his men." The tailor's son glanced at the body on the road, the blood still leeching slowly into the dirt. "What we have to do is talk him into using Orym's Legacy."

"He won't. We can't ask that of him."

"How long do you think we can hold them back?" Rinn demanded. "We don't have the arrows to mount another mass attack. Those we do have won't last much longer. I think we've done fairly well, considering. Our soldiers have slaughtered nearly three-quarters of the forces the enemy's sent against us so far. But they'll only send more. How many men have we left?"

"I don't know." Marten rubbed a hand over his eyes.

"We've lost at least half."

Rinn sighed. "You and I, milord, will either soon be dead . . . or swearing fealty to another king with swords at our throats."

"*I'll* be dead," the earl said, his jaw tight.

"Well, I'd rather be neither. I'm going to do what I can to get His Majesty to use Kingslayer. Let's find your tent, so you can rest."

"We can't leave him. . . ." Marten gazed at the dead man.

"We must, for now anyway. We've left far more behind in the pass." The tailor's son shifted the bow and quiver on his shoulder. "Davi and the king are likely at your tent already."

Fortunately the tent was close, because Marten insisted on stopping to encourage, and commiserate with, every band of soldiers along the way. Rinn followed, his mind elsewhere. A glance up showed him a beautiful summer sky, with the tops of the trees rustling in the hot, dry breeze. It somehow made the war seem distant . . . until he looked down again and found the dirt stained with blood.

* * * * *

Near Marten's shaded tent on the knoll, the king dismounted Davi's horse from behind. The duke slowly swung his right leg over the back of the saddle and dropped to the ground. Immediately Gaylon shed his cuirass and chain mail, desperate to let the cool air beneath the trees reach his sweat-soaked skin. There were a hundred little itches that demanded scratching. Davi pulled his gloves off, his movements stiff and slow.

"Here, let me help," the king said shortly and began to unbuckle Davi's cuirass, then knelt to loosen the greaves that protected the boy's shins. The right one had trapped a great deal of blood. "You've been injured. . . ."

The duke of Gosney ignored the accusatory tone. "A pike thrust. The mail parted, but the wound isn't deep."

"It's bled awfully well for not being deep. Get the chain mail off so I can better look."

The hauberk, its broken links thick with coagulating blood, was also shed, and Gaylon ordered the boy to seat himself on a small, rounded boulder in the shaded grass. There the man tore the one leg of Davi's breeches up to the wound in the thigh.

"Not deep," the king snarled. "You might have bled to death."

"It always looks like more blood than it is," Davi countered.

"Well, this is all the excuse I need to send you to the surgeons."

"No," said the duke, resolute.

"No to what?" Karyl asked, making his weary way to the top of the knoll, his own armor carried awkwardly in both arms. He eyed Davi's leg. "That looks nasty. Better have it taken care of." The king's cousin dropped his load with a crash and caught up a water flask beside the tent, then sank to the ground while taking a long drink.

"There're bandages here." The duke stood up. "I can wrap the leg as well as any gods-forsaken surgeon."

From behind Davi, the tailor's son and Marten Pelson trudged into view over the hillock, leading a single horse.

"Rinn! Marten!" Karyl, despite his exhaustion, leaped back to his feet and rushed toward the two men.

"Brilliant ambush," the royal cousin told Rinn and gave him a quick slap on the shoulder. "That had to be your idea."

Embarrassed, Rinn nodded. Marten silently found the water flask and drank deeply, then began to peel off his armor.

The king, his attention momentarily diverted from the insolent duke, agreed with Karyl. "You diverted disaster

with that clever ploy, Rinn—first baron of Greenwood.
And this time you can't refuse my offer."

"I'm too tired to refuse, Sire." The lanky blond man
found a seat in the trampled grass. "But I haven't diverted
disaster, only postponed it—and not for long. Our supply
of arrows is nearly spent. After that—"

"After that," Marten said dully, settling beside Rinn,
"the vales become the battleground."

An elderly man arrived at the tent with a pot of venison
stew, which was placed on the ground near His Majesty.
Bowing, the old fellow left them. Across the small area,
Gaylon noticed Davi determinedly wrapping his own leg.

"Not too tight," the king snapped and glanced at the
others. "We should eat something if we're to have energy
to fight."

No one moved. They hadn't even the energy to eat. All
around them, campfires crackled and smoked under the
trees that lined the valley. Exhausted men in bloody, ragged clothing clustered near their tents. Gaylon finally allowed himself the luxury of sitting. To see his friends
assembled here only made him all the more aware of
Arlin's absence.

"We knew from the beginning that we had little
chance," the king muttered. "That we've survived this
long is a miracle. Does anyone have a suggestion on how we
should face this next attack?"

Rinn raised his head. "With Orym's Legacy, Sire."

The ugly sword still hung from the duke's saddle. "If I
do," Gaylon began, "there'll be so much more death and
devastation. . . . You can't begin to understand. Orym ex-
terminated not just his enemies, but his own army as well.
I've felt his madness, preserved by Kingslayer. I don't want
to add my own insanity."

"But if we've already lost this war," the tailor's son per-
sisted, "then let no one be the winner."

"Do you hear yourself?" Marten demanded. "If you

wore the Sorcerer's Stone, Rinn, would you be willing to kill so many?"

"Enough." The king closed his tired, reddened eyes. "Which of you has the strength to assemble the men?"

"I do," Davi answered immediately.

"No, not you. Stay off that leg."

Karyl dragged himself upright. "I'll go."

* * * * *

Roffo, king of all Xenara, was furious. The sun on his armor was slowly parboiling him in his own sweat, and on every hand, he found incompetence. It had taken him ages to locate the high priest in all the confusion. Tek had managed to find the one scrawny tree on the whole southern slope. He sat in the shade of it now and refused to move, even for his king. Roffo, with his retinue and Tydus Dorenson, were left to cook. At least here, at a higher elevation, the sun didn't quite have the power it did on the plain below.

"Where are these terrifying spells your god has promised?" the king demanded. The horse under him shifted its weight, causing the jointed armor to pinch in half a dozen places. "We should have annihilated the Wynna-myrans by now. Instead, we've lost nearly thirty thousand men. Explain this to me, Tek. How can three thousand kill thirty thousand?"

"Be calm, Your Highness," the high priest said. "Mezon has not forsaken us."

"Then why do your warrior-priests cower here? They should be fighting!"

"Gaylon Reysson must first take up Orym's Legacy. Through the weapon, the god will destroy him."

The old king glanced at the second litter, also set out in the summer sun. Arlin D'Lelan's eyes were closed, his face pale and drawn, his hair matted with sweat. Roffo's lip

curled in distaste. Through this hapless creature, Tek
hoped to destroy the Red King.

"Well, get on with it," Roffo snapped.

"In the god's time. . . ."

The god's this and the god's that. The king was sick of
the sound of it.

"If I might suggest," Tydus Dorenson began. He was
suffering nearly as much as the king in the grand, heavy
robes he wore, yet his stately demeanor remained
unchanged. "Perhaps, if you were to take the third battalion of your army and send them through to deplete the
enemy's supply of arrows, the—"

Irritated, Roffo glared at the man. "If I do, you'll lead
them." Dorenson's mouth clamped shut, and the king
turned his attention back to the priest. "Another thing,
Lord Tek . . . If Kingslayer is so powerful, why hasn't Reysson put the thing to use?"

"The Red King has a conscience, Sire." Tek smiled.
"And that will be his downfall."

Eighteen

Covered in a smothering suit of chain mail, Karyl hung the heavy, bloodied cuirass across his chest, and tried to blindly line up the straps and buckles. Marten came to help, his own armor already securely in place. Somehow they'd all found that last small reserve of energy, and none too soon. There was an ominous quiet in the foothills beyond the valley where the archers made careful use of the remaining arrows. But their brave defense would soon fail.

Davi, trying to hide his limp, crossed to his horse and pulled the battered two-edged sword from the saddle. Then he hooked that belt over the one already at his waist, though on the opposite hip. The weight alone would be troublesome, but to have the weapon knocking against his bad leg would bring misery.

"Why do you keep lugging that old thing around?" the royal cousin asked, then noticed the curious stares that the question brought. "What'd I say?" he demanded of his comrades.

"Is it possible," Rinn said in wonder, "that he doesn't know?"

Marten finished the last buckle on Karyl's cuirass. "He must. He's a descendant of the Red Kings."

"Know what?"

"That's Orym's Legacy, you clown," the tailor's son said irritably. He had discarded his bow for a sword and drew a sharpening stone along the blade's edge. "Karyl, how can a royal cousin be so royally dense?"

Unoffended, the redhead peered closer. "I thought the blade was his father's. Doesn't look like much for so evil a reputation."

"Let's go," the king called from the road just below the knoll. He led a sorry excuse for a horse behind him, saddled and ready. The animal's long ears flopped sideways like a rabbit's.

"Come on, come on," Marten said, impatient with the others. He took up a long banner pole that Gaylon had asked him to carry.

Despite all that he'd been through and all that he faced, the royal cousin plunked his helm over his matted red hair and winked at Rinn.

"Not a mark on us, eh, tailor's son? The gods are still smiling."

The earl of the Lower Vales snorted. "Not Mezon."

The king's companions mounted and sent their weary animals down the slope to meet their lord. Foot soldiers and cavalrymen gathered along the road, the rattle of weapons and armor the only sound.

With Davi and Marten riding on either side of him, Gaylon brought the tattered remnants of Wynnamyr's army to face the enemy on the southernmost edge of valley. The archers, their supply of arrows all but gone, descended from the foothills to join their comrades. Taking up sword and pike, they swelled the king's forces to nearly fifteen hundred men. The earl held the banner pole upright, tucked between thigh and saddle, and a strip of white cloth fluttered from its tip in the hot afternoon breeze.

Roffo's horde rolled from the pass in greater numbers than ever, though more orderly than before. They came at an unhurried pace, certain of their victory but leery all the same. Among the Xenarans were separate troops from Turvia and Benjir that Gaylon recognized by their garb and shields. Noro tribesmen and women, their hair in long braids, their bodies scantly covered by furs, rode rangy desert horses near the fore. Many of the lesser foreign companies were unknown to the king.

At sight of the white flag, their enemy slowed and stopped, then parted near the center of the front line. A band of Mezonite priests came forward through the gap, almost as if they had anticipated this moment. The king threw out a hand to halt his own men, aware that a heavy silence had fallen.

"Will you treat, Red King?" one priest shouted.

Gaylon considered his answer carefully. "No," he shouted in return. "I haven't come to treat, only to warn. Orym's Legacy is with me, and its power is mine. Your god's magic will not save any of you! Take your great army and leave this land or face destruction."

The same warrior-priest gestured behind him, and a litter was brought forward, then tilted on end. The king of Wynnamyr saw the white-robed man tied upon the wooden platform and knew this hostage instantly.

"Arlin!" he cried and spurred his mount. Davi grabbed a rein and held him back.

Hot sunlight glinted off a dagger blade in the priest's hand. "Listen to me! My lord Tek has sent you a message, Red King. He says that this man, Arlin D'Lelan, has been consecrated to Mezon and will be sacrificed to ensure our victory. If you would save his life, then you must offer yourself in his stead. Bring the sword and surrender to us now or watch him die."

Davi never gave his king a chance to decide. Before any could stop him, he drove his tired gelding forward and grasped the hilt of Kingslayer. Left-handed, he dragged it from the scabbard. Orym's Legacy answered his touch immediately, though not with the searing blue-gold energy that a Sorcerer's Stone would create.

The sword's song was muted, but nevertheless, Gaylon

could hear it—could see its effect on the boy. Davi's exhaustion had vanished. Weapon held high, he threw back his head to let loose an ungodly scream of fury and joy. Even in his fear for the lad, Gaylon longed for that feeling of omnipotence.

As one, the king, Marten, Karyl, and Rinn raced after the duke, heedless of the Wynnamyran army that also surged forward with them. Roffo's forces closed around the priests of Mezon and their captive, and the duke of Gosney slammed into the lead soldiers, bowling one horse over, running another man through with the ancient blade.

"Davi!" Gaylon screamed.

But Kingslayer had completely swept the boy up in its savage rage. He killed and killed again, never slowing, as if determined to hack his way through the wall of flesh that kept him from Arlin. Gaylon saw the enemy, confused and afraid, fall back under the young duke's onslaught. Davi's comrades and countrymen followed in his wake, adding to the bloody destruction.

The final battle was truly begun.

The priests, carrying D'Lelan, slipped deep within the enemy army, and the duke followed. Gaylon rushed after him, desperate to catch the boy and find some way to wrest the blade from his hand. Too late the king recognized the danger. The Mezonites had used Arlin to purposefully lure the Wynnamyran leaders away from their men. Gaylon watched the Xenaran ranks close about them, but Davi, unaware, continued his methodical destruction, cutting a swath of death through the foe. No one could touch him; his moves were too sudden and violent.

A warrior-priest appeared momentarily between Gaylon and Davi to shout in Xenaran. Weight dragged at the king's leg; a gloved hand wrapped around his ankle and another around his calf. Next came a prick at the back of his knee, something sharp and small enough to pass through the links of mail. Twice more he was stung.

Gaylon swung his sword. A soldier fell back screaming, both arms severed at the elbow, but more of the enemy closed from every direction. Their hands and arms snagged the Red King and wrenched the sword from his grip. Terrified, he reached inwardly for the power of his Sorcerer's Stone.

The Stone refused to answer, though, and a familiar lethargy filled him—the same foul Mezonite magic that Baron D'Loran had used. Under the pull of a dozen men, both the king and his lop-eared horse toppled to the ground.

"To the king!" someone cried distantly. "To the king!"

Gaylon was dragged from the saddle and the mailed glove on his right hand jerked loose. Then unseen fingertips pried gently at his ring, careful not to touch the Stone. A small, sharp blade began to slice into the skin beneath the gold band. Somehow, the Red King found the strength to clench the hand into a fist and heard a squall of pain when the Stone touched another's bare flesh. Already the weakness was fading.

"To the king!"

Karyl's voice, close by, sounded the alarm, over and over. The royal cousin, no thought to his own safety, arrived to dispatch three of the enemy with his sword. The rest scrambled away out of reach and left Gaylon on the ground, struggling against exhaustion and the magical residue of the Mezonite spell.

"Sire," Karyl said breathlessly, his attention on the scuffling knots of men around them. "Are you hurt?" He reached out a hand to the king. Suddenly he stiffened, and his eyes unfocused. "Milord?"

That one word was whispered, barely heard over the skirmishes. The young man dropped to his knees and fell forward, a pike buried deep in his back.

"Karyl!"

Marten and Rinn came at last. The earl dispatched a

Benjiran spear wielder, while the tailor's son battled a pair of the Benjiran's blue-kilted comrades. With the skirmish raging on all sides, Gaylon Reysson cradled his cousin in his arms, helpless and heartsick. Blood bubbled slowly over the redhead's chin.

"Not a mark on us," Karyl murmured. Smiling faintly, he died.

Gaylon moaned, "No. . . ." Tears of outrage stung his eyes.

"Sire!" Rinn cried as he defended his sovereign against the forces that crowded closer. "Best find your sword while you have the chance."

The blade lay in the dirt nearby, half hidden under a body. "Where's Davi?" Gaylon demanded as he scooped the weapon up. His horse had disappeared.

Marten answered, "Over there."

He pointed, and the king followed that gesture out across the contending armies. Near the center of the field, the duke of Gosney had laid waste to everything in reach. He wheeled his exhausted horse around and around in search of a foe, Kingslayer held high. Even the Wynnamyran soldiers stood at bay, afraid of the boy's madness. Arlin and the priests of Mezon were nowhere to be seen.

Leaving his cousin's lifeless body behind, Gaylon fought his way into the crush, his sword used to chop a bloody path. Rinn and the earl of the Lower Vales followed close behind, guarding his back.

* * * * *

Kingslayer seemed to have fused itself to his fingers, but Davi no longer cared. He'd given himself over to the weapon's influence and would gladly pay any price for the power that coursed through him—for the quickened reflexes, the incredible physical strength, the heightened senses.

And the hot sweet blood that soaked his gloved hands.

The weapon fed on death insatiably. He'd taken up Kingslayer to save Arlin, but all reason had been quickly lost to the bloodlust. The duke spun his mount, searching out new prey, but the soldiers fled from him over the bodies of their fallen comrades. Their fear only enraged him all the more.

"Dogs!" he screamed at them. "Cowards!"

Someone stepped into his circle of carnage. A familiar tall form came toward him, and the dim memory of his Red King made the duke of Gosney hesitate.

"Give me the sword," the red-bearded man said with infinite calm.

Davi shook his head. "No. It needs me."

"*I* need you, my duke."

Jealous, Orym's Legacy hummed the louder to block the voice and sooth this descendant of the Dark King into submission. Its song filled Davi's head, demanding the blood of this man, as well. When Gaylon Reysson reached up a hand to take Kingslayer, the boy suddenly swung the blade high. Then something buried itself deep in his upper right arm, twisting him sideways out of the saddle. His elbow and hand felt as though they were on fire.

Davi hit the ground hard enough to empty his lungs of air, and the sword fell away from useless fingers. With its loss came incredible agony and horror at the memory of all he'd done. Through the fiery pain, Davi saw Rinn on the edge of the circle, crossbow in hand.

"Forgive me, Sire," the duke rasped when Gaylon knelt beside him. "I might have killed you."

Sorrow and anger and fear mixed together in the king's face as he knelt beside the youth. Rinn and the earl came to stand over them, watchful guardians, though the tailor's son had tears on his face. No one challenged them. This was the eye of the storm—at least for a little while. Davi shifted uncomfortably.

"Be still," Gaylon snapped and began to unbuckle the

young duke's cuirass.

Marten collected Orym's Legacy now, holding it gingerl
by the blade. "Do you see what the boy did with thi
sword? Some of these men have been cut completely i
half."

The king, crouching over the fallen duke, didn't react t
that awed statement, but Davi's heart thudded in his ches
and caused the pain to quicken.

"How bad is it?" asked the tailor's son as he handed th
king a small dirk.

"He'll survive," Gaylon said grimly. "Hold him tigh
while I cut it loose."

"I couldn't let you go, Sire," Davi muttered as Rinn
caught his upper arms in a firm grip. "I had to try to sav
Arlin. I—" A searing agony in his arm made him bite hi
tongue.

Late day shadow had found its way into the foothills
and behind the rumble and clatter of battle came a skirling
melody—not the low, vibratory song of Kingslayer, but the
sound of many voices blended in perfect pitch. The invocation of the priests of Mezon. Hands smeared with Davi's
blood, Gaylon froze at the sound.

"There, Sire!" Rinn pointed off to the south, where the
pass lay.

Another green cloud rose slowly into the sky, much higher than before. This was not a threat, the king sensed, but a
challenge and a guide. There, beneath the godfire, he'd
find Arlin and something more. Gaylon stood abruptly
and strode to Davi's sweated horse, catching up a trailing
rein.

"Defend the duke," he told his two comrades, then
swung into the saddle, a hand outstretched to Marten.

The earl brought Kingslayer, his face contorted with
doubt. "Milord, please . . . *Your* safety is our first duty."

"Your first and only duty is to obey me." The king took
the ancient sword in his left hand, unwilling to give the

blade life through contact with his Stone, or control over him . . . just yet. "Whatever happens, keep Davi safe. Take him back to Castlekeep and Jessmyn."

"No!" the boy cried and managed, white with pain, to get to his feet. "You can't leave me!"

Rinn took an elbow to steady the youth. Gaylon closed his ears to Davi's pleas and put the spurs to the tired gelding. The horse responded sluggishly, but the king turned him west, pushing him on through whatever breaks in the throng that could be found. More than once Orym's Legacy was used for defense, always with the left hand.

The worst of the fighting continued mostly on the flat ground along the coach road. His easiest passage south would be on the hillsides, and there the king sent his mount. From this higher vantage, he saw the actual size of the struggle for the first time.

In the trampled, sun-yellowed grasses along the road, small knots of men beat at each other with weapons. Their cries of anger and anguish created a wretched counterpoint to the Mezonite song. Bodies lay thick on the ground, Xenaran and Wynnamyran soldiers stacked in common piles, while others moved feebly in their own pools of blood.

The death and pain repulsed Gaylon. He had brought about the destruction of so many lives and was far from finished. On his finger, the Sorcerer's Stone shone with a steady blue light, while the god's green fire led him on toward the Sea Pass and into its peaceful confines.

Only here did he find the peace of death. Nothing stirred in the narrow rocky channel. Bodies, in pools of clotting blood, lay everywhere across the shadowed floor of the pass. The gelding, forced to step over and on them, shied continually. Each time, Gaylon spurred the animal brutally, for at the southern end of the pass, he saw the king of Xenara, armored but helmless, seated upon a huge white horse. Arlin's litter rested on the ground beside him.

The Mezonite priests were also in attendance, singing gently, their neat rows in a semicircle behind Roffo and their sparkling emerald godfire anchored high above them. The elderly priest who had confronted Gaylon at the temple was not among the others.

"Ho, Red King!" Roffo boomed, the echoes of his deep voice covering the sounds of battle in the distance and the incongruously sweet song of the priests.

"Roffo." Gaylon halted the gelding a short distance away and laid the ancient sword across the pommel of his saddle.

The naked blade and the less than courteous greeting displeased the old man. He scowled. "We are ill met this bloody day, young lord."

"I see no blood on you, sir."

"Come, come," Roffo snapped. "Let's end this now. Another great battalion of soldiers waits on the plain below. Your army has fought valiantly, but the war is lost. Give up yourself and the sword, and save those few Wynnamyrans left on the field."

"Why should I?" The Red King had noticed the fine sheen of sweat on the old man's face, even here, in the cool shadows and sea breeze.

"You can't be such a fool, boy. How many more deaths will you carry on that young head? If you use Orym's Legacy, you'll be more reviled by future generations than the Dark King ever has been." Roffo raised his great double chins. "And then there is the weapon's curse. Your death is assured in any case. Let these good priests end your suffering for you."

That brought a wry smile to Gaylon's lips. "How can I refuse such a kind offer?"

Bound to the litter, Arlin D'Lelan turned his head slowly and opened his eyes. The old king heard the captive stir and glanced down.

"His life will be spared as well. I swear it."

"No. . . ," Arlin managed, voice hoarse and cracking. "He lies, Sire."

"I never doubted it," the Red King answered.

Roffo flushed a deep red, but offered no denial. The sweat began to trickle down the sides of his round face.

Gaylon, heart heavy, turned his attention back to Arlin. "Look what I've done to you, my friend. Look what I've done to Wynnamyr."

"End it, *now* . . . milord. Take up Kingslayer and . . . end us all." The young Southerner lapsed into an exhausted silence.

The old king's face had gone impossibly white. "The man's delirious. He can't know what he's saying."

"But he does." Gaylon gazed at the white-robed men who stood unmoving behind the king of Xenara, voices still blended in quiet, beautiful harmony. "Where's your high priest, old man? Surely, he has something to say in this."

Roffo's jowls began to quiver, and he rolled his eyes. "Tek promised me . . . there would be no danger . . . so long as I stood here beside D'Lelan."

"You'll notice that Tek himself stands elsewhere," the Red King observed and stepped down from his horse. "But there's nowhere to hide from Kingslayer, not even for him."

The Red King wrapped the fingers of his right hand slowly around the ancient sword's lacquered grip. As his ring touched the hilt, the star stone appeared between the quillons, needle beams of colored light streaming from it. Orym's Legacy blazed into life at the same instant, and the king's Sorcerer's Stone flared a brilliant, blinding cobalt in answer.

Behind Gaylon, a voice cried out—Davi's, he thought—but that no longer mattered. Kingslayer sang a terrible song of power, and the king had already lost himself in it. The music of the stars swelled, enveloping him, filling

him, and all his senses heightened. A figure shimmered
into existence before the king—a black-bearded man in
long dark robes, his tangled mass of curls caught in a heavy
gold crown. Mad Orym. He raised an outstretched hand
fingers tipped with long, ugly nails.

"Use my knowledge. Let me aid you," the Dark King
called, his voice drifting on Kingslayer's song. "Let me live
again in you. Together we can crush this world and make it
ours.

Behind Orym, the light faded and images flashed by—
memories of a thousand years past. Gaylon saw Wynnamyr
in flames, saw its forests devoured by fire, its towns and
people destroyed. These were Orym's promises of power,
but an ancient minor holocaust meant nothing. Unim-
pressed, the young king turned away.

"Listen to me!" Orym shouted. "Kingslayer will kill its
master. Only I can save you. Only I can keep you from the
fate that befell me."

"Begone, old fool." Gaylon let the sword's energy course
through him, building in intensity. "There's nothing you
have that I want." Kingslayer thrummed in his hands, and
Orym, face contorted with rage, faded away.

Unseeing, Gaylon stared beyond the shadows at the far
end of the pass. Why had he denied the sword so long?
Why? His inner vision soared, and all things became crystal
clear. How infinitesimal was humanity, how great the universe. This tiny moment in the flow of time meant nothing, just as the lives of the multitude meant nothing. He
and the Stone and the sword were one, as destiny commanded.

Kingslayer continued to sing. Its voice spiraled upward
until Gaylon's ears ached, but the pain went unnoticed.
Time had ceased to flow, yet endless future possibilities
raced through the king's mind. He saw Wynnamyr's mountains barren and treeless, but not because of fire. The trees
were taken to build great cities that sprang up along the

rivers and in the valleys. Civilization spread in every direction, and where it went, the land died, the air grew foul.

The inner visions altered. Other cities rose, and machines raced along stone roads or flew through the clouds. A great white light flared, rolling over the land and leveling everything in its path. Hot ashes the color of snow fell endlessly until the world was buried.

The Red King floated far above the earth, but not alone. Man had somehow found a way to build his cities in the night sky, suspended in the void. Silver and gray and twinkling with lights, huge wheels rolled lazily against a black universe. There was beauty and dignity in their slow dance.

Variation after variation of this future dream fled past Gaylon's eyes, and after each, civilization died horribly from some disaster—natural or manmade. There would be powers even more terrible than Kingslayer's in the ages to come, but here and now, such power was the king's to use as he pleased. Gaylon brought the sword under control, and the visions ended. A blue fire raced the edge of the golden blade, circling back to the hilt. The song fell quickly to a low, vibratory hum that tingled through the Red King's body.

Only once before, in the bowels of the keep, had Gaylon felt Orym's Legacy unleash its power. This time the energy arced violently into the air first, a great jagged bolt of lightning that dove immediately to ground. The sword rumbled as the king pointed it upward, and blue-gold energy flashed into the green cloud that still writhed high above.

Godfire rained down on the priests of Mezon. Filled with a dispassionate wonder, Gaylon watched them scatter. The old king's mount reared and leaped away, leaving the fat man in his armor on the stony floor of the pass. Arlin, still bound, had no way of escape and cried out when burning debris struck him.

The Red King frowned, troubled briefly by the Southerner's pain, but there could be no regret. The solstice sun

westered, and great clarity of mind brought greater understanding. Gaylon Reysson was hereafter above the laws of
men and gods. Behind the feeling of omnipotence, Orym
still whispered slyly. That long-remembered and cruel essence would linger with the sword forever, an immortality
of sorts. So the weapon sang to the Red King as it once had
to the Dark King.

A distant thunder welled on a hot, dry wind, thousands
of voices in cacophonous discord. Behind the shouts came a
melody, faint but sweet and magical. The Mezonite priests
had joined Roffo's final division, and now that army
rushed up the steep slopes from the Xenara Plain to exact
the god's revenge.

Orym's bloodlust began to jibber in Gaylon's ear.

* * * * *

Arlin watched, helpless and in pain. Whatever he had
imagined about the fabled sword of Orym did not even
come close to the reality. Gaylon, transformed and limned
now in an aura of brilliant blue-gold, held the weapon
high above his head. The blade's throb of power vibrated
through the very stones of the pass.

"Help me," Roffo sobbed from the ground near the litter, caught like an upturned tortoise in his silver shell of
armor. His white steed had deserted him as quickly as the
priests.

Behind the Red King, soldiers entered the Sea Pass from
the vales, friend and foe alike, drawn by the light and the
pulsing energy of the enscorceled sword. The boy-duke,
Davi, came well ahead of the others, on a lathered horse
taken from a Xenaran lancer. Gosney flung himself off the
animal before it had a chance to halt and crossed the last
bit of ground to the king at a staggering run.

"No!" Arlin croaked, unable to make himself heard.

The boy's hand caught at Gaylon's wrist, and the king

looked down into the young face without recognition. Davi clung to him, and, annoyed, the Red King flung the youth aside. Rinn appeared on foot to dart past Gaylon, running toward Arlin, knife in hand.

"Idiot! Go back!" the Southerner croaked, but the tailor's son ignored him and the floundering Xenaran king, as well.

The little blade severed the ropes from Arlin's ankles, then from his left wrist. Behind Rinn, Davi struggled back to his feet as the king swung Orym's Legacy in a long, slow stroke toward the southern mouth of the pass, where Roffo's last battalion came flooding through. Rinn cut the cords on the Southerner's other wrist and dragged him upright—too late.

"My brave, foolish friend," Arlin murmured to the tailor's son just as Gaylon loosed Kingslayer's terrible power.

Thunder boomed, and the earth heaved under their feet. Then a searing, golden wave swept over and through them. For Arlin D'Lelan, that final moment of agony seemed to last an eternity.

Nineteen

A heavy liquid fire erupted from the sword's tip, dense and brilliant as star matter. The molten river of light flowed swiftly toward the southern threshold of the Sea Pass, and those touched by the flames died shrieking, the flesh melted from their bones like wax.

The Red King watched the destruction of Roffo, of Rinn and Arlin, and felt nothing, neither sorrow nor joy. Even Orym's voice had been silenced. All that remained was the song of the Stone and the Legacy. Viscous sunfire struck rock walls, curling back into the main current, then poured onward.

The Xenaran troops turned to run, but found themselves trapped by those who came behind. The shimmering blue-gold flood engulfed them, and the wails of terror and agony from so many finally shattered Gaylon's inner calm. He pulled back sharply on the sword's power, fighting for control.

Momentarily sated, Kingslayer obeyed. The weapon grew heavy in his hands, and the point dropped earthward. A similar heaviness dragged at the Red King's limbs, but the madness still churned inside. Flames flickered and died, the river of light evaporated, and Gaylon beheld the devastation with a clear, cold eye. A skeletal king commanded a small skeletal army scattered across the floor of the pass. Every bone had been gleaned of flesh, every piece of armor, every metal weapon fused to the stones.

The Legacy hummed quietly now, at peace until its master chose to wake it once more. *Soon*, he promised the sword, *soon*, and felt Orym nudge at his consciousness. Much of Roffo's army gathered still on the Xenara Plain, and many more soldiers would die before the king was done.

"Sire . . ."

Slowly Gaylon turned and even more slowly focused on the blood-and tear-streaked face of the duke of Gosney.

"You've won, milord. Wynnamyr is saved. Roffo's men retreat." The boy's shaking, tentative fingers touched the Red King's wrist and his voice implored. "Let me take the weapon, Sire. You've no more need of it. I'll keep the Legacy safe."

A sudden mirthless laughter echoed from the high rock walls, then ended abruptly.

"Leave him be, boy!"

Davi searched the stone ledges for the source of that voice, and found a little man in blue-black robes above them on the eastern wall. With pointed chin and dark eyes and long sheep's wool hair swept back in the sea breeze, the boy knew him for certain—Sezran, twin brother to Misk and creator of Kingslayer.

"Leave him be!" the wizard cried again. "He's far from finished."

"No!" Davi shouted back and brought himself a stab of pain from the wound in his arm. He tried once more to catch Gaylon's attention. "Milord, please. The task is done. Give me the sword."

"He'll never give up such power," Sezran called. "You ask too much of him, son of Daryn. He's made his sacrifice—and all before the solstice sun has set. Run away, boy, while you can. Find some distant place to hide. Go to ground and stay there, for soon there'll be little left of this world."

The young duke, face upturned, glared at the wizard. "You want him dead. You want Kingslayer for yourself, but you'll never have it. Never!"

Beside him Gaylon stirred, and Orym's Legacy woke, its hum deepening. Desperate, the youth wrapped both hands around the quillons of the sword's hilt and tugged.

The king simply snapped an elbow forward into the side of Davi's head. Vision grayed, and the boy fell, his right arm striking the ground first. Agony exploded behind his eyes. Through the pain, he heard the king's bootsteps on the stone. Sezran's laughter skirled, then vanished. Aware that Gaylon, too, was gone, the duke drew his knees under him, sobbing in despair.

"The bleeding from your wound has worsened," Marten said gently, voice filled with a heavy sorrow. He crouched beside the boy. "Best do what the old wizard says, Davi. Let's leave this place."

The ache in his chest far outweighed the pain in his arm. "I can't leave him."

"He doesn't know you. He'll kill us as thoughtlessly as he killed Rinn and Arlin. We're all that's left of the king's inner circle, Davi." The earl paused. "Everyone's gone. Roffo's soldiers have scattered through the vales, along with our own men." He snorted. "They were quick enough to ask him to take up Kingslayer, our brave little army, but the reality has sent them in a mad dash to escape."

"Where's the king gone?" Davi asked, scrubbing tears from his face.

"Toward the southern mouth of the pass," Marten said, troubled. "I think time is swiftly running out. Can you stand? I'd carry you, but . . ."

The boy struggled to his feet and saw the reason for Marten's hesitation. The fourteenth earl of the Lower Vales had taken a sword stroke to the upper arm. While the mail had stopped the edge of the blade, the strength of the blow had badly broken the bone.

Marten's tone was grim. "First the leg, now the arm, and all on the same side. I've still got my good right hand, though. Perhaps we can assist each other to Arbor House."

"Go on alone, Marten," Davi told him. "I'll be there as soon as I can."

"Don't do this!" The earl caught his elbow. "Gaylon's mind is gone. He warned us this would happen. I don't want to be the only one left alive."

"Then come with me."

"Gods!" Marten snarled and got himself upright. "It'd probably be less painful if we just cut our own throats, here and now."

The duke ignored his comrade's grumbles. He'd already begun a hard passage through the Legacy's destruction. Roffo's bones were encased in silver, while Arlin and Rinn's lay in an anonymous heap. Beyond them, though, death had claimed at least a thousand souls in the mouth of the pass. There was no way around. Davi stepped into the jumble and felt brittle bones snap underfoot. Marten followed, cursing.

"Where? Where has he gone?" the earl growled.

Davi suddenly knew. The Red King would find some high vantage, someplace from which he could cause more destruction. The Legacy craved lives, and those would be found even now scattering across the Xenara Plain.

"This way!" the boy cried and broke into a ragged trot.

Exhaustion and pain dogged him along the bone-strewn path that led to the outcropping that overlooked the Xenara Plain—the spot where Sezran had first shown himself. All the while, Davi heard Kingslayer's hum, a low, ominous vibration felt through the soles of the feet. From somewhere even more distant came the song of Mezon's priests.

"Davi! Wait for—"

Marten's shout was cut short by an inhuman shriek, a wail of power that shook the earth. The duke fell back, sliding the rest of the way down the steep trail through the boulders, hand clutched to the wound in his upper arm. Out on the point, Gaylon gathered the forces once more. Late afternoon sunlight touched him, burnishing his red beard and sandy hair while blue fire raced the edge of the Legacy's blade. Davi watched the Red King swing the weapon over his head, then with a heavy stroke, chop the air in front of him.

Panicked soldiers, the remains of Roffo's great army, fled on foot and on horseback over the plain below, headed for the distant red-tiled roofs of Zankos and the shining Inland Sea. Only the priests of Mezon held their ground, white robes tinted yellow by the setting sun. Near them stood a mounted man, white-haired and in familiar red robes. Tydus Dorenson, no doubt seeking safety in the priests' magic; yet their ranks, too, had diminished. Even from so far away, the young duke could see the raised chins, the open mouths, though their song was lost behind Kingslayer's thrum.

This time no writhing green cloud formed above them, but a huge dense ball of fierce emerald light that flew at Gaylon just as he loosed the Legacy's storm of sunfire. The energies met in midair with a force that slammed Davi— only a dozen paces from his king—back against the rocks. Blue-gold flame and green godfire rebounded off one another. The priest's cloud shot skyward, striking a nearby mountain peak, while Gaylon's river of fire was deflected down toward the earth.

Davi dragged his attention from the blazing mountain overhead to the plain below. There, Kingslayer's diverted molten wave swallowed the priests and rushed on in all directions, growing deeper, wider. Orym's Legacy spewed an endless, bright flood over the salt dirt. Again, every living thing it touched died horribly. Even though they were made tiny with the distance, Davi could see men and horses blacken and shrivel, their screams of agony brought

o him on the wind. The huge army camp with its thou-
ands of tents vaporized, and still the energy swelled and
pread.

Sickened, the duke looked to his king. Gaylon Reysson,
ooted to the earth, held the sword out before him with
igid arms until even the distant city of Zankos was taken in
Kingslayer's fiery embrace. Flames engulfed the tall build-
ngs, raging above the horizon until the iridescent river
ouched the Inland Sea at last, and billowing clouds of
team rose to blot out the southern sky.

Only then did the Red King bring the forces under con-
rol, his face contorted with effort. The blade tip dropped,
and the shimmering inferno flickered and died. Zankos,
lone, continued to burn, its thick black smoke roiling
high above the horizon. The screams had been silenced,
and the wind brought only the stench of charred flesh. In
he empty quiet, Davi drew a heavy ragged breath, sud-
lenly aware of the sobs that threatened to choke him.

Marten arrived then to drag the young duke deeper into
he sheltering boulders, but Davi struggled free finally, his
yes still on the plain. In the midst of that barren bone-
trewn landscape, one man stood unscathed, his gold-
rimmed white robes fluttering in the breeze. He raised his
hands above his head, then opened his arms wide; at that
moment, the wind gathered him up into the air. The priest
ose higher and higher, coming closer to Gaylon's promon-
ory. His beautiful voice floated to them.

"I am Mezon, the god incarnate," he sang, the words
and tone hypnotic. A greenish aura limned his body and
his glowing countenance radiated an awesome power.
'Every life you have taken has greatly pleased me. All that
you have done has been by my will. You are mine. The
sword is mine. Come to me, Red King."

Gaylon, face peaceful, eyes empty, took a mindless step
oward the edge. Kingslayer rumbled quietly in his grip.

"No!" Davi screamed.

His voice was echoed by Sezran's. The wizard had found
a perch on the mountainside high above them, where he
could watch and wait in relative safety. "My sword! Mine!"
the little man wailed, but made no move to stop the king
or challenge Tek.

"Milord," the duke shouted.

The distance was too great for him or Marten to overtake
Gaylon quickly enough. Davi grabbed up a rock with his
left hand and threw as hard as he could. It struck the king
of Wynnamyr on the cheek. Stunned, Gaylon jerked his
head back, his serenity instantly transformed to rage. The
sword's hum spiraled upward into a shriek once more.

The creature that had named itself Mezon transformed
as well. The human form exploded, and flesh and bone
rained out of the sky with tattered bits of bloody cloth.
What remained was anything but beautiful and godlike.
Davi heard Marten cry out in fear behind him. Unlike the
statue in the temple, this Mezon had leathern wings and a
shape only vaguely human.

Far too large to have hidden in the priest's body, Mezon
stood over three times the height of a man. Thick, gray-
green scales covered the god's skin where it showed from
between enormous pieces of dull metal armor. A kilt fashioned with strips of the same dark metal covered it from
waist to knees, and it held a massive sword tightly in its
clawed hands. Worst of all, were the eyes—enormous,
black, and glittering with hatred.

The creature hovered momentarily over the plain, held
aloft by the thermal updrafts under its broad wings, then
drove suddenly at Gaylon, blade raised and poised to
strike. Davi cried out, thoroughly terrorized by so grue-
some a vision, but Orym's Legacy thundered in response.
Mezon easily parried the brilliant blue-gold gout of flame
that gushed toward him, sending the energy back into the
mountain under the Red King's feet.

Gaylon dived to safety just as the promontory collapsed

but the god-creature followed, sword ready. The king only had time to raise his own weapon to stave off his enemy's blow. A sickly blue-green fire erupted as the two swords met. Then Mezon reached out a huge scaled hand and grasped Kingslayer at the very base of its blade. Gaylon bellowed in fury and tried to wrench the weapon free.

The god only laughed, dragging both man and sword into the air. The backwash of its wings drove dirt and grit into Davi's eyes, but still he saw the Red King release the hilt with one hand—but only so he could jam his Sorcerer's Stone against Mezon's forearm. Light flared at the contact point. Roaring, the god dropped his burden.

Gaylon hit the ground running, only to find himself cornered against the mountainside. As the creature descended on him, the king of Wynnamyr brought Orym's Legacy over his head once more, but not in defense. He turned suddenly and dashed the flat of the golden blade down hard against a boulder. Kingslayer gave a discordant shriek, sparks flying, but Gaylon struck the rock again with even greater force. This time the sword shattered in his hands. An uncontrolled firestorm engulfed both god and king. Mezon, leather wings aflame, tried to rise above Gaylon's holocaust, but the fire wrapped white-hot tendrils around the monster's legs and dragged it screaming into the blazing chaos.

Under Davi, the earth bucked and swayed, and it seemed the whole mountain would crumble. The roar of Kingslayer's unchained energy pounded his ears, yet Sezran's wails of despair at the destruction of his sword could be dimly heard over the cacophony.

"Keep your eyes covered!" Marten shouted as the ground finally stopped shaking. "Don't look into the fire."

The boy ignored him. On his knees, he watched the inferno grow brighter and brighter, until the searing heat blistered his skin. Deep inside that glowing furnace, he saw one small figure, encased in a faint blue nimbus. A sense of

strong certainty filled the duke—Gaylon lived. Of the god
Mezon, there was no sign, and Davi prayed it had been
destroyed.

The radiant energy began to shrink into itself, growing
hotter and denser, until a brilliant light pulse flashed outward. The concussion threw the youth against Marten and
carried them both backward into the sheltering rocks.

An unknown time later, the young duke roused in bless-
ed coolness. Night had fallen, so complete that not a single
star flickered in the sky. Marten stirred beside him, groaning.

"Milord?" Davi called into the empty darkness. "Sire?"

"I see him," the earl said, voice heavy with pain.

"You can see him?" The duke rubbed at his eyes with
shaking fingers, suddenly aware of his blindness. He
reached out and touched Marten's mailed sleeve. "Does he
live?"

The man said nothing for a long moment, then, "Your
eyes. Davi. . . ."

"Take me to him, please."

Every stone tripped him, every moment brought him
closer to panic. Finally Marten pulled Davi down, and
sightless, he found the still form of Gaylon Reysson with
his blistered fingers. They stripped away the cuirass, and
the boy pressed an ear to the king's chest. No air filled the
lungs. The heart was silent.

"He's dead, Davi."

"No, he can't be. Where's the wizard?" The boy raised
his head. "Sezran! Help us!"

"He's gone as well," the earl said tonelessly.

"No. . . ." The word nearly strangled Davi. "He must be
here."

"There's nothing here, lad. There's no one left alive on
this side of the pass, no one but you and I." Marten
groaned. "Gods, the devastation. It looks as if the whole
world has been put to the torch. Fires light the night sky."

The earl paused, then sighed. "We'd best move on." His
and cupped Davi's elbow. "Let me take you to Arbor
House. Then I'll somehow find help and come back for
Gaylon. We'll make him a funeral pyre befitting a sorcerer-
ing."

The duke shook his head. There would be no pyre for
Gaylon Reysson. "He goes home to Castlekeep."

"But that's insane. It's summer. The body will . . . pu-
refy. Besides, you're blind and I've got only one good arm.
How can we possibly manage?"

The burns on Davi's face and hands had slowly become a
source of agony, overcoming the pain from his other
wounds. Exhaustion and thirst brought their own form of
misery, but none of that mattered. The duke of Gosney was
determined to perform this one last duty to his Red King.

"I don't know, but we will."

Twenty

If not for the pregnancy, Jessmyn might have given up
For the baby's sake, she ate the food brought to her and
took morning and evening walks in the gardens, though
there was little left of the lawns or flowerbeds. So it was this
evening as she took herself to the center of the dry brown
sward and stood, deserted and alone.

Gaylon had left her nearly a month before, not on the
morning he'd ridden away, but a fortnight later when the
war had finally been fought. In the same dusky light as
now, she had lost her sense of him. There was only emptiness where his love had been. Oddly, though, tears had deserted her as well. Jessmyn rubbed slender hands over her
swelling belly. Even with him lost to her, something of the
king might live on.

Wynnamyr had been struck hard by its military losses
Those few who had returned home alive from the Sea Pass
brought stories of slaughter and of Kingslayer, of the weapon's horrendous powers. Fearful, they would say nothing of
the king. Karyl, Arlin, and Rinn were dead—that much
the queen sadly learned, if not how. No one would tell her
what had happened to Davi or Marten, either, or how Gaylon had died. Perhaps no one knew.

As day after long day passed and no Xenaran forces arrived to exact revenge, Jessmyn reckoned that this had been
a war without a victor. So it had been in Orym's day, until

the people of Wynnamyr had risen up to slaughter the Dark King's kin and purge the land of magic.

The hot summer evening closed in around her now, and the queen tried to put aside her fears. Bats and nighthawks swooped through the crepuscular air in search of flying insects, and among the trees below the castle grounds, the first town lights came to life.

"Ho, the keep!"

At the shout, she turned toward the road. The shadowy forms of two horses with riders, one behind the other, moved slowly toward the deserted stableyard.

"Hello!" Jessmyn called in return and hurried past the weapon's yard to greet them alone.

"Your Highness?"

Marten Pelson, left arm splinted and his clothes little more than rags, dismounted stiffly, then managed a bow. The queen felt the first tears welling in her eyes, uncertain whether they were of joy or sorrow. The duke of Gosney sat the second horse, but between the two animals, a litter was fastened. She stared at the shrouded form on the crude structure.

"You've brought him home to lie with his family among the cairns."

"No," Davi said sharply. "The king is not dead."

The earl shook his head. "Neither is he alive, milady."

Heartsick, Jessmyn stripped back the thin blanket that covered Gaylon Reysson. How gaunt and pale he was. She imagined his hazel eyes opening, but it was only a trick of the dusky light. His red-bearded face was cold to the touch, far colder than the night air. She leaned to press her lips to his—the promised kiss on his return, but the emptiness in her soul remained. Davi had also dismounted and, with fingertips, followed the staves to the litter frame until he stumbled and bumped into the queen.

"Davi? What's wrong?" Tears slid unnoticed down her cheeks.

"He's blind, milady," Marten answered.

"Not entirely," the youth said defensively. "I can see some shapes in bright light."

"Well. . . ." Jessmyn laughed to hide her pain. "I have a duke who's not quite blind and a husband who's not quite dead. Things are definitely better."

"Is Misk here?" Davi demanded, impatient as always.

"Yes."

"We must take the king to her immediately."

The queen thought that she could manage to carry half the weight of the litter, but the earl, concerned by her pregnancy, refused to let her. She was allowed only to lead Davi, while the young duke struggled with his end of the burden and the uneven stones of the bailey. Marten, behind, said nothing though his splinted arm must have hurt. Within, Jessmyn found some of the few male servants left in the keep and ordered them to take the litter, then sent another to care for the horses and a maid to search out Misk. The tiny woman would already know, of course, and would come in her own good time.

They took Gaylon to his empty chambers and laid him on the bed, then dismissed the servants after the candles had been lit. The queen looked down on her husband, his face slack.

"He's dead," she murmured softly, certain of that now.

Davi ground his teeth. "The body would have corrupted long before this. I swear to you, the king lives."

"He Dreams," Misk said, her voice coming from the air around them. She winked into existence at the center of the floor, startling Marten. "Something he's not willing to face has sent him far beyond the normal bounds of the Dreamer."

"Bring him back," the duke begged, blind eyes searching for her from the chair Jessmyn had seated him on.

"I'm afraid that's a magic only a Sorcerer's Stone can achieve."

Davi groaned. "No. . . ."

"Where is Kingslayer?" the tiny woman asked.

"Destroyed," Marten answered. "His Majesty used the weapon to obliterate every living thing on the Xenara Plain . . . including Zankos. I'm told the city held half a million souls, men, women, and children. The god, Mezon, came afterward to take the Legacy, only Gaylon shattered the blade. A great, searing white fire enveloped them both. We found the king like this, but nothing of Orym's Legacy or the god."

"That's how you lost your sight, Davi." Misk turned to the duke. "Too foolish to close your eyes or look away. You should have covered them once the damage was done." The boy bowed his head. "Perhaps your sight can still be saved. You may have the power to heal yourself."

"I care only for my lord's healing. There's nothing left for me . . . without the Red King."

"But you must have a care for your life, Davyn Daryn-son. Other lives depend on it—even a young Red King, one day." She caught up one of Davi's hands and pressed the palm to his face. "Cover your eyes." Reluctantly he did so. "Now . . . envision a glowing orange light within your head. That is a healing color and draws the necessary energies. The eyes will grow warm. . . . Do you feel the heat?"

"No . . . Wait, I do feel warmth."

"That gentle heat is always the sign that healing has begun. Eventually you might teach yourself to use this skill on others, though there are limits to such power. For now, be content to use it on yourself. Complete healing will, of course, take time, but you should have some vision returned immediately. What do you feel now?"

"The warmth is fading."

"Good. Uncover your eyes."

The youth did so, blinking rapidly in the candlelight.

"Do you see?"

"A little," he replied dully, his attention on Gaylon.

"Perhaps too much."

Jessmyn crossed the chamber to rest her hands on the young duke's shoulders. "There's nothing more you can do, Davi. You need rest, and Marten's arm needs tending. I'll send for Girkin."

"Wait." Misk put out a hand and tilted her silver head as if listening.

The queen sensed something then, a pulse on the air, a breath of salt moisture. Next a whirlwind spun suddenly in the center of the floor. Marten, of them all, had no real knowledge of Sezran, and his eyes grew fearful as the little man formed on the stone flags. The wizard's Stone glowed brilliantly on the chest of his robes, and Jessmyn saw a faint glitter in answer from Gaylon's ring. For the first time, she allowed herself a small hope.

Sezran stepped to the bed. "Again too early for the funeral, I see."

"He's lost in Dreaming," Misk said gently. "Fetch him back, Brother. Please."

"It's too late," the wizard growled.

"Daryn Dreamed longer and survived."

"To my regret."

"Do this for me. . . ."

"No!" Sezran said, suffused with mercurial fury. "Let him die! The star gem is gone, destroyed. Without it, the ship can take us neither where nor when we need to go. We can never return home, Misk."

"Then accept your fate, Brother, and be generous. There's nothing more to strive for, to hope for. Put your energies to better use."

"No." The wizard smiled down on Gaylon. "As you've often accused me, I've only come to gloat. A momentary pleasure, but it will have to suffice."

Davi stood up, and the low rage on his face frightened Jessmyn. "You—"

"Be seated," Misk commanded him. "Sezran refuses because what I've asked is beyond even his abilities."

"Oh, very good, Sister," the little man chortled. "Shame me, appeal to my pride."

"I would if you had any, but there's no room in so withered and shriveled a spirit. Go away, miserable old creature. You are unwelcome in my presence, now or ever again."

Those words were imminently cold, but instead of anger, Jessmyn saw doubt touch the sorcerer's eyes.

"Misk," he said softly. "You can't mean this."

"But I do."

Anger reddened the old man's face briefly, then he paled. "This is foolish. We've argued and fought throughout the past millennia, but I've always loved you. We two are alone in this world forever. You can't shun me." The tiny woman turned her back, and Sezran did the same. "You're right. This task is beyond me. Out there are stars beyond counting. To find one lost Dreamer . . . is impossible."

"I ask only that you try, Brother. You taught him to Dream. Is there nowhere in the universe that the young prince favored? Is there nowhere Gaylon Reysson might seek brief happiness and refuge before he dies?"

The wizard grew thoughtful. "There was a place, once, that attracted both Daryn and the prince . . . a place with no sun and no sound. I might be able to find it again." He stepped toward the center of the chamber, then paused, turning back to the tiny woman. "I do this for your sake, Sister, not the Red King's. You tried to stop me when first I forged Kingslayer, and the star gem pulled you loose in time. For all that's transpired in this world since then, I do accept responsibility. My love for you has never dimmed, though I've been cruel and self-serving, always, and may always be. I can offer no excuse, but . . ."

When his voice trailed off, Misk continued for him. "But such power is hard to resist."

"Will you forgive me?"

"I forgave you long ago, Brother."

The old sorcerer glanced at the others, once more cold and imperious. "Do not bide, any of you. There's little hope in this venture. If I fail to find him on that one world, I'll look elsewhere . . . for so long as life remains in the Red King's body. Best to count him lost, though, and go about your own lives."

The wind stirred his robes, then whipped them into a frenzy, and Sezran began to spin. Blue light shone within his small tornado for an instant until man and glow vanished.

Marten had seated himself on a wooden chair and now leaned forward. "What sorcerous things does your brother speak of? A ship, a star gem to take you where . . . and *when?*"

Misk ignored the earl's questions, instead taking the queen's hand to lead her to the bed.

"You also have a task, my dear. Call to Gaylon with your heart and mind, give him reason to return."

"Will he hear me?"

"We must hope so."

The empty boyish face on the pillows was pale, and Jessmyn felt empty, too. She crawled onto the bed, only vaguely aware that Misk had gone to tend Marten's broken arm. The queen could hear their low voices, but couldn't make sense of the words. Misk finally sent the earl to his own chambers, but Davi refused to leave. The duke watched the king intently from his chair.

Jessmyn curled herself around the pillows, cradling Gaylon's head against her swollen stomach, then placed one hand flat upon his chest. There, she detected the first true sign of life, the faintest rise and fall of the ribs, very slow, but steady.

"My lord . . . come back to us," she whispered, finally letting go of long-denied sorrow and despair. The pain it brought was nearly unbearable, though tears once more refused to come. Her father dead, her mother and sisters lost in Zankos. These were family members little known in her life, but they had died at Gaylon's hand . . . along with thousands upon thousands of others. From this horrible deed her husband had fled and might never return.

What could she say to alleviate his guilt, to prove her love and guide him home? Jessmyn pulled the king's ringed hand to her and wove her fingers into his. His left hand, closed in a fist, lay tucked against his thigh. Head pressed to his shoulder, she murmured hope and peace into his ear all through the night.

Morning arrived, and Gaylon's condition hadn't changed. Near despair, the queen continued her quiet monologue while Davi paced endlessly back and forth before the hearth. Misk, as serene as ever, insisted Jessmyn eat and drink to keep up her strength.

Three days passed, and still Gaylon refused to respond to the queen's touch or her voice. A deep hopelessness settled over her, and she gave in, at last, to sleep. Her dreams brought no peace, though. In them, she followed her husband through a dark woods—a tall figure that remained always out of reach no matter how she hurried.

A gentle shift of the mattress startled her awake just before dawn of the fourth day. Jessmyn sat up, rubbing her eyes. The candles had burned well down, and a hush lay over the room. On Gaylon's hand, the Sorcerer's Stone suddenly blinked with a tiny, but pure blue light, then an ocean wind stirred the tapestries and drapes. Davi, asleep in a chair, woke as Sezran materialized in the center of the floor.

The king's fingers flexed slightly, and Jessmyn took a sharp breath. His eyes were open, staring into some distant place, empty still. Then understanding and horror filled them.

"My lord, no!" the young woman said quickly, before

Gaylon could withdraw into Dreaming once more. "Wait,
I beg you. . . ."

"Listen, Gaylon Reysson." Misk leaned over him, commanding his attention. She held his head and tilted a water
cup to his lips. "For you, the past is gone. Be glad of that
and let it go."

A weary anger touched the king's face. "I can . . . never
let it go." His voice, rough and weak, caught. "Leave me to
Dream in peace."

"Leave you to the peace of death?" the tiny woman demanded. "I've thought of you as many things, child, but
never a coward. Listen to me. Whatever the price in lives,
you've destroyed Kingslayer, so the weapon may never kill
again."

"But I haven't destroyed it . . . not completely," Gaylon
whispered. Trembling, the king turned his left hand over
and opened the fingers. Tiny colored lights sparked deep
within the oval black stone on his palm.

"The star gem." Sezran's eyes widened in wonder. He
reached for the stone, his own fingers shaking.

"No," Misk said sharply. "The Red King has won this
prize. With it, he'll undo a dark age that's lasted one thousand years." She laid a hand on her brother's sleeve. "We
have debts to pay, you and I."

"This *is* a truly wondrous power," the king muttered.
"With the gem I've seen the future. . . . I've seen cities
that stretch from horizon to horizon and machines that fly
in the sky." Exhausted, he paused.

Misk smiled down on him. "That's a future you'll help
to bring about."

"No. I don't want that future," Gaylon continued, tired
and saddened. "I've also seen the land die and the air grow
foul. So many more people, so many better ways to kill
them. Such weapons . . . ones that chain the power of the
stars and bring even more devastation than Kingslayer."

A shiver rippled through Jessmyn at that bleak description.

"I've told you," Misk said gently, brushing the hair from his face. "Such growth is always costly."

The king closed his eyes tight. "Worse than all those things . . . that future has no magic. . . ."

"Not so," the tiny woman insisted. "Simply a different sort. None of that will come to pass in your lifetime, though. Your particular magic is safe. But change will come eventually. It cannot be denied."

"Sezran." Gaylon held out the star gem, then let his shaking hand fall back to the blankets. "If that future is inevitable, I would rather it come as slowly as possible. Take this and return with your sister to your own world. I don't want to be tempted by such power ever again."

Misk shook her head. "Think what you say, child, of what you sacrifice by this."

"I have. Accept my gratitude, good lady, for all you've done, but accept the star gem as well. With your own kind, there's hope of healing . . . unless you enjoy wandering in the unwoven fabric of time."

"There's no pleasure in that," Misk admitted. "I'd thought we'd come to the end of our time, my brother and I, but it was only the end of our time on this world that I saw." The tiny woman managed a faint smile. "Or failed to see."

Sezran dared to take the gift, his fingers trembling worse than the king's. "So long I've waited. You told me once, Sister, that Gaylon would hand me the stone."

"Did I? I don't remember." The woman looked at Jessmyn. "Is this goodbye, then? I had hoped to see the baby, but it's best we go quickly, before I think of all that I love in your world." Fading away already, she leaned to kiss the queen's cheek, then whispered, "Have no fears. It will be a fine, healthy son."

In the silence, Sezran clutched the gem tightly.

"Shall I thank you and wish you well, Red King?" the old wizard asked, a sly glint in his eye. "No . . . I've hated you too long." He took a step back from the bed and caught his glowing Sorcerer's Stone in his other hand. "I've often wondered if my Stone will have power beyond your miserable planet. Think on that, Gaylon Reysson. If the Stone does keep its power, you may see more of my kind one day. Our race has always fancied such baubles."

A sea storm swirled about him, and, grinning wolfishly, Sezran was gone. They were alone now, king and queen and duke. Jessmyn took her husband's hand once more. His eyes still held a certain bleakness, but his love had been returned to her, stronger than ever before.

"Davi," Gaylon said and waited until the boy came to the edge of the blankets.

"Milord?"

"I couldn't have hoped for a more worthy duke of Gosney or a more valiant comrade-in-arms. Such devotion deserves reward."

"No, Sire. To serve the Red King is reward enough."

"I fear it will have to be. Kingslayer is gone, but a sorcerer-king still reigns—one who's laid waste to his realm and to much of his neighbor's. History will revile me as it does Orym."

"Never," the boy said stoutly.

"You think not?" Gaylon offered him a thin smile. "There'll always be danger in my service, Davi. You might reconsider the peaceful life of an innkeep." When the duke's young face set stubbornly, his king smiled again. "So, together we'll find some way to build a new, stronger nation on the ruins of the old . . . but that is for tomorrow. Today, we rest. Go, Lord Gosney, find your bed and sleep well."

"Yes, milord." Davi gave Jessmyn a courteous bow. "Milady."

The queen reached out to catch the boy's hand. "Thank you for defending your lord . . . and for bringing him home to me."

Wordlessly, Davi glanced down. The months of hardship had marked him deeply, but not so deeply as the war. His face was etched with a grief that would most likely never leave him. His green eyes, so newly healed, were filled with pain, though a faint smile touched his lips. Silently Jessmyn mourned the laughing, mischievous child that had arrived on their doorstep the previous winter.

The young duke managed another graceful bow, then turned away. She watched him leave the chamber, his back straight and chin held high, despite his obvious exhaustion. The queen returned her attention to her husband. His expression had darkened with misery again.

"Don't think upon it, my lord." Jessmyn stroked his forehead gently. "Do as Misk said and let the past go."

"If you'd seen his eyes, you'd know why I can't."

"Whose eyes?"

"Arlin's. He knew I had to loose Kingslayer and that it would mean his death. He understood me better than any of the others. . . ." Gaylon's jaw tightened. "Arlin urged me to end the war whatever the cost, but there at the last, I know I saw hope in his eyes. Despite everything, he wanted to live. He wanted me to save him."

Tears began to leak from the corners of the king's eyes. "My friend trusted me, and I failed him."

His desolation tore at Jessmyn, and she felt her throat constrict with emotion. "My lord, don't think of it. Please."

"Look what I've done to you, lady wife. Your father and mother are dead at my hands, your entire family destroyed. When I close my eyes, I can still see the fire spreading like a flood over the plain. Zankos burned, and I could hear the screams of children even from so far away." Gaylon's tone grew angry, almost vicious. "I can still see Arlin and Rinn, their flesh seared and melting—"

"Stop it!" the queen cried. "If it will ease your pain to inflict those memories on me, then I'll accept them, but I would rather you consider what you still have, not what you've lost." She grabbed his hand and pressed it to her stomach. "You have this child and a wife and a kingdom, however poor. You have Davi and Marten, who suffered through the war and love you still. They don't blame you for what happened. You told the duke you would build a new Wynnamyr on the ruins of the old. Let go of the self-condemnation and do so."

The king closed his eyes. "Could it be that simple?"

"No, Husband. Nothing will ever be simple for you." Jessmyn touched his cheek. "But when the sorrow and grief grow too heavy to bear, let me share the burden." She leaned near. "I gave you the promised kiss on your return, but I doubt you remember it . . . so let me remind you."

His lips were cold and unresponsive at first, but then his fingers touched her cheek.

"My love," he whispered. "Hold me, please."

Gladly Jessmyn gathered Gaylon in her arms and held him close, determined to make him forget his pain—at least for a little while. No, nothing would ever be simple for the Red King or his queen. The young woman knew that misery would likely dog them all their lives, and any happiness would be fleeting. It hardly mattered. She could endure anything so long as they were together.

Epilogue

The Lower Vales had been used as a military cemetery for ages, and so it was again. Common graves had been dug in the fields so the bodies of the soldiers might feed the crops that had once fed them. Those survivors who wished could scratch the names of loved ones and comrades in the stones of the boundary fences. On his return to the valley, Marten Pelson added the names of Arlin, Karyl, and Rinn.

The seasons turned, summer passing into autumn and then into winter. Within Castlekeep's cold walls, the queen of Wynnamyr gave birth to a tiny red-haired son. The child was named Thayne after his father's great-grandsire, and Gaylon found some joy in this new arrival. Much of the madness had passed, but the deaths of his friends still haunted him. Even so, the king kept faith with his countrymen and set about to restore Wynnamyr in the aftermath of war.

On a lonely sward overlooking the Western Sea, Seward Castle lay in ruins, gutted by some tremendous force that had left a wide blackened hole in the earth where Sezran's home had stood. Only the fisherfolk of a nearby village had witnessed the slow rise of a huge fiery ball that summer night. Multi-hued beams of light had flashed suddenly from the ball, swelling in every direction as the orb leaped away into the sky. Soon, it had dwindled to a mere pinpoint of color—one tiny star lost among all the others.

SORCERER'S STONE

L. Dean James

For a thousand years, the Red Kings guarded the magical sword Kingslayer. Now a young prince is the only one who can hope to master the blue light of the Sorcerer's Stone and control the mystical blade in time to save his kingdom and his life.

Be sure to read this exciting prequel to *Kingslayer*. On sale now!

B·O·O·K·S

The Nine Gates
Phillip Brugalette
Gopal, the prince of Goloka, sees his teacher burst into flames, then the many-armed Virabhadra go on a rampage. Gopal decides he must perform a sacred test but needs help from a centuries-old mystic to survive. On sale August 1992.

Half-Light
Denise Vitola
Commander Ariann Centuri's betrothed is killed by the Bat-faced Benar, and she is stricken with a terminal mind-bending disease. Suddenly she finds herself wedded to the Viceroy of the Galactic Consortium of Planets . . . and fighting for her life. On sale December 1992.

Thorn and Needle
Paul B. Thompson
When two intriguing travelers journey to Miyesti to investigate the Brotherhood of the Fact and destroy a strange new god, powerful forces collide. On sale now.

novels

Vampire of the Mists
Christie Golden

Jander Sunstar, an elven vampire, is pulled into the newly formed dark domain of Barovia and forms an alliance with the land's most powerful inhabitant, Count Strahd Von Zarovich, unaware that Strahd is the very enemy he seeks. Available now.

Knight of the Black Rose
James Lowder

The cruel death knight Soth finds his way into Ravenloft and discovers that it is far easier to get in than to get out--even with the aid of the powerful vampire lord, Strahd. Available now.

Dance of the Dead
Christie Golden

Larissa Snowmane is a dancer on a magical riverboat that journeys to the zombie-plagued island of Sourange. The music is chilling, the captain is sinister, and Larissa must master the Dance of the Dead to save her own soul. Available June 1992.

Heart of Midnight
J. Robert King

Casimir, who inherited his father's lycanthropic curse, fled from both his home and his heritage. Now the young werewolf must embrace his dark powers to prevent his own death and to gain revenge on his monstrous father. Available November 1992.

BOOKS

The Cloakmaster Cycle

Beyond the Moons   David Cook
When a spelljamming ship crashes into Teldin Moore's home
on Krynn, a dying alien gives him a mysterious cloak that
makes him the target of killers and cutthroats. On sale now.

Into the Void   Nigel Findley
Teldin is plunged into a sea of alien faces when his ship
is attacked by space pirates. The mind flayer who rescues
him offers to help him learn how to use the powers of the
cloak--but for whose gain? On sale now.

The Maelstrom's Eye   Roger E. Moore
Teldin allies with a gypsy kender and is reunited with an
old friend, but they must fight to find a genius slug to learn
more about the cloak. Both scro forces and the elven
Imperial Fleet are in hot pursuit. On sale May 1992.

The Radiant Dragon   Elaine Cunningham
A radiant dragon who also possesses a key to control of
the *Spelljammer* joins Teldin in his search for the legendary
ship, but the quest is interrupted by the coming of the
second Unhuman War. On sale November 1992.

Invaders of Charon Series
A New Dimension in
Outer Space Adventure!

The Genesis Web Book One
C. M. Brennan

Follow the adventures of Black Barney, from his birth
in a RAM laboratory to his daring escape from his evil
creators and beyond, into a world of danger and
intrigue. On sale April 1992.

Nomads of the Sky Book Two
William H. Keith, Jr.

The mysterious, dreaded Space Nomads take Vincent
Perelli prisoner, forcing him to fight a ritual battle for
survival before he can seek the Device, a missing
RAM artifact that may save the life of Buck Rogers.
On sale November 1992.